Dream Chaser

Pat Spears

Twisted Road Publications LLC
Tallahassee, Florida

Twisted Road Publications LLC

Printed in the United State of America

This is a work of fiction. Any resemblance to real events or persons, living or dead, is entirely coincidental

www.twistedroadpublications.com

In memory of my sister
Mary "Cotton"

Acknowledgements

I was fortunate enough to be born into a rich tradition of oral storytelling. I never tired of the stories told to me by my Granny Bailey. She could neither read nor write, but by God she could spin a tale. And my dad, who was a fine storyteller in his own right.

I wish to thank Lorin Oberweger, Connie May Fowler, Sandra Gail Lambert, Glenda Bailey-Mershon, Margie Craig and Jackie Shumate for reading and offering invaluable feedback on the multiple versions of the manuscript. Thanks to the organizers of the Southern Women Writers Conferences at Berry College for giving me my earliest opportunities to read my work publicly. Thanks to the various editors who have selected my short fiction for publication.

Thanks to Dorothy Allison for her special gift of friendship and encouragement over the long years when despair could have easily defeated me.

Thanks to Joan Leggitt, my first reader and publisher for her vision and diligence in turning my manuscript into a book, and for everything else.

Dream Chaser

ONE

Jesse drives the eight miles into town, his brain paralyzed by dread, and he's rejected every notion of what he might say to his son. He wishes Dodie was here. She'd know what to say. But if she hadn't left, Cole would have been in his room, sleeping with his iPod blasting, and none of this would have happened. He wants to make his misery her fault, but he knows better.

He parks three blocks east of Sheriff Buddy's shiny new jail; a white steel building with family-friendly green shutters framing its barred windows. It's the only new structure to have gone up on Main Street in the last five years. He gets out of the truck, crosses the street, and steps onto the busted sidewalk, weeds creeping up between its cracks. He walks past what was once the local newspaper office, its fate written in the faded real estate signs plastering the dirty plate-glass window. The tiny shop next door was Miss Fanny's flower shop for two generations. Today, it's an antique shop that just sells junk.

He pauses at the entry to the town's square, its remaining centerpiece the paint blistered bandstand that once shimmered in brightly colored lights, and he wants to feel again the promise he felt when he and Dodie slow danced on warm summer nights to the off key music of home grown bands. Perched in a nearby magnolia, a thieving mockingbird sings some other bird's sweet song, and he wonders when he and Dodie stopped believing in the dreams they once shared.

The front office is a fluorescent flash of bright orange plastic and tarnished chrome chairs occupied by four worriers who look as if they've had the night he had. The room smells of their tension, fast food, and bitter coffee. He nods in passing and approaches the female deputy.

She gets off a chair to stand behind a chest high counter with one of those cheap motel sliding glass business holes. Stuffed into a dark green uniform, she packs a 38-caliber handgun holstered in a wide black belt, and a hefty roll rides its top edge. The effort of smiling would likely crack her face, and he figures she's heard every excuse known to men like him.

Still, he says, "Morning, ma'am. I'm here about Cole McKnight," in a hopeful voice. He glances at the sign behind her head, warning that he's not to lean on the counter, and steps back, arms hanging awkwardly at his sides. It's hard not to feel like a criminal.

"You his daddy, are you?" She squints at him from behind the thick glass, sizing up his worth as a father, he thinks, and her scowl speaks to her doubt.

"I'm afraid so." He fakes a half-assed grin. From behind him someone snickers, getting that he only means to turn aside his embarrassment. But the deputy's eyes narrow into slits above her round cheeks, and it's clear she took his remark in a way he hadn't intended.

She studies the clipboard and reads: "Jesse Cole McKnight, age sixteen, arrested August 28th, charges pending." She peers at him over the top of the clipboard.

He exhales, his hot breath forming a perfect circle of regret on the glass and he steps back, away from her intensity.

"What you got there in the sack?"

"Shoes. He got off without them." He twists the top of the paper bag tighter.

She steps from behind the counter and tells him to leave them and follow her. He sets the bag on the counter, concerned that the shoes may not be there when he and Cole are ready to walk out of this place.

"You were told that your son's awful sick?" She bites down hard on each word.

"Yes'um. You might say we're all sick."

She frowns.

"By that, I mean his mama and me. He's got two little worried sisters at home." He wants her to know that the name on the arrest report isn't some pitiful runaway but that he has a real family. Maybe a bit splintered at the moment, but a family just the same.

"He used his one call to phone a young lady. She came earlier. I took her back myself. I believe she said her name was Sarah."

Jesse nods with intent, trying to hide the fact that lately he knows little about his son, and even less about a girl named Sarah. But the deputy isn't fooled.

"Pretty sure he won't want to look at anything alcoholic for some time. Report says he downed nearly a fifth of Night Train."

"No, ma'am. For sure that stuff ought to be called Train Wreck." His failed humor bounces off her, as if she calloused over ages ago, and in no way is he to find a forward gear with the deputy. Maybe he should have told her that, as far as he knows, Cole doesn't even have a learner's permit, and he's dead certain he has never before as much as tasted wine or anything else. He knows this because his boy is determined not to become his old man.

Thirteen months ago, he'd have argued that he was at least a passable dad. But that changed the day he picked up the pink slip that severed him from his job of fourteen years; the same job his boss promised would be waiting for him at the end of his tour in Iraq. But all deals were off after the company bigwigs pulled up stakes and took one hundred eighteen good-paying union jobs to Mexico. That loss, courtesy of a room full of smooth-talking sons of bitches he never as much as laid eyes on, screwed with his head, right along with everything Iraq taught him about country and truth.

He follows the officer through a heavy metal door and onto a long hallway, flanked on each side by cells. An aging drunk flashes a vacant smile, and a couple of shirtless inmates cat call to the officer. He glances at their muscled chests and upper arms and tries not to think about the prison rape scenes he has seen on cable TV. He rubs his sweaty palms on his jeans, and stares at the back of the deputy's head.

She says over her shoulder, "Didn't move him over to the new juvenile facility after the Sheriff said you were coming to take him home." It's the second time she's left him an awkward space to fill as to why he hadn't bothered to do the expected. It isn't that he doesn't see her point, hasn't second-guessed his decision not to pick him up last night a thousand times, but that's water under the bridge, and he can't undo what's done.

She unlocks the cell door and he steps inside the steel cage measuring roughly four manly strides square. Behind him, the metal door slams shut with a certainty that sends a quiver along his spine, and he can't bring himself to speak to the hump that is his son lying on a narrow metal cot beneath a stained blanket. Rather, he focuses on the names and phone numbers of women, along with the names he takes to be past inmates, scribbled on the walls. Someone penned Jesus wept, while another wrote screw Jesus.

When he dares, he looks without wanting to see. He can't know if Cole senses his presence, for he doesn't move or make the slightest sound. Jesse draws closer, placing an uncertain hand lightly on his son's shoulder, quietly calling his name.

Cole screams, "Get the fuck off me," twisting to sit upright on the cot. He stares wildly, as a child might when awakening from a nightmare filled with bogey men, and Jesse guesses Cole has seen the same TV prison horrors.

"Steady, son, it's me." He draws back. "I've come to take you home."

Cole stares blankly, clutching the blanket beneath his chin, and he moves to the far edge of the cot, his back to the wall. His face is the color of paraffin; gray and waxy, and Jesse thinks that maybe Cole doesn't even remember where he is. He takes a seat on the cot across from Cole to give each a moment to catch their breath.

Cole swings his legs over the side of the cot and sits with his head bowed, staring at his tightly clasped hands, and Jesse notices anew how small and delicate his son's hands are. He wears blue jailhouse slippers, and Jesse can't say why, but something about those slippers makes him want to cry. Maybe it's remembering little boy footie pajamas of the same color, and the sound those little boy feet made as Cole ran toward him, squealing to be picked up and lifted above his head.

He calls his son's name, and Cole looks at him with the same turtle-eyed sadness he thought only belonged to Dodie. He studies Cole's young face, and thinks that maybe what he feels isn't regret, or even fear, but something much deeper.

"Why, Dad? Why Iraq? You never cared about any of that." There are no tears, but his voice is thick with all that he holds back. "Mom said you were never ready to be a father."

"Lord God, Son." He's caught off guard. "What does Iraq have to do with any of this? That was years ago."

"Mom said you went because you didn't want us."

"Cole, that's crazy."

"Why's it crazy?"

"Because your ass is in a sling and you pick now to bring up Iraq. Forget what I did. I ain't the one in jail." No sooner are the words out of his mouth than he regrets having pushed all the blame onto Cole.

"And when did you ever own your own shit?" Cole springs to his feet. Swaying, he bends, clutching his middle, and rushes past Jesse, dropping onto his knees in front of the toilet. Jesse offers Cole a wet cloth, but he pushes it away and slumps back onto the cot, his head resting on his drawn knees.

Maybe Cole's right that things started to go wrong with his deployment to Iraq. When Dodie learned she was pregnant with Katie, his National Guard unit was already in Iraq. Like most of the guys, he'd signed up to soldier on weekends for the extra cash. No one, least of all him, was gung-ho to become a real soldier, but that's nothing any of them would have admitted. Trust was all a guy had over there.

"Cole, I admit nothing's the way it used to be. But you've got to know it ain't about what you want. Or what I might want." He shoves his hand into a pocket of his jeans, fingering the worn folds of the note she left behind. "It's what she ... your mom ... did."

"You're a liar. Mom would never leave us kids." He flings his arms as though he means to hammer his words into something he can accept. "She left you, not us. You drove her away with your drunken threats."

"I'd had a few drinks, but I wasn't drunk. And it wasn't like that." He stood at their bedroom door, pleading for the chance to explain missing her birthday party, but she told him to go away. That she'd given up on him. He believed that after they both slept, he could once again smooth things over with her. After all, their fights were practiced, which might explain his having missed the finality in her voice. But Cole's anger is new. At least he hadn't seen it coming.

"What happened between me and your mom ain't as bad as you think I could've fixed things if she'd given me a chance." Now it's his turn to beat back the truth.

"Which part, Dad? Blowing off Mom's birthday? Or pissing away the only decent job offer you've had in over a year? And tell me why the great Jesse McKnight would do that?"

He'd come to hate gatherings at her mama's, sticking his feet under Cora's table, listening to her blather on about the existence of jobs if only he wasn't so picky. Maybe Dodie believed she'd sweetened the pie with the notion of a job offer from her Nazi brother.

"It's enough to know there's bad blood between your Uncle Jake and me."

"And it's got nothing to do with your fucked up pride."

"Shut your mouth, boy. You don't know what the hell you're talking about." Cole knows plenty, but no man wants to hear of his transgressions from his son.

They're winded, and like boxers, arms locked and leaning, neither risks the killing blow.

"If you know where I should start, I promise I'll do what I can to find your mom. But right now we're in the eye of a shit storm. You need to come with me or Buddy has no choice but to keep you locked up."

"No, I don't trust you."

"You do know a trial date could take weeks." He's not sure about what is ahead for Cole, but he's scared for him.

Cole doesn't look at him, but lies back down on the cot, turning his face away and pulling the blanket over his head. Jesse understands that his son does so against his every lie, his every broken promise, and he sags back against the cold, metal bars.

Accepting that there's nothing more he can say to change Cole's mind, he buzzes the officer. She returns and it's clear she expected to walk two McKnight males from the cell block.

Jesse pauses, watching for the slightest sign that Cole was bluffing. He remains the same gray hump, lying still as death, and Jesse walks from the cell block. Behind him, the heavy metal door slams shut.

He hurries from the jail, taking refuge in his truck, and for the first time in a long while, he feels a pain stronger than his own.

TWO

Jesse drives the town square, looking for what, he isn't sure. Maybe it's nothing more than wishful thinking that has him pulling the truck to a stop in the dirt lot opposite Dodie's beauty shop. A flock of pissed-off crows scatter no farther than the overhead power lines, perching there and squawking down at him.

He kills the engine and checks the street for her brown Datsun, but there's only Sally's candy apple red Firebird. Sally's single, right on, and has little to brag about other than that fast car. Unless she counts the married guy who stays over when he's through town, looking for sex to go, but it's fairly well known that Sally treats men and cars the same, wearing off the new and looking to trade up. Whatever is going on with Dodie, he knows she's different.

He needs to know where to start looking for his wife, anything he can use to prove to Cole that he means to keep his word, convince his boy to come home with him. He swigs the last of the cold coffee from home, searching his fragmented recollections for clues, pieces of the bigger puzzle he'd missed on his last visit to the shop.

At the sound of him entering, Dodie had looked up at his reflection in the wall of mirrors, and before he could open his mouth, he heard, "Dear God, please don't tell me you've lost another job?"

He explained that his forklift broke down and the boss sent him home. She didn't turn to face him, but did her talking to his reflection; joined by the old blue-haired woman he knows only by reputation as the town's queen meddler.

He'd needed no reminder that he was already short hours that pay period, and yes, it meant Katie was stuck with shoes that pinched so her toenails turned under. Still, he asked his wife to go with him to Hardee's where they could get coffee, and maybe talk about anything other than the stack of overdue bills piled on the kitchen counter. Something was always coming due, and he wanted their marriage to be about more than that.

He watches the crows, and while he can't remember her exact words, he clearly remembers the hard way her otherwise pretty mouth twisted into icy contempt. She said something about him having time on his hands, but she had a perm coming in and that they needed every dime she could make. But he'd insisted until she said she would go with him if he could tell her he had money for the utility bill and she wouldn't need to borrow from her parents.

The change in his pocket wouldn't have fed a parking meter. He felt trapped in the tiny room, his nostrils burning from the nasty smell of chemicals, while he pleaded with his wife for her favor by way of a mirror. He'd turned to leave when the nosey old woman piped up with her notion of how much more Dodie could charge for her perms in places like Tallahassee and Valdosta.

He squints into the early morning sunlight, and thinks that the truth of Dodie's intent was masked in the hardness of her tone. "Sweetie, you can forget what makes perfectly good sense. My husband's joined at the belly button to this pathetic town. And for God's sake, don't get him started on the McKnight legacy."

He hated how easily she talked about their packing up and leaving behind everyone and everything he'd ever known for whatever good she imagined awaited them someplace else. He'd stayed alive in Iraq, thinking about home.

He's unsure what's left of the love he and Dodie had or how far back they'll need to go to find that good. But, what he does know is that he means to keep his promise to Cole. He'll find her, take a stab at convincing her that it's too early to quit on him. Remind her that he was once a steady worker and if they can hold on a little longer, a position is bound to open up at the warehouse. He's proven himself with his boss, and he has a good shot at landing a full-time job.

He gets out of the truck, hurries across the street, and walks into the shop. Sally is loading diet soda into the small fridge, and it strikes him that a bunch of the shop's patrons must drink diet sodas with their Little Debbie cakes. She looks up at the sound of the door, and he gets a good look at the dread in her face.

"Hey, Jess. You're up early." She straightens and closes the fridge.

"Tell me what you know." He's tight as a tick; embarrassed to be asking Sally for answers about the disappearance of his wife. Then she's likely had an earful from Dodie on his many failures as a provider, maybe even as a husband. But he isn't here to bolster his ego; he wants to know where to find his wife.

Sally forces a stalling grin. "Why you here pumping me? She's your wife."

"Damn it, Sally. I ain't playing." He takes a quick step toward her and she throws up her hands and backs against the shampoo bowl.

"Okay, okay, settle down."

He stops. "Sorry, I didn't mean to come on like that. I'm a bit raw on that point."

"That's all right, I get it. But you've gotta believe she never said a word about leaving until day before yesterday. Said I was to keep the shop open and deposit her share of the receipts. I swear that's all I know." Her shoulders slouch and she twists the empty container she still holds. "You've got to know it was my damn job on the line."

"All right, take it easy. I'm just trying to puzzle things out." It figures Sally got jammed, but she knows more than she's giving up. A little draw on their shared past might open her up.

He pours her a cup of coffee from the freshly brewed pot. "You take sugar, right?" He plays her, but what he and Sally had was groping high school sex; nothing special. Then she'd given it up to half the football team.

"You know I do."

He gives her his most disarming smile and backs off.

"Maybe she talked about someone." He turns, his back to her, and pours himself a cup.

"Her? You're kidding, right?"

He exhales, relieved. Still, he'd feel better satisfied had he seen her face.

"All right, then. How about a particular place? Worried about not having money enough for food, gas and motels?" If she'd split their pitiful savings, it means she'd likely withdrawn less than a hundred bucks. That won't buy many nights at Motel 6 and a steady diet of tacos.

"No, not one word, I promise. But I can tell you Roy did a hurry-up service on her car, maybe even a brake job. I dropped her and Cole at his place after we closed here. Now, she did worry about being late for her birthday party and her mama bitching that her efforts went unappreciated. But that went on a lot with her."

"Cole?" Maybe he knows more than he'd let on.

"Yeah, he needed a ride home. Said he missed the school bus."

"Did you notice what Roy charged her?" That fat grease monkey screws road-desperate women in exchange for reconditioned auto parts. Even when he isn't thinking straight, Jesse knows Dodie would ride out of town on the back of a jackass before she'd make such a trade with Roy.

"No, but she took money from the cash register. Ninety-three dollars and eighty-four cents, and paid him out of that. Said I'd need to wait for my share out of this week's receipts. Down to one chair, I can tell you I'll walk to work, farting beans the whole way."

"I hear you. There's a bunch of us in that pity-parade."

Ninety-three dollars and eight-four cents worth of repairs won't take her far. A brake job had cost her that much. Forget worn hoses, a rust-clotted radiator, and the tread on all four tires smooth as the palm of her hand.

He leaves Sally standing in the middle of the empty shop, the coffee cup clutched in her hand. He didn't much like leaning on her, but he learned enough to suspect that Dodie had a full-blown plan for leaving, and her brother Jake's job offer was more likely bait than real. She counted on his absence at Cora's to spring her trap. She abandoned her kids, and he'd made it possible for her to take the high ground.

Down to what Sally can do, after expenses, Dodie's bank account dries up, and soon. She'll need a job and her best bet will be her trade. How many shops are there in the area? He doesn't have time to play detective. But making the effort at a few local calls might satisfy Cole.

THREE

Jesse wakes to the sound of girlish giggles, and he feels the sting of guilt for having slept late. He pulls on yesterday's jeans and shirt, and drags into the kitchen. Sky sits alone at the table, an overturned bowl of Rice Krispies neatly piled in front of her. With her tiny index finger, she pushes grains of cereal into the outline of a red hibiscus print on the tablecloth, and if she notices his presence, she doesn't let on.

Katie, trailed by a panting Beau, slams into the kitchen from outside. The dog goes straight to lapping water. Katie's cheeks are bright red, her tee shirt streaked with sweat and dirt.

"Good lord, girl, where've you been? You're supposed to tell me when you leave the yard."

"Shoveling manure." She removes her Braves cap and tosses it onto the counter, her red curls springing into a tangled freedom. She squints up at him. "If you ain't forgot, I'm eleven almost. I don't have to tell you everything. Mama never made me."

"Yes, you do, when you leave Sky all alone. Remember, she's only four." He cringes at the thought of awakening alone in the house to her screams.

"I didn't leave her alone. You're here."

"Right. But I still need to know." She's showing a rawer edge than normal and it's justified. Her only free time before now was when Sky napped.

Katie cleans stables for Dee and Susan in exchange for riding lessons, but he hasn't wanted the girls to go next door until after talking to both women, especially Dee. He told himself he needed to pick the right time. Maybe even take something. Women like flowers, and they might work for Susan, but Dee would likely throw them back at him. Maybe just saying he's sorry. Then 'sorry my son stole your car' isn't exactly what he thinks of as an over-the-fence, neighborly visit.

He sets about brewing a pot of coffee and considers that the biggest headache in herding kids is that the job never lets up. He already wants to slip off to some cool place and sleep without an ear cocked for disaster. Maybe Dodie's motive for leaving is as simple as her needing a break, and that her disappointment about him not showing for her birthday was the straw that broke the camel's back. The car brakes had needed fixing for months, and maybe the timing for her trip to Roy's was nothing more than coincidental.

Jesse fills his cup and sits at the table. He's a fool, and denial doesn't change the facts.

Katie pours dry cereal into a bowl and pushes it and the nearly empty milk jug across the table. He mumbles his thanks, but what he really wants is four fried eggs winking at him from atop a pile of hot grits, with country sausage and home-made biscuits riding the edge of his plate.

He opens the cabinet, takes down a box of grits and goes to the fridge. There are two eggs and a single, dead turkey wiener, its ends pale and shriveled. He slams the door shut.

"It's Sunday. Don't you ever get tired of snap, crackle, and pop?"

"You've looked." Katie nods toward the cabinet. "It's what we've got."

He glances at the clock, and realizes Hank would have called hours ago had he planned to take the day to go fishing and needed him to work his back-hoe. Another week without the extra pay.

"How about we go to your Uncle Clyde's and see if he's got new pups. I bet Miss Marlene will make us a real Sunday breakfast."

Katie gives him a high-five and sets about pouring dry cereal from their bowls back into the box. Sky doesn't protest, but sweeps her cereal art from the table onto the floor, gets down off the chair, and runs to stand at the front door. Beau chases about, his pink tongue a welcome vacuum cleaner.

He looks at Katie.

"Don't you know Sky loves baby puppies better than anything?"

Jesse hunts cleaner jeans and an unstained tee shirt while Katie explains to Beau that he can't come. Clyde's stud dog, a champion Beagle, attacks Beau on sight. Clyde claims the dog's still pissed with Beau's unfaithful mama, and hates her bastard offspring. It's enough to say that Beau's peculiar looks have to figure into the equation, but Jesse doesn't dare say this to Katie.

When they're in the truck and well on their way, Katie wears one of her serious old lady looks, and he dares to ask what's put such a sourpuss look on her face. He expects something about her missing their mama, or even a second tirade about how wrong Cole was to steal Ms. Susan's car and that he belongs in jail.

"I'm mad at Grandma."

He glances over at her. "Thought you two were tighter than Mama Trudy's girdle."

"Daddy," she giggles. "It's mean to talk about Mama Trudy's big butt."

He'd swear Sky frowns.

"Come on, you know I was kidding. I love Trudy better than chocolate cake. Why are you mad at your Grandma Cora?" Without working at it, he could name a hundred reasons he dislikes the old hen.

"She said I shouldn't call Uncle Clyde uncle. That he's not our real uncle. That he's not nice because he owns a place where bad people go to get drunk." Hers is an expression of willing defiance, yet perceptive enough to register doubt, and to raise his discomfort. Cora thinks of him and Clyde as peas of the same pod.

"What do you think?"

"That I don't care what she says. He's funny. And I like him. And not just because he's your best friend ever." She nods in the decisive way that for her seals the deal, and he's certain neither he nor Clyde can uphold the standard Katie requires for men and beasts alike.

He and Clyde Parrish go back to first grade, when he'd swapped Clyde fried egg sandwiches for dime cans of sardines. They'd fallen in love with their pretty sixth grade teacher and might have stayed in sixth grade forever, had she not jilted both for a traveling Bible salesman. High school was a triumphant swirl of eager girls and gridiron glory for both of them. Neither had cracked a book, except to stay football eligible.

Nothing much good has happened to Clyde since he tangled with the freight train that landed him, a man in his prime, full-time in a wheelchair. He claims that the loss of his legs isn't the worst part, but rather the fact that dead nerves don't fire along his spine, which keeps him from getting a hard on, though he swears he still can in his mind. Exactly how that works, Jesse isn't sure, although he thinks about the mechanics of Clyde's claim, especially since Marlene stayed on when the stoned band boys she'd arrived with two years ago moved on.

THE AROMA OF COUNTRY SAUSAGE fills the air as they make their way toward the four-room cabin that serves as living quarters for Clyde and Marlene. He reminds Katie to keep quiet about her mom and Cole until he's had a chance to talk to her Uncle Clyde. She nods and runs toward the house, Sky in tow.

Then it's unlikely that either Clyde or Marlene will question Dodie's absence, although Clyde's regret will show in what he doesn't ask. Dodie blamed Clyde for Jesse's heavy drinking during the first six months or so after his return from Iraq. But she was wrong. Had it not been for Clyde, he might still be hiding inside his drunken stupor.

Even when his drinking slowed, Dodie had refused to visit, although they had been best friends since junior high. Lately, he's reasoned that her dislike of Marlene figures into the picture somehow, likely stemming from her Baptist upbringing. He was raised the same, but it seems a lot of his didn't take the way hers did. As far as he can tell, whatever Clyde and Marlene have together works for the betterment of both. When he's not jealous, he's glad for Clyde.

The ancient collie taken in as a stray gets up off the porch steps and trots toward them, barking a toothless welcome. Clyde waves them on from his wheelchair parked on the screened porch. Marlene comes from inside to stand with a hand resting on Clyde's shoulder. She calls a warm greeting, and he notices right off that she's wearing cut off jeans beneath her bib apron.

"Nice outfit." He teases, liking the way she smiles and curtsies. All the women he knew growing up wore the same style cotton print apron.

Katie gives Marlene a hug around her waist, and Clyde reaches to pull her into his huge arms, bristled with red hairs. Sky doesn't speak, but her dark eyes, more black than brown, search about expectantly. Suddenly, Jesse remembers the pups he promised she'd see.

"Come get breakfast girls, and then I have a special treat for Sky."

Sky doesn't look at Marlene, but he does. Her eyes shine, and he wishes he could remember the last time he'd seen that same playfulness in Dodie's eyes. Maybe then he'd know how far back he'd need to go if he's ever to have a chance at turning things around with her. But first, he'll need a real plan for finding her.

"Don't bother with Little Brother, here," Clyde calls to Marlene. "He's likely had some fancy French omelet and can't eat a bite." Clyde winks at Jesse.

"Kiss my boney ass, you lucky dog." Jesse stoops to hug Clyde's massive shoulders. Clyde has called him Little Brother since grade school, although Clyde's six months younger. But his extra eighty pounds gained during high school made the nickname stick.

Jesse leaves Clyde to pick grits from his teeth with a broom straw and goes inside to the tiny kitchen. Marlene turns from the stove where she's frying more eggs and hugs him with a hot flipper in her hand.

"Four fresh yard eggs, over easy, right?"

"A man can't help but love a woman who remembers how he likes his eggs." She's warm against his chest, and he's slow to let go. He steps back, arms at his sides, and he feels high school foolish.

If she notices his awkwardness, she doesn't let on, but turns back to the sizzling pan. He fills his plate with hot grits, biscuits, and pork sausage. She places four eggs on top of the mound of grits, looks at his plate, and shakes her head.

"I really do appreciate you taking a little just so I don't get my feelings hurt."

"I'm a nice guy, in spite of what people say." He bends, kissing her pink cheek, and walks back onto the porch, savoring the lightness he feels. He passes his plate under Clyde's nose before taking a seat across from him at the makeshift table.

"Lord, I do believe a shot of Jeritol might help boost your appetite."

"Marlene's cooking is all my appetite needs."

Sitting across from Clyde fades the lightheadedness he felt in the kitchen. His friend gets a puzzled look on his face, but turns to bitching about Georgia's loss to Florida. Jesse eats like the starved man he is, slowing only to nod in apt agreement with Clyde's Sunday morning quarterbacking, while silently celebrating having won five bucks in the football pool at work.

Marlene comes onto the porch, pours a round of coffee, and places a plate of hot, homemade cinnamon buns on the table between them. Clyde leans his shaggy red head back between her breasts, a look of satisfaction playing across his face. She tenderly rubs his head, and Jesse searches for the smallest clue that she feels what Clyde feels, but she gives nothing away.

"While you two visit, I'm taking Sky and Katie to see the newest pups."

Sky runs to the door and Katie follows.

"Hold up there, young ladies. Before you take off, these dirty dishes need to be walked into the kitchen."

Clyde squints at him. "And when did you turn into a nagging mama? These girls don't need two mamas."

"He's not our mama, but sometimes he sounds like her." Katie takes Sky's hand, and Jesse notices Sky's thumbnail is bleeding where she's bitten it into the quick. Why hadn't he noticed before that she's a nail biter?

Marlene and the girls walk toward the kennels, Katie leaping ahead and Sky walking next to Marlene without touching her. Clyde calls the kennels the Doggy Hilton, and rightly so. The kennels cost considerably more to build and equip than the four-room cabin.

Clyde justified it by saying he doesn't have a pedigree to match that of his dogs.

They sit for a time, neither having much to say until Clyde declares, "All right, Little Brother, spit it out before you choke."

He isn't sure he means to tell Clyde everything, especially about his fight with Cole, but he can't remember the last time a secret lodged between them for longer than it took either to open his mouth.

He blurts, "Dodie left me."

Clyde gets a big don't shit me look on his face. "Do those two little ones know?" He glances in the direction the girls went.

"Sure they do. It ain't something easy to hide."

"What'd you say to them?" He swings the chair around closer, his stare intense.

"Not much, just that she was going away for a while. Like the time when their Aunt Teresa had twins. There wasn't much more I knew to say."

Clyde turns away, stares through the rusty screen wire into the woods beyond, then back at Jesse. "Leaving you, hell yeah, I can see that. But leaving those babies with you? Don't make sense."

"What the hell are you saying? Maybe you've forgot I'm their daddy. Who the hell else was she going to leave them with?"

"Law says you're their daddy, all right. But for some time now, your head's been so far up your own ass, you've been worthless to them kids."

"And what do you know about being a daddy?" He leaps to his feet, and the old dog stands between him and Clyde's wheelchair, its hairs bristling.

"Not a goddamn thing. And that's the truth. So stop your pitiful blustering and sit the hell down. You're making me feel short." His gaze is still steady, but less hard.

Jesse notices that Clyde's big hands tremble. He sits back in the rocker, wiping sweat beaded across his forehead on his shirt sleeve. The porch shrinks, and he thinks about bolting, gaining fresher air.

"What else, Little Brother? You know I can read your messed-up mind like the Sunday funnies."

"Cole went crazy over his mama's leaving. Got himself roaring drunk. Took Susan's Lincoln and drove onto the interstate."

"Took, as in stole? Cole? Why? What'd he say?"

"Claimed he took it to go look for his mama."

"Why'd he need to steal a car? Why weren't you the one looking?"

Jesse stares at the floorboards between his boots, and he has no kind of answer Clyde won't toss back in his face.

"All right, but where's Cole now?"

"Locked up at Buddy's. Since about three Saturday morning."

"Then why are you here? Why not on Buddy's doorstep, talking your boy out of that cesspool he runs?"

"He won't talk."

"What? Buddy won't talk? He'll talk or I'll snatch his balls out his nose holes." Clyde's powerful arms flex, and he lifts himself off the seat, as if he means to do just that. He growls like a trapped animal and falls back onto the chair.

"Don't go gunning for Buddy."

Clyde squints, his brow a rub board.

"It's Cole. He won't have my help."

Clyde nods, as if what he heard makes sense and that it comes as no surprise. "It's the gospel truth. Two stubborn jackasses don't haul worth shit."

Katie runs back onto the porch, Sky in tandem.

Clyde smiles at Sky, his mood a hundred and eighty. "How'd you like them babies, little darling?"

Sky tugs at the hem of her tee shirt and looks to Katie.

"She thinks they're pretty as a picture."

"Girl, you need to hush. How's that sweet thing going to learn to talk if you're all the time butting in?"

Sky goes to stand at the far corner of the porch, facing outward.

"See what you did." Katie goes over and takes her sister's hand, leads her back.

Jesse gives Katie a hard look to say watch your manners. He means to talk to her about her mouth, but he thinks it's hereditary.

"Then how'd you like the pups, Miss Katie talky-butt?"

"Told you."

"That you did, Missy." Clyde reaches out and draws her onto his lap.

Sky squats onto her heels, her hands covering her eyes, and Clyde watches her over the top of Katie's head. His face is a mix of bewilderment and sadness, not unlike what Jesse feels.

"It's okay. She does that when she wants to do something real bad but it's too scary."

"Get that way myself." Clyde backs the wheelchair away from the table and spins the chair in his rendition of a wheelie. Katie laughs, her arms wrapped around Clyde's thick neck, her hair tangling in his beard.

Marlene comes onto the porch, beaming, and the air sparks with their good energy.

Jesse wishes he could put off his trip to the detention center. But he believes Cole's sober now, and has had time to think better of his decision.

"You girls thank Miss Marlene for breakfast and for showing you the pups. We've got to go."

"No, I don't want to. I'm mad at Cole for stealing …." Katie covers her mouth. "Sorry, Daddy."

"It's okay, baby." He's surprised that the prospect of seeing her big brother in jail scares her so. Clyde's right. There's much that he doesn't know about reading his kids.

Marlene inhales sharply, the sound of her shock, and he looks at her in the way of an apology. He stands to leave and feels bad that she's to hear the news about Cole secondhand, and that she's to hear Clyde's version. His bluntness can put a bad face on "good morning."

"Daddy, can we stay?"

He wants to avoid a set-to with Katie, but decides she and Sky can sit in the truck while he visits Cole. He doesn't have gas enough for a second trip and to make work tomorrow.

"Come on, man, leave them. One of us will see they get home."

Jesse drives the truck slowly away, Katie waving and Sky standing next to her sister, but she doesn't wave.

FOUR

He tells the disinterested woman at the counter that he's here to visit his son. She gives him an empty smile and tells him to make himself comfortable in the visitors' lounge. He takes a seat, but it will take more than a large room made up to look like a normal living room for him to be at ease. The set of double glass doors labeled Juvenile Detention Center squeezed all the comfort right out of him.

Unlike the uniform-clad woman deputy at Buddy's jail, the officers are dressed in casual clothes; navy blue knit shirts with a tiny logo and pleated tan slacks. As if visitors are someplace other than a fancy jail for kids. An officer stands with her tanned arms locked behind her nice butt, rocking heel to toe, her trained gaze focused on the indifferent space above visitors' heads. Although she's trying to blend in, her bored expression separates her from the other worried women.

He has chosen a maroon side chair, away from the family members seated in the dark brown couch and matching chair, encircling a sniffling boy in a sky-blue uniform. After a wait of twenty minutes, a second officer, reversibly dressed in tan on top, navy blue on bottom, walks toward him. She whispers his name, and he stands, glancing about, wondering who isn't supposed to hear. He shakes her pale hand.

"Mr. McKnight, I'm afraid your son declines a visit. He's complaining of a headache and stomach cramps." She pauses, and her upturned face invites him to ask a question that all concerned parents would know to ask. When he only stares, she sighs and shifts her weight, and he's certain he failed some kind of parental test.

"We've scheduled an appointment for your son with the visiting physician for tomorrow at three. You can, of course, come by at that time and talk with the doctor."

"Why does he need a doctor?"

"Strictly routine, I assure you."

Routine isn't a reason and he distrusts her smile, a mere extension of her uniform; authority over common sense.

"Ma'am, I can't miss work." Miss a Monday and the boss writes a man off without asking why. Blames the weekend the man had too much of.

"I see," she replies, her tone heavy with disrespect, and his resentment flashes hot. The sanctimonious bitch doesn't *see*, but he wants a favor.

"Then maybe you can pass along this little notebook. It's the kind he carries. A Five Star, but with lines. He uses these to ... draw in." He pauses. "You might say he's an artist-type. Draws wildlife, mostly. Tell him, if you would, that I tried for the one without lines, but ...." His throat tightens, and he feels he'll strangle on his ineptitude. He spins into a quick about-face and rushes back through the double doors.

He drives to the seedy side of town where he can buy beer on Sundays. He's misread Cole. Settled for an easier notion of a teenage boy pissed and popping off. But Cole's anger is fueled by something bigger, more complicated than he first thought.

He pulls to the window and tells Charlie what he wants and shrugs, agreeing to the ten percent service fee Charlie pockets for breaking the county's blue laws. He turns off the engine to save gas, and waits.

Out by the store's dumpster, a circle of men sit on overturned crates, a quart-size brown bag making the rounds. A slender man, the color of burnt toast, jumps to his feet, his rough hand jabbing the hot air, driving home his message. Laughter follows with another pass of the bag. A second man leans in and another story begins.

Jesse doesn't know these men, but he knows their tales of woe. He wants to take a turn with a painful truth of his own; one buried deep within the whopping lie he'd tell. In Iraq, liquor and laughter became his antidotes of choice for all the misery and regret he'd known.

Charlie returns with a six-pack of Pabst, and Jesse pays with the money he intended to leave with Cole for snacks or toothpaste or whatever his keepers allow. He drives back onto the highway, three-quarters down on the gas gauge, and heads west onto I-10, bound for the rest area he favors. The place doesn't have day or night security, the kind nervous travelers tend to avoid in favor of the illusion of safety the rent-a-cop provides at the Tallahassee rest area, twenty miles east.

He pulls the truck into a parking space overlooking the slow, churning brown waters of the Appalachicola River, and a bout of longing washes over him. Maybe coming here wasn't such a good idea, but he needs a quiet place where he can drink in peace.

He slips the damp bag under his arm and walks the short distance to the river bank, settling on the familiar grassy knoll beneath a giant water oak.

He and Dodie went all the way for the first time, here on this slope. Afterward, she cried softly against his shoulder, and he didn't know why. He'd believed she wanted it as much as he did. He isn't proud of the way he handled the news of Cole, but she's wrong to have held that against him for all these years.

He drains the second beer and opens a third, pressing its wet coolness to his warm right temple, his thumb touching the three inch scar.

Clyde had cursed his lack of manhood, smashing his big fists into his face, opening up the cut. He swore that if he was too damn selfish to do right by Dodie and his unborn kid, then he'd gladly marry her. He never believed Clyde's threat, but the licking shamed him into accepting what he'd known was his only real choice. He dropped out of school, forfeiting his life-long dream of playing college ball. He and Dodie moved in with his parents, and he joined his dad in a four generations long struggle to squeeze a meager existence from the family's small farm.

Jesse blinks hard, his eyes watering, and there's no disavowing the jab of guilt for having wished for a different choice.

He stands, gathers the empties, tucks the remaining beers under this arm, and starts for his truck. He slows next to the green trash container and tosses the three remaining beers. If he means to learn how to walk back his regrets and earn a second chance with his wife and kids, he'll need to do it sober.

He starts the engine and speeds onto the eastbound ramp, pointed homeward. He glances at the falling gauge, kicking his butt. Gas would have been a better buy than beer. He'd once seen a thirties movie where a couple of bootleggers poured liquor in the tank of a Model T and drove away, the engine spitting, but the old truck moving just the same. Pabst is damn fine beer, but it won't run a thirteen-year-old F-150.

HE DROPS ONTO THE SAGGING FOLDS of the couch, rank with the smell of dog and kids, figuring on catching a short nap before the girls return. He points the remote and the screen flashes and it's everything the western channel isn't.

Six feet from his face and worlds apart, a beautiful dark-skinned woman moves like a wisp of smoke to the rhythmic throbbing of Latin music, and her sizzling heat drives his. He unzips his jeans, takes his eager dick in hand, and puts his head back, closing his eyes.

The blaring of a car horn in his driveway snatches him up short of his moment of full relief. He moans in agony and pushes up from the couch, his jeans riding his hips, and shuffles his way to peer through a front window. Holy crap, Dee's Laredo sits in his driveway. He fumbles with his fly, tucks in his sweat-stained shirt, and runs his fingers through his too long hair. The horn blasts again, and he considers the penalty for failing to answer should she stop with her earsplitting racket and actually knock on his door like a civilized human.

She gets out of her car and leans on the front fender, and he gets a bad feeling that she means to keep it up until he shows himself. He pulls on his boots and steps onto the porch, taking the steps like the shaken man he is.

He advances and she straightens, but doesn't make a move toward him. Her eyes are red, and her face seems swollen. He imagines tears from Susan, but never Dee. He's known her since first grade, and he's never known her to cry, not even the time bully boy, Roy, pushed her off the playground slide. She got up off the ground and kicked the bark off Roy's sorry hide, the entire third grade cheering her on. He can't remember anyone stupid enough to try her again.

"Had no real plan to look you up just yet. I stopped because I need to settle things with Cole. Don't want to lose a good friend over this insane mess." She folds her arms across her breasts and leans away, back against the Jeep.

"It's fine, I'm glad. Been meaning to get by your place to say I'm awful sorry about what happened. Can't say exactly what got into Cole."

"I wanted to spare him this awful ordeal, but I don't lie to the law, even for him." She kicks at a tuft of crab grass with the toe of her hand-tooled cowboy boot. "More importantly, it would have sent the wrong message to Cole."

"Oh, hell yeah. You're right. No way did I expect you to lie for him."

"Where's Cole now? The sooner we talk, the better for both of us."

"He's not here just now."

"Okay, then where do I find him? I mean to put this behind us."

The look on her face says she'll go wherever, and that she intends to do it now. The best kind of lie will only bring her back ready to kill. Still, he hesitates, considering whether or not he owes her an answer. It's true, she and Susan were wronged. Still, Dee's the last person he wants to know that Cole picked detention over coming home with him.

"Went along with Buddy's notion that a little jail time might just teach Cole a hard lesson."

"He's there?"

"Oh, no, not with Buddy. The juvenile detention center. Just left there. The place ain't all that bad. Not like a real jail, I mean."

"Is that the best you can do? Let me get Cole a pro bono lawyer. I know several good ones I can call on." She steps closer, puts her hand out as though she means to touch him, but then drops a clinched fist to her side.

Jesse nods. "Maybe, but first I need to see if Cole's going to come around."

"Come around? What does that mean? Come around to what?"

"Figuring this thing out. Learning from it, I guess." He feels exposed: a dried insect pinned to cardboard.

She looks beyond him, toward the row of Leyland cypress standing tall and straight along the property line they share. She turns back, and he'd swear she considers taking out the 45 semi-automatic she's licensed to carry and blowing him away.

"Listen, you stupid asshole, don't bully Cole on this. Get him a lawyer before the so-called juvenile justice system messes him over."

Without another word, she gets back into the Jeep and speeds away, leaving behind a thick cloud of sand and gravel. He brushes grit from his face, remembering the first time she'd stomped his balls to Jell-O. He asked her for a date to the freshman dance, his first ever, and she'd snarled her disgust, turning him down flat. It would appear her opinion of him hasn't changed for the better, and that it has nothing to do with the fact that she favors women.

He takes a seat on the top step, and Beau comes from around the house as if he, too, has an axe to grind. The dog sits near, back on his haunches, his head tilted to one side, right ear standing, left ear drooped.

"Shut up, dog. I ain't interested."

Beau cowers, moves to the bottom step, and sits, his back to Jesse.

"Aw, forget it, dog. I was kidding." He pats the floor next to him, and Beau turns his head, thinks about it before taking up the space. Jesse tugs at Beau's drooped ear. "Your ears ain't all that bad.

There was this guy in my unit, name of Arnold. Boy had a blue eye and a brown eye. Claimed both his parents had green eyes."

MARLENE'S BEAT-UP BUICK approaches the lane, and he doesn't want to admit it, but he's glad it's her and not Clyde.

Katie runs toward him, shouting his name, Sky at her heels. "We've got Happy Meals. And you got a Quarter Pounder and biggie fries."

Marlene balances a tray of drinks in one hand and carries a bag of food in the other. "Hope you can stomach easy for supper. It's what the girls wanted."

"No, no, around here burgers and fries are eating high on the hog." He takes the tray of drinks and invites her in. He follows her into the kitchen where the girls sit at the kitchen table, their food spread before them. Beau stands on his hind legs and barks. Katie rewards him with a fry dipped in catsup.

The girls quickly finish their food and wander into the living room to watch TV, and he glances a time or two over his shoulder, as if Dodie's ghost hangs over the kitchen. Marlene suggests that they go to sit on the back door steps. She follows him and they resettle.

"Would offer you a beer, but I had a couple and tossed the balance in the trash." The back of his neck heats up. She's likely to think tossing perfectly good beer was the action of a crazy man.

"That's okay. I'm trying to cut back." She frowns, and he wonders if the demons she brought to Clyde's still haunt her.

She sits with her elbows propped on her knees, her chin cupped in her palms. Neither talks much, each appearing to shift through layers of thought while the day quietly melts into a sunset of deep orange and gold.

"I sometimes want the sun to linger on the very edge of good days. I love hanging out with Katie and Sky. They're great kids."

"Yeah, they are, most days. Still, Katie can be a pain. And when it comes to Sky, I'm at a loss. Don't know what to say or do."

"Patience, I think."

"Yeah, I hope you're right." He wonders if she ever married. If maybe she had kids sometime in her past. He considers both questions to be off limits. The kind of story a woman tells a man on her own terms.

They return to watching the first fireflies of the evening sprinkle soft light across the back yard. It's the kind of unexpected good that makes it feel okay to confide in her.

"I'm guessing Clyde told you about Cole's troubles."

"Yes, he did." Her dark eyes liquefy, and she fights back her tears.

"A lady guard told me he was too sick to see me, but I didn't believe her. He blames me entirely for his mom leaving."

"You can't know that for sure. I'd rather think he's hurt and confused. He needs more time to sort things out." Her words are gentle, and her kindness shows in the softness of her face.

"If my dad had tried visiting me in that place, I would've crawled on my belly, begging him to kick the shit out of me and just let me go home."

"Even though I didn't know your dad, I'm sure you're different, and Cole's different from you. We aren't meant to grow up to become our parents." Marlene stands and looks west, toward home.

"Don't go. It's still early." He wants to hear more of what she might tell him about his son.

"I'd love to stay, but Clyde's cooking his famous chicken and dumplings. He makes a big show of setting the table with the good dishes. He even lights candles."

"Damn, he does all that?"

She smiles. "Yes, he can be very sweet."

He believed he knew everything there was to know about his oldest friend, forgetting that a man's different with the woman he wants to please. Although Clyde's never said as much, his feelings for Marlene run deeper than Jesse had though before now.

He stands in the driveway, watching as Marlene's car disappears over a slight rise, and he feels calmer than he has since discovering Dodie's departing note. From the house, Katie's playful giggles float out to greet him, and he's struck by the notion of her resilience. And although he doesn't remember Sky making a sound, he decides that she liked seeing the pups.

FIVE

Six weeks pass and Cole continues to refuse Jesse's visits. He's had no direct word from Dodie, unless he counts the brief phone message she leaves weekly for the kids. Today, he and the girls come home to: "Mom loves you very, very much and I'm working hard to make things better for us. I'm coming for you soon. Bye for now."

It's the same message as always, from a blocked phone number, recorded at times when the girls are either at school or Trudy's after-school care. But it isn't her words he studies. He listens for the slightest crack in her voice; one that might tell him she's lonely, regrets her decision, even fearful of being alone. He doesn't trust her hyped promise of making things better; her miracle cure for all the misery she left behind.

Upon hearing her mom's first message, Katie looked at him, her lips parted, and she made a strange sucking sound, as if her breath came hard. Now she just listens, doesn't look at him or make the slightest sound, but rushes outside, straddles her bike and peddles hard, her head down. She doesn't stop until she runs out of lane. She stares east and then west along the highway, as though she means to choose a direction and ride on.

Sky pushes the replay button nine times, and when he can no longer bear it, he turns off the machine. She screams, her tiny face distorted by what he can't know, and he's helpless to know how to comfort her. She joins Katie at the end of the lane, and he's ashamed of the relief he feels. Still, he wants to know what, if anything, they are saying about their failed parents.

He's sure Sky's fits are on the rise, or maybe it only seems that way since he's around all the time. Just last evening, he walked out in the middle of one, her hands flapping while she spun in tight circles, screaming. He knows he can't keep walking out, leaving Katie to tend her. He means to talk to Trudy. She's the one adult, other than Dodie, Sky trusts. She'll know what he should do.

Katie's teacher sent a note home, concerned that her attention had started to wander, and that her usually excellent classroom work was suffering. She wanted to know if Katie's parents were aware of any reason why this problem might have developed, and if so, they were to call. Her tone suggested that responsible parents would have called already, but he has nothing he's willing to say to her.

After supper, the girls bathed and into bed, tomorrow's school clothes pressed, he places a call to Buddy. Trapped into listening to a political speech disguised as instructions, Jesse leaves a message. He remembers an earlier time, before automatic secretaries, when Buddy's front desk person would have picked up the damn phone, and if Buddy was out on patrol, she would have radioed him.

Too tired and sleepy to chance piling up on the couch to wait for Buddy's call, he pours the last of the coffee and sits at the kitchen table. He takes the court summons from his pocket and studies their names: Jesse W. McKnight, Jr. and Delores Jean McKnight, parents of Jesse Cole McKnight. The only other time he's seen all three names on any official document was on Coles's birth certificate. The gnawing pain in the pit of his stomach is the same as then. He puts his head down on the table and dares to close his eyes. He's unsure how long he's dozed when he's startled awake by the ringing of the kitchen phone.

"Hey, Champ, whatcha' need?"

"Got this summons and I don't know what to make of it." He knows he's to appear with Dodie in court, but beyond that, he's clueless.

"Uh huh, and who's the judge? White or Davis?"

Jesse reads the name into the phone.

"That ain't good. Wanted Davis. She's liberal. Loves boys in trouble. Believes they all can be reformed."

"All right, but what about White?" Jesse pictures Buddy spitting a nasty stream of tobacco juice in the tomato can he hides beneath his desk.

"That old sonofabitch is tougher than shark's teeth. Let Cole wise-off just once, it's the slammer. Lessons in becoming a hardened criminal, courtesy of Florida's taxpayers."

"How about first-timer, top grades, perfect attendance? Hell, Buddy, the boy's on the … on the debate team. That's got to count for something."

"I hear you. But I'm here to tell you a handwritten note from God Almighty, hand-delivered by Jesus Christ, won't make a tinker's damn."

"Holy crap, the damn sky's falling." He pitches his cup against the far wall, and it smashes to the floor, spilt coffee running down the wall.

Buddy is calling his name.

"Yeah, I'm good. Let you know how it comes out."

"Daddy, Daddy, what happened?" Katie stands in the kitchen door, Beau trailing.

"Nothing, baby. I spilt coffee. You and Beau go on back to bed."

He grabs a dishtowel and scrubs the wall. Katie gets the mop, and together they clean up his mess.

There's no hope of sleep after what he's heard, so he sets up the ironing board in the kitchen. He applies a hot iron to a damp dish cloth in an attempt at steaming away the heavy creases aged into his best trousers. It's three when he finally sets the clock and turns in.

Two hours before he's due in court, he's dressed in his best: a blue button down collar shirt, the freshly pressed gray slacks, and his good shoes polished to a parade shine.

Never mind that Katie turned up her nose, declaring that he looked as though he stepped off Noah's ark along with the extinct dinosaurs. He ignores her confusion, right along with her argument that he should at least wear a tie. The last two times he wore a tie, he'd buried his mama, and then his daddy six months later. Ties are bad luck.

JESSE DRAWS EVEN with the red brick courthouse, slows the truck, and searches for a glimpse of Cole among the handcuffed boys filing off a county van. When he doesn't see him, he comes to a complete stop, and behind him, an impatient driver sounds his horn. He mentally gives him the finger, and drives on without ever seeing Cole. Maybe he waits in the van. Surely if Cole's hearing date had been changed, he would have gotten a notice.

He parks the truck and searches among unopened final notices, candy and gum wrappers, and Katie's most recent school work, yet unsigned and unreturned, when he remembers putting the summons in the glove compartment. He scans the summons and exhales. He hasn't screwed up, but he still worries that he hadn't seen Cole among the others.

He takes the rumpled sack off the seat and steps onto the sidewalk, pausing to admire the wash job he and Katie did on the truck. He wants to believe that, by driving a cleaner truck, dressing in his best, and showing up after six weeks of sobriety, if he doesn't count three beers, he can charm lady luck. What he knows is that big and small breaks come down to the luck of the draw. Which side of the bed the judge got up on this morning may be all that counts. Yet the effort helped keep his worst fears at bay.

Forty-five steep stone steps to the courthouse entrance, and when he reaches the top, he's breathing hard. He passes through heavy double doors and climbs a second set of stairs to the second floor.

A row of metal folding chairs lines the hallway, pushed against the wall opposite the judge's chambers. He leans against the opposite wall, and across from him there are mostly women, years of dread chiseled into their faces. He recognizes the musty smell of steamed clothes, for these women have also worn their best.

Near his right foot, a toddler squats. The boy stares up at him and picks at gum stuck to the floor with a chubby index finger the color of a tootsie roll. Jesse leans and whispers, "Better find your mama before you end up like that gum."

A girl, five or six years older, her hair braided and fastened with dozens of red plastic ties, takes the boy's hand and drags him screaming toward a set of outstretched arms. Jesse looks at the young woman now holding the boy and nods, wanting her to know that he was only teasing. Her fixed jaw says she isn't interested in what he intended.

Jesse looks away, following the path of a palmetto bug the size of a hotdog bun, skittering along the long corridor of office doors with frosted glass insets bearing names and domains of authority painted in tall, black, stately lettering. He hopes the bug plans on taking his nasty business under the door of Judge White's kingdom.

At the end of the long hallway, a second set of double doors swings open and heads turn, a breathless hush falling over those waiting. Old women push onto pained knees while younger women, babies riding on their hips, call to other children scattered about. They gather pocketbooks, diaper bags, and crumpled brown paper sacks. He joins them, and like human boxcars, they shuffle toward the double doors.

When it's his turn, he answers, "My boy's shoes." Jesse opens the bag and Cliff peers in. He worked with Cliff before the plant closing, and the man seems surprised at seeing him at the hard end of courthouse business.

"Just the same, Jess, you're gonna need to leave 'em." He offers a stingy grimace, caught between duty and the ridiculous. "I'll see they get to the charge officer should he need them."

"Right." Jesse surrenders the bag, *should he need them* taking fire in his brain. He enters the courtroom and takes a seat near the back. He glances at the woman sitting next to him, and she leans and whispers, "There, through them doors."

Jesse spots Cole, fifth in a tightly formed line of three white and six black boys of varying sizes and hues, each clad in bright orange jumpsuits. Without a backward glance, Cole sits with his shoulders drawn and head bowed. Worried about how his son might react at seeing him, Jesse pushes back in his seat and slumps.

The rank smell of their fear fills the room, and a deep hush falls over the courtroom as an officer of the court announces the approach of the honorable Judge Solomon White.

The courtroom groans with the complaint of aged wooden benches under the sudden shift in weight. They stand and wait for the sound of the gavel to release them. The judge looks over the courtroom with a scowl, and only a village idiot would expect a break from this man.

Jesse strains to hear over the hammering of his heart what passes between the judge and a smooth-faced attorney, his deference focused directly on the judge. Jesse scoffs at the notion of a rookie lawyer brokering a favorable deal with the man Buddy described. Still he watches, pushing back hard on Dee's warning that, without a lawyer, Cole was fodder. He'd just as soon she hadn't gone off in his face, but as the young attorney hurries the pale-faced boy from the courtroom, he has a sinking feeling that she wasn't just whistling Dixie.

"Jesse Cole McKnight, step forward." An officer leads Cole to stand before the judge, removes his handcuffs, and steps back.

At the sound of Cole's name Jesse's scalp feels as if it lifted from his skull, and he tastes backed up coffee in his throat. He swallows hard, shifts onto the front half of the bench, and waits.

When he hears his name, he stands and steps onto the carpeted aisle. Suddenly, his mind seizes, and for an instant he's no longer in the courtroom, but back in Iraq. Fear of his next step pushes into his legs, and he falters. A large, black hand reaches to steady him, and their eyes lock in an intense look, neither speaking, but Jesse knows they likely share the same sleepless nights.

He stands with his left shoulder inches from Cole, who glances at him. His eyes are those of little boy, and he's holding back tears. Jesse moves closer, and Cole doesn't move away.

"Mr. McKnight, I ask you again. Are you the boy's father?" The judge's look bores down from the bench.

"Yes sir, Your Honor, sir, I am," He looks straight at the judge, his trembling hands hidden inside his pockets, until he realizes that his slouched stance could make him into a brash fool. He withdraws his hands and straightens.

"Mr. McKnight, where is this boy's mother? And is there reason I should not find Delores Jean McKnight in contempt?"

Jesse hesitates, working his way through a maze of consequences. If he tells the judge she knew of the summons and refused to comply, the judge would issue a warrant. The law would find her, force her back, and she might stay. But Cole would never forgive him.

He presses a sweaty palm to the pocket of his shirt where he placed the note he'd found propped innocently as sweet baby Jesus against the salt and pepper set the morning she left. He's shared the note with no one. The full weight of its meaning remains a mystery, making it doubly hard to know how to answer honestly.

"Hell fire, man, find your damn tongue."

"Your Honor, sir, I can't say exactly. You see ... we're ... separated just now." He doesn't think he lies, and he's sure the judge needs to hear that their separation is temporary.

"Then I take it you're a single parent?"

It sounds to him like a trick question; one smart lawyers get paid big bucks to know how best to answer. Single parents are women, and he doesn't think men are trusted in that way.

"Mr. McKnight, it's a simple question, requiring either a yes or no. Again, is this boy's mother in or out of the picture?"

"Yes sir, I'm afraid so. Out, I mean."

The judge shakes his head, and Jesse is pretty sure he didn't hear what he needed to hear. Still the man looks down at the folder open before him.

Jesse remembers the contempt he heard in the voice of the deputy at Buddy's jail, and that of the woman at the detention center. Had their cut-downs made their way into the folder the judge reads?

"Mr. McKnight, your son has waived his right to council and pled gulity to grand theft auto juvenile, driving under the influence, driving without a license, and reckless driving."

Jesse is stunned. Cole sags against him, and he whispers, "Steady, son. Don't give up."

"Maybe six weeks of detention gave your boy time to think about what he wants to do with his life." The judge shifts his attention to Cole and his gaze probes. "But, unfortunately, I find many young men are either too hard-headed or stupid to learn from their mistakes."

Jesse allows himself to take heart in the notion that learning from one's mistakes could include leniency. He thinks this is likely an opening to say more on behalf of Cole. But what exactly, he has no idea.

The judge leans toward Cole. "Young man, which are you?" His voice, low and steely, wipes away all inkling of compassion.

"I'm neither, sir, hardheaded nor stupid, I mean. Please, I'm sorry for taking Miss Susan's car. She's always been nice to me. I swear I'll make it up to her."

"Young man, I'm afraid your obligation goes beyond the good neighbor you wronged. There are the innocent lives you endangered and the laws you broke."

"Yes sir. I know." Cole wipes at his eye with the back of his hand.

"The arrest report says you claimed to have taken your neighbor's car to go look for your mother. Is that right?"

"Yes sir. I needed to talk her into coming back home." Cole glances at him and back at the judge, and since his talk with Sally, Jesse believes Cole may have had a bigger part in his mom's plan; may have known where to look.

"Mr. McKnight, do you have anything to add to this boy's story?"

"No sir. Only that we got into it pretty hard … and both said things. But I do believe he's telling the truth about what he meant to do … the part about looking for her, his mother, I mean." The back of his neck flushes hot, and he wishes he'd put it better.

"Mr. McKnight, the file indicates that you made frequent visits to the detention center."

"Yes sir, I did."

"Young man, I understand you refused your father's visits. Why was that?"

Cole's chest rises and falls beneath the loose smock, and he stares at the floor between his feet.

"Young man, I need to hear from you. Now I asked you a question, and you're going to need to look at me. And you will answer truthfully."

Cole lifts his chin, tears forming in the corners of his eyes, and he doesn't blink. "Sir, I was so angry I couldn't think straight. Right then, I hated my parents for messing up my life, and that of my little sisters." Cole sucks air, and Jesse fears he has gone too far with the truth.

The judge nods. "And now, what do you have to say?"

"I still get angry. And confused." He pauses, but continues to look the judge in the face. "But, now I'm more ashamed than anything. I can't change what I did. But I want a chance to make good with those I've wronged."

"Am I to believe that includes your parents?"

Cole hesitates, and then he says, "Yes sir, my dad. Where that's possible."

The judge studies Cole's pale upturned face, and he appears to look for some reason to trust him. "Your school record is commendable. Then, I've sent plenty of smart boys to jail."

Cole's shoulders sag, his weight shifting onto Jesse. He places an arm around his son's shoulders.

"Mr. McKnight, if I should decide to place your son on probation and release him into your custody, I'd expect you two to work out whatever needs working out between you. And I'd need your solemn word that you'll be around to hold this boy's feet to the fire. That means I'd better not hear of your son being as much as tardy for homemaking class. And from you, not even a parking ticket. You get my drift?"

"Yes sir, you have my word."

Cole inhales sharply, and Jesse figures it's about the worthiness of his word. There's no doubt, the judge has tied Cole's fate to his promise.

"Young man, I need to hear from you. Otherwise, I have no choice but to put you behind bars, and I can guarantee you that your life will go straight to hell." The judge's tone aims to melt any defiance Cole may still harbor.

"Yes, sir, please. I don't want to go to jail."

The judge cocks his head to one side. "Mr. McKnight, I've got a feeling about you, and it isn't altogether good. Still, I'm going to take a chance on you and your boy."

"Yes sir, thank you." It was the miracle his praying mama would have called upon.

"Jesse Cole McKnight, I sentence you to twelve months probation and three hundred hours of community service to be worked out with your probation officer. Go with the officer and change out of that uniform. Then you're free to go with your father. Mr. McKnight, you will be informed by an officer of the court as to the terms and conditions of your son's probation."

He and Cole thank Judge White, who doesn't as much as nod, directing the clerk to call the next boy. Cole goes with the officer, and Jesse leaves the courtroom, drained of the juices needed to propel him along the corridor. He thinks he knows how it will feel to be old.

He locates the room, signs the release papers, and puts his copy in his shirt pocket. He takes a seat, sandwiched between two women, one older than he feels.

The older woman leans and whispers in the booming voice of the deaf, "That boy of yours is mighty lucky. Judge don't turn many loose, no sir, he surely don't. Then he's powerfully big on daddies and their promises. Any caliber of daddy bothering to show goes a long ways. Told my boy that, but he don't listen."

"Yes'um, he is. Lucky, I mean." He wonders about her luck, but doesn't want to start a public conversation with a deaf woman.

"Uh huh, lucky. But then white don't hurt." She crosses her arms over her sagging breasts with a finality that he suspects comes with a lifetime of truth-telling.

He nods, not sure what he can add. Still, he likes knowing that his presence in the courtroom may have influenced a better outcome. Maybe even wearing his unlucky tie would have been okay, but he's glad he didn't run the risk. Maybe now, even Dee will let up, admit that he did okay by Cole.

Cole precedes a deputy through the door, and he's wearing his shoes with no socks and the rumpled shirt and jeans he wore the night he ran from the house. Jesse wishes he'd remembered to bring clean, pressed clothes.

They exit the courthouse, and Jesse glances upward into a cloudless sky. The noon heat bears down and they stand for a moment, blinking against the bright light. They descend the steep stairs, and it has to feel good to Cole to step into the flow of ordinary people going about their day.

"What'd you say to a double burger and fries? You've got to be half-starved."

"Yeah, thanks, I've been hungry for six weeks. Jail's everything you've ever heard … and more." Cole's last words trail off, absorbed by street noises, and he short steps a sidewalk crack, as if he momentarily slips back into the innocence of his childhood.

SIX

They enter Cole's favorite burger joint, and Jesse waits until his son has ordered, tallying the tab in his head, before ordering a single burger, coffee and no fries. They take their orders, slide onto orange plastic benches at a table the same color, and begin to eat in strained silence. When Jesse finishes the burger, he leans in, deciding to risk asking Cole the question that has gone unanswered.

"Something you said back there in court caused me to wonder how it was that you headed east onto I-10. Buddy mentioned that you'd tried talking his deputy into looking for your mom on the Tallahassee leg of the interstate."

"Are you asking if I knew where to look?"

"I guess I am." He knows he risks any goodwill that might have built up from the trial.

"No, I wasn't in on her leaving, if that's what you're thinking. Remember, I heard it first from you."

"Okay, but did you take Susan's car straight away?" Jesse remembers the barking dog he later decided was Beau. He isn't sure why, but a timeline of Cole's movements before his decision to drink looms big in his mind.

Cole nods. "Then I went to Grandma's. Thinking Mom would go there."

He doesn't say "like before," but his hard eyes do. An earlier fight sent his mom there, he and his sisters in tow.

"When she wasn't there, I figured the worst. Her leaving without Grandma knowing didn't make sense."

"Did you talk to her, your grandma, I mean?"

"Hell, no. I didn't want to be the one to tell her."

"She can be a handful all right."

"Drove by that dumpy trailer park on the chance Mom might have stayed the balance of the night at Sally's." His lip snarls.

"After leaving you at … Buddy's …."

"Jail, Dad. Say it and get used to it. Your son's an ex-con." Cole looks away, but not before Jesse sees his eyes water.

Jesse nods. "Talked to Sally myself. But I didn't get much."

"Did she tell you I was with Mom?"

Sheepish, Jesse thinks, but nothing more. "How'd that happen?"

Cole shrugs. "I skipped the bus ride. Stayed to talk to my physics teacher. Then I walked over to the shop."

"You go home with your mom?"

"No, she offered to drop me at James's. He drove me to Grandma's for Mom's party."

"Did you think that was odd?"

Cole doesn't answer, and Jesse takes that to mean he doesn't like the obvious. Dodie regularly pitched fits about Cole's friendship with James. She swore his twice-divorced mother's live-in boyfriend dealt drugs. Her evidence was beauty shop gossip, which is not to say the kid's a saint. He has a record stemming from a failed runaway and one count of shoplifting. What sixteen year-old boy hasn't considered running, or for that matter, fleecing a six-pack? It was hardly up there with grand theft auto.

"Did you even bother looking for Mom?" Although Cole omits *the way you promised*, his jaws lock and his resentment holds steady.

"Called around to different beauty shops in Tallahassee, asking for an appointment with her. But that didn't pan out. Tried talking to your Aunt Shirley. And I think you know that didn't have much of a chance."

"Does that mean you're done looking? What if she's out of money and can't get back home? You see that all the time. Stranded people begging for gas money. You want that for Mom?"

"No, and I think you know that I don't. But that's not what's going on with her." Jesse pauses.

"What then?" Cole slouches, his eyes uncertain.

"Sally's staying on. Paying overhead and depositing the balance in your mom's account. That's their deal."

"Deal?" Cole's glance is perceptive beyond comfort, and he twists the plastic cup in tight circles as though he scrambles for any rational counter-argument he can shape.

Jesse thinks about pulling out the worn note he carries, maybe settling this argument with Cole once and for all. But he knows his and Cole's differences are much greater than the way in which his mama left. That talk will need to keep for a time when their wounds are not as raw.

Jesse glances at the clock on the opposite wall. "Guess I best drop you at school and head to work. Make what time I can."

"Do I just go back? No questions asked?" Cole's face shows his dread. Like he said, he's returning, not as an honors student, but as a jail bird. There's surely a better way to color what he faces, but a fancier label won't spare Cole its consequences.

"I'd like to wait until tomorrow, if that's okay."

Judge White said he should be tough with Cole, but the pleading in his voice stops any hard line Jesse thought to take.

"Should be all right. The school day's mostly shot. But you heard the judge. School attendance is a big deal."

"Maybe you didn't notice, but school is a big deal. And that's not about to change." Cole wraps the burger and bags it.

"It's true I missed a lot. And you've got a right to be pissed. But you're dead wrong about me not being proud of your school work."

"Why'd you keep coming after I wouldn't see you?"

Jesse reads Cole's tone not as one of disrespect, but of confusion. He slips his keys back into his pocket and pushes back onto the seat.

"I've thought a lot about that. And I'm guessing a big part was my guilt at letting bad blood build between us. Then there was me wanting to do what I could to make your time easier." He wishes he knew more to say, but he has too many unanswered questions of his own.

Beneath the florescent light, Cole's brow glistens with tiny sweat droplets, and he twists the top of the burger bag tighter. "You stopped being proud of me when I didn't turn out to be a super jock. What those old rednecks at Willie's Barbershop think means more to you. Can't you be proud of me for who I am?"

"Good Lord, Cole, you're my son."

"But not the son you dreamed of." His fine jaw squares, and it's clear he doesn't intend to back away.

"Quitting cold-turkey the way you did was hard to swallow. You didn't bother talking to me. I had to hear it from your coach."

"I wanted to tell you, but I knew you'd try talking me out of my decision."

"What happened to the kid who bragged he'd break my school records?"

"I grew up, Dad. I don't want that anymore."

Maybe not, but that was the son he knew how to be a father to, not the bookish boy who sat for hours drawing. Among the three generations of McKnight males he's known, not one ever took up a pen for more than signing a bank note for the next round of crops.

"Sarah says I can't change how you feel. Only screw up my own life."

"Sarah? Why haven't I heard about her?"

"She's been my best friend since sixth grade." The softness that settles around Cole's mouth tells Jesse that, if he's lucky, Sarah is likely to be the subject of future talks.

"Sarah sounds like a real smart girl. And I bet she's pretty, too."

Cole blushes.

He and Cole walk from the restaurant, and upon reaching the truck, Cole stops, a slight smile playing across his handsome face.

"Damn, I didn't remember it was blue. Just dirty."

"A spiffed up dude like your old man is expected to drive a clean truck."

"Yeah, right, Dad." His smile holds.

Jesse exhales, the weight he carries lifting a bit, his breath coming somewhat easier.

SEVEN

He drops Cole at home, changes into his work clothes and boots, and hits the road. Down two hours into his shift, he pushes the old truck to seventy and the front end suspension shakes, forcing him to cut his speed. Still, he pulls into the warehouse gravel parking lot feeling better than he has in some time. Cole's a smart kid, the kind the judge spoke of; one who learns from his mistakes.

He punches in and goes to the locker area for his safety equipment and work gloves. Through the Plexiglas and metal enclosure that passes for a break room, he notices the boss sitting alone at one of three red plastic snack tables, and he waves him in.

"McKnight, take a load off." The boss motions to a seat across from him at the table.

Jesse sits, his knees bouncing to the rhythm of his racing heart. In his gut, he feels the way he had waiting for the ball to fall through glaring lights into his open hands, while the noise of the hopeful was deafening.

"Heard about your boy's troubles. How'd it go?"

"A damn sight better than I expected. Got probation and a shit-load of community service."

"Yeah, I'd say. White put my oldest boy's ass in the junior pen for three years. Then I can't fault the judge. Damn fool kid was selling dope two blocks from a junior high."

Jesse nods, and he feels the boss switching gears.

"McKnight, work load being what it is, I've got to lay off a part-timer and go with a full-timer." He drains his coffee cup and reaches into his pocket, coins jingling. "You want some of this goat piss?"

Jesse declines and works at spinning what he's heard into good news for him and rotten news for some other poor bastard.

"A guy with more experience got picked over you." He stands and puts change in the coffee machine.

"Why's that? I operate a forklift as good as any man here."

"Yeah, I know, but there's the other."

"What other?" He has a clean safety record and doesn't drink on the job.

"This boy's solid. Married with a good wife at home." He pauses. "You raising kids on your own—you're bound to have more no-shows."

"Today's the first time I've asked for time off. And I've got after school help."

"I'm sorry, McKnight. Two more weeks, that's all I can promise."

An office worker comes to the door. The boss picks up his clipboard, and without another word, he walks out to take a phone call. Then, how many different words are there to say screwed? Although Jesse feels like a rat drowning in a bucket of slop, he walks out of the break room and climbs onto the forklift.

When his shift is over, he punches out and heads for his truck.

"Hey, McKnight. Hold up."

He turns to his shift supervisor. The very asshole that likely passed him over.

"Look, I'm sorry about what happened."

"Right." He turns and walks on.

"Listen, I know about a job."

Jesse turns back.

"Atkins Lumberyard fired an operator yesterday. The job's part-time. But, if you're interested ...."

"Better than a damn kick in the teeth." He grins, but doesn't feel it.

He gets the time and the name of the guy he's to talk to about the job.

"Tell Rufus I sent you. The fat fuck's my brother-in-law. And I guarantee you'll despise him before lunch time."

"Yeah, thanks. I've worked for plenty of guys I'd never date."

He's driving the speed limit, sipping the last of the bitter coffee from his thermos and cursing his bad luck, when a fancy woman driving an S-Class, silver-gray Mercedes speeds past. She flashes him a look that he takes as her disrespecting him, his truck, and everything about his piss-poor station in life. A fit of pure rage erupts, scorching his reasoning. He overtakes the Mercedes, pulls the truck alongside, and screams profanities through the open window.

Nestled in the protective cocoon that is the luxury Mercedes, the woman can't possibly hear his rant, serving to increase his outrage. He sets down on the horn and she looks in his direction, her eyes stretched wide. He thinks about backing off, settling for having given the snotty bitch a good scare, but he wants more. He swerves the truck's rear bumper, forcing the terrified woman onto a steep shoulder.

That's when he spots the sleeping child in the safety seat. A corner of fuzzy pink blanket catches his eye and he thinks it must be a girl.

The woman struggles to control the speeding car, finally managing a safe stop, and they're both damn lucky she's driving a Mercedes. Through the rear-view mirror, he watches her, bent over the steering wheel, and he can no longer see the baby. He's sure the tiny girl was jarred awake, her face now twisted in fear as she cries.

Slowing the truck, he considers going back and apologizing, explaining that he isn't sure what came over him, only that he'd gone momentarily crazy. He wants her to understand that he isn't the type of guy who risks the lives of a woman and her child. But could she believe anything other than he's a stupid redneck who willfully endangered her and her baby? She's probably already placed a frantic cell phone call to the highway patrol.

Forget going back, he needs to worry about his own kids. The judge's stern threat echoes through his head, and he realizes that his moment of insanity could send Cole to prison, the girls to their Jesus-freaking, hard-ass of a grandmother, and Beau to the pound.

He drives on, his after-stupidity consequences pounding against his temples, and tries to lose the picture of the crying baby. If the woman called the law, then she likely described the vehicle as a beat-up pickup, maybe once dark blue or black, driven by an unkempt man wearing a dingy tee shirt; the description fits half the county's male population and their vehicles. With everything happening so fast, she probably didn't get a good look at his expired tag. Still, he needs to pick up the girls and get off the road.

He slides the truck to a quick stop in front of Cora's, fifteen minutes late, and braces for Katie's chorus as predictable as pancake syrup and sticky fingers. Times like these, he's shamefully grateful to have only one kid with a motor mouth. Katie gets into the truck, dragging Sky onto the seat next to her.

"We've got to go to Wal-Mart and get Sky new shoes."

"No, I've had a shitty day and we're going home." He looks over at Sky's right shoe, and sure enough, she's blown the sole.

"Oh, no, if Cole's still in trouble, he'll need Mama to talk for him."

"It's not about Cole. He's home. You'll see."

She pauses, appears relieved to hear that her brother is no longer in detention.

"Okay, then we'll hurry home as soon as we get Sky's shoes. It'll only take a minute." Her voice lifts. "I know exactly where to look for her size."

"No. Give it a rest. I'll super-glue the sole. It'll be fine. You'll see."

Katie shakes her head. "You know it won't stay fixed. Sky needs shoes the other kids don't laugh at."

He turns up the radio and speeds on, working at ignoring her. She sets her jaw in a hard line, flips the radio dial to a station that plays the kind of music she knows causes him to grit his teeth. For a fleeting moment, he thinks about the sweet relief of pulling the truck to the side of the road and putting her sassy little behind out, leaving her to find her own way home.

It's true he's never been the parent to handle the kid's crises, big or small. He was in Iraq when Katie was born. Clyde drove Dodie to the hospital and sat in the lobby for ten hours, waiting for Katie to make up her mind.

ENTERING THE HOUSE, Jesse expects Cole to come from his room to greet his sisters. When he doesn't, he goes onto the back porch, the anxious dog trailing his every step. Cole isn't sitting at the picnic table beneath the pecan tree, where he likes to sketch in the little pocket-sized notebooks he carries in his hip pocket.

The kid's been out of jail for less than six hours, and already Jesse can't account for his whereabouts. This isn't what Judge White meant by holding Cole's feet to the fire. When he's run out of places to look, he goes back into the kitchen where Katie stands in the doorway, her hands on her hips, and he sees her as a miniature replica of Cora.

"So where is he? You said he'd be here."

"School assignments, I think. He'll be here for supper."

She squints up at him, and he's sure she doesn't trust his answer.

"What's James's name?" It won't hurt to call.

"James." She shrugs. "That's all I know." She opens the fridge door.

"Dang it, he's been here. Puts empty milk cartons back. Makes you think there's milk when there's not." She continues to stand in the open door, shaking an empty carton.

"Shut the door and make up some of that blue powdered stuff." It tastes like crap and looks like it's extracted from old people's veins.

"Sky won't like it. And we'll hear about it." Katie slams the door. Spotting the can of corned beef on the counter, her wider pout becomes a reminder of his failure to uphold her mom's Thursday night ritual of fish sticks that taste like fried sawdust, served with frozen French fries.

He dumps the congealed glob of corned beef into the hot skillet with chopped onions, peels and dices white potatoes into a pot of boiling water, adding plenty of salt. Tomorrow, he'll go to the store, buy a few things they're out of until his grocery money plays out.

A horn blasts and the fool kid, James, has driven onto the patchy lawn as if Cole walking ten yards might kill him. Cole waves to James, who hangs out a window, shouting, as he spins away on bald tires. Cole comes through the door and Katie, trailed by Beau, runs to meet him.

"Hey, shrimp turd. Danged if I don't think you've grown. Dad's cooking, right?"

She pushes a finger down her throat and makes an awful gurgling sound.

Cole's heavy backpack hits the floor. He and Katie stand in the doorway of the kitchen, Katie hanging around his waist and Beau circling the table, barking.

Cole leans and pulls back the tablecloth, peering underneath where Sky sits, tearing paper into tiny strips, piling it into three neat mounds. She doesn't bother looking up.

He shakes his head. "I see all's normal with you, baby sister."

"Ripping paper's more fun than sucking Beau's ears." Katie giggles.

"Come on. Don't give her ideas. And get her to the table. Supper's about ready." Jesse doesn't think she meant to be mean, but only to impress her big brother, and maybe she does mean to separate herself from Sky's peculiar behaviors.

The water in the pot of potatoes boils over, and the tea has steeped too long by the time he yells for Katie to get the tea bags out. She stops dragging Sky from beneath the table and glares, as if to ask just how many hands he thinks she has, but she holds her tongue.

"Cole, I'm thinking you might need to stay clear of James for a while."

"And maybe you're forgetting I don't exactly fit in with the born-again crowd or the jocks whose crimes are fixed by boosters. That leaves geeks and ex-jailbirds."

"Okay, I get it. But, there's the judge's warning. A loud fart and we're back in court."

"No, Dad. It's my ass back in jail. So, if you don't mind, I'll pick my friends."

They stare each other down over a steaming skillet of over-cooked corned beef and onions.

"You weren't here and I needed my backpack from Sarah's. Afterward, James drove me to meet my parole officer." His tone softens, and Jesse senses he's trying. "I would've called, but my cell phone has no service."

"Had to let the cell phones go." The disconnect notice included a penalty for fudging on the contract. "The house phone still works."

"Great, I'll remember that the next time I need to call home."

"Your parole officer?"

Cole's smirk says all Jesse needs to know. "The lard ass is a total loser, but I drew the animal shelter after school three days a week, plus half a day on Sundays. Three cheers for separation of church and state, right?"

Jesse sets aside Cole's comment about the parole officer, thinking that scraping dog mess out of cages, any day of the week, has a way of humbling even a smart-ass kid. Still, he has concerns about James. How long before he'll drag Cole into one of his scrapes? It's bad enough that he already looks to dodge the law.

Because it means fewer dishes to wash, Jesse serves their plates directly from the stove. Katie and Sky take potatoes, corned beef, and canned garden peas. Cole takes only potatoes, scraping the last of the peanut butter from the jar, declaring it to be protein, unlike canned corned beef consisting of congealed fat, rat shit, and slaughter house sawdust. He had a right to expect a meal worthy of a get-out-of-jail celebration, but at their table, decent meals for any occasion are, at best, a fading memory.

After supper dishes, Jesse asks Katie to bring Sky's busted shoe. He applies super glue and holds the upper shoe and sole together with a wood clamp from his toolbox. If it doesn't rain, maybe it will stay glued until his next paycheck. He thinks Katie may feel a bit guilty that she got new shoes three paychecks back.

"Daddy, Daddy, come quick," Katie screams.

"What the hell?" He hurries to the laundry room.

"Everything's pink!"

He pulls wet clothes from the washer and throws them into the laundry basket. She's washed underwear, socks, and his favorite red knit sport shirt in the same load.

"Tell me how I'm supposed to replace all this? Buy shoes? Groceries?" He's yelling and he can't stop.

A tearful Katie runs down the hall, a screaming Sky and barking Beau at her heels. Their bedroom door slams behind them. Cole shouts something about detention having been quieter.

In his panic, he calls Marlene, and although he knows he can't expect to call his best friend's lady every time something goes haywire, he cringes at the thought of her not answering. After seven rings, he pictures Clyde's place overrun with demanding drunks calling her name.

Clyde leaves her alone to run the joint while he drives the beat-up '87 Chevy van that the two of them rigged with hand controls and a lift, outfitted to haul dogs, into the woods. He rides his motorized wheelchair, equipped with oversized tires, clear to the edge of a boggy swamp where he sits, swigging Ancient Age, while waiting for the return of his hounds and their trainer.

Jesse once remarked, after he and Clyde had been drinking heavily, that he should leave the stragglers to find their own way home. Clyde had pulled himself up, suddenly sober, leaned across the table, and declared that, if a hound was to hunt and not ramble, it had to want to come back to where he dropped it. His side of the deal was to be there when it did. Without another word, he'd rolled the wheelchair through the door and into a freezing night.

Marlene picks up, and she's breathless.

"Hey, I'm sorry. I know you're busy. But I wanted to tell you about Cole getting probation."

"I was so happy to hear. He'll be fine. I'm sure of it."

He's surprised that Cole has already called and he wonders how often they talk and whether Cole had allowed her a visit while he was in detention.

He explains his second reason for calling, and she speaks calmly about losing the shirt unless he likes pink and that he should rewash the whites with bleach, explaining that it may take several washings to get all of the color out.

"Don't worry. You'll look hot in pink underwear." She laughs. "Maybe you and the kids could use a home cooked meal. What do you say we celebrate Cole's homecoming? How about Sunday afternoon in your back yard? I'll bring food and drink. What would you like?"

"Anything, but if it's all the same, could we please have something other than corned beef hash and stewed potatoes?"

"Okay, you've got it."

When she hangs up the phone, an odd feeling passes over him, and he feels her absence as though she'd stood next to him while they talked. He restarts the washer and calls Cole into the kitchen.

"I'll need you to get yourself and the girls ready for school tomorrow and to the bus stop on time." He's told no one, not even Clyde, about the layoff. If he gets the job at the lumber yard, then no one needs to know.

"What's wrong that you can't do it?"

"Nothing's wrong. I just need to be somewhere before the bus runs."

Cole looks skeptical. "Okay, but what do I have to do? Sky won't listen to me. And Katie can be a butt."

"Yeah, I know. But Katie will see to Sky. There's Rice Krispies and milk. Just get yourself and those two on the bus."

"Okay, but I'll catch hell from that bunch of morons on the bus."

EIGHT

When he arrives, a line has already formed. He finishes off the last of the cold coffee, gets out of the truck, and joins the hopefuls, looking to go home the winner. The line stands sixteen men deep, and he doesn't like his odds. Still he squares his shoulders and tries calling up the swagger he once owned.

The door swings open and a fleshy, rouge-cheeked man wearing a shirt gapped over his belly orders the line to move back against the wall. Jesse leaves his place in line and approaches the man he expects to be Rufus. There's justified grumbling from those ahead in line, but he doesn't retreat.

"Your brother-in-law from over at Watkins sent me. I'm a damn fine operator, a steady worker, and I need a job." Begging sticks in his craw, but no worse than Sky needing shoes.

"Mister, every damn one of these guys got sent by some bastard or another who laid him off." The man's sarcasm gets a sucker you're screwed look from those he passes on his way back to the end of the line.

An hour later, Jesse has worked his way to third from the door when the man, who isn't Rufus, announces, "Hiring's done, boys. Ya'll free to go on back to watching porn."

"Sonofabitch is funny, ain't he?" The disheveled man behind Jesse looks as though he lives in his car.

"Oh, yeah. He's a hoot, all right."

Grumbling men fall out of line, their coarse jokes meant to cover their defeat. Others, who've been at this longer, slouch and walk away, their desperation showing in their bowed heads. Jesse pulls himself up and walks back to his truck at a pace intended to say he's got other options.

He sits behind the wheel and thinks about a nice, cool place where he can know the comforting, sweet-sour scent of bourbon filling his nostrils. It was moments like this that had caused him to carry Jim Beam under the seat of his truck.

Ahead, captured in the frame of the truck's bug-stained windshield, a tiny girl Sky's age approaches with a man Jesse takes to be her father. As the two draw even with the truck, she looks up at the man and smiles. It's a smile he's yet to know from Sky, and he wants to earn that smile more than he wants a drink.

He starts the truck and drives across town, pulling to a stop in front of Trudy's Child Care, operated out of a small wood frame house painted flamingo pink and trimmed in lime green. He searches for Sky among the kids scattered like patches of wildflowers over the playground, cluttered with swings, kid-size tables, and sandboxes. Two girls and a lone boy sit at a purple table, the girls pretending to bottle-feed dolls while the boy looks on. Two older boys swing higher and higher, their toes pointed to the sky, double-dog dares tattooed on their young faces. But Sky is not among any of them.

On the screened porch, Trudy sits in a rocker, mounds of flesh spilling between the chair rounds. She watches the kids playing in the yard while rocking a young one, a bottle propped against her large breast.

He gets out of the truck and walks toward her.

"Morning, Daddy Jess," she calls. "I got a serious bone to pick with you." She shifts the blue-eyed boy to a shoulder, gently patting his back. "Where's my baby girl this morning?"

Jesse points across the street. "She didn't get off the bus with Katie?"

"No, and since Katie didn't come off the bus, I figured you were bringing them."

He pivots, looking again toward Katie's elementary school, and he thinks he must look like a swirling fool.

Trudy rocks herself forward to the front of the rocker. She holds the boy firmly against her shoulder, and with her other hand, she pushes her bulk out of the rocker.

"You wait right there, and let me put this boy child down." Tiny puffs of air escape her mouth as she hurries into the house.

His mind darting wildly about like bats at twilight, he fights off his near panic. But he doesn't know what to think. It's simple. They missed the bus. Kids do it all the time, but never Katie. Where was Cole? How did he let this happen? He can't keep his worst fear at bay.

Behind him, he hears the hurried scuffing of Trudy's house slippers as she rushes from the house and back onto the porch, while from the direction of the street, he watches as Dee's Jeep slides to a full stop next to his truck. He hurries to meet Katie, who rushes toward him. Sky trails her sister, her face red and blotchy.

"Daddy, Daddy, I tried." Katie's voice is pitched high with relief. "Sky wouldn't get on the bus." The insides of her forearms appear red as if blistered.

Jesse stoops and hugs Katie while Sky stands back, a hand now rubbing the top of her head in quick circles. He calls to her, but she runs to Trudy, who scoops Sky into her arms.

"It was the substitute driver. I tried, but Sky wouldn't get on the bus."

Dee approaches, looking altogether like a pissed off mama gator. Her critical gaze settles on him. She rests a light hand on Katie's shoulder, asking in a quiet voice if she needs her daddy to come with her to school to explain why she's arrived late.

"No ma'am, I'm on red, and it won't matter what anybody says." Katie squares her shoulders, turns, walks away, and doesn't look back. It's clear she doesn't do a lot of second-guessing.

Jesse watches Sky, her arms wrapped around Trudy's neck, and he worries anew that Dodie's absence means that he'll need to put aside his fears, learn from Katie and Trudy the secret workings of Sky's mind, and find his own ways of reaching her.

He turns to Dee, resenting that she always seems to think he owes her an explanation for his shortcomings. But, right or wrong, he owes her.

"I thank you for what you did." He pauses. "You're a good neighbor."

"You do know Cole would have been late on his first day back at school if he had stayed with the girls."

"Are you saying him being tardy is more important than his sisters' safety?" He remembers the judge's warning, but it still feels good to back her into a corner.

"He didn't abandon them. He called me."

"Daddy Jess," Trudy calls from the porch. "Who's coming after school? I need to know what's going to happen with my babies."

"Cora," he answers, turning back to Dee, who's getting into her Jeep. He calls to her, but she doesn't as much as look his way.

JESSE CASHES HIS LAST CHECK for two weeks of work and goes directly to the cooler for a gallon of pricey whole milk.

He grabs a ten pound bag of potatoes, macaroni and cheese, grits, yellow rice, five pounds of ground beef, store brand corn flakes, and the cheapest brand of dry dog food. He decides against a package of light bulbs, figuring they can keep moving the working ones around.

He rounds the corner into the next aisle and nearly bumps into Roy Griner. He's pushing a fully loaded cart with four sixteen-ounce T-bones riding on top, a testament to his habit of over-charging. Roy pats his wife's plump behind, and Jesse thinks he does so to rub in the fact that Dodie left town driving a car Roy made road-ready. In his mind, that makes Roy an accomplice.

"Damn, man," Roy taunts, "you need help getting to your truck with everything you got there?" His obliging wife giggles like the look-the-other-way wife she is.

"Thanks, Roy. I don't want you straining."

Roy laughs. "Wait up now. If you're still looking, I got a line on a good job."

Jesse knows better, but he stops and turns back.

"I hear Tallahassee sanitation had a bunch of coloreds quit." He laughs big, and his fat wife whines a half-ass protest.

JESSE PUSHES THE CART to the truck, his blood pounding against his temples, and he wants to go back and kick Roy's ass. Then again, all Cole needs is for him to get into a fight at the Winn-Dixie to bring Buddy's bunch down on his head.

Half way to Cora's, he slams on brakes, pulls to the curb, and realizes he forgot the main reason he stopped at the store. Swearing, he pounds the steering wheel a hard pop. He hopes Katie has forgotten fish sticks and French fries, but he knows she never forgets a promise.

He stops the truck at Cora's, removes his cap and wipes his sweaty face on a dirty sleeve, sets it back on his head and pulls the bill low. He gets out of the truck, his slow approach weighted with dread.

"We're getting Sky's shoes?" Katie calls, twisting free of Sky, who runs with a hand rammed inside her sister's back pocket, making her look like a miniature pickpocket.

"Not here, we'll talk later."

She squints up at him, but slips her hand into his and they step onto the walkway bordered by perfectly shaped boxwoods, evidence of Cora's forced order on all that comes under her command. She stands on the porch, wearing a scowl, her bulk plugging up the doorway. He watches the way her fleshy hands ride her wide hips and remains convinced that Dodie didn't risk telling Cora she was leaving her grandkids with him, although she likely asked her mother for money. Doing so would not have raised suspicion. She'd done it often enough.

"Afternoon, Miss Cora." He touches two fingers to the bill of his cap.

She grunts a feeble greeting, her glasses resting cock-eyed across her sharp nose, her left ear slightly higher, and he thinks that may have a bearing on how Cora views the world. From inside the house, he hears the muffled sounds of TV news, which means Dodie's dad will stay in his recliner. Since retiring from the post office three years ago, Hank has watched CNN twenty-four seven, and Jesse has yet to hear him repeat any of what he's heard. Then if the second coming showed up on some radar screen, he'd need to interrupt Cora to issue an early warning.

The girls gather their backpacks, each clutching a zip-lock bag filled with oatmeal-raisin cookies, a reminder that Cora deals sweets like approval.

He turns the truck around in the street and heads toward home.

"Want one?" Katie pokes a cookie under his nose, the good smell wafting. He can't remember when he last ate, and his stomach answers back.

"Your grandma meant those for you kids."

"It's okay. Grandpa says what she doesn't know won't hurt her." Katie giggles, dirty fingertips pressed to her lips. He thinks Sky's dark eyes lighten, if only for a second, and he gives her a wink. But she looks away, grabbing the toes of her shoes.

He takes a cookie, relieved that the girls and Hank have their own conspiratorial ways of dealing with Cora.

"See, Sky, I told you." Katie searches the grocery bags he stashed behind the seat.

Sky looks up at him for a fleeting moment, and he knows he can't explain away a broken promise by what happened in the store.

"Look, I messed up, but we're going home with whatever's in those sacks."

"No, we can't. What about Sky's shoes? You crossed your heart."

Sky picks at a scab on her knee until blood trickles down her leg, staining her sock.

She was wrong. He hadn't crossed his heart. "Maybe tomorrow, okay?" He stares ahead and doesn't look at either of the girls.

"No, we got to go back." Katie pulls at the sole on Sky's shoe and it flaps as loose as her tongue. Her voice goes all whiny, and he can't believe that after everything she's stared down, she's going to cry over his failure to buy fish sticks and French fries. Sky starts to cry, and he doesn't know if she's only joining her sister or understands that she isn't getting new shoes.

"For chrissakes, Katie, you make it sound like I deliberately lied. I forgot, and that's different in my book."

"Mama never forgot a promise." Katie kicks the dash, and right on cue, Sky's crying ratchets up a notch.

His head pounds and the two cookies he wolfed down spin in his stomach like tiny tornadoes. He can't handle another word about what their mama would have done. He's here and she's God knows where, doing God knows what.

He makes a sharp turn onto M. L. King and speeds the four blocks to Trudy's. She's always been there for his kids, and for that he worships her as though she were two hundred pounds of solid gold.

Calling back to the girls to stay put, he rushes toward Trudy as if his ass is on fire, unsure how to put what he's come to ask.

"I'm guessing the fire engine will be along shortly?" She doesn't smile, and he thinks she already smells disappointment.

"I know you'll think I'm off my rocker, but I need for you to take the girls overnight. I'll pay you extra soon as I can."

"Boy, you real sure that's the help you need?" Her deep frown includes the two daredevils in the nearby swings, and it's enough to slow the smarter boys.

"Yes'um." He thinks about throwing in more repairs she might need, but he's already behind on work promised. Then she isn't asking about broken promises to her.

"Get out. Both of you. You're staying the night with Trudy." His tone is harsher than he intends. Katie gets out of the truck, still clutching Sky's hand.

"I'll be back …."

"I don't care if you never come back. Mama said she would, but she lied. Me and Sky want Mama Trudy to be our real mama."

"Jesus, Katie, I've got somewhere to go, and I can't take you and Sky."

"To Uncle Clyde's, to get drunk." The insides of her forearms are flaming red.

Trudy looks at him and shakes her head, and a heavy sigh escapes her lips. "Am I right that you know the cost of what you're about to do?"

"Yes'um." It isn't that he doesn't know he's wrong to leave the girls with yet another broken promise lodged between them. But right now, he doesn't have the will to stay and make things right.

"Then you girls come on with me. Let your daddy get on with his rat killing. I'm going to make us a special supper. Then I'm going to let you pick out a movie to watch."

"Do you have fish sticks and French fries?"

"You know what? That's exactly what I had in mind. I've even got popsicles. But I'm afraid I've only got strawberry." Trudy plays at frowning.

"Strawberry's my favorite. Sky's too."

Through the rear-view mirror, he watches Katie and Sky squat to pet the circle of strays Trudy calls her sometimes borders. Katie stares in the direction of the truck, and the hurt on her face is enough to turn any good man around, but he heads for the relief of a place where no one calls him daddy.

NINE

Jesse drives across the state line into Georgia, stopping at a seedy bar he'd noticed only in passing. He parks his truck under a shattered security light and rolls down a window, inviting thieves to take what they will, sparing himself the busted glass.

The bar smells of stale beer and sweaty armpits, and it has no air conditioning. But something about the damp darkness and the rhythmic clacking of overhead fans makes it feel cooler than it has a right to. He straddles a wobbly barstool and motions to the barkeep, a pencil-thin man sporting a Poncho Villa mustache. He's leaning across the bar opposite a woman, her eyes half-shut, and Jesse decides she's either drunk or bored.

"Sorry, bud, I don't run tabs for strangers," the bartender calls back along the bar.

"How 'bout you walk your boney ass down here. Me and you get acquainted." He pulls a wadded five from the pocket of his jeans and slaps it onto the bar. "That cover a Pabst, you think?"

The bartender snatches a beer from an old-fashioned ice cooler, plops the bottle in front of him and takes up the five. "Guess you'll want change."

"Hell, yeah. Do I look like the United Way?"

The cold beer is instant relief to his parched throat, and he's flushed with the pleasure of a cool, dark place where no one knows his name. If that's not a country song, it ought to be. When he's downed four straight away, paying as he goes, he pushes a twenty across the bar and orders a double shot of Wild Turkey.

"Damn, bud, I do believe you came here with something to drown." The asshole shifts into instant congeniality, waving off his money, saying he'll run a tab after all. Jesse liked him better without the pretense.

After the double Turkey, he heads straight into the drunk he came for. The one that promises to ease his losses, level out his thinking, and wrap his shitty day in a blur. By now, the girls have had their fill of fish sticks and the frightened mother in the shiny Mercedes has had several glasses of expensive wine in some fancy restaurant. He hopes she feels safe again.

On the barkeep's next trip, Jesse asks, "You got something besides that damn wrist-cutting music? Irish jig, maybe?"

"What you're hearing is what there is. Folks don't come here to celebrate."

He isn't here to celebrate, but he'd like music that could remind him of better times. He watches as couples take to the tiny dance floor, and it reminds him of late night dancing in the living room, after the kids were asleep, and Dodie saying that those evenings made her feel romantic.

She taught Cole to dance, readying him for his first school dance. They'd pushed back the living room furniture, rolled the worn rug, and she'd smiled as Cole's two left feet found their rhythm, his stiffness melting under her praise. Katie stood on his feet and they stumbled about the room, her giggling. Afterward, they practiced party manners, dipping strawberry Kool-Aid from a large mixing-bowl with a measuring cup, Cole fetching for his unnamed date. He now wonders if Cole and Sarah dance, and if so, has their dancing led them to sex.

There had been no father and son talk about safe sex, or sex of any kind, between him and his dad. But now days, he thinks dads know what to say to their sons. He doesn't watch tell-all TV, but Dodie did, quoting Oprah the way Cora does the Bible.

The Friday night crowd pushes in and the bar fills with loose-jawed men, a few sporting ladies his daddy would have called floozies. At the opposite end of the bar, Jesse overhears a loud-mouthed guy in a plaid western shirt, the sleeves cut off at the shoulders, talking big about a genuine mustang mare that he bought off an old geezer for a song. He offers the mare to any would-be cowboy for two hundred dollars.

Jesse gets off the stool and walks over to the guy. "What's this about a cheap horse?"

"Pure mustang, straight out of the old West." He laughs and slaps his buddy on the shoulder.

Jesse doesn't like the man, figures him to have a mean streak as wide as the interstate. His instinct is to back off, yet he asks, "Where's this prized horse, anyway?"

The guy offers to haul the horse from North Georgia for half the price now, and the balance on delivery. He jokes about throwing in the whip for free. Jesse wants to ask what he means, but the guy turns back to the woman he's hitting on, the one the barkeep had cornered when he first came in. Up close, there's a discernable numbness about her.

"Evening, ma'am. What do you think about what you've heard here?"

She stares straight through him as though he's part of her fog, and for reasons he can't name, he pities her. Then she's right as rain. She's none of his business.

He returns to his seat at the bar, and even though he's drunk, he recognizes a shaky dealmaker. Still, he's never going to get another chance to buy a horse this cheap. Katie's eleventh birthday is two weeks away, and the mare could make up for years of broken promises. He'll fix up the busted corral and ask Dee and Susan for help; they know everything there is to know about training horses. What animal could resist Katie's touch? Maybe he's shit-faced and loco to boot, but he means to surprise her.

He goes back over to the cowboy, pulls three wrinkled twenties from his pocket, and asks if he'll take sixty on the spot and the balance on delivery. The dealmaker grins, showing an uneven row of teeth with a sizable gap in front, and Jesse hopes some horse is to blame. The man slips one of the twenties between the woman's breasts, and the deals are cut.

Jesse gives directions from I-10, and in return, he gets a receipt and phone number for Jake Madison scribbled on a scrap of paper. He reclaims his seat, orders what he intends as his last drink, and works at fending off his buyer's remorse with thoughts of redeeming himself with Katie.

Behind him, through the foggy mirror, he notices a balding, middle-aged man, wearing the only suit in the place, working two women at a nearby table. He studies the two and makes a private bet that the chubby blonde will break first. After more talk, the dude flashes a touchdown grin as he and the blonde head for the door. She turns back to the woman left sitting alone at the table, waves, and follows the man through the door. Jesse doesn't think the woman means to say that she's necessarily won the door prize.

The hands on the red, white, and blue Budweiser clock hanging from the wall behind the bar click toward two o'clock. Those lucky enough to score have moved on, and those giving up have drifted out as well, leaving the place to the few whose fate is as yet unknown. Jesse glances in the mirror, and the woman still sits, and he's sure he can't make it through another night alone. He stands and leans against the bar, steadying his knocked out legs, and motions to the bartender.

The barkeep slides two drinks across the bar. "That's all she wrote, bud, make your move. Twenty minutes and I'm folding the joint."

"Don't call me that. I'm bud to a guy with a limp dick who lives in a fucking wheelchair. And don't look at me like I'm some damn loser."

"Whoa down, sport, I don't know you."

"That's right, you don't."

He takes the drinks, goes deep into his wallet to settle his tab, then slowly crosses the floor and stands next to the woman. A lone candle in the center of the table flickers and dies, trailing a slender thread of smoke upward, and Jesse hopes that isn't a sign of things to come.

She doesn't look at him, but mumbles something he doesn't catch. She's so drunk he believes they could go at it on the table and she wouldn't remember. He's glad he isn't that drunk.

She's several years older, maybe forty, give or take, and she might have once been fair looking, but he can't picture her as ever pretty. She's bone-thin, and the sagging skin under her dead eyes is dark and puffed. When she feels his presence, she tries a smile, but it slides off her face before completely forming.

"Hey baby, you're shopping late, ain't you?" She motions toward a chair.

"Yes'um, you might say that." Jesse pulls out the chair and sits, pushing a drink across the table, and she takes the drink straight to her lips.

"Know that I'm cheap, but I don't do kinky shit. You got that?"

"No, ma'am. I ain't thinking about … nothing like that." He's never bought sex, and although he's unclear about what she might consider kinky, he's pretty sure what he needs isn't anything like that.

Just now, he felt as though his balls shrunk to pea-size, and he thinks it may be that he's never heard a woman talk that way about herself. He's embarrassed for them both; him for buying, her for selling. Still, he looks around the near empty bar and he's about to ask her price when he begins to gush that his wife left him with three kids and doesn't stop talking until he sucks air, his cheeks flaming with embarrassment. He's told his miserable story to a hooker. But she has his gratitude for seeming to listen.

She leans back in the chair, lights a cigarette from the one in her hand, and tilts her head back, exhaling a cloud of blue smoke toward the light above the table. She looks across at him, her eyes half-closed against the smoke. "How long ago did you say she left?"

"Uh, a damn long time ago."

The woman blinks hard. Her eyes clear as though she draws upon some still sober brain cells, and she places a hand on his forearm, her painted nails slowly twisting the long dark hairs.

"Baby, you're too sweet for any sensible woman to leave for good. Go on back home and wait. You'll see." She stubs the butt in the over-flowing ash tray, reaches under the table to slip her shoes back on, and gathers her purse, half-empty pack, and lighter.

He liked hearing something nice about himself, even though he'd left Dodie's side of the story untold. Then there's little truth to stories told in bars, and she's right about his needing to wait. Still, he offers her a ride home and helps her to stand. The bartender winks, and Jesse lays two fingers to the bill of his cap, allowing him to believe whatever he wants.

He helps her into the truck, and she gives him directions to a roadside trailer park before passing out against his shoulder. He likes the feel of her against him, even if it's only one way, and sits for a short while in front of the trailer before nudging her awake.

She opens her eyes, blinks hard, and for a split second, hers is the startled face of innocence.

"This it?" he asks, and she nods.

"I didn't catch your name, sweetie."

He tells her, certain that she won't remember beyond the trailer door, and that's just as well.

"I'm Elizabeth. My mama named me for the English queen. Promised I'd have a good life because of it." Her sour laugh carries a weight no one needs to shoulder alone.

She slides off the seat and stands next to the truck, gathering herself before stumbling across the cluttered yard toward the naked light hanging above the door. He regrets that he failed to call a proper goodnight before she disappears inside.

Back on the road, an amber moon lights his way, and he tries to picture Katie and Sky snuggling together on one of Trudy's beds, his wrong forgiven. But no amount of alcohol can erase the truth he remembers stenciled on Katie's face. His deliverance rests with a great deal more than a horse he knows nothing of, except for the cynical warning hidden in the sidekick's sucker laugh. Still, he wants to believe it's some kind of a fresh start.

TEN

Jesse stands in the shower, cold water running over him until
he shivers. He shampoos his hair but doesn't take the time to shave;
he needs to hurry if he's to make it to Trudy's on time. He dresses
quickly and thinks about coffee, lots of coffee. But first, he pulls
the wad of bills from the pocket of yesterday's jeans and flattens
each out on the dresser, sorting by denomination. He figures he's
short a hundred bucks.

Music comes from Cole's room, and Jesse realizes he'd totally
forgotten Cole when dumping the girls on Trudy. Cole is sitting on
the floor with a large sketchpad across his knees and several of the
small notebooks open and spread around him.

"Whoa, man, you look like warmed-over death." Cole slips the
charcoal drawing he's working on beneath a bigger pad, but not
before Jesse catches a glimpse of a pretty girl.

"Right. Coming back from the dead ain't easy."

"Where'd you dump the midgets?"

He answers.

"Just hope Grandma doesn't get wind of it." Cole looks down
at one of the notepads.

Jesse weighs Cole's words and wonders if he means his drunk or Cora's rant that Trudy's neighborhood is unsafe. His son's tone felt more like a mental shrug, signaling that he's lived up to expectations. Then maybe his guilt bothers him more than Cole's judgment.

"You had breakfast? There's stuff in the truck. I'll get it."

Jesse takes the bags from behind the truck seat, and there's nothing for breakfast but corn flakes. He leaves the box on the table, puts the gallon jug of milk in the fridge, and refills Beau's bowl. He steps out on the back porch and whistles, and when the dog doesn't come, he goes back into the kitchen and starts coffee.

Cole comes into the kitchen and takes a bowl out of the dish drainer. He pours cereal and milk into a mixing bowl and sits at the table. "Crap, the milk's spoiled." He shudders, making a face, and dumps the contents into the sink.

"I'll pick up more after I get the girls." The damn stuff costs a frigging fortune, but nowhere near the price of his drunk.

"Glad you at least remembered Beau's food. I fed him leftover corned beef. Did you know he can separate the onions from the stuff that passes for meat?" Cole eats dry cereal scooped from the box.

"Where is Beau?"

"He slept on the girl's bed last night. But I don't remember seeing him after I let him out earlier this morning. If Dee and Susan are outside with their horses, Beau's with them. Oh, yeah, Susan called last night to remind you the girls are invited for lunch and riding today."

Jesse pours a cup of steaming coffee to go and grabs his truck keys from the peg on the wall. He takes a wrinkled Hamilton from the dresser, and puts the pitiful balance away. On his way out, he asks Cole if he wants to ride along, but he has make-up work.

THE GIRLS HUG TRUDY good-bye while he stands condemned, guilty as sin, soliciting a list of chores in exchange for her help with the girls. Trudy doesn't respond, her keys jingling from her hand. She's dressed from head to toe in purple, her feet overflowing her dyed-to-match pumps, looking like two royal loaves of brown bread, going late to her grand-niece's wedding. She's never shy about laying blame where it belongs.

Katie chatters about the four baby kittens born under the house that she rescued and put in a laundry basket. "Mama Trudy said that the mama cat didn't scratch me 'cause she knew I meant to help her babies. Like her looking after me and Sky when you'd rather get drunk." Katie's red curls, pulled back into a ponytail, bounce with each declarative nod.

"Trudy said that? The part about me not looking after you two?" Guess he pissed her off pretty good.

"No, I did." He looks over at her and she doesn't as much as blink.

"About that. I was wrong. I'm sorry."

She studies him, and what he sees in her stern look is far from the face of forgiveness. Maybe at best a truce, but even that seems doubtful.

They drive for a time in precious silence, until she reaches and slaps him on the thigh, asking what he thinks. He looks at her.

"About Sky's almost new shoes. You like them? They fit fine. They're from Mama Trudy's lost and found box." If it bothers her that her sister is wearing hand-me-down shoes, it doesn't show. Trudy must have kid shoes and clothing of all sizes, colors and for all seasons, stored away for just the right moment of need.

"Yeah, Sky, I like your new shoes." He looks over at her and winks.

She grabs the toes of her shoes and rocks back and forth. He doesn't know what it means to her, but at least he spoke and she didn't go nutty on him.

He doesn't stop at the house but drives directly to Susan and Dee's place to the sound of Katie's loud cheers. As they approach the barn, Dee looks up from brushing one of the quarter horses and waves. Beau scampers from beneath the wooden fence, racing toward the truck.

Katie hugs Beau and runs to Dee, grabbing her around the waist. The two spin around a hitching post as if it were a May pole. Beau chases a noisy circle around them.

Sky gets out of the truck and stands behind him, but doesn't touch him, nor does she respond to Dee's greeting. She squats and hugs Beau, who licks her face. Jesse cringes when she licks the dog back.

Dee walks toward him and his cringe deepens. He never knows what to expect from her.

"Hey, I owe you an apology. The name-calling was out of line. I was worried about the girls, and that Cole arrived late his first day back." She removes her work glove and extends her hand, her grip firm and strong. "I also need to let you know that I called in a favor with the school superintendent. He's a client, and I know more about his business than the IRS." She smiles conspiratorially.

He must look puzzled, but only about Cole's part. Dee cut her teeth on backroom deals. Her daddy, a local politician, bribed his way into the state legislature, and found a home among thieves for over five terms.

"Longley's a total ass. Unexcused absences meant Cole was disallowed makeup work. It would have killed his chance at a college scholarship."

"Glad for your help." He's embarrassed that Cole hadn't come to him, but what leverage would he have had with the school principal?

"Enough talk for now. Stay and have lunch with us. Susan invited Cole to join us, but he has plans to go over some debate preparation with Sarah." She winks.

"Yeah, he mentioned that." Jesse hesitates, for she's never invited him for a meal. Susan comes out of the house onto the wrap-around porch and calls them inside. She's wearing a floral skirt and a white sleeveless blouse, her light brown hair pulled back into what he thinks is a French twist.

"Yes ma'am, thank you kindly. I'm happy to join such a fine company of ladies."

Dee attempts to hide her smirk at what he's sure she considers his corny country manners. Still, his spirits lift. He squares his shoulders and Katie slips a hand into his, and they walk toward the house. He stops and says to Sky, who trails behind, "Come on. We can't keep Miss Susan waiting."

He's pleased Sky follows, and she may have even skipped a step.

Susan leads the way through a large, airy kitchen onto a sun porch. At the end of the porch nearest the kitchen there is a round oak table surrounded by matching chairs and covered by place mats and matching cloth napkins held by dragonfly shaped rings. An arrangement of garnet and gold daylilies occupies the center of the table.

He stands awkwardly, uncertain as to whether the social skills he learned apply at a table headed by a woman. He seats Susan, then remains standing until Dee seats herself and motions for him to sit.

"I hope you like Quiche Lorraine." Susan reaches for his plate.

"Yes ma'am, I'm sure I do." He fears he can't keep as much as soda crackers down.

Both Katie and Sky sit upright, and when Susan reaches for Katie's plate, she says a proper thank you. He's proud of her ease in the presence of finer ways. Sky picks black olives from her salad and lines them up on the edge of her plate, and he's sure he should say something to her, but neither Dee nor Susan appears to object, so he avoids a break in the good he feels.

The quiche stays down, and, to his relief, most of their talk is about plans for expanding the barn in preparation for the birth of their first foal in February. He offers his help and Dee accepts, but only after Susan glares at her.

Everyone helps to clear the table, and Susan encourages Dee to take the girls and go ready the horses for their ride into the National Forest. When Dee balks, Susan pops her bottom with a wet dishtowel and the girls giggle.

Jesse studies a framed charcoal drawing of two mourning doves feeding from the ground, and something about the drawing feels familiar. "Danged if those things don't look like they could fly right off the wall."

Susan has come back into the room and is standing at his elbow. "It's as though you can expect to hear the light, airy whistling sound they make on takeoff. You do know the drawing is a gift from Cole?" She points out his signature at the lower right-hand corner. "His wonderful way of saying he deeply regrets having betrayed a trust."

Jesse nods, and he's surprised that his eyes suddenly sting. "Guess the law saw it different."

"Yes, but the law is designed to judge adults. Cole was never a thief, but rather a hurt and confused young man." She touches Jesse lightly on the forearm.

He nods. "Still, it's hard settling on a McKnight man choosing art."

"Oh, I like to think that art chose him. It's a rare and precious gift entrusted to Cole, and he accepts it, fully understanding that it comes with certain burdens."

Jesse likes hearing her talk about Cole. He wants the good in the moment not to end, and would like to ask her what more she could tell him about his son.

She looks into his eyes for a brief moment, and then takes his arm. Together, they walk onto the porch to the sound of the girls' giggles coming from the barn.

He thanks Susan for lunch while wishing he knew how to thank her for the more important part. He steps into the bright sunlight, to the feel of drier air on his skin, a welcome relief from the humid heat of the demanding summer.

ELEVEN

Jesse wakes before dawn, makes coffee, and sits at the kitchen table, scanning the employment ads. As badly as he needs work, he can't focus. The house looks as if a garbage truck dumped its load, and he means to right it before Marlene and Clyde come with supper. He goes down the hall, shouting threats until the kids drag themselves out of bed.

Katie and Sky make cheese toast while he separates two weeks of laundry into six mounds, piled knee high on the back porch. Cole agrees to pick up accumulated clutter from the living room and run the vacuum should he actually uncover the carpet. He hauls kitchen garbage behind the storage shed to overflowing trash cans, but only after agreeing that the stench is better outside than in the kitchen. Katie washes, dries and puts away the dishes, and the kitchen counter surface gets cleared for the first time since Dodie left. Sky sits under the kitchen table, humming a tune Jesse doesn't recognize, while she feeds Beau tiny bites of toast.

He goes to the shed, pulls out the grill, and cleans the racks, then rolls the grill into the back yard beneath the shade of the pecan tree and takes folding lawn chairs from the storage area on the porch. He wishes for a cold beer, but after tossing spoiled food he'd left overnight in his truck, he has yet to make a return trip to the store. He can't believe he's thinking about making a shopping list. All he needs is a bib apron.

Mid-afternoon, he strolls through the house, pleased with the way it looks, and that they've turned dirty laundry into fresh stacks of folded clothes. Still, he wishes for one of those sweet-smelling sprays to cover the lingering odors of the kids and Beau.

When he emerges from the bedroom freshly shaven, wearing clean jeans and a neatly pressed sports shirt, Katie teases, "Gee, Daddy. It's only Miss Marlene and Uncle Clyde."

"Come on, Katie. Don't you know today is dress rehearsal for the Governor's visit?" The corners of Cole's mouth turn up slightly and he, too, has spiffed up.

Beau barks and runs toward the driveway seconds before Jesse hears the crunch of gravel beneath tires. Clyde rolls his chair with the wider, outdoor tires off the ramp into the backyard while Cole and the girls help Marlene carry containers of food into the kitchen. Jesse brings the heavy cooler, and when Marlene has taken out more food, he carries the cooler with iced beers into the backyard.

Clyde sets up at the open end of the picnic table and Jesse stoops to hug his friend's shoulders, putting a cold beer into his hand.

Clyde nods next door, his fake smile fixed.

"Knock it off, will you. I'd be up shit creek without the help of those ladies." He sometimes thinks the wheelchair has made Clyde jumpy about any woman capable of changing a flat.

"Nothing from Dodie?" His brow gathers, and he gets that far away look in his eyes.

"Not unless I'm to count messages she leaves for the kids." He hates coming home, the blinking recorder his empty welcome.

"You figured out what you'll say when you get the chance?"

"Starting to think I won't get that chance." He takes a seat next to Clyde.

"That's bullshit and you know it." He shifts his weight in the chair. "Her leaving your selfish ass is no surprise. But get ready. She's coming for her kids. And without something good …."

"What?"

"Face it. You could lose both her and your kids."

"I don't mean to lose them. I can still make things right."

"Well now, I'm glad to hear that. But you just might want to consider telling your kids as much. They deserve to know you plan on sticking around."

"I'm here. What more do they need to know?"

"Lord, Little Brother. It ain't that I don't know you're flying blind through a shit storm. But that's exactly the thinking that may satisfy the moment, but ends up costing the likes of you and me everything. Whatever sent her running wasn't about you missing some damn birthday party. Or even hiding in a damn bottle. She forgave you for that."

"What the hell do you know about it?"

"When was the last time you did more than bargain sex? Don't you think she deserved more from you? And just maybe she looked elsewhere for what she needed."

"Damn you. There's never been anybody for her but me, and you know it." Clyde's accusation jars him, and he thinks back to their first fight over what he owed Dodie and an unborn Cole. He stares across at Clyde, the one face he believes he reads better than his own reflection. But what was always open to him before is tight and closed, prompting him to ask, "What the hell do you know that you aren't saying?"

"I ain't saying. I'm asking." Clyde studies his clenched fists as if he imagines them belonging to someone other than him.

"I told you what I know. And unless you know something I don't …."

Clyde squeezes his eyes shut, and when he opens them, they're clouded with pain. It's the kind Jesse's seen only once before, on the morning after his accident when he heard the word paralyzed for the first time.

"No, hell, Little Brother, I don't know a damn thing worth saying, and that the truth."

Jesse pushes back in his chair and stares across the pasture next door, recalling Dodie's brightness when she declared that Stuart Brown had returned to join his father's law practice. At the time, it meant nothing to him. Now, he wishes he'd paid more attention.

Clyde reaches and takes a cold beer from the ice chest, pops the top, and passes it to Jesse. He takes the peace offering, for he too wants their heat to cool. He'd often wished his and Dodie's arguments could have ended the same. Theirs had only built greater resentment, disappointment and hurt; left to smolder, never cooling.

From the kitchen, faint sounds of Marlene and the kids fill the silent spaces between him and Clyde, and the sound of their voices brings Jesse a surprising pleasure; one that makes the hairs on his arms tingle.

"Truth is …."

"Which truth is that?"

Clyde's eyes narrow, as though he comes to something anew. "That you might've sung sweet as a canary, and it not changed a thing." He pauses, runs his big hand along his bearded jaw. "I've come to consider women as a lot like the weather we get."

"How's that?"

"A man thinks he can predict what's coming, but he can never be sure. Sunshine or rain, we men just ain't built to know." He blushes above his red whiskers.

"Uh huh, and you're the same fool who told me girls didn't get pregnant their first time."

"I was considerably off on that." Clyde shakes his head. His big grin breaks through and they laugh.

Cole comes out and places a round of hamburgers and wieners on the grill. Only politeness passes between him and Clyde. Clyde's never said as much, but it's likely about Cole quitting football.

Katie runs from the back porch and scrambles onto Clyde's lap. He nuzzles her neck and she giggles and plays at twisting free, squealing that his whiskers tickle.

Jesse can't help but envy the easy way Clyde has with Katie. He makes her smile that special smile, full of the brightness Jesse covets, the one that breaks his heart with love.

She jumps from Clyde's lap and brings her bike over for him to tighten the chain. She asked Jesse to fix it days ago, but with all he's had to do, he hadn't gotten around to the bike.

"Jess," Marlene calls from the porch. "Can you watch the food while Cole helps me finish up in here?" She hands him a large platter, leans closer, and whispers, "The house looks great, and so do you and the kids." Her presence is quiet and still, her smile lingering.

"You too," he stammers. Her hair, the color of summer sea oats, is pulled back into a French braid, and he likes her in the white shorts and red tank-top. Her legs are long and tan, and she presses upon him so gently, his erection surprises and embarrasses him. He'd wished only to touch her, but now he worries that any gesture would be either small or too much.

He turns away, and Clyde is watching him. Not in an accusing way, but with the slow deliberate gaze he'd use when determining the will of a dog to hunt.

Jesse covers himself with the platter and hurries past Clyde, mumbling something about tending the meat. Jesus, he's gone without for so long. His erection was nothing more than an act of nature. Then a man has to own his thoughts, and for that he's guilty.

What had Clyde seen? Nothing. His back was to him. He's a
fool. Clyde didn't need to see. He reads his mind.

When he has taken deep breaths and calmed down, he calls,
"Grab another beer, big guy. Food's nearly ready to take up." His
voice carries the high pitch of guilt.

"You might not want to overcook those burgers." Clyde leans
and takes a beer from the cooler.

Jesse brings the platter of burgers and wieners to the table, and
everyone takes a seat. Beau picks a spot between Clyde and Katie,
and they take turns feeding him bites of food from their plates.
Jesse's careful to limit his remarks to Marlene to her homemade
potato salad and cucumber pickles, and to rave about the baked
beans, chips, and all the trimmings. He brings over another round of
patties and wieners and encourages the kids to load up, reminding
them that beef hash and boiled potatoes are in their future.

"This food is a life saver. Dad's cooking sucks."

Katie rams her finger down her throat and pretends to gag.

"Shut your ungrateful mouths, both of you."

Cole's off-hand compliment brings a satisfying smile to
Marlene. There's so much good in what they share, Jesse's shame
swells up inside of him, and he wants a "take back," the easy kid
way he and Clyde had of settling their differences. But this isn't
high school, and Marlene isn't some hero-worshipping teenage girl
they'd shared.

Marlene insists that he and Clyde stay put while she and the
kids clear the table. She sends Cole with a pot of fresh coffee, and
Jesse takes a second piece of the lemon pound cake to sweeten a
cup.

Katie asks to take cake next door to Dee and Susan. Jesse
agrees, but tells them they're not to take time with the horses. He
and Clyde watch Katie and Sky ride away on their bikes.

Clyde cocks his head to one side. "It's one of theirs Katie's got her heart set on, right?" He gets that gleam in his eye, and he's about to hatch a plan.

"Yeah, but the mare's a registered quarter horse worth more than my truck."

"Hell, a castrated goat's worth more than your truck."

"Yeah, well, even if I had the money, Dee's not about to sell me one of theirs. Take a look at that barn, corrals, and twenty acre pasture. And they're building a second barn. Rivals the Doggy Hilton."

"You got a point there, Little Brother." Clyde laughs, and it's the one that promises an easier way through the balance of the evening.

"Katie's birthday comes up in two weeks, and you know how she's dreamed of her own horse."

"Yeah, I do. And I ain't missed a birthday ever."

"Right, and this time she ain't going to be disappointed."

"Oh, yeah, and how's that? You aim to rob the Flying J?"

"I got her a horse. It'll stand right there in that corral on her birthday."

Clyde turns and looks toward the broken corral, then back at Jesse.

"Oh hell, Clyde, wipe that scowl off your ugly face. I know it needs fixing." He pauses, waiting for his friend to get on the bandwagon, but his frown only deepens.

"This horse is a pure mustang mare, straight off wilderness grassland. Cheaper to own and cheaper to keep. Nothing like those pampered horses next door."

"Lord God a'mighty," Clyde mutters. Shaking his head, he stares down at his hands, clenched into fists. "Why didn't you come to me beforehand? Between the two of us, we might have come up with a way for that little darling to have a horse she has a chance of ever riding."

Jesse looks away, deciding that this time he doesn't want Clyde's help.

He shrugs. "Aw, forget it. The dude had a woman hooked, needed the money to close the deal. Truth is, I likely bought him a fuck and there is no horse." Lying to Clyde is his worst option. But he means to earn Katie's special smile.

"And if it's legit? What then?"

"What makes you so sure this horse won't work out?" The cowboy's guarantee to deliver the horse was the one thing he'd taken at face value. The man will show and he'll be ready.

"Because you don't know jack shit about training a horse. And any horse, mishandled, could hurt her. Did you ever stop to think about that?"

Jesse worried that, because Katie had her heart set on the mare next door, she might not, at first, like the mustang. But he never considered the mustang might be dangerous.

"I want to hear you say you'll call and tell the asshole the deal's off. We'll figure out something that'll get that baby a good horse." Clyde's eyes narrow, his broad jaw line set, his mind made up.

Then, the decision is not Clyde's to make. Jesse leans and pulls a clump of crabgrass and grinds its roots beneath the heel of his left boot.

Clyde inhales sharply. He knows a lie unspoken, especially from him. He swings the wheelchair around closer, and is about to get up into Jesse's chest, but the squealing noise of the screen door stops him, and they each look in its direction.

"Is a woman allowed in on this hush-hush conversation?" Marlene's voice holds her concern.

Clyde waves her out. "Come on. I want you to hear this damn fool story."

Jesse cringes. If he's the fool Clyde thinks, he'd just as soon she not know. But better she hear about the horse from him than Clyde.

She sits quietly, her attention focused, and no judgment shows on her face, not even deep sighs marking the places in his story she plans to come back to, the way Dodie would.

When he's run out of words, she says, "I knew a man back in Texas who trained mustangs to be cow ponies. He claimed some were among the best he'd ever worked." Her voice flattens, trailing off as she loses faith in her words.

Still, he's grateful for her easy let down, even if she couldn't side with him.

"Truth is, that old cowboy knew which end of the horse to bridle. And Jesse here," Clyde's slap to the shoulder is patronizing, and Jesse feels to cuff him a sharp one, "ain't one of the James brothers."

Clyde laughs, and maybe he means to prick the bubble of tension that hovers like a bad blister, but Jesse suffers the raw sting of his friend's ridicule. Marlene doesn't say, but her silence aligns her with Clyde. Faith in his decision takes a hard hit, and Jesse wants to believe that he's more than pig-headed.

Katie comes onto the porch steps and calls, "Miss Marlene, do you want to call out my spelling words?" Weekly spelling tests are always on Fridays, and Katie easily learns a list of twenty words in one evening. No doubt she misses her mom more than she's willing to admit.

He and Clyde watch the two disappear back into the house, Marlene's arm around Katie's shoulders, her arm wrapped around Marlene's waist.

"She's awful tight with my kids. Let her keep that up, and those three will turn her into a mom."

A curtain of silence drops between them like an undertaker's shroud, and the only sound is that of cooling coals until Jesse says, "I'm sorry. I didn't mean ...." His regret is real, though his resentment fueled his hard push back.

"Oh, hell, Little Brother. That good woman takes in strays and mothers cripples." He pauses. "Why you think that is?" He glances down at his lap, and back at him. "Can't fuck her."

"Jesus God, Clyde. Why say stuff like that? You know I didn't mean nothing like that."

"I'm thinking she must like that I don't track up her clean floors." Clyde doesn't acknowledge that he's heard his apology. Rather, he points in the direction of a squawking blue jay perched on the nearby birdfeeder.

"Jays are mean, selfish bastards." He turns toward Jesse. "You ever notice they steal from the nests of other birds?" The underside of his freckled arms turn red, an odd trait of his, and a clear measure of how far removed they are from the simple "take back" he wants.

"It ain't right, dragging Marlene into our argument about a horse you've never laid eyes on."

"And you have?"

"No, but I mean to give Katie and this horse a fair chance."

"You're a fool. And if that baby gets as much as a bruise, I'll whip your sorry ass within a breath of your last. And that's a promise." Clyde spins the wheelchair away from the table and rolls toward his van.

Jesse sits through the sound of the wheelchair ramp striking the ground, the horn blasting, the slamming of doors, and the crunch of sand and gravel beneath the tires of the van.

He looks to where Dee and Susan's horses graze contentedly, and he pictures Katie's mustang mare standing knee deep in tall, sweet, summer grass. He intends to hold onto his dream. If he's wrong, he'll swap the mustang for a more suitable horse. Either way, Katie gets a horse and he gets a second chance at winning his daughter's trust.

Then there's the cowboy's wisecrack about throwing in the whip for free, and his gut tells him he should overtake Clyde, give each the peace of mind they want.

TWELVE

Jesse folds the last of the lawn chairs, puts them back into storage, and leaves the hot grill to cool. He goes into the kitchen and it's spotless. The fridge is filled with a gallon jug of milk, butter, two dozen eggs, a package of bacon, and leftovers from the picnic. There is a large covered dish of meatloaf with directions for warming written on a card attached to the aluminum foil. Marlene could not have known beforehand that he'd blown a week of grocery money on a drunk and a doubtful horse. His gratitude mixes with his humiliation.

Cole comes into the kitchen, cuts a hunk of pound cake, pours a tall glass of milk, and sits at the table.

"Where you putting all that food?"

"Jocks aren't the only boys with big appetites."

"No, I once saw a four-foot dwarf swallow a cow."

"A dwarf cow, right?" The corners of Cole's mouth turn up.

"Got me there." Jesse welcomes the ease of their give and take. It feels normal.

"What pissed Clyde off? Stormed out of here like his ass was on fire. I hate the way he treats Miss Marlene."

"He can be rough. But I don't think it was more than having stayed too long. He's training a new pack of dogs for a state competition."

Cole tilts his head and squints. "So that's what he does nights when he leaves Miss Marlene alone to run that crummy bar?"

"They got some kind of deal about that." How does Cole know about Marlene's nights alone at the bar? Then he isn't in the mood to defend Clyde to Cole.

"I believe I'll have another piece of that cake while it lasts." He drains the last of the coffee and sits across from Cole. "How're you doing with all that makeup work?"

"All good so far. But I've got a big trig test coming up."

"Don't look to me for help. Would've flunked Algebra I flat if your mom hadn't slipped me her homework."

"No way. Mom cheated?" His eyes brighten, and Jesse thinks Cole might like hearing a secret.

"She was on track to be valedictorian." He wishes he'd left it with their cheating. "I guess Sarah's helping you catch up?"

"Not so much. Mostly James."

"James? You're kidding."

"No, James beats both Sarah and me on tests. He doesn't care about grades or getting into college, so he never bothers with homework. Says it's boring."

"What does he care about?"

"Getting the hell out of his mom's craziness. He'd rather come with me to shovel dog shit than listen to her loser boyfriend brag about how much money he makes."

"You ever run into this boyfriend?" If there's any truth to what Jesse has heard, Cole needs to follow James's lead.

"Hell, no. The crazy bastard cooks meth."

"James's mom in on any of that?"

"Not unless you count using."

"Damn, that's rotten." He could never picture Cole as a user. But he knows a teenage boy walking around with empty pocket to be an easy target. He and Clyde made extra money running whiskey for his bootlegger uncle until coach got wind of it and threatened to throw them off the team if they kept it up.

"About that deal Miss Dee cut with the superintendent … I didn't go to her for help on that. She asked me how the makeup was going. And I told her Longley meant to screw me over."

Had Cole known at the time he chose detention over coming home that he was putting his dream of college at risk? If Jesse had to guess, he'd say not.

"I'm working hard at squaring away. I mean, I'm …." Cole's voice cracks.

"You're doing fine." Smart as he is, Cole doesn't speak the tough words any better than his old man. In that way, at least, they are alike.

"Need a ride to the shelter?"

"No, James is picking me up."

"Let me know when you get in."

Cole nods.

JESSE WAKES TO FIND JAMES rolled like a giant mummy in a tattered sleeping bag on the floor of Cole's bedroom.

"What the hell is this?"

"Shit, what time is it?" Cole flings back the covers and stands.

James sits staring, the sleeping bag draped around a set of shoulders Superman could envy. His round, child-like face sits oddly on his thick neck, making the kid laughable if he didn't look so lost.

"His mom locked him out. Had no place to go."

"Never mind. You guys get up. Breakfast in ten minutes."

Jesse scrambles a dozen eggs and fries a pound of bacon before walking Katie and Sky to the bus stop, waiting there until

Sky gets on the bus. Back at the house, he takes a call from the office manager. She tells him that he need not bother coming in. The regulars are caught up with shipments.

He wants to tell her that it's only a bother when he doesn't come in, but instead he thanks her and asks about tomorrow. She says he should call first, hinting that maybe he'll want to take the day and go fishing. There was a time when he might have said the same to a man without knowing how wrong it was. The boss's promise of two weeks of work only counts when work backs up.

To get out of the house, he decides to drive into town, knowing there's only one place where loafers are welcome. He walks into Hardee's, and near the back wall, three guys drink refill coffee and bitch to each other about shit that regularly happens. He knows these guys and they were once steady workers. Today, their yards are cluttered with for sale signs taped to late model pickups, boats and motors, lawn tractors; anything they can unload to make the rent or mortgage on a doublewide they can't sell for a third of what they owe.

His grandpa had bragged about surviving the Great Depression while his neighbors went on the public dole. The old man believed that his land and his back were all he could count on. A generation later, his daddy went to his grave owing the local bank for his last low-interest farm loan.

A disinterested young woman flashes him an empty PR smile and pushes a steaming cup across the counter, and he pays with change gathered from the truck's ashtray. He picks up a discarded copy of today's newspaper, takes a seat, and scans the Employment Opportunities section. He searches for jobs he can do, and when he doesn't find one, he looks for jobs he can claim to do. Coming up empty, he glances at the stock market page, not that he knows how to read it, and wonders just when that trickle-down effect is to make its way to the bottom.

"Hey there, sport. You playing hooky?" Sally slides into the booth and flashes a come and get it smile, settling across from him. The steam from her coffee drifts to the perfect V shape between her rounded breasts, and he thinks Sally's done even more fine growing since high school.

"Not exactly hooky, Sal. How about you? Who's turning ugly to beautiful?"

"Uh-huh, and you might say I'm fresh out of miracles. Got tired of talking to myself, so I flipped the door sign. And here I am."

"Got my sign flipped earlier today too." He grins.

The guys in the back corner stare, figuring they know something when they don't.

"How're you making out?" She sticks a bright red fingertip into the icing atop her Danish, making a show of licking it away. "I'd hoped to see more of you." Her red lips pucker into a tease.

"Keep that up and you just might." He tries ignoring the slow rub of her sandal-clad foot along the inside of his right calf. But he loses his battle against what comes naturally. He squeezes the cup, jostling coffee onto the table.

She gives him the same sexy look he remembers from high school, and when she's satisfied with her power over him, she quits with the hot foot rub and looks out across the highway. When she looks back at him, her mood is altogether different. "Sorry about your job."

He shrugs. "Come easy, go easy–ain't that what we say?"

"I'm paying the shop's bills, taking my pitiful cut, and depositing the balance in Dodie's account."

She'd told him the same the morning he'd shown up at the shop. She's going somewhere with this, but he isn't sure where.

"While it ain't much, I'm willing to skim a little from hers for you and those kids. Ain't fair, they're hers too."

"No way, that money's hers. I don't want a crying dime." He feels the back of his neck burn, embarrassed at sounding so damn self-righteous. "Hell, don't get me wrong. Last Tuesday, I stuck up a homeless grandma."

"And the old gal was blind, right?"

They laugh.

"Okay, sweetie, it's your call. If you need anything, anything at all, you know where to find me. Maybe you'll just change your mind." She leans across the table, catches a tuft of forearm hair, twisting it with her painted nails. "Me and you had some good times. We could again."

"About that ...." His rational brain scrambles to find a way back, but the promise of sex is far more tempting than money for overdue bills he's mostly stopped worrying about.

She glances at the clock. "I got nothing back at the shop for an hour."

"Not there. I hate the smell of that place." He doesn't think he could there. Dodie's ghost would lurk in every inch of the place.

"I remember you used to like it under the stadium bleachers. The new one's off the beaten track. Not like before."

"You want to leave first? Me follow?" He glances over at the guys still bunched in the corner and they're watching him. Why should he care what they think? The jealous sons of bitches all have wives at home.

Sally crosses the parking lot, the sway of her rounded behind all the incentive he needs to risk discovery. He watches her straight through a second rotation of the town's one traffic light.

To his left and directly behind him, he hears, "Good morning, Brother Jesse. I pray God's blessings on you in this glorious morning He has created."

Cora's pocket-sized preacher stands next to the table, his bald head shining under the bright florescent lights. He wears a sanctimonious fake smile with the power to turn stomachs.

"Preacher. Oh, yes sir. Thank you, sir. That He has."

Loud hoots of laughter come from the men.

He walks to his truck and doesn't look back. When he starts the engine, the radio blasts hip-hop. He grabs the dial, but it twists off in his hand, which shakes so he has trouble threading it back on. He turns off the radio and sits, trying to breathe normally.

He pulls into the new stadium parking lot, shuts off the engine, and looks around for potential spies. In a town this size, a careless noon-hour tryst won't go unnoticed. He glances at his watch, then stares in the direction he expects Sally to have taken from the shop. He wishes he had just a nip to settle his nerves.

Sixteen years of marriage and he has cheated only once. He remembers how wronged he'd felt when Dodie refused to go with him to a respectable bar with live music on Saturday nights. He pictured them dancing the way they had before things between them got hard. To her credit, she never liked going to bars. Said the rowdy crowds made her feel cheap.

He thinks now that he should have told her about the traveling woman he'd danced with and followed to her motel room. But he felt slighted that Dodie never as much as asked where he'd spent the night. Maybe she'd stopped caring long before he noticed.

He takes an old blanket, smelling of its years of riding behind the truck seat, and walks toward Sally. They meet on the fifty yard line and he looks toward the south goal, remembering the best moment of his young life happening in the end zone of the old high school field. But that was a lifetime ago. Sex with Sally will make him twice unfaithful to Dodie, but he can't forfeit what's already lost to him.

"Cold feet, Champ?" She cocks her hip, her pelvis open to him.

He reaches for her hand, and she takes hold. Beneath the bleachers, sunlight filters through the spaces between the rows, creating a pattern of light and dark, and Jesse remembers Cole jump-stepping sidewalk cracks. He'd thought it odd, but he now understands Cole's ambivalence. Jesse spreads the blanket in the quiet secrecy and pulls Sally against him.

WHEN THEY STEP BACK into the bright sunlight blinking, Sally says, "Maybe I'll see you around again." He's unsure what he thinks about a next time. Still he's grateful that she doesn't need him to speak of meaning. This was sex alone, and for each, sex was enough.

She surprises him when she takes a folded note torn from one of those pink pads and presses it into his open palm.

"Thought you might want this. It's a number where you can reach Dodie." She touches his forearm, turns, and walks in the direction she came.

"Thanks," he calls. "Thanks for everything."

Sally stops, turns, and calls, "Shit, Jess. I ain't the Easter bunny, and it sure ain't Christmas."

"God, Sally, I'm sorry. I didn't mean nothing like that." He's so embarrassed he can't look at her.

"Forget it. If it doesn't work out, you can still give me a call. You're still pretty damn good." She shrugs and walks on.

He climbs to the top of the grandstands, a mere forty rows, his breath labored. He doesn't know if he should blame his poor conditioning or the humiliation he suffered. He watches Sally's car pull away in the direction of the shop, then unfolds the note and stares at the unfamiliar number.

A groundskeeper, or an automated timer, activates the field's sprinkling system, and he watches tiny rainbows of reflective color in the sunlight. For weeks, he's told himself that if he only knew where to look, he'd find her and talk her into coming home. His kids need their mom, and he promised Cole. But now, after all this time, he's confused about what he wants.

THIRTEEN

Jesse takes a seat on the unmade bed and removes the folded note from his pocket. Pressing it against his thigh, he traces its two-way creases with his fingertip, smoothing the paper, working to gather his courage. He punches in the number and holds his breath, the way he did waiting for an opposing team's punt to sail skyward to its pinnacle and then drop through an electrified night into the cushion of his waiting hands. He forces himself to breathe deeply and exhale slowly through five rings of the phone. A machine picks up and he hears, "Hi, leave a message at the tone for Joyce, Sharon or Delores."

Who's the woman with the too cheerful voice? He slams the phone down.

A message takes his element of surprise, although he dreads the thought of restarting his nerve. Clyde said he needed to know what he'll say to her, but he has no idea what she wants to hear. He needs a sure-fire plan. Something she hasn't heard from him—something that will cause her to believe he's changed.

He walks into the kitchen, takes a beer from the fridge and three aspirin from the bottle in the cabinet. He takes a seat on the back steps and ponders the name change. Does Delores mean she intends to lose everything in her past that reminds her of him, even the nickname he tagged her with in junior high?

Beau follows him onto the porch and sits back on his haunches, his head tilted to one side, his rat face wearing what Katie calls Beau's frown. The dog sniffs him, his so-called frown deepening.

"Get the hell back, dog. It's none of your business." He refuses criticism from a half-breed mutt. Beau blinks, and Jesse considers that a "take back." He wishes Dodie could be as forgiving, but he likely has a better track record with Beau. He dreads coming face to face with her, even over the phone.

He leaves the porch and picks his way back down the hall littered with coloring books, blunted crayons, scattered pieces of a board game, and an assortment of girl clothes in varying shapes, colors and sizes. He should pick up a bit, maybe empty the sink of dirty dishes, but instead he goes into the bathroom. At the sound of the phone, his hand jerks, a stream of urine spattering the rim of the commode. He flushes, letting the mess go for all the times Dodie bitched about the messes he left behind.

He picks up the phone.

"McKnight, the asshole I told you about? Wants more money than the job's worth. If you want it at ten-fifty an hour, it's yours."

His tongue grows thick, his throat dry, and he takes a quick seat on the bed.

"McKnight, what the hell? You still there?"

"You bet your sweet ass I want it."

"Uh, you do know it's the graveyard shift?"

His enthusiasm slips away—how the hell is he to manage working nights—but he can't turn down full-time work. "Nights ain't a problem. My wife's back. What I mean is, her sister don't need her help with the new baby."

The boss grunts into the phone. "Uh huh, ain't that timely?"

"When do I start?"

He has two days to come up with a plan.

Hanging up the phone, he leaps onto the bed, a victory fist raised in the air. When he drops onto his back, breathless and giggly, Beau leaps onto his chest, licking his face. He catches the dog's head between his hands and shouts, "How about that, you little rat-faced sonofabitch. I've got an honest to God full-time job again."

He had to say it out loud to believe it, even if only to Beau. He now has a plan. Their financial worries aren't over by a long shot, but Dodie will have to see that it's a start.

HE PULLS THE TRUCK to a quick stop in front of Cora's, and Katie and Sky are waiting on the porch, Katie wearing her grandmother's long face.

"You did it again."

"What'd I do?"

"Forgot Bible study and prayer meeting night. You're late and Grandma's royally pissed." Katie gets into the truck and Sky climbs in behind her.

Cora sits behind the wheel, the engine running, and she leans through the window, motioning for him to clear the driveway.

He smiles big and waves, allowing the girls to take their sweet time settling before driving away.

"Can we get hamburgers for supper?"

"Nope, not tonight. You had hamburgers Sunday."

"That's not fair. You and Miss Sally went to Hardee's. Why do you get to go and we don't?"

"What the hell … how do you know about … that?"

"Preacher told Grandma. He saw you there with her." Her face mirrors Cora's suspicion, and he worries that his face wears its own confession of guilt.

"What'd she say?"

"Just that. But she did that eyebrow thing she does when something isn't right. So why were you there?"

"It was business. Something Miss Sally needed fixing. At your mom's shop."

"Okay, but I still want to go."

"No, we're going home." Blackmail and he isn't falling for it.

Katie sulks and Sky plays with her shoestrings. He's pissed at Cora's bitching to Katie about him running fifteen minutes late. Maybe making her late to prayer meeting wasn't all she had to say about him. The preacher saw nothing, but he and Cora are the type to see sin in others. It distracts them from their own. Then it's likely neither Cora nor the preacher have ever had sex under the stadium bleachers.

They pull into the yard and Beau runs to meet the girls. Katie drops her backpack on the ground and runs across the yard, Beau barking at her heels, and Sky chasing Beau.

Jesse picks up their backpacks, steps onto the porch, and a friendly reminder from the utility company hangs from the door. It warns of a power disconnect unless he pays what he owes. He stomps into the house, swearing, and when his fit passes, he searches for the phone book.

"Hey, man, McKnight here. Yeah, I'm good, them too. You still do cut offs for the utility company?"

"Yeah, hated leaving that note. Know you've had some troubles lately."

"That's fine. It's just that payday falls a day short."

"Look Jess, if it'll help, I'll get Ruthie–you remember she was a grade behind us–to sit on the order for a day. But I can't do no better than that. Otherwise, my ass is in a sling."

"Sure don't want that, but a day's all I need." He's not sure one less night in the dark is all that much better, but maybe something will turn up.

Supper, a nasty concoction made from a quarter-pound of browned ground beef, a chopped onion, tomato sauce and elbow noodles, is ready after twenty-five minutes. They sit down at the table and when he serves the girls' plates, Sky starts to whimper. He pours real milk, not the powdered blue stuff, into the glass she favors, setting it next to her plate. But now she's no longer whimpering, she's squealing like a pig in the grip of death. He looks to Katie, and understands from her gathered brow that passing the buck to her won't play.

"What? For chrissakes tell me, maybe I can fix it."

"You're not going to like it."

"Try me."

"Mama makes spaghetti with long, skinny noodles. Sky won't eat crooked noodles." Katie pushes back in her chair and cups her hands over her ears as though there is no relief coming.

"Sky, I'm sorry. I know it's not your mama's spaghetti." He's shouting over her screams. "You've got to understand. Your mama's gone. My spaghetti is what you've got."

Sky lets out another brain-bending squeal, louder than before, gets out of her chair and runs down the hall, Beau barking at her heels.

Katie's cheeks flush and the insides of her arms turn pink. "Bet you're sorry we didn't stop at Hardee's."

They sit at the table, Sky's screams continuing while Beau chases back and forth from bedroom to kitchen, barking and circling the kitchen table. Katie finally yells for Beau to shut up, and the anxiety-driven dog drops as though she axed him.

Jesse can't bear to listen to her screams any longer, so he escapes to the backyard. He squats on the ground, rocking back on his heels, his hands cradling his throbbing head.

He asked Trudy about how he should handle Sky's fits in Dodie's absence. Sky needed time, she said, to make up lost ground caused by the nasty ear infections she'd suffered. That even a short loss of hearing can throw off a child learning to talk, and that learning to talk is like climbing a ladder, one rung at a time.

Trudy didn't say, but he accepts that the damage came with the delay before taking Sky to a pediatrician. He'd argued that earaches were as common as snotty noses and insisted Dodie use warm sweet oil, a remedy his mama had used with six kids.

But what explained those awful fits, he'd wanted to know. Trudy had smiled and said, "Lord, darling, it's hard for a mama to say no to a sick baby. Our baby girl learned how to get her way, and she's good at it."

He's relieved that she'll someday catch up, learn to talk. But what is he to do when he feels as though the entire house is under siege?

Katie and Beau follow him outside and sit on the ground, each watching him, and he has no answers.

"What did your mama do?"

"Like us. Waited her out." She shrugs.

He and Katie sit without talking, the first stars of the evening coming into view, while Sky's muffled screams slow and finally stop. She's either worn herself down or lost interest. He looks over at Katie, and she's pinching the tips from grass blades and staring off across the pasture next door.

"Besides having fits, does she ever just say what's bothering her, maybe just talk?" He tries to imagine what Sky speaking would sound like.

"She talked to Mama. But now, she just talks to Mama Trudy and me. I think she knows Mama's not coming back."

He knows he should say something reassuring, but he doesn't want to lie to Katie. "Why won't she talk to me?" Sometimes, he felt she thought about it, but still held back.

Katie stares at him without flinching. "You don't want to know."

He sighs. Maybe she's right. Trudy said that Sky had drawn her family, "… right down to that funny-looking dog she's so crazy about," and that she'd drawn him, "… way tiny, set apart to nearly falling off the page." He'd wondered at the time which color Sky had chosen for him, but he'd been too afraid to ask.

"Yeah, baby, I think I do want to know." He's never even yelled at Sky, much less raised a hand to her.

"Remember when you'd come home drunk and you and Mama yelled? Sky got real scared. I think she was too little to know that sorry meant you took the names back and Mama forgave you." Blinking, she looks away, causing him to think that maybe she means to include some of her own fears.

"Katie, if you're thinking I hit your mom, I didn't. I never did that." He wants her to know he'd never forced himself on her mama. He'd only meant to persuade her. But how do you say that to your young daughter?

"But you yelled mean names and beat on the door until Cole made you go away. "

"You girls heard all of that?"

"Dad, what'd you think? We're little kids, but we got ears."

He lifts his gaze to the stars, and he has no words that he trusts just now. He hadn't realized that she and Sky heard his argument with Cole the night Dodie left. He hadn't been able to make out Cole's features in the dark hallway, but he'd heard him sucking air like he'd run a long way. He yelled for him to leave, and it was only then that he made out the baseball bat in Cole's hand.

Katie rubs the white spot between Beau's ears, and she seems willing to wait for as long as he may need.

After some time, he manages, "Katie, do you remember our playing tag in the front yard?"

"Yeah, and all of us falling down on the ground, rolling around and getting our legs and arms tangled like noodles."

"And your mama giggled so hard when you kids tickled her that …."

"She had to run to the bathroom." The corners of Katie's mouth turn up ever so slightly. "But all that was before Sky."

"Really? Are you sure?"

She nods. "That's why I used to think it was all her fault."

"But why did you think it was Sky's fault?" He realizes he's asking Katie for answers he doesn't have.

"Sky cried all the time, and Mama was too sad."

Dodie had cried through most of her pregnancy with Sky. He doesn't know how she was when she was pregnant with Katie. He wasn't around for any of that time. He saw Katie for the first time at about five months. He laughed and asked if she'd had a head full of red hair at birth. Dodie cried and left the room. Katie grabbed his uniform cap from his head and tried putting it atop her wild curls. He'd fallen hopelessly in love with her in that moment.

"Katie, I don't know why things quit being fun. I just know I want the fun back."

"Can't you go find Mama and tell her that?"

"I may have a chance. And I promise you, I'll try."

SKY HAS FALLEN ASLEEP on the floor, and Jesse lifts her into his arms. It's the first time he remembers holding her in such a long time. He puts her onto the bed, removes her shoes and socks, and covers her.

He and Katie go into the kitchen, and he makes peanut butter and jelly sandwiches and pours the last of the milk in a glass for Katie. They eat in front of the TV, making it through the first half of E.T. before Katie falls asleep. He lifts her and carries her down the hall into the bedroom. Beau jumps onto the bed and settles. Jesse thinks about Beau's fleas, but decides what the hell. The dog had a rough evening too.

The front door opens and closes, and Jesse hears the fridge door slam back. He goes into the kitchen, and Cole looks up from his scavenging for food.

"What's there to eat? I'm starving."

"You eat crooked noodles?"

"Hell, right now, I'll eat anything that doesn't eat me first."

"Good. The pot there on the stove."

Cole dishes food onto a plate and when he's warmed it in the microwave, he sits at the table. "It's awful quiet. Midgets in bed, I'd wager."

"You'd be right."

Cole stuffs food into his mouth like it's his last meal.

"I'm headed to bed. How 'bout you?"

"Yeah, I'm wasted. Scraping dog shit has lost its charm."

"I bet."

Sitting again on the edge of what he still thinks of as his and Dodie's bed, he tries the number he called earlier, and this time the cheerful voice is real. He tells her his name, and holds his breath through a long pause. The woman tells him Delores is out for the evening, her warmth cooled.

He thanks her and asks if she'll please ask Dodie … Delores … to call home. No, he doesn't care how late.

It's ten o'clock, and he wonders why she'd be out so late. Is she seeing someone? No, she isn't like him, and he wants to believe she has a good reason.

He stretches out across the bed and closes his eyes. Dodie isn't E. T. and maybe she won't phone home. He wishes he'd told the stranger on the phone that there was an emergency with one of the kids. Maybe Sky. No, he wants her to believe that he's taking such good care of their kids that they're safe even from emergencies.

Although it's warm in the bedroom, he draws the sheet beneath his chin and lies awake in the darkness. If she doesn't call back tonight, then he'll keep trying until she decides to talk to him. Maybe a job loading semi-trailers isn't much to brag about, but it's full-time, and things could start to level out over time. It's bound to make a difference in how she feels about their future.

The phone startles him, and he answers too quickly. But she has to know he was waiting by the phone. At the sound of her voice, he gathers a pillow to his chest and squeezes his eyes shut.

"Is something wrong with one of the kids?" A mother's fear echoes in her voice, but why has she not called before now, felt the same fear?

"No, not if you mean right this second." Everything is fine unless she considers Cole's stint in jail, Sky's fits, and Katie playing mama around the clock. But he isn't about to whine to her, for himself or for the kids. There's a pause, and he works at controlling the anger churning inside him.

"How is Sky?" Her voice is thick with the kind of dread that comes with already knowing the answer.

He pushes his fingertips to his left temple, and echoes of Sky's screams still make him light-headed.

"Did you know she hates elbow noodles?"

There's a longer pause.

"Jess, I'm sorry I left the way I did. I was afraid you'd try talking me out of leaving. I couldn't risk that."

"You're right. I would've tried."

"Then you know I didn't even tell Mama. I told Sally only because I needed her to stay on at the shop." Even after all these weeks, she is weighing her every word, intending to cover any cracks in her doggedness. He starts to feel a little better about his chances.

"Yeah, the old lady's still giving me fits." He's surprised that she doesn't have more to say about Sally, but grateful if she means to let the question of how he got her number go unanswered.

"I'm sure. Then you've never been among her favorites." Her voice softens, and although he knows better than to push, he can no longer avoid the question they've both circled like a coiled rattler.

"Is this … thing … for much longer?" He can't say separation because it sounds too decisive.

"I want badly to see the kids."

"I could bring them to where you are."

"No, I'm coming Thanksgiving to see them."

"Thanksgiving's weeks away. Why not now?"

"Jesse." There's the familiar impatience in the curt way she says his name, and he senses a shift in momentum.

"Can I at least come where you are? Maybe talk things out?"

"No, I'm not ready."

"I promise I won't ask you to come back." He remembers Cole swearing that she'd left him and not him and his sisters. He chucks his pride and cuts straight to where she's the most vulnerable. "Please, I've got to know how I'm supposed to answer our kids' questions about what your leaving means for them." No matter how she feels about him, she has to be handling a load of guilt.

She whimpers. "Okay, but only this once."

It was dirty of him, but her turnaround means he succeeded in breaking her will, and for that reason, he decides to save his good news. Use it to his best advantage when he sees her.

"Meet me tomorrow at noon in the cafeteria at the tech school in Valdosta." Her voice is stronger.

"Valdosta?" A little over a hundred miles away. That isn't the decision of a panicked woman running into the night. It's a destination. He was right all along.

"Yes, Valdosta." Her voice confesses as much.

"I'll be there."

"And don't call again unless there's a real emergency." She hangs up without another word.

He wishes she'd left things the way they were.

HE MAKES HURRIED ARRANGEMENTS with Trudy to keep the girls overnight, then calls Cora, telling her that he'll get the girls after school. He lies to keep from having to listen to her tired old arguments that leaving the girls with Trudy is unsafe. Cora believes that safety comes only to those behind white picket fences.

He withdraws his last fifty dollars from savings, feeling helpless against the unexpected, despite having known that fifty dollars wouldn't cover an emergency of the size he has. Still, he thinks it may have been his white picket fence.

He drives out of town and heads north, then east for a couple of hours before reaching Valdosta in record time. He stops and gets directions to the tech school, and drives the twelve blocks to the main entrance. When he locates the cafeteria, he parks the truck in a space marked student parking.

He buys a large coffee and takes a seat near the front where he has a clear view of the entrance. He sips coffee from a thin Styrofoam cup cradled between his palms and stares at every woman who comes through the door, regardless of her age, size or hue.

When Dodie doesn't come right away, he makes a game out of pressing his palms against the hot cup, releasing only when his pain from doing so becomes too intense. Physical pain is much easier to bear than the silent kind that crawls like giant killer worms in the pit of his stomach.

Glancing at a clock on the wall, he wishes he'd driven slower, arriving closer to the appointed hour. Over the noisy clatter of food service, chairs scraping across the tiled floor, and loud greetings, he makes out bits and pieces of serious conversation, largely foreign to his ear.

Crowded around tables stacked high with books and loose papers, males and females of all ages and colors listen intently, their solemn faces sometimes giving way to pinched smiles and nervous laughter. Why has she asked him to meet her here, rather than one of the fast-food joints he passed? Maybe she works at the small beauty shop he noticed in a nearby strip mall and she's taking her lunch break. It makes sense that she doesn't want him to know where she works until they've had a chance to work through their differences. Yet he feels oddly out of place, less and less sure that what he's come to offer can matter.

His anxiety increases, and he senses her presence moments before he sees her standing near the entrance. The two women flanking her on either side stare in his direction, and he tries remembering their names from the message machine. He stands and Dodie flashes a strained recognition, then waves the women to a table across the cafeteria. They move away, but continue to stare, and he equates their intensity with that of middle linebackers he had faced off against. He's wearing his best sports shirt, the one he wore at the picnic. He touches the hair that curls over his shirt collar and wishes there had been time for a trip to Willie's.

She speaks his name in a flat tone, as if they're strangers forced into a blind date. She shifts her load of books and he reaches for them, placing the stack on an extra chair, inviting her to sit opposite him.

She runs a quick hand over the buttons on her blouse, and her discomfort causes him to glance away. Her posture is erect, her arms crossed, resting on the table between them.

Her hair is different, cut short, and it's back to its natural brown. She looks even thinner, but he can't be sure. He says she looks good, even though he liked her hair long, and she thanks him while each measures the mood of the other.

"Why here?" Of all the questions on his mind, he feels safer starting with one he believes to be inconsequential.

"I'm between classes." She shifts in the chair and crosses her left leg over her right knee, swinging her left foot the way she does when she's about to say something that's going to hurt.

He glances at the books, thinking the cafeteria is convenient all right, and even Thanksgiving makes sense. He drains the last of the cooled coffee and concentrates on all the ramifications of what's left unsaid.

"I've started a new life here." She twists her wedding band as though it no longer fits or even belongs. "I hate that my leaving has made everything so hard ... especially for the girls. They're so young and there's so much they can't understand."

He's unclear what her starting a new life means for him and their kids. All he knows is that the life they'd promised isn't the one they're living.

She stares at him, and in a flat tone sounding more like thought than speech, she says, "The problem with marrying someone you grew up with is that you never stop to ask the really hard questions. Before I got pregnant with Cole, I believed I knew everything I needed to know about you. But I was wrong."

"Oh for chrissakes, Dodie, not that again." The three chatty women at the nearest table fall into an inquisitive silence, and he regrets having raised his voice. Yet he hates more that she has started whatever she has to say with their oldest argument, and like all the times before, he feels the emotional ground shift beneath him. He runs his sweaty palms along his thighs, and it's never meant more to him than now that she believe him.

"Dodie, I swear on our children's lives, I never meant to do anything but marry you and have Cole. Please come home with me. It's not too late. We can fix things."

Her chest rises sharply, and she exhales, three quick puffs of hot air much like a choked scream. "No, stop. I won't go back. I'm thirty-four years old. I have to do what I can to make a better life for our kids and myself. Otherwise, we're stuck in that miserable town, barely scraping by. Me doing what I hate. You brooding over the imagined glory I cost you. Neither of us with a chance of happiness. I can't, and I won't, do it."

"Does that mean I'm to tell our kids they had a mama, but now that everything's tougher, they don't? Jesus, Dodie, that's too fucking hard." If she'd been there to see Cole puking in a jailhouse toilet, Katie wearing Sky like a hangman's noose, and Sky screaming herself into an exhausted sleep, she'd know hard the way he's come to know it.

"No, of course not. That's ludicrous and you know it. I fully intended to find a place near the campus for the kids and me, but rent is too high. I'm barely making ends meet sharing rent and utilities. No one wants to share with a mom and her three kids."

"Then come home. The kids need you." In a controlled voice, he tells her about Sky's fits and that Katie's grown quieter, that her grades have slipped. "And I worry about Cole's future."

"Cole? What on earth do you mean?" Her tone mocks what she can't know. Cole isn't her perfect son anymore.

"He insisted on knowing where you were. When I told him I didn't know, only that it appeared that you'd planned for a time to leave, he blew up."

"Oh, Jess, didn't you show him the note? What about the messages?"

"No, but I don't know that the note could've changed what happened."

She cries softly through his story of Cole's arrest, the hearing, and the judge's decision to grant probation. When she does speak, her voice is raspy with strain, and the veins of her slender neck show like taut rubber bands under her pale skin.

"Oh, God, I don't think I could have handled hearing that my sweet boy spent even one night in jail."

For a moment, she sits quietly, and he's relieved that she doesn't search his face for the truth about Cole's detention. He's certain she could never forgive him for having failed their son.

She leans away from him, her hands tightly wadded in her lap. "As terrible as things are now, what I'm doing, I'm doing for their future."

"About that …." He tries sounding hopeful.

"Jesse, please."

"But things have already turned for the better. I've got full-time work now." He's played his ace, and he hopes she'll latch on to its promise, the way he has.

"You don't get it, do you? Even if I could bear the thought of ever touching another woman's hair, there's no future in a two-chair shop in that God-forsaken town."

She squares her shoulders, tightly folding her arms across her breasts. The softness in her brown eyes hardens to fired clay. The woman across the table from him is the same one who ran away weeks ago. He slides to the front edge of his chair and struggles to come up with anything that will undercut her determination.

"You know I'm a damn good worker. I'll get raises. Then you can sell the shop. We'll save on childcare and gas." He hears the smallness in what he offers. "Baby, please don't ask me to leave everything familiar. I survived that in Iraq. I can't do it again." He squeezes his eyes against the tears building behind his eyelids.

"Don't you understand? I'm not asking you to move. I want a divorce." Her voice is low, but strong. "I'll ask the court for full custody of the children. When I'm done here, I'll be a certified court reporter. I can provide for them in ways you can't."

He has no doubt that she means what she says. Yet the words on the note she left, "Dear Jess, I think I may still love you," never sounded like divorce.

"Is there someone else?" Clyde's warning jabs his consciousness like an ice pick, and every absolute he'd once held about him and Dodie spins in his head as though caught up in the fury of a sand storm.

"If you're asking if I'm leaving you for someone else, my answer is no." She doesn't look at him but glances at the women she came in with, and he's overpowered.

"You know Iraq wasn't my fault, any more than losing my job was."

"You're right, neither was your fault. But you had to know that I'd stopped loving you." She pauses, the tiny heart shaped necklace he'd given her when Cole was born rises and falls with her rapid breathing, yet her rejection is as real as a bolted door.

Standing on knocked-out legs, he stumbles his way across the crowded cafeteria and doesn't see the woman until he reels from their impact, her food tray crashing to the floor. He doesn't stop to apologize, but swings open the door.

As he speeds out of the parking lot, the orange parking ticket tucked beneath a wiper blade tears loose and catches in the wind.

FOURTEEN

Jesse maneuvers through heavy traffic, the near-rotted wiper blades scraping a narrow view of the highway home. He wants to believe that he's left Dodie standing in the parking lot, pleading that he should come back so she can tell him she's changed her mind.

He brakes hard, steering the truck to a skidding stop onto the muddy shoulder of the road, enraging the driver who had been riding his bumper. He gets out of the truck, the engine idling, and squats next to the off-road rear tire. His mind races, searching for the slightest missed clue, but no matter how hard he tries, he can't undo, "full custody." He drops onto the wet ground, his knees drawn to his chest, and he's grateful that at least the panic that sent him into flight has eased. Even so, he can't shake the strangeness he feels, like a small boat cut loose from its mooring, left to float rudderless on waters shrouded in heavy gray fog.

The rain lets up, and he's mindful that he's soaked to the skin and shivering. He pushes up stiffly from the ground and gets back into the truck. Suddenly, he does what he didn't believe he could. He weeps for all that he imagines he's lost, and for all that he now fears for himself and his kids.

AFTER TWO HOURS along a road he barely remembers, he pulls the truck into a local gas station and waits his turn at the pump. Through the rearview mirror, he catches sight of James's battered green pickup turning into the parking lot, the radio blasting. Cole and a pretty girl Jesse believes to be Sarah are passengers.

The truck idling, James hurries into the store, and Jesse watches Cole and Sarah, their backs to him. She leans into Cole, rests her head on his shoulder, and Jesse wishes he could see his son's face. Would he see his own face at seventeen, the way he'd looked at Dodie? Is Sarah crying the way Dodie had?

Behind him, he hears the squealing of rubber, and a red Mustang spins to a stop next to James's truck. A short, muscular boy, maybe a body-builder, gets out of the car. He leans into the driver-side truck window, and there's yelling between him and Sarah, but Jesse can't make out whether or not Cole gets into the argument.

Sarah gets out of the truck and into the Mustang and the car speeds away. James exits the store in a run, holding three drink cups and a big bag of chips. He swears, flinging a soda cup in the direction of the departing Mustang, then gets into the truck and he and Cole speed away in the opposite direction. Jesse takes a deep breath, relieved that whatever Sarah's troubles are with the boy, Cole and James had sense enough not to chase after the speeding Mustang.

Jesse pumps ten gallons of gas, grabs a dozen donuts and a half-gallon of milk, and pays the clerk. He can't put his finger on exactly what bothers him about what he just witnessed. Nevertheless, his gut churns. Cole can't help but get drawn into Sarah's troubles. But how much is he willing to risk for this girl? And James is primed for any excuse to kick someone's ass.

He pulls the truck into the yard, gets out, and strides onto the porch where Cole stands brushing loose dog hair off his jeans. His backpack is on the floor. He's been home only long enough to greet Beau.

"Look, we need to talk." Jesse puts his key into the dead bolt, and Cole picks up his book bag and follows him through the door. They circle each other in the middle of the living room. An all too familiar squall gathers behind Cole's dark eyes.

"What was that back there at the station?"

"You spying now?" Cole stares in the way that presses on Jesse's last nerve. Still, he remembers Clyde's remark about two jackasses can't haul.

"I stopped for gas. Saw ya'll pull in. Couldn't help but see some of what went on."

Cole walks into the kitchen and Jesse follows.

"I need to know. I'm worried."

"Forget it. It's her problem. And I'm staying out of it." His eyes cloud, and it's clear Cole's up to his neck in whatever is between Sarah and the boy in the Mustang.

"Staying out could get tougher than you think. Keep it up with that girl and that asshole will bring it. Then what?"

"Sarah. Her name is Sarah. Is that so damn hard?"

"All right, Sarah. But that don't change a thing."

Cole walks to the fridge, searches its pitiful offerings, and comes away with a tub of margarine. He globs margarine on a stale hot dog bun and woofs it down in three quick bites.

"Don't mean to get over in your stuff. But …."

"Then back off. I know what I'm doing."

Cole has no idea how far his feelings for Sarah can push him. But, no matter how much he wants to save him from what's coming, Cole can't hear any of what he might say. He means to butt with his own stubborn head.

"All right, I will, because I've got a big-ass problem I can't handle alone. But first, go out to the truck and get that bag behind the seat while I start a pot of coffee."

Cole sighs, obviously relieved to have the evil eye off him in favor of someone else's problem. Jesse puts on a pot and takes a seat at the table. Cole returns with the bag and pulls out the box of donuts, then pours himself a glass of milk. He takes a seat opposite Jesse, pushes back in the chair, his brow furrowed.

"Let's eat first. I'm starved."

After they've each had three quick donuts, Jesse feels he can begin. He decided on the drive home that he would tell Cole the truth about what happened between him and Dodie.

"First of all, I've got something real hard to say and harder to hear. But I figure, with all that's gone down around here, you're old enough to hear it."

"Please, cut the melodrama, will you?" Cole draws his arms tighter across his chest and slouches, as if he tries for invisible.

"Sally gave up your mom's telephone number."

"Her? Why, after all this time? What changed her mind?"

"Don't know why. It's enough to know that she did."

"Yeah, right, if you say so." Cole sneers.

Jesse runs his sweaty palms along his thighs, blaming his own guilt for having heard more in Cole's hint of infidelity than he likely intended. "Your mom agreed to see me. That's where I'd been when I saw you at the station."

Cole pinches sugar granules from the tablecloth, puts his fingertip to his lips. He says nothing, perhaps even better at deflecting his emotions than his old man.

"Valdosta … the whole time."

Cole lifts his head, his face still a pale mask, and he doesn't show surprise.

"Shares rent with two other women. Money's a big part of why she hasn't come for you kids."

Cole's chest expands, and he gathers himself, pushing up straight, his tailbone wedged against the chair rounds. He leans on the table, his hands squeezed into a double fist.

"She's signed up for classes there. *Court Reporting Techniques* was the title of one of the books she carried."

"Dad, I don't give a damn what courses she's taking. I don't care who she's living with. I want to know what this means."

Jesse fumbles with the donut box, and when he's aligned the fastener into the slot, he pushes the box aside. "I now know that you were right all along."

"She talked about divorce? Actually said the word?" Cole leans closer.

"Clear as can be said. And it wasn't the kind of thing said in the heat of an argument that you later regret." Jesse passes a quick hand over his chin. "I tried, but nothing I said made a difference. Her mind's set, maybe as early as before she left here."

"What about us kids?" His voice cracks, and Jesse wishes he could tell Cole that his life, and the lives of his sisters, won't change.

"No doubt it'll mean a move." He can't bring himself to speak of full custody in the cold, absolute way she had.

"Does that mean you're agreeing? Just like that, it's all settled?"

"Cole, I can't say what's settled and what's not. I need time to think about what all this can mean." The boy deserves something more from him, but he's unable to give that just yet.

Cole comes to his feet and slings the empty milk glass at the sink. "I hate the cowardly way she left. And that you're so messed up you don't know what you want. Before I'll agree to go with her, I'll go live next door. Miss Marlene will take the girls. Those two can never be separated."

"Just wait a damn minute before you go deciding you know my mind. Maybe you knew all along, but I heard divorce for the first time less than five hours ago. You've got to believe I went there still thinking I could convince her to come home. If not for me, then for you and the girls. I thought that's what you wanted."

Cole turns to him, tears in his eyes. "Can't you at least tell me what you want?"

"I can, but I don't think …."

"Just tell me what you want."

"She's your mom."

"And you think that lets you off the hook?"

"Off the hook? If I intended that, would I have been here? Doing what little I know to do? This whole mess is a giant fuck-up, and I'm sorry."

"You haven't been all that bad." A sly smile.

"You mean you want to stay, even with all the shit that's flying around this place?"

"Sometimes I pray that you're more blind than stupid. Then you open your mouth." He shakes his head in disbelief.

Jesse sags into a chair, his body convulsing in the kind of hysteria that swaps tears for laughter.

Cole watches him, his face brightening, and he too begins to laugh.

Jesse wipes tears on the back of his hand and chokes out, "She's cut her hair. Shorter than mine. And it's back to its natural color."

"No way. What color is that?"

"Your grandpa McKnight called that color brown 'chicken shit brindle.'"

Their laughter is genuine. Cole calls Beau away from the broken glass. He brings over the broom and dust pan, sweeps glass into a pile, and scoops it into the garbage.

"There's more news, and it's mostly good. But I'll need you to step up for it to have any chance."

Cole's eyes narrow, and he's back to wary.

"I've got full-time work at the warehouse. Comes with overtime and some paid holidays." He's unsure about the last, but can't resist inflating his success. He glances at the clock and then back at Cole. "It's the graveyard shift. It starts tonight."

"No, no, I can't." Cole sucks air through his mouth and he looks as if he may stage a runaway.

"I know. And I hate to put this on you. But I'll get them into bed before I leave. All you have to do is be here. I can't afford Trudy, and Cora's out of the question."

"There's Miss Dee and Miss Susan. Can't you ask them?"

"That's too much to expect from neighbors, even good ones."

"Katie's okay, but what if Sky wakes up screaming and freaking out the way she does?"

"I don't know what to tell you except to say if things get crazy you'll have to do what I do."

"What you do? Meaning I should push her off on Katie? That's not fair."

"You're right. But there's nothing about any of this that's fair."

Cole puts the remaining milk away and stands looking out the kitchen window for a time that seems too long to be good news. He turns back with an anxious expression. "Okay, but if I feel I'm screwing up, you've got to let me back out."

"Fair enough. I've got to get the girls from Trudy's, and I'll pick up something good for supper. You got a request?"

"How about fried chicken, mashed potatoes, and gravy?"

"I'll stop by Margie's Chicken Coop and get a bucket with all the sides." He'll use the extra money he'd taken to Valdosta, just in case he needed the price of a motel room, and splurge on take-out for their supper instead. For a man who just heard that his wife of sixteen years wants a divorce, he feels better than he expected.

FIFTEEN

Jesse makes his first week on the job with little left in his tank. He drives home in an exhausted fog. He steps onto the porch thinking about hitting the sack for a few hours before the girls and their noise make sleeping wishful thinking.

Sky and Katie are still in their pajamas, sprawled on the couch in front of the TV, and neither looks up from Saturday morning cartoons. He slips down the hall, setting aside their mom's hand-wringing that too much TV will make them fat and shrink their brains to peanut size. If all of that were true, he'd care, but he still wouldn't have the energy to walk over and turn the damn thing off.

Cole lies face down across his bed, fully dressed, a pillow pulled over his head. There's no doubt his first week as night guard carried every bit as much fatigue. There's good reason working nights is called the graveyard shift. It should come with a pre-paid burial plan.

He drops his jeans and shirt on the floor and falls across the unmade bed, burying his scratchy face into a pillow that smells too much like him. He flips it for a fresher side, but no such luck. He can't think about the list of chores that awaits him. He sleeps or he dies.

Mid-afternoon, Jesse wakes and squints through sleep-caked eyes at the wavy numbers on the clock face. He sits on the side of the bed and feels a twinge of guilt at having slept so long. He takes his jeans from the floor and chooses a cleaner shirt from the pile in the corner, then stumbles into the bathroom and pees, deciding not to shower and shave until he's had a start on chores. But first, he needs coffee.

The house is scary quiet. Beau snoozes on the girls' bed, and Cole isn't in his room. Jesse takes a cup from a sink of dirty dishes, a cold greasy skim floating on top. He runs cold water over the cup, fills it with yesterday's coffee, and turns toward the sound of footsteps from the back porch.

Cole appears with a sketchpad under his arm and a fistful of colored pencils.

"Thought you'd died." He has dark circles under his eyes.

Jesse grunts. "Where's everybody?" He sits at the table.

"Miss Marlene took Katie and Sky to Tallahassee to get birthday presents."

"Birthday? Good lord, I forgot." He glances at the clock and tries to remember if there was talk about a time. Where did he put the paper with the Georgia cowboy's number? He pats his hip pocket. "Shit, where's my damn wallet?"

He hurries back into the bedroom and searches. The balance he owes for the horse is in his wallet. He stands in the middle of the room, mentally retracing his steps, when he spots his wallet on the floor. He checks the secret flap where he put the money for safekeeping and pulls the bills out of hiding. The condom he'd hoped to use in Valdosta drops onto the floor, a silver flash rolling across the floor.

Cole stands in the doorway, and Jesse overtakes and plants his bare foot on the runaway disk, aflame with embarrassment. "Went prepared, that's all. Then you know how that worked out." He wishes he didn't have the thing with Sally on his conscience. He avoids her like a leper. And that's wrong, but he doesn't trust himself.

"Give me a break. I don't want to hear stuff like that. Not about you and Mom … you … and anybody."

"Yeah, sorry. That was lame."

Cole walks away and he's blushing too, but not as much as Jesse thinks he should. The father and son talk with Cole about sex is long past due.

He tosses the rubber in with his tie and makes the call to the number in Georgia. A woman answers, telling him the men pulled out before daylight, headed his way. He thanks her and calculates the distance and time for a truck pulling a horse trailer, and estimates they will arrive within the next hour or so. He looks out at the corral and wishes he'd had the time and money to make it stronger. But it'll have to hold until he can get together the price of boards.

He makes cheese toast, but the knot in his stomach swells to the size of a green plum, and he feeds the toast to Beau. Clyde's warning pounds like a hammer against the sides of his skull, and he tells himself that he still can turn the deal around. Give the cowboy the money in his wallet and let him keep the horse. He could offer the guy extra for gas, if he had it. The cowboy can't lose. But Katie loses her dream of a horse, and he loses his second chance with her.

At the sound of a vehicle approaching, Jesse walks off the porch and crosses the yard to the corral. A white, late model Chevy pickup hauling a rusted trailer slows, pulls off the highway, and turns onto the lane.

From where he stands near the corral, he can't see the horse, but he can hear loud thuds. The truck draws closer, and the sound he heard is the horse's hind hooves striking the metal door of the trailer.

Cole comes to stand propped against the corral fence, and although he's lost much of his sullenness, he watches the rig approach with his face twisting in what Jesse reads as dread to match his own. Likely Cole has already sized up his purchase of the horse as flying downhill without brakes.

"That there's where you figure on holding her?" The man jeers more than asks. He leans across the cab and says something that Jesse can't hear to the man riding with him. The two laugh. He recognizes the second man from the bar.

The driver maneuvers the rig into position, backing the ratty trailer even with the corral gate, the trailer width plugging up most of the opening. He shuts off the engine, and it spews a cloud of oily smoke.

Jesse walks to the back of the trailer, getting his first look at the mustang mare. Her head is pulled up short, a heavy rope tied to a metal rod runs behind her haunches. She has raw rope burns, and he imagines her struggling in that position for the duration of the trip.

At the sound of Old Blue approaching the lane, Jesse looks away from the horse. He'd hoped he would stay away, but Clyde's been with Katie for more birthdays than he has, and has never missed a single one. A fight between them wasn't cause enough for him to miss this one.

Clyde pulls the van to the side of the corral, and Jesse waits for the sound of the ramp engaging, and for Clyde to maneuver himself into the wheelchair and to the van door. He rides the motorized chair down the ramp and onto the ground.

Jesse leaves the horse, deciding to face Clyde's scorn and get it behind him for the moment.

"She ain't much to look at, but that'll change. Katie's gonna have her eating sugar out of her hand. You'll see. Don't worry." The last time he'd felt this big a lie, an old woman lay dead at the feet of a grieving kid soldier under his command. The boy had taken his own life with the same gun.

"Ain't got time for a family reunion," the man calls. He gets out of the truck and approaches along the side of the trailer.

The mare's ears point straight at him, and when he gets behind her, she pulls against the halter ropes, sawing the rope across her bleeding haunches. She shifts her weight from side to side, rocking the narrow trailer, and she's caked in sweat. Her hide ripples across her shoulders.

"You can look all you want. But she's yours, fair and square. So what you say to forking over my money. Let me get the crazy bitch unloaded and me back on the road." He shows the gap-toothed sneer Jesse remembers.

Clyde calls to Jesse from his chair near the corral. "I don't know a damn thing about horses, but that poor critter's scared half crazy."

The cowboy stares down at Clyde, his contempt clear. "She'll settle when we've unloaded her," he snorts.

"Not if she has to contend with the likes of your sorry ass, she won't." Clyde's upper lip curls.

Jesse steps toward the chair and raises his hand. The man can't know that Clyde carries a semi-automatic in the side pocket of the chair. Claims it's for snakes and other varmints.

Jesse has seen enough of the mare to know that he's screwed, but just how badly he isn't sure. Even he sees the work needed to gentle the mare, forget the training he doesn't know anything about. He prays for a case of good old-fashioned love at first sight between Katie and the mustang. But even with the blindness of first love, the mustang is no match for the mare next door.

The mustang is smaller than the quarter horses, but it's reasonable that a horse raised in the wild would be smaller. At best, this horse is ordinary, and he'd describe her over-all as leather brown with a white blaze the shape of an upside down pear between her eyes. The mustang may be a two hundred dollar horse and never worth more, but if Katie can put this mare first in her heart, it still could make everything okay between him and Katie and give the abused animal the breaks it hasn't had.

"Goddamn, Jesse. Give the man the money. Let 'em get that pitiful animal out of here before Katie sees her. We'll find her a decent one."

"Unload her. Here's your damn money." He takes the folded money from his pocket and the man counts it out before placing it in his shirt pocket.

"Be damn quick with that gate." The cowboy spits on the ground and Jesse believes he sees fear in the man's eyes.

He stands ready to swing the gate shut when signaled.

The cowboy walks back to the cab, leans in and talks to the second man. He gets out, and the two draw the mare's head up tighter against the front of the trailer, one side of her head slammed hard against the metal frame.

The trailer gate drops onto the ground, and the mare tries to turn toward the noise, but the ropes hold her blind to the action behind her. It's clear she's terrified of any movement in a direction she can't see.

"All right, Hank, ease up on that haunch rope. But don't give the bitch her head."

For the first time, Jesse sees the scars across the mare's body, along with fresher wounds caked with blood and dirt. She is matted to her knees in dried manure.

The horse kicks free of the rope beneath her haunches and dances in place, again rocking the trailer side to side with her weight.

Working together, the two men release the mare's head and begin shouting, waving their hats.

The mare tries to rear and pivot, but the space in the trailer is too small. She loses her footing and stumbles down the ramp and out of the trailer.

The two men continue running at her, and the mare runs to the far end of the corral, spins back, and faces the men. She's completely awash in sweat, the whites of her eyes rolled back, and her tail slashes back and forth in a frantic whipping motion.

"Shut the damn gate." The man shouts and runs toward Jesse.

He swings the gate shut, fastening it with a chain and hook.

The man sucks air, his face covered in grimy sweat.

"Hold her and there's likely a bonus in it for you. Not that I give a damn."

He takes off his hat and wipes his sweaty face on the sleeve of his shirt. Placing his hat back on his head, he walks to the truck, gets behind the steering wheel, and drives away in a cloud of dust and exhaust.

Jesse watches as the truck and trailer rattle onto the highway, nearly sideswiping Marlene's car, and any sensible thought he might have had about sending the horse back with the cowboys vanishes with the sight of Katie waving from the window of Marlene's car.

Marlene stops in front of the house, and Katie jumps out and runs toward him, calling, "Daddy, Daddy, is she mine?"

He watches her, and his heart swells with his love for her. Behind him, he hears the mare's frightful screams. Clyde shouts his name, but he can't make out what he's saying. He turns toward the corral, and what he sees takes his breath, turning the love in his heart to fear.

"Oh, my God, what've I done?"

The mare stands with her nose nearly touching the ground. Her ears lay close to her head. Her tail lashes from side to side and she rears, charging the fence.

"Jesus God, get back," Clyde shouts. "She's coming over."

Jesse sprints toward Katie, who has dropped to her knees. He doesn't look back at the sound of splintering boards or the pounding of hooves, but drops onto the ground, covering Katie with his body. Beneath him, he feels the ground rumbling up through her body and into his heaving chest. She struggles against him, and he shouts for to her stay down.

A rush of heat and energy hangs in the air above him like smoldering lightening, along with a sickening scent he takes as his raw fear mixed with that of the mare. He squeezes his eyes shut against a swirl of dust and loose sand from the mare's flying hooves, and prays for deliverance.

The panic passes and a fragile curtain of stillness drops around him and Katie, and it's as though they exist inside a dome. He hears only his heavy breathing and Katie's muffled crying.

He raises his head and looks in the direction of the fleeing mare. She runs with her neck extended, her nose in the air, and her ears turned backward to the corral.

He pulls Katie to her feet, and they stand watching as the mustang cuts away from the fence line and gallops toward the National Forest. He worries that only an explosion of hot lead to her brain can stop her now.

Tears run a dirty track down Katie's flushed cheeks, and with the tail of his shirt, he tries wiping her stained face. But she pushes his hand away and runs into Marlene's arms. Her look of despair is the same as Dodie's in the moment just before she asked him for a divorce. He felt the pain of her loss, but nothing like what he's feeling now.

He turns at the sound of Cole calling his name. Cole is standing over Clyde, who is lying face down in the sand. The wheels of the motorized chair are stuck. From the look of the loose ground, Clyde tried crawling toward where he and Katie were hunkered. He too was in the direct path of the escaping horse. Jesse runs to Clyde's side and takes hold of his arm in an attempt to help him sit.

"Get the fuck off me." He doesn't look at Jesse, but keeps his face down.

Jesse steps back.

Clyde lifts his torso with his massive arms, twisting his hips to sit. He reaches and lifts his legs, extending them. He wipes at his wet, gritty face; a mix of tears, sweat and sand.

"Boy, get me that bitch of a chair, will you?"

Cole needs Jesse to help free the chair from the sand. Jesse steadies the chair, and Clyde lifts and drags himself into it. His chest rises and falls from his exertion.

"Clyde … I was wrong. Bad wrong. I nearly got …." Jesse chokes and he can only stare at his old friend, searching for the smallest gesture of forgiveness. But he thinks he may have reached Clyde's limit.

"Shut up about who's right or wrong and go see to our girl. She's had her heart broken." Clyde looks away, meaning to hide his tears, something Jesse has never seen before.

He walks to where Katie and Marlene sit on the ground. Marlene strokes Katie's springy curls and whispers what he knows to be a tonic for pain. He reaches to touch his daughter's shoulder, but she pulls away.

"I think we should go back to the house. I left Sky napping. I wouldn't like for her to wake to an empty house."

"Thank you for that … and …."

She touches his hand and it's the gesture of shared willpower he wanted to feel just now from Clyde. He pulls her to her feet and watches as she and Katie cross the yard and enter the house. He turns back to where Clyde and Cole sit near the busted corral.

"For damn sure Jesus saved us." Clyde glares at him. "That had to be your all time best piece of stupidity."

"Don't you think I know that?" Jesse steps toward the truck, calling back to Cole. "You coming? I don't plan on standing around, listening to his rant. I'm going after that horse and bringing her back."

Cole strides across the open ground toward the truck.

"Hold up there, fools. What do you think you're doing? You can't chase a mustang through the forest with a damn pickup."

"I mean to take feed out there, dump it on the ground. And when she's hungry enough, she'll come to it. And … and this time, by God, I'll be ready."

"Fool, she ain't Trigger and you ain't Roy. So forget her eating out of your hand. She'll be happy to graze free. You saw those scars. She was bad hurt by that sonofabitch who left out of here laughing his ass off."

"Yeah, she was. And you bet I want to run him down and put a thirty-eight slug through his rotten heart. But I can't change what he did."

Clyde looks in the direction the mare fled, and then back at Jesse. "You mean to go on with this, don't you?"

"Yeah, I do. That mare's out there somewhere. And it's the way you said, Katie's in there crying her eyes out. I can't stop now." His desperation swells up so thick in his throat, he feels he'll choke.

"All right, I hear you, Little Brother. You do know you've got a better chance at winning the lottery. But if you're fixed on seeing this through, your gut ain't enough. Granted it's against your nature, but you've gotta go about this smart-like if you're to have a snowball's chance in hell of pulling it off." Clyde sits back and exhales. His face is relaxed for the first time since their parting shots at the picnic.

"And, God help us, you're getting ready to tell me you know smart."

"I don't know a thing about recapturing a wild horse. But I'd have sense enough to ask for help from them two gals next door. Just in the time it took you to get your ass in this sling, they forgot more than the three of us know turned end to end."

"No, I don't think. . . "

"Don't think? If it's saving face, you can forget that. They already know how screwed up things are."

Jesse wants to ram his fist down Clyde's throat to shut his big mouth. But he knows he's right, and that stings.

"But what do I tell Katie?"

"Go tell our little darling one of your sweetest lies. Tell her you've got a fool-proof plan that can't miss." Clyde reaches with his big paw, gripping the back of Jesse's neck, and he shakes him the way he might one of his disobedient hounds: strong and with forgiveness. "Come on, we can't sit here licking our wounds. Marlene's got a party planned. Let's go party with that kid even if it about kills us." He rolls toward the house.

Cole takes a portable ramp from the van, and Clyde steers the chair onto the porch and through the kitchen door.

"Where's the dang party? I feel like dancing."

Marlene looks up. Her eyes are red, her face swollen, and she forces a smile.

The nasty oilcloth has been removed and the table covered in a birthday tablecloth, a pink cake with eleven candles centered on the table. There are matching plates, cups, and napkins for serving deli wraps, hot wings, potato salad, and pink lemonade.

"Katie invited Dee and Susan. There's more than enough food."

Jesse nods and mutters his thanks for all she's done, excusing himself to clean up.

He stands in the door of the girls' room, but Katie doesn't look up. She wipes her nose on her sleeve and pulls at Beau's floppy ear, as though she means to at least correct one wrong.

"Katie, I'm sorry about what happened. I meant to surprise you."

She catches up the corner of the bed sheet in her hands and twists it into a knot, but still doesn't look at him. Sky moves closer to Katie, placing a hand on her arm. Her tiny fingers spread, stiff like wood, she pats Katie's arm. He swallows hard, unable to recall a time before when he's seen her attempt to comfort, even Katie. Beau whines and licks Katie's flushed cheeks.

"Katie, please. Can I come closer?"

"Why did she run away? I would've loved her."

He takes a seat on the side of the bed. "The mare needs to be gentled. I think what she knows about people is all bad. She couldn't know you're different. She was afraid. And when animals are afraid, all they know is to run away."

"Was her other owner mean to her?"

"Yeah, he was. Bad mean."

"I hate him. I hope his old truck turns over and he spills on the ground."

He agrees that the man deserves nothing better. "I know. But I don't think we want to be mean like him."

She nods. "But can you get her back?"

"Yes, I promise. I'll find her and I'll bring her back."

"Cross your heart and hope to die from a vampire sucking your blood if you're lying?"

"And I'll eat a can of purple worms if I am."

She makes a terrible face, but holds back that perfect smile he so wants. Clear through to the marrow of his bones, he knows he must deliver on his promise or all the good that has ever passed between him and Katie won't matter.

"Can you ask Uncle Clyde to come here?"

He steps into the hallway and calls Clyde. He works his chair though the narrow hallway to the door of the bedroom. Katie gets off the bed and climbs onto his lap, her arms around his neck, and she whispers. "Will you please help Daddy bring back my horse?"

"Little darling, I don't exactly sit a horse too good of late. But don't you worry. I'll strap on spurs and ride this blame chair wherever I need to go to get your horse back. But for now, I think I remember somebody saying some little gal's having a birthday party. Would that be you?" His face lights up in the way only Katie can elicit.

She giggles. "I'm eleven. I ain't little. Sky's little."

Katie turning to Clyde for reassurance isn't lost on anyone, least of all Jesse, and he looks to each for a measure of their confidence. Marlene and Susan smile cautiously, while on the faces of Clyde and Dee, Jesse reads talk is cheap. Cole looks away, and Jesse accepts that he's earned their distrust. He means to recapture the mare and wipe away all doubt, most of all his own.

SIXTEEN

Jesse arrives in Dee and Susan's barnyard a half hour early, and although there are lights in the kitchen, he decides against knocking in favor of waiting outside. He takes a seat on the tailgate of his truck, wondering if Dee has had second thoughts, maybe third, on the plan she agreed to only after Susan pleaded. Dee is big on planning, but he'd pushed her, wishing to make a show of action. Anything to prove to Katie that he intended to keep his promise.

The two come through the door, each holding a steaming cup of coffee, and Susan calls a greeting from the porch. She offers to bring him a cup, but he's coffeed out.

"Dee invited along a friend from work who adopted a mustang last year." Susan walks up to him and gives him an encouraging smile.

"Adopted? People adopt horses?"

"Oh, yes. Katie's mustang mare likely came through such a program."

Susan patiently explains the federal government's program for the removal of mustangs from grasslands in the west. She hesitates and looks over at Dee.

"We're worried that the mare may have been badly handled. Not necessarily cruelly, but in the hands of an inexperienced owner, damage can be done." She looks to him for reassurance, but he's unwilling to tell her what he saw of both horse and owner.

"Can't say about that. He was a stranger. The owner, I mean."

"Did you at least get a title transfer from him?"

"No, nothing like that." He can't remember as much as a handshake. But he'd just as soon leave the barroom transaction out of their conversation.

"You mean you bought the mare without knowing her history?"

"That's about the size of it." Cornered between her badgering and his ignorance, he thinks about calling off the search and looking elsewhere for the help he needs. Then he doesn't know what kind of help he actually needs, much less where to go to get it.

"It's especially true with horses that ignorant buyers pay for their lack of knowledge. Can you at least tell me how she looked?"

"Hell, Dee. The horse is ordinary brown. Not much to look at, I'm afraid."

Dee swears and stomps off to stand next to her Appaloosa gelding. She rubs the horse and speaks to it in the way she might Katie and Sky.

"Uh, Jesse, sorry for the confusion. She doesn't mean color, but whether or not the mare looked well cared for." Susan smiles, only gently mocking.

He hesitates, wishing to side-step more ridicule. "I can't say she was, and it was clear she hated her owner."

"Poor baby. That's terrible."

Susan looks in the direction Dee has gone toward the barn, and he isn't sure whether she means the mare or Dee. Both, he decides.

"I don't want to upset Dee any more, but the horse had cause to hate that mean bastard."

"It helps to know that she was abused. It'll make a difference in how we approach her recovery."

Jesse nods

"Excuse me. While we wait for Fred, I need to get a couple more canteens." Susan walks into the barn where he imagines Dee kicking everything in sight that remotely resembles a male ass.

Jesse climbs onto the corral fence to wait.

Across the pasture, the first light of day breaks on the distant horizon, and the dew soaked grass reflects as smooth as glass. His mama believed that the arrival of each new day held God's promise of a new beginning. He'd once believed he knew what she meant, but now he isn't so sure. He'd been a part of too much wrong in Iraq to believe in such certainty. Susan had said recovery rather than recapture. Did she mean to draw a line, one meaning different from the other? If so, maybe one carries the weight of punishment, while the other a chance to right a wrong.

A late model red pickup towing a horse trailer turns onto the driveway and stops. A tall man dressed in faded jeans and a pale blue western shirt gets out of the truck. He walks up to Jesse at the same time Dee and Susan come from the barn. Susan carries two large canteens over her shoulder.

Fred hugs Dee and Susan, and Dee introduces him.

Fred is friendly enough, but judged on looks alone, he doesn't live up to his billing. They shake, and Jesse notices the white softness of Fred's hand. He may know roping, but Jesse doubts he's done much of it. His gear, including his horse, is likely more for show than real work. Granted, he knows nothing about horses or horsemanship, but he knows a working man, and Fred doesn't even come close.

"Jess, you take the dark bay. She's the best with casual riders." Dee winks, and he's glad for her effort at easing up.

"I'd better lose some of this coffee first." He motions toward the barn.

He steps into the tiny bathroom, hoping the three have mounted when he returns. He doesn't want to admit he doesn't know which horse to mount.

When he comes out of the barn, the dark reddish-brown horse with black mane, tail and legs stands with an empty saddle. He approaches the horse and she turns her head to look at him. He swears she sighs, but she stands perfectly still, making it easy for him to haul himself into the saddle.

Dee rides the Appaloosa gelding toward the back pasture gate, Fred next to her. Susan drops her horse back into position, riding along with him. Her horse, a rich red golden with mane and tail the same color, side steps and tosses its head.

Jesse grabs the saddle horn in case the horse he rides decides to join in the frisky play.

"Relax, Lady is just that. She's twelve and perfect for trail riding, not afraid of anything we're likely to encounter. It's Lady that Katie rides. She's a very good rider for her age."

He takes a deep breath and tries to relax, works at matching his motion to the rhythm of the horse. He now thinks the mustang is a lighter bay.

They ride for a couple of hours along a woodland trail, and when they don't find any sign of the mare beyond the tracks where she entered the deeper forest, Fred suggests they check out the nearest water sources and any open areas where grass is plentiful. They turn east and ride for another hour before Dee leads them to a natural spring that forms a pool of clear water. They stop to water and rest the horses.

Fred takes a long drink from one of the canteens and then passes the reins of his horse to Dee. He walks around the edge of the pond and into the woods for fifty yards or so. Squatting on his heels, he passes a flat palm over the tops of the grass and then looks out across the grassy area into the tree line. He stands and waves Dee over.

She hands the two sets of reins to Susan and walks to where Fred waits. She nods as he talks, and for the first time this morning, Dee's face relaxes a bit. She walks back to where he and Susan wait with the horses.

"There's a spot near the edge of the trees where she might have rested. Cropped grass nearby, but that could just as easily have been deer. The mare's smart. She's staying off any worn trails."

"What about droppings?" Susan shades her eyes against the glare.

"No horse, just deer."

"Is she likely to come to these horses?" Jesse looks to Dee.

"Not after we've scented the place."

"What if we left a horse here? Like a decoy."

"That would be damn stupid."

"Unsafe. It would be unsafe for the horse, tethered." Susan mounts her horse and looks over at him. "Don't mind her. She accepts that your intentions are good."

"I'll believe it when the mare is standing in a decent corral." Dee reins her horse about and rides forward, leading Fred's horse.

Jesse feels the heat under his shirt collar, and he's glad Susan rides ahead. Lady stands patiently for him to mount, and when he's in the saddle, the mare follows Susan's horse.

Fred suggests that they pair off and each ride a half circle around the grassy area, doubling back to meet at the pool. He thinks this is the best chance they have of actually spotting the horse. The women take the north half, and he and Fred turn and ride southward. They ride without talking for some time before Fred asks the question Jesse has dreaded.

"Why'd you decide on a mustang for your daughter?"

"Didn't really. I guess you could say I got snookered by the price." Jesse is grateful that, if Fred shares Dee's opinion, he holds off saying so.

"Mustangs can be good horses. This one's smart, may have been a dominant mare. Some old timers say it's much harder to gain their trust, but that they can reward your patience."

Jesse looks at Fred and invites more.

"They lead the herd to good grazing, water, and shelter. The stallion breeds and protects his mares from other stallions."

"Is she bothered by going it alone?" If the mare is anything like him, she does.

"You might check around to see if any of your neighbors have stallions. I've had one or two go through pasture fences to get to mares in heat."

"I can believe that."

They ride on and Fred gets off his horse several times, studying signs. He's walking along a narrow animal trail, leading his horse, when he suddenly stops and turns back to Jesse.

"A horse came this way, and recently."

He swings back into the saddle and tells Jesse to stay behind until he can take a better look. Fred rides off slowly into a heavy cover of brush and trees. Jesse dismounts, glad for any time out of the saddle. He ties the reins around a small white oak and walks off a ways, peeing long and hard against a fallen tree. He walks back to where he tied the mare and stands rubbing the horse's nose. She accepts his hand, and when he stops, she rubs her nose against his sleeve. He's beginning to see the added value of a well-trained horse.

He sits on the ground beneath an ancient Florida holly and his head drops on his chest and he nods off. He doesn't know how long he dozes before the horse whinnying startles him awake. He's rattled, but certain there's movement at the edge of the tree line. Lady stomps in a tethered circle around the small tree.

The sound of pounding hooves reaches him before he sees Fred's horse galloping into the open from among the trees. Fred holds a lasso rope, and he's lost his hat. He shouts for Jesse to mount up.

Jesse unties the reins and passes them over the bay's head, and with one foot in the stirrup, he hops around on the other foot trying to mount the horse. He lifts himself onto the saddle, and the horse starts for the tree line in a full gallop. Squeezing his tired legs hard, he manages somehow to stay in the saddle. When he catches up to Fred, he's standing on the ground next to his lathered horse, gathering his lasso rope and quietly swearing.

The bay slides to a quick stop, and Jesse hangs on to her mane and leans back, his toes way out in front, along the horse's shoulders.

"What was that?"

"She flashed into the open, but when I set out after her with this rope, she headed for cover in those trees instead of trying to outrun me."

"I reckon I didn't buy a stupid horse."

"Nope, she's smart all right. I'd say you're going to need a team of experienced ropers to ever have a chance of catching her." Fred mounts and they continue the agreed upon route back to the spring without seeing further signs of the mare. When they arrive, Susan and Dee are sitting beneath a large live oak. Their horses are unsaddled and tethered in the grassy area.

"How'd you do?"

"Located her, but never had a chance to get a rope on her. She easily outsmarted me." Fred dismounts and leads his horse to the pool to drink. Jesse follows with the bay.

Dee swears and walks thirty yards or so into the clearing, stands and looks off into the woods, her hands resting on her hips.

"I'm afraid that doesn't sound promising." Susan looks up at Jesse from where she kneels on the ground, unpacking sandwiches and homemade sugar cookies.

They sit beneath a large bay magnolia at the edge of the pool to eat, and Jesse thinks this might otherwise be pleasant. After they have eaten, they pass around a canteen of lemonade, and it's Susan who breaks their silence.

"What do we do now?"

"Start back when the horses are rested, and call around before next Saturday, asking for more ropers." Dee glances over at Fred and he nods.

"There's a regional Bureau of Land Management office in Dothan. Jesse, you might call them for help."

"Don't know if he wants the feds in on this just yet." Dee looks at him as though he has something to hide.

"I'm slow to call in the feds, but in this case …." Fred looks to Dee and not to him.

"I doubt they'll let him keep the mare unless he can provide papers, and even if they were agreeable, they'd demand much better facilities. He'll need proper shelter and a bigger, stronger corral to contain the mare if we're fortunate enough to recover her."

"Then I guess I'll wait on that." Dee's right, but he thinks he knows what Sky must feel when Katie insists on being her mouth piece.

The women walk off into the cover of the woods, and he and Fred stand behind a tree. Jesse rubs the insides of his thighs.

"Remind me, I've got something back in my truck for that." Fred grins.

Jesse figures he'll get plenty toughened before he's through chasing the mare. He worries about what he'll tell Katie when he returns empty-handed. Maybe having sighted the horse will be enough to keep her hopes up until he can do more.

In the distance, Jesse hears what he decides is the roar of small engines. He looks over at Fred. "That racket what I think it is?"

"Kids on ATVs."

"They're allowed in the forest?"

"I'm afraid so. They do tons of damage to the vegetation and wildlife."

"What about the horse?"

"They can't catch her, but they can run her. Increase her fear of humans. And on those damned machines, they can keep it up for hours at a time."

"But they sure as hell can't slip up on her."

The women return, and from the worried looks on their faces, they've heard the noise.

"Let's get out of here. I'll call Gerald with the forestry bunch."

Dee mounts and they follow suit. Jesse remembers Gerald from high school, and unfortunately for the mare, he'd screwed the girl Gerald was sweet on. He hopes Dee doesn't mention his name when asking for a favor.

They ride back along the trail toward home, the fading noises of the ATVs in the distance. Jesse pictures the horse running through the woods, whooping kids and loud machines making a game of her fears. He vows to catch the mare and bring her to safety, even if she never stands under a saddle.

Back at the barn, they unsaddle the lathered horses, and when they've hosed and rubbed each down, Fred loads his horse. Dee and Susan lead theirs through the pasture gate and stand watching as the horses roll and shake before moving on to graze. The bay looks back at Jesse, and he thinks the look means she's glad to rid herself of him. Fred calls Jesse over to the truck and hands him a white liquid in a brown bottle.

"Liniment. Try a little for the soreness, but go easy. It can burn your tender spots." He winks.

Jesse puts the bottle on the front seat of his truck, then walks back to where Dee still stands at the gate watching the horses.

"I hope the bay gets over being pissed at you for having to haul my sorry ass all day."

"Oh, forget it, the mare's fine. A day of poor horsemanship won't ruin her training. But you might need to stand for a few days." The corners of Dee's mouth turn up the tiniest bit.

"You're right about that. It's a shame a grown man has to suffer something akin to diaper rash. I thank you for all you've done."

"Don't thank me yet. The job's far from over." She gazes into his eyes, and all hint of her earlier amusement has melted.

"Am I in some kind of trouble about those papers?"

"I'm not sure. I'll check before we go out again."

Driving away, he glances back at the two women. They stand, their shoulders touching, and they seem perfectly at ease. Whatever the truth is about those two, they make no apologies, and while that's a quality he admires, he remains confused. Not so much about those two, but what he thinks in general.

WHEN HE ENTERS THE KITCHEN, Katie is working at maneuvering a roaster holding a pot roast, potatoes, and carrots into the oven to warm. Sky sits at the table, spinning a fork and humming the tune Jesse still doesn't recognize.

"Daddy, you're back." She hurries past him, through the front door and down the steps, before stopping at the sight of the empty corral. When she turns back to him, he braces for what he knows will be a flood of questions.

"Where's Dakota?"

"Lord, baby girl, you didn't think we were going to bring her back today, did you?"

Katie looks up at him, and her disappointment makes it clear that she'd allowed herself that much hope.

"She's hungry, I know."

"No, Katie, there's plenty of good green grass and a deep pool of cool water. And Miss Dee's friend said the mare won't leave such a good place and wander too far off."

"Then why didn't you catch her?"

"It's going to take more men and ropes than we had. She outsmarted us."

"If she's so smart, why doesn't she know we won't hurt her? Beau would never run away."

"She doesn't know us. Beau's been in our family since he was only two weeks old."

She looks at him and her eyes narrow, and then slowly, she nods.

He reaches a hand down to her, and she walks back up the steps and takes it in hers.

"Cole pulled some boards off the old chicken house and nailed them up where the broken ones were. I helped him, and Beau played with Sky so I didn't have to watch her."

"That's good, Katie. What's cooking? I could eat a road-kill skunk."

"A pot roast from Miss Marlene. She showed me how to warm it and she helped me with my science project. You want to see it?"

"After I clean up and we've had supper." He needs a hot shower and some of the white stuff in the brown bottle before he can sit comfortably long enough even for pot roast.

WHEN KATIE AND SKY ARE IN BED, he wanders into the living room to watch Sports Center, then remembers the call Dee talked about. He steps to the kitchen phone and punches in Jake Madison's number, then slides down the wall and sits on the floor, counting the number of rings.

"Hello," a woman answers.

He explains that he's down in Florida and that he's the one who bought the mare.

"That's my husband's business, you understand." A nervous silence follows; the kind that comes when an honest woman lies for a husband who makes a habit of lying.

"Ma'am, nothing's wrong with the horse. She's just fine. But I hoped you might agree to send me the government papers that came with her."

The woman pauses, and he hears her muffled voice talking to someone. "Mister, tell me again your name and all, and I'll send them papers on to you next time I'm in town at the post office."

"Do you think you could send along with that something to prove I paid your husband for the horse?"

"What kind of proof? He don't intend on no discount or nothing. That wasn't in the deal."

"No, ma'am. I just need something that says I didn't steal the horse."

There's the same hand over the phone sound again, and Jesse figures the woman's old man is sitting right under her nose. In a moment, she comes back on the line and agrees to send what he needs.

He gets off the phone and glances up at the clock. It's too late to call Dee and Susan, but he does it anyway. Susan answers, and he apologizes for calling late.

"No, we aren't in bed."

He thinks about what being in bed means, but forces the notion out of his head. "I wanted you and Dee to know that the woman's sending the papers on the horse."

"That's good news. They will tell us where the mare came from, and help to answer many of our questions."

He hears Dee in the background. "That's all, I guess. Good night." He hangs up the phone and thinks to call Marlene and Clyde to let them know a bigger plan is in the works. But he's weary of thinking about the mare, and Clyde, like Katie, will have more questions he likely can't answer just now.

He pours a glass of tea and sits on the back porch. A chilly wind works the yellow leaves on the pecan tree, announcing flannel shirt weather is upon them. It helps to know that, among the mare's troubles, the mild winter of north Florida won't make the list. But the kids on four-wheelers worry him.

Cole comes onto the porch and takes a seat in the rocker. "How'd it go? You look like you're the one rode hard and put up wet."

"Feel it for sure. But we, that is, Fred, the roping dude, got a look at her. I never got close enough. He says she's smart, maybe too smart for a rope."

"Why not leave her there. She'd be fine, wouldn't she?"

"She would until a bunch of knuckleheads riding ATVs decided to play cowboy and run her to death." Jesse spits through the screen.

"This is messed up. I wish you'd never …."

"Yeah, it's messed up all right. And I wish I'd had sense enough to walk away from what I wanted to be a lucky break. Hell, I don't even believe in luck."

"What's next?"

"Dee and Fred agree we go after her with more ropers. But damn, I hate the thought of that. If they try and fail, it could make the whole thing harder."

Cole nods. "I know you're trying for Katie. But do you really think you can save the horse?"

"Save her?"

"I read on the internet that horses filled with such hatred for humans can't always be rehabilitated." He sighs and leans forward, wrapping his arms tightly across his chest as he shivers.

"Destroyed, you mean?"

Cole nods. "It'd kill Katie."

"I ain't ready to give up on the mare. Not just yet, anyway."

The prospect that the mare could end up dead is new. Then, to go on trying, he can't afford anything approaching Cole's kind of hard deduction.

Beau comes to stand at the screen door, wanting out for his late night prowl. Cole opens the door and offers to wait up for Beau's return.

"Good, this tenderfoot's taking his raw ass to bed."

In the near darkness, Jesse can't make out Cole's face, but he feels the warmth of his slight smile.

SEVENTEEN

Since the mare's escape, the foliage of the pecan tree has turned a dull yellow and drifted to the ground, leaving the branches bare. Jesse has gone into the forest with Susan, Dee, Fred, and two of Fred's friends who claim to be ropers, four straight Saturdays to catch only glimpses of the mare moving through the heavy tree cover like a ghostly whisper. Each time, they find fresh evidence of the boys on their machines, and on their last ride deeper into the forest, Fred pointed out the tracks of what he worried was a pack of wild dogs.

Still, the mustang outwits and outruns all her enemies, including them. The more he chases the mare, the more confused he becomes. There are encounters when it's hard for him not to cheer for her, even against them. Then there's Katie standing on the front porch, her face twisted in anguish, each time he comes home without the mustang.

Jesse punches out at work and drives into another Saturday morning breaking, the sky smeared in colors ranging from tangerine to deep purple. He sips the last of the cold coffee from his thermos and fights off the chronic weariness that has wracked his body and mind for these long weeks. Saturday rides into the forest have come before sleep and the mountain of household chores piling up.

Today, he's grateful that Dee and Susan are out of town for the weekend, flying, Susan said, to Burlington, Vermont with two friends who are getting married there. Going all the way to Vermont to get married must have something to do with honeymooning in snow country, although he can't imagine what the weather has to do with staying in bed. Right now, he craves sleep even more than sex.

He stops on the road for yesterday's mail and pulls out an envelope addressed to him in sloppy handwriting scrawled with a dull pencil. He rips it open and it's from the woman he talked to in Georgia. Dee turned the pursuit of these papers into a holy crusade, maybe now she'll get her foot out of his ass.

The papers include a copy of an original Application for Adoption, dated February 10, last year, and a record of Mr. George Washington Madison taking delivery of a ten-year-old mustang mare on August 17. There is no bill of sale or transfer of ownership between Mr. Madison and the cowboy. Had the cowboy sold him a horse he didn't own?

Jesse looks at the handwritten receipt enclosed showing he paid Mr. Jake Madison one hundred and forty dollars. He briefly wonders about the sixty dollar down payment, and remembers the guy depositing a twenty with the woman at the bar. It figures the wife never saw that sixty. Weeks of waiting, and he's no better off for his time and trouble.

He calls Clyde and explains his predicament. "I'm no closer to getting a certified title."

"What do you want to do?" Clyde's voice is thick with either sleep or too much whiskey the evening before.

"Don't know, exactly. The original owner skipped the last step to ownership. I'm thinking that, when you get right down to it, the mare still belongs to the feds unless he returns this form."

"If I was you, I'd let a sleeping dog lie. The feds don't want that horse. Get them in on it and they'll likely shoot her. A bullet's faster and cheaper than hiring boys with ropes."

"What if they want money from me to get her back? I'm the damn fool that let her get loose." He rejects Clyde's notion that killing would be the fed's way of dealing with her. The program is about saving the mustang.

"You don't want the feds messing in it. Before you could jerk off, they'd have you eyeball-deep in red tape."

"I'm driving up there and beating the crap out of this Madison asshole if he don't sign this paper showing he's got the horse and she's eating sugar out of his hand."

"You sure them federal boys don't eyeball horses before they issue title?"

"I don't know that they don't. But I'm between a rock and a hard place here. And there's something else."

"Go ahead on, I'm already sitting down."

"I need a vet to sign off on the horse's health. Even if he was willing, that old boy can't do that under the circumstances."

Clyde grunts, and he likely knows what's coming.

"Can you get Doc's help on that?"

"No, I won't do that, but I'll get Susie in his office to stamp a signature. That way, if things come up stinking, and they will, Doc can swear he didn't know nothing and tell the truth."

"What about Susie?"

"Remember, she's his bossy wife's niece. Doc ain't about to fire her. But if it blows up in our faces, you can count on him being up our asses over it."

"I'm willing. You?"

"Hell, ain't that what I just said?"

"Can you do it today if I meet you there with the form?"

"No, I'm waiting on a buyer, but I'll call ahead and sweet-talk Susie. I bet Marlene will agree to meet you at Doc's and be the one to walk the paper in the office. That way, you stay at arm's-length. Ain't that how all the crooked politicians work it?" He laughs.

"If we get this done, I'm heading out tomorrow." Jesse pauses, and when Clyde keeps his silence, he says, "You willing to go along?"

"Yeah, I'm thinking you'll likely need my diplomatic skills to pull this thing off."

"Too bad Washington ain't hired you to untangle their messes." He hangs up the phone.

"Daddy, are you okay?" Katie asks from the kitchen door. Her face mirrors some of the despair he feels.

"Yeah, baby. I'm okay. I just got business in town. Need to hurry."

"I'll get the laundry together. And don't worry. I remember how to sort so you don't get pink underwear."

He sighs, and she slips inside the circle of his arms.

"Why aren't you looking for Dakota?" Katie has taken to calling the mare Dakota, but he's unwilling to think of the horse by name.

"Can't today, got no help."

Her arms tighten around his neck, and she whispers into his collarbone, "I love Dakota, and I want you to get her back more than anything."

Jesse holds her close, but doesn't try for more words. Over her shoulder, he sees Cole coming along the back fence from the direction of Susan and Dee's place.

Cole steps onto the porch. Sweat runs along his temples, and he smells like horse manure.

"Where you been?" Jesse's sharp tone backs Katie out of his arms.

Cole stiffens. "Next door, why?" He answers in the same tone and glares back.

"He's taking care of their horses." Katie takes a tentative step toward her brother.

"Shut up, Katie. I'm not Sky. I talk for myself." Cole turns and walks into the kitchen, begins slamming cabinet doors.

He has a right to be upset, but not at Katie. Why is it that half of what Jesse says lately, he wishes he could take back? He goes into the kitchen and leans against the counter, waiting for the worst of the slamming to stop. Katie stands just inside the kitchen door, and even Sky leaves the TV and comes to stand behind Katie.

"I'm sorry. It's just that I've got business in town. And I need you to watch the girls while I'm gone."

Cole looks up from the cereal bowl he's overrun, corn flakes spilling onto the kitchen floor. "You sure you can trust me? I might take a notion to sell that bright penny for kiddy porn. I hear cute, milk-skinned girls with red curls fetch top dollar."

"Okay, okay, cut the bull crap. I hard-mouthed you, I know."

"I've got seven teachers, a principal, a parole officer, and most of the kids at my school waiting for me to screw up. I sure don't need it from you." Cole slams the jug of milk onto the counter, turns, and walks out of the kitchen.

"What's kiddy pone? Would I really be good at it?"

"No, forget it. He didn't mean it."

He follows Cole down the hallway and knocks on his door.

"Cole, I was wrong. It just seems every way I turn, I get new shit slung in my face. Like what you just talked about in the kitchen, with everything flying at you. That's how I feel, too. I don't want to fight."

"Okay, but I've got the SAT next Saturday and I'm not ready. I can't be bothered with those two midgets day and night."

"Maybe I can get help with the girls, but you're on your own with the SAT."

Cole sighs and nods.

"And do you think you could cap the kiddy porn comments? It'll be her teacher or Cora she asks next."

"Yeah, I get it." He gives up a weak shrug. Jesse backs out of the room, meaning to quit while he's ahead.

JESSE EASES THE TRUCK into the space next to Marlene's sedan. He leans and calls to her through the open window. "Hey there, pretty lady. I believe I'm the lucky guy you're here to meet."

She marks a page in the book she was reading and places it on the seat.

He opens the car door, and for a moment they stand pressed close within the space between the frame and open door. She places a hand on his forearm and where her fingertips touch, his skin burns and he feels light-headed.

"You look tired. Are you getting any rest?"

"Enough, I guess." He sighs. "I'm still managing to keep my feet." He steps back, embarrassed that his hands tremble.

"Clyde said you'd explain what I'm doing here."

"You got time to get a cup of coffee? Just there, across the street." He points to Ruby Jean's Cafe. "Nothing fancy, but Ruby's always got good coffee."

Marlene glances at her watch.

"But if you're in a hurry, I'll understand."

"No, I have time. I'll want to be back in time for the homecare nurse's visit. Clyde likes for me to be there. He's more comfortable, I think."

"Didn't know he needed that. He's not worse or anything?"

"No, it's just that he's too heavy for me to handle alone. Baths are difficult, even with her help."

Jesse nods and a sudden uneasiness passes over him. He hasn't allowed himself to think much about Clyde and the everyday difficulty in something as ordinary as a bath. What else does he need help doing?

They cross the street to the cafe and take a booth near the window. His thoughts are still on the logistics of two women moving Clyde, stripped naked, lathered and slippery, in and out of a bath. His preoccupation with the task helps him to avoid the more painful thoughts of what he imagines as Clyde's embarrassment.

"What's that?" He turns to the waitress standing at his elbow, her sharp hip bone cocked forward, a pot of steaming coffee in her hand.

"Coffee? I asked if you want coffee."

"Sorry, yes. We want coffee." He looks at Marlene.

She nods to the waitress, who pours two cups, takes sugar and tiny tubs of cream from her apron pocket, and walks away.

"I've never thought enough about him needing that kind of help. Guess I'm not much of a friend. If I was, I'd think more about what he might need from me."

"No, he doesn't want that. A show of pity would break his heart. He's a man who uses a wheelchair. And yes, he does need special care. But he wants you to think of him as the man you've loved since you were boys."

He meets her gaze, and she appears to study him. Her expression is one of understanding something important, maybe for the first time. He wants to know what he sees in his face. But most of all, he wants to ask her how he's to think about her. Then he doesn't want to hear her speak of the love for Clyde he reads in her face.

"Now tell me. What's the great mystery about this visit to the vet's?"

"Seems stupid didn't stop with my buying a wild mustang. The seller never got a proper title to the horse. My guess is the mare still belongs to the feds until they say otherwise."

Her chin draws downward, and he plows on, trying to convince her of his plight. He takes the form from his shirt pocket and places it on the table in front of her. "Gotta have a vet sign off on the horse's good health. With that form, I plan on talking the seller into applying for a title, making his sale to me legal."

She looks at the form and begins to read. Her jaw sets in a hard line, and he feels her taking a step back.

"If you're not sure about this, I'll understand." What he's asking her to participate in is forgery. But it's either that or he calls in the feds and gives up on Katie ever owning the mare. The fate of the horse will be out of his hands.

"And this way you think Doc can't be blamed should it not go well?"

He nods.

"Okay, I'll do what you ask." She stands and walks out of the café, crosses the street, and enters Doc's office.

He'd feel relief if it didn't come at the price of using a good woman to do a bad thing. He pays and walks back to his truck.

After what seems an eternity, Marlene exits Doc's office and places the form in his hand. He folds the paper along the same two creases and places it in the envelope.

"Thank you for what you did. With any luck, this will get Katie closer to actually owning a runaway horse." He forces a half-assed smile, but she doesn't return his gesture.

"Know that, from now on, I'm a reformed lawbreaker." She turns and gets into the car. "Have Cole call me if he needs help with the girls."

He calls his thanks, but he isn't sure she hears. He sits in the truck after her sedan disappears into traffic, and he thinks Clyde may have asked Marlene, and she may have agreed, not because of anything he'd said back in the cafe, but to save Clyde from asking an old girlfriend for a favor while riding a wheelchair.

He pulls the truck into traffic and points it in the direction of home, and ahead, dark clouds gather.

AFTER A QUICK SUPPER of yellow rice and black beans, Katie pleads with Cole for help with a homework assignment, but he goes into his room and locks the door. She pouts until Jesse offers his help. He reads the assignment sheet twice, and together he and Katie gather the ingredients for making a flour-paste map of Florida.

"Oh no. Rat dooky." Katie's hands fly to cover her mouth, and Sky rolls a black weevil around under her fingertip.

"Good gosh, girl, they're harmless bugs."

He pours weevil-infested flour into a mixing bowl, grateful that at least they aren't wasting good flour. The flour, salt, and water mixture overflows the mixing bowl and there's enough dough for a map of the world.

"It needs more salt. Teacher said it keeps the flour from being gooey." Katie has sticky fingers and flour smudges on her face and in her hair.

He pours more salt into the bowl and stirs until she's satisfied with the consistency. She spreads the paste onto a flat piece of cardboard inside an outline map of the state and painstakingly spreads it into the shape of Florida.

Sky climbs onto a kitchen chair and pats the dough until Katie pushes her hand away, shouting, "Stop, you're messing it up."

Sky stomps up and down in the chair, slinging dough onto the table and floor around the chair.

"No, no, Sky please. Here, make your own map." He pours some of the mixture onto a sheet of waxed paper and dares to place his hand over hers.

He guides her hand and she doesn't resist, and his blood pressure levels out. He works with her, liking the warmth of her tiny hand under his, and leans closer. She turns and looks up at him, then smiles.

"Katie, look. Look at us. We're making a map of the whole world. Ain't that right, Sky?" He's a grown man playing in flour paste, and he thinks he must sound like another kid.

Sky pats the gooey mess, her fingers spread, goo squeezing between them. She grabs his wrist and turns his hand over, patting the paste on his palm, and giggles. He places his hand over hers, sandwiching it between his palms. She pulls her hand out and begins to patty-cake. He watches her and realizes she means to teach him. He follows her lead, and sings, off key, as much as he remembers of the rhyme, "patty cake." Sky pats along with him, but she doesn't sing.

"Dang, Dad. You sound like a drunk bull frog."

"What do you know about tipsy bull frogs?"

When Katie has painted the Gulf of Mexico and Atlantic Ocean in royal blue, wishing aloud for two shades of blue, Jesse places both wet maps in the center of the table. It'll need to dry before Katie can label key cities, rivers and place a star at the state capital.

"Can you take us to school? Some of the mean boys on the bus might mess it up." He agrees, and Sky pulls on his shirttail, a gesture he takes to mean she wants him to take her map to Trudy's.

He looks at her. "Okay, but only if I can get a smile."

Sky takes the tail of her shirt in hand and pulls it over her head. "Where's my smile?"

Sky climbs out of the chair and runs, Katie and Beau trailing her. Maybe she didn't smile, but he feels better than ever before about his chances with her.

Cole comes into the kitchen. "What the hell happened? Tell me you weren't trying to make biscuits." He searches the cabinet.

"Nope, Sky and I made a map of the world."

"Great, as long as it wasn't made with peanut butter. I'm starved."

"I know this is sudden, but I'm driving to north Georgia tomorrow. Won't be back until late."

Cole slams the peanut butter jar onto the counter, his face a building storm. "No way. I've got the horses next door to look after. And Miss Susan said I could use her computer to input my position paper. I can't be in two places, and I sure as hell can't take those two with me."

"Hold on before you mount an all-out assault. You can call Miss Marlene for help with the girls."

When Cole has put together three sandwiches, he returns to his room, and Jesse faces the mess map making has made. He wipes the flour from the table and remembers Sky patting the sticky paste. He wants to believe Trudy's notion that Sky will be fine in time. There are likely plenty of books about kids like Sky, but he's never had much faith in learning from books. What he has learned is that the best times with his kids seem to just happen and that he can't sit on the sideline.

Turning out the kitchen light, he follows two sets of two-legged prints and one four-legged one along the hallway into the bathroom. He jiggles the handle on the toilet tank, thinking he needs to replace the float mechanism and stop wasting water.

But, at best, he may get to those things that are actually broken. Preventive repairs don't have a snowball's chance of making it onto the list he keeps in his head.

He places the call to Clyde. "Hey, sorry to call so late, but I've been up to my armpits in flour. How about I pick you up at five?"

Clyde chuckles and Jesse hears, "Our boy's baking now." Five is good, but he insists they take his van. "That's unless you intend on toting my fat ass wherever we stop."

"Guess it don't smell that doggy."

He hears Marlene's voice in the background and he wants to disown the surge of jealousy he has no right to feel.

EIGHTEEN

After five hours of hard driving north on I-75, he and Clyde reach Atlanta and take the by-pass to I-85. Jesse remembers the way those two cowboys had the mare's head tied up so close. Traveling in that open trailer along eight lanes of deafening steel and chrome would have been plenty of reason for her to run the first chance she got.

Three hours later, Clyde steers the van off a county road onto a deeply rutted dirt lane toward a weathered farmhouse. An old, grizzled-faced man stands propped on a cane near a rusted-out tractor that looks as though it was last parked decades ago. Waist-high weeds grow around other discarded farm implements scattered about the barnyard.

"This ain't it."

"How do you know?"

"I know because he ain't the man who sold me the horse."

"Ask him anyway. Everybody knows everybody around here. Go on, do it."

"Afternoon, sir. Can you tell me where I might find Mr. Madison?" Jesse calls through the passenger window.

The old man hobbles toward the van. "Where's that you're headed?"

"That old geezer's deaf as a stump. You're going to need to shout."

"The Madison place, sir." Jesse winces.

"In that case, sonny, you've found it, unless you're here to sell me burial insurance or some other version of the Bible. I'm the third George Washington Madison in the flesh. Yes sir, and still kicking after ninety-seven years. Folk I'm of a mind to let get this close call me Wash." He motions with his cane for Clyde to shut off the engine and for the two to get out.

Jesse glances at Clyde, somewhat relieved to have found the mustang's original owner without having to deal with the asshole cowboy.

Jesse steps toward the old man with his hand extended. "Afternoon, Mr. Madison. I'm Jesse McKnight, from down in Florida." He expects the man to know about the telephone conversation he had with Mrs. Madison, but it's clear from his blank stare that he doesn't have the foggiest notion. Still he pumps Jesse's hand and smiles, revealing just enough teeth to count on one hand and still have a finger to pick his nose.

"Poppy," a woman calls from the back porch of the house. "Have them men to come in. I've got hot coffee and a fresh cobbler."

"Love to, ma'am, but my buddy rides a motorized chair, and it might be a little hard for him to get up on that high porch." Jesse breathes easier, deciding the woman must be the one who sent the letter.

"Don't matter, there's a ramp from before Mrs. Madison passed." She points to the far corner of the porch.

Clyde maneuvers the chair into position, lifts himself into it, and rolls to the side door of the van. Mr. Madison watches with great interest, and when the door slides open and big Clyde appears, the old man pounds his cane on the ground.

"Howdy, Mr. Wash. Yes sir, ain't I just a human marvel?"

"Get them legs in the war, son?"

"Yes sir, battle of Bullshit Run it was." Clyde grins big.

Mr. Wash leans against the van and watches in pure admiration as Clyde puts the chair into a NASCAR spin. "Damned if my hat ain't off to you, sonny boy. Come on in the house. My daughter-in-law bitches aplenty, but she makes a decent cobbler." He slaps Clyde on the shoulder.

Jesse asked Clyde along for company, but now he knows that anything he wants from the old man, Clyde can likely get. Then the daughter-in-law may not give in to Clyde's humor.

The tall, raw-boned woman takes a golden brown cobbler from an old-fashioned kitchen safe and places it on the round oak table cluttered with homemade jellies, jams, pepper sauce, pickled okra, and a jar of congealed pig's feet. She's wearing a cotton print dress covered by a bib apron, and her stringy brown hair is pulled back into a bun that's mostly slipped the knot. Although she isn't old, she looks as though she stepped from a depression era issue of *The American Farmer*.

"Bless pat, ma'am, I do believe that's a better looking cobbler than even my dear old granny made. God rest her sweet soul." The earnestness in Clyde's voice could melt steel hinges, and Jesse knows that Clyde's grannies both died when he was still sucking his mama's tit.

"You gents pull to the table. I don't hold with serving food in the parlor." She pushes chairs back to make room for Clyde's wheelchair, then dishes out large bowls of cobbler and places a sweating pitcher of cold milk in the center of the table. She removes her apron and brushes down the front of her dress before hanging the apron on a wall peg.

"Now what exactly are you wanting here? You'll need to talk up since his hearing is poorly."

Jesse takes the government form from his shirt pocket and passes it across to the woman. "I'm told I'm going to need this paper signed before I can lay claim to the horse."

She takes a quick look before saying, "I just sent you this in the mail."

"Yes, ma'am, and I thank you for your trouble. But I need Mr. Wash's signature since the horse was adopted by him." He sits back, short of breath, worried that he'd sounded more like a door-to-door salesman than an honest man should.

"Lord, Poppy don't want that horse back. Besides, my husband sold her to you fair and square. He won't like it a bit if I go dabbling in his business." The woman stiffens and leans back in her chair.

"Oh, no ma'am, and he surely did. That is your husband did. Fair and square, like you said." In the moment, he's stuck on what he should say next. He waves his spoon in the air, working at finding the words to win her over and leave with what he's come for. But she doesn't as much as glance at the paper.

"Ma'am, I do believe this is the best cobbler I've ever had. Do you think I could get just a little more?" Clyde gives the woman his best Sunday school smile.

"Clyde, if you could just hold off a minute. I'm trying here …."

"Well thank you, Mr. Clyde. I don't get near enough compliments. My men folk eat aplenty, but they don't say much." She takes his bowl and refills it, leaving barely enough room for milk.

"My goodness, out there in the yard, just now, Mr. Wash raved about your cobbler. Said that in all of Georgia we'd come to the right place."

She looks at Clyde's big kind face, and her eyes glow for a moment, and although Clyde's one hell of man when it comes to winning over women, she folds her arms across her breasts and loses her earlier pleasure. Something's working on her, and because he's seen the scars on the horse, he decides she's more scared than disagreeable.

The woman turns to Jesse. "Leave that paper with me, and I'll tell my husband what you said when he gets back off the road." She stands and begins clearing away their dishes.

The old man strikes the table a sharp lick with his cane. "Damn it, Maude, give the boy whatever he's come for. What do I care if I piss off the gov'ment? The cause's lost. Everything worth anything's done lost."

Jesse looks at the old man, and he isn't sure which cause Mr. Madison spoke of, unless it's the one the old timers at the barbershop still call the war for southern independence.

When the old man has scribbled his barely legible name on the form and they've bid proper good-byes to the woman, Jesse and Clyde follow Mr. Wash into an old barn that matches the neglected house. In a back stall stands the finest strawberry roan quarter horse stallion Jesse has ever seen, in real life or the movies.

"That old boy took first place in roping at the state rodeo three years straight with my grandson in the saddle. Stands at stud since the boy got killed in a car wreck over on Highway 129." The old man taps the dirt floor with his cane and grows misty-eyed. "Then again, this old horse grins a heap, and the mares go out of here looking plumb satisfied."

"If I was him, I'd be tickled with the work." Clyde winks at the old man.

"Can you get it up from that chair?"

"No sir, I can't. But I ain't never stopped feeling it."

The old man nods, his hazy eyes smiling with a sudden brightness.

"That brings me to ask what you meant to do with the mare."

"Figured to do no more than settle her enough for breeding. Mustangs can make fine roping horses. Turned her in with the stallion back last December, I believe it was."

"If you don't mind me asking, how does the fellow I bought her from figure in?"

"He's my only son. A wife-beater and a drunk. My grandson was the only good that ever come from those two. Then, back a while, his drunk driving got the boy killed."

"Awful sorry about that."

"He got his due."

"How so?" Clyde asks.

"Bragged he could break the mare, but he's a proven fool when it comes to horses. That little mare damn near stomped him to death, and I can't say I blamed her. It was all over for her after that. She remembers every hateful thing he ever done to her. My grandson might've got her over her fears … but he was gone by then." He studies Jesse for a moment. "I'm afraid you may've come on the mare too late."

They shake hands all around, and Jesse and Clyde drive back down the lane. The old man stands in the yard and waves his cane while hanging onto the fender of the rusted-out tractor.

"Strange, the hands we're dealt. And I reckon that goes the same for horses." Clyde's face clouds, clearly meaning the mare's bad hand as well as his own.

Jesse considers the mustang's fate compared to that of the four horses standing in Dee and Susan's pasture. He feels drawn to the mustang's plight in a way that surprises him.

"Hell, boy, my next round, I want the stallion's life. Did you see the cock on that sucker? Thing's bigger than my damn arm."

"Not a half-bad calling." Jesse welcomes Clyde's humor, for it works to pull him back from the pity path he was about to take in his head. Doing without can put a man in a bad state, he knows all too well, and Clyde has been in that chair for nearly ten years. He wonders if some of those drugs advertised on TV would do Clyde any good. He might risk asking if he had any idea about what he'd say if he had to hear there's no help for his friend.

They drive for the better part of an hour without talking much, each with his thoughts, until Clyde chuckles and pounds on the dash. "You do know, don't you, that I came within a hair of winning over that poor woman back there."

"Yeah, you had her there for a minute. Too bad she's scared of that sonofabitch." He looks over, and Clyde wears the same silly grin Jesse knows from their glory days.

"May not slow dance, but I can still charm the pants off the ladies." The big grin stays on his broad face, and he begins beating out a slow hand crossing rhythm on his dead legs, singing along with Rod Stewart: "... Fill my heart with gladness, take away all my sadness, ease my troubles, that's what you do ...."

Jesse wonders if Clyde sometimes blames him for the accident, the way he blames himself. He'd been less drunk than Clyde the night the two celebrated his return from Iraq. Yet Clyde insisted on dropping him off at home. Twenty minutes later, his truck stalled out on the railroad track, him too drunk to restart it. The next morning his phone rang before dawn and Buddy told him about the accident.

"Remember them Daisy Duke Posters?" Clyde abandons Rod and reaches across the seat to slap Jesse on the shoulder.

"The one you jerked off to starting in fourth grade?"

"Remember how we'd lay on the floor and look up at Daisy, sprawled on the hood of that Trans Am, and take nickel bets on who could get it up first? I've still got those posters."

"No, hell you don't. Not on the ceiling, you don't."

"No, fool. I put Daisy away. But I still got a picture of the red Corvette we were going to steal and cruise Route Sixty-Six."

He pauses. "Gave up on convertibles. Don't exactly fit my image."
Clyde stares out the window at a field of soybeans.

Then Jesse goes to the shared memory that has always
saved them. "Hey, Clyde, you remember being down four in the
championship game with forty-seven seconds on the clock?"

"And in the huddle I shouted that a touchdown meant the team
got to go to the best little whorehouse in all of north Florida."

"And old Buddy winked and said 'crank the bus.'"

"And I said, all right, you pussy linemen, slobber-knock them
bastards snorting on the other side of that ball. I'll clear a way for
Little Brother, and me and him will spring for the tickets."

"Damned if Buddy and the linemen didn't block to a man."

"And you waltzed your puny ass into the end zone without as
much as a scratch."

"Over the two deep men you pulverized. You should've had
that MVP trophy and that's the God's truth." The Parrish legend,
a mix of fact and tall-tales, was that Clyde was a man who'd run
naked through hell never getting as much as a blister.

They sit through a song or two, neither talking, maybe just
feeling the good of sharing what was their finest moment.

"How'd we know the cheering would end? Hell, we believed we
were indestructible. Samson and the Hulk rolled into one."

"Then I tried my hand at blocking a freight train. Went from
Friday night hero to crippled bootlegger. Now I live with a skunk
stuck in my grill, scheduling shits with strangers and making do
with only memories of sweet pussy."

Sickness stirring in his stomach, Jesse steals a glance at Clyde,
who stares ahead through the windshield. His profile is caught in
the dim dashboard lights, and Jesse turns away, his anger huge. He
wants to ass-whip God until He begs for mercy and cuts a deal that
would have the freight train switching tracks and Clyde walking
away whistling.

They leave the interstate and drive south on 319, the darkness broken only by streetlights in small towns where silent homes and shops crouch in the veiled cover of night. Their storytelling dropped off back up the road, as though the present bled the joy out of their stories.

"Been thinking about what that asshole said about a bonus, and then what Mr. Wash said about putting the mare in with the stallion. Could be that two wild horses are running loose in the forest. If that's the case, then I'll wager that catching her just got some easier."

"How you figure?"

"If there's a baby, we'll have a better chance of catching it and using that little one to bait the mare out in the open."

"You don't mean to hurt the foal?"

"No, fool. I mean to turn the mare's natural instinct against her. You still want to catch her, don't you?" Clyde looks at him like all the other times when he's been slow to agree on a given.

He gets it, he just doesn't like it.

Thirty miles to go, he is surprised when Clyde asks to pull over so he can take a leak. He doesn't move to position the wheelchair, but opens the passenger door, then uncaps a tube taped to his leg. When he's drained the bag, he re-tapes the tube.

"Now ain't that easier that shaking the snake?" His sarcasm is steeled in bitterness.

Jesse stops the van in the front yard and quietly lets himself in the front door. Marlene dozes on the couch. He touches her shoulder lightly and she blinks up at him before he pulls her to her feet. They stand close for the time it takes him to properly thank her.

"The kids are all fine. Katie finished her Florida map and Cole's paper is excellent. Sky showed me her map. And before I forget, there's a message from their mom. It came while we were helping

Cole take care of the horses next door. I didn't play it for the kids. I thought you might want to hear it first."

Clyde and Marlene drive away in separate vehicles, and Jesse steps back into the deep silence of the house. Although he's bone-weary and not of a mind to deal with Dodie, he presses the blinking button on the answering machine and braces himself.

"Hey, my darlings. Mama's sorry to miss you, but I hope you're having fun. I'm still searching for an apartment. Mommy loves you very much. Bye for now."

He's considering erasing the recording when he hears the scuffing of tiny feet. Sky stands rubbing her eyes, and she points at the machine.

He sits on the floor, Indian style, pats the space next to him, and she sits, taking up the same posture. He plays the tape over and over again until she falls asleep, her head resting on his thigh. He cradles her in his arms and carries her back to bed. Beau raises his head and blinks, but Katie sleeps soundly.

NINETEEN

Jesse picks up a copy of the Tallahassee newspaper from a vacant table, and it doesn't matter that it's a day old. Yesterday's news is still news to him. He orders a large coffee, takes a seat in the back, and out of habit, turns to the classifieds. He wouldn't mind picking up an odd job or two on weekends or afternoons after he's caught a few winks. When he's read the short list of jobs, he notices an ad for Welsh Corgi pups and figures that's a breed Clyde wouldn't take into the woods against Marlene's wishes. He copies the number on a napkin, deciding to pick up the girls after school and surprise them with a trip to see the pups.

He's searching the paper for the missing sports section when he looks up to admire a Ford F-350 dually, hauling a double horse trailer, pull into the parking lot. A tall man wearing a Stetson gets out of the truck, takes a long look at his load, brushes off his jeans, and turns toward the door. The rig's top of the line, and it clearly set the cowboy back a pretty penny. Jesse figures he's not playing, but the real deal.

The man orders the biggest breakfast on the menu and a large coffee, and takes a seat at a table near Jesse. They exchange polite nods, and Jesse goes back to the paper, searching for the outcome of last night's Spurs game, just in case he should happen upon Marlene.

"Them Washington bums called off that damn war yet?"

"Don't say exactly."

"Handwriting was on the wall, but good folks were so pissed off, they looked the other way."

Jesse hates talking politics, but he sure would like to pick the man's brain about any ideas he might have on recapturing the mare. He leans across the table, meaning to keep him talking.

"Where you headed?"

"Home. Got a little spread northeast of San Antonio. Been on the road longer than Willie," he laughs easily. "But I bet he never travels with just a couple of mares for company. Man needs a little something more than that, if you get my drift."

"I do for a fact." Doing without is a subject he's come to know all too well. It has sent him to the very edge of calling Sally for her favor.

"Hauled those two mares to a quarter horse stallion down in Ocala."

"What can you tell me about mustangs?"

"I'd say a sensible man ought to stay the hell away from them unless he's got lots of time and know-how." He stuffs eggs into his mouth.

"That right?" Jesse considers walking out on the conversation.

"Don't get me wrong, some make real good cutters if a man's got the patience. They got little hard hooves, making them quick over rough ground, and they can stop and spin on a cow patty." He shoves more food into his mouth and chews. "Then the really smart ones can be too smart to be of any real use. Want to take the bit."

"I think I had one like that. Busted out the same day I took delivery. Been chasing her for what seems like forever."

"Run off where? Here about looks too damn crowded for people to live decent, much less a mustang." The man's gathered brow and piercing blue eyes cause Jesse to trust that what he heard is genuine concern. He recounts every effort to recapture the mare, and half way through his spiel the man pushes aside his tray.

"My buddy and me figure to bait her if it turns out there's a foal."

"Yeah, well what you've done up to now's make a bunch of mistakes. A weekend cowboy astride his under-worked horse is no match for a mustang. Chasing her could cripple a horse and its rider. I'd lay off with them weekend cowboys and their ropes."

Jesse welcomes the man's frankness. "I figured as much, but I'm right desperate. My little girl loses hope every time I come back empty-handed."

"What's your girl's name?"

"Katie. It's short for Katherine Elizabeth, but she'd pout for a week if she knew I'd told even a stranger."

A warm smile crosses his weathered face. "Katherine was my wife's name. Bone cancer took her at thirty-four. Twenty-six years ago last Tuesday, and if it hadn't been for my horses, I'd have stayed more lost than not, likely turned out to be a total drunk." The old cowboy swallows hard and stares at a cloudless, sapphire sky visible through the dirty plate glass window.

"I'm sorry. Your wife passing, I mean." He likes the misty-eyed cowboy, and wishes for more of what he might say about the mare.

He turns back to Jesse. "If it's done right, a captured foal tethered in a catch pen can work. Still, I've heard of mustang mares refusing to come to a trapped baby."

"Why's that? Figured instinct would kick in."

"It does, but separation plays a second to a mare's fear for the herd's survival. If you think about it, the survival of a newborn in the wild is a long shot to start with. You could say the mare plays the odds."

He goes on to explain that the mare's habits must be carefully studied, including where she grazes, where she's willing to leave her feet to rest, where she drinks and how far she ranges. "When you know her habits, a sturdy catch pen can be set up in a place where she's likely to return. Then you wait downwind, hoping the baby wanders in. If it does, you've got bait. After that, you wait some more."

"How long? Tied up, I mean."

"Depends on the mare."

"So far, I figure she's had her smarts and my ignorance working for her." Still, Jesse dreads such an ordeal for the mare and her baby.

The old cowboy sits, draining what's got to be cold coffee. He glances out at the trailer and then back at Jesse. "Tell you what, I've got loose time coming up, and if you want, I'll take these mares on, come back and give you a hand. This old boy I know owes me a favor or two. He's one of the best with mustangs."

"God knows I'd be grateful, but I can't promise you much for your trouble, maybe a place to stay over, a little on gas and road expenses. Would do better if I could, but I'm flat busted."

"Here, let's swap numbers. We can work all that out when the mare and her foal are someplace safe."

"Damned if we ain't done all this talking and I don't believe I introduced myself. I'm Jesse McKnight, from right here all my life."

"Curtis Dobbs, Jesse. If that little girl of yours can hold on a little longer, we'll come back and catch her horse for her."

Jesse writes his number on a napkin and they shake hands. Curtis walks in long easy strides through the open door, mounts his big rig, and pulls onto Highway 90, heading for I-10 westbound.

Jesse tucks the business card in his wallet where he keeps Dodie's number. He doesn't know if he's heard a Texas-size lie or the gospel truth, but, either way, he figures he's better off for having met Curtis Dobbs.

If what he heard from Dobbs is true, it will mean cutting away from Dee and Susan. They'll never agree to go along with his plan; it's far too cruel. But it may be the best hope he has of recapturing the mare.

TWENTY

The sleep Jesse needs is filled with a dream of chasing through a dense forest in search of Katie and Sky, only to discover that they were carried away by a vicious animal the size of a dinosaur. Jarred awake with his heart pounding, he sits on the side of the bed, his head resting in his palms, waiting for the fog to clear. Beau scampers into the room and jumps onto the bed, licking his hot face.

"Holy shit, dog. That was some scary dream." To his surprise, tears well up, and he strokes the anxious dog, calming both.

He glances at the clock, and he has an hour until time to drive to school and Trudy's. He stumbles into the kitchen, Beau at his heels, and the dog still wears an anxious look. Searching the fridge for something to eat, he settles for strawberry Kool-Aid and peanut butter on Ritz crackers, which he shares with Beau while standing over a sink full of two-day-old dirty dishes.

When he's cleared the sink of dishes, stacked them on the drain to dry, he still has time for a quick shower and shave. He stands under the hot water, questioning his decision to take the girls to see the pups he has little chance of affording. But he's determined to go ahead with his plan.

KATIE SPOTS THE TRUCK and quickly takes her leave from a covey of giggling girls, not bothering to hide her surprise.

"Daddy, what's wrong? Where's Grandma?"

"Why's something got to be wrong? Can't a daddy pick up his kids? And yes, Miss Worry Wart, before you ask, I called."

They leave the truck parked at Katie's school and walk across the street to Trudy's to pick up Sky. He tells Katie about the ad in the paper and that he's taking them to see the puppies. She looks puzzled, but interested.

"My, my, but our Sky's improving. Just today she asked to have her artwork put on the display board. She's never wanted that before." Sky is hanging at Trudy's knees like his granny's old knotted stockings. He dares to touch her shiny hair, risking that he may pop the pretty bubble Trudy just blew his way.

He's relieved when Sky doesn't scream or run away.

Katie coaxes Sky into the truck and tries pushing past to take the middle seat. "Dang, Sky, I sit next to Daddy, you don't."

Sky pushes back against the seat, her legs straight out in front of her and she doesn't give ground. He smiles at her, but she turns away, sucking her bottom lip.

"Daddy, I want you to start picking us up. I like that you stay and talk to Mama Trudy. Grandma never does. Not even when Mama Trudy tries showing her Sky's drawings."

"Baby, that's a tired old story, and if your grandma high hats Trudy, then she's wrong."

"Can I tell her she's mean?"

He thinks about what that might sound like and settles on Cora deserving Katie's scorn. "Yeah, you can, but try being polite."

"What's a nice way to say butt-hole?"

"Fanny hole." Sky giggles.

Her voice comes sweetly to his ears, so much so that his eyes water. She steals a glance—her large, round eyes shine—and he wants to believe that she's allowed him a glimpse into her tiny world. He swallows hard, knowing that his voice would shake should he try to speak.

"Right, Sky. That's good, don't you think, Daddy?"

He winks at Sky, and she turns toward the window as though she expects something of interest to fly by wearing a bright red tail.

Katie studies him for several blocks, and he decides she's making up her mind about something. "This pup's for Miss Marlene, right?" Her voice is low, as though she's talking R-rated, unfit for Sky's tender ears.

Does Katie think of him and Marlene as some kind of secret? He glances over at her, and her expression carries a harder question.

"Because of what happened to Sylvester, right?"

He's a bit relieved that it's now Clyde she has pinned and not him. He'd asked Marlene about the pup's disappearance. The little guy had hung out nights with her, sleeping in a laundry basket behind the bar.

"Maybe, if we find the right pup at the right price."

"Good, 'cause I've already got the best dog in the world. But Miss Marlene's really sad, and I'm mad at Uncle Clyde." She stares at him, her mouth drawn hard like a line in the sand. Clyde's guilty of a mortal sin in the Book of Katie.

"You're right, it was wrong of your Uncle Clyde to take the pup into the woods when Miss Marlene asked him not to. But the snake bite wasn't his fault."

"Nope, you're wrong. But I know he's your best friend."

He decides that she means to hold her peace and has no plan to get up in Clyde's face. But he worries that Clyde will view the new pup as meddling, him taking sides on what happened to Marlene's pup. Buying her a pup of her own could work without pissing off Clyde if he thinks it was Katie's idea.

They drive into one of the older but well kept neighborhoods of small frame houses with tidy yards nestled behind picket fences.

"Why can't we have a pretty house with lots of flowers?"

"There's nothing wrong with our house that a couple coats of paint can't fix."

"Can we plant lots of flowers? Maybe build a fence like that one?"

"Not any time soon."

She frowns at what she's come to expect from him.

After six blocks of more questions he can't answer, he spots the house. It's a single story, painted silver-gray and trimmed in a darker shade, surrounded by a picket fence the color of the trim. Beds of daylilies banked with pine straw and a double row of Cannas, nipped by an earlier frost, run the length of the fence. Beneath a shedding sycamore, an older woman sits on the grass among a pile of playful puppies. She waves, but doesn't smile. He shuts off the engine, figuring he's made a mistake bringing the girls.

Katie hurries out of the truck and reaches back for Sky's hand. Jesse tucks in his shirt and waves as they enter the gate, approaching along a crushed oyster shell walkway bordered by Japanese boxwoods.

"Afternoon, ma'am. That's a mighty fine bunch of pups you got there."

The woman is wearing faded jeans and a worn flannel shirt over a Save the Manatee tee shirt. She struggles to gain her feet, and he reaches a hand in her direction but doesn't take her arm.

"I got it young man, thank you." Her matter-of-fact tone eases his awkwardness, and she looks first at Sky, who hangs back. The woman's leathered face softens, and he introduces himself and the girls.

Katie sits on the ground and six pups try climbing into her lap. Two of the six chew the bright buttons on her shirt. The seventh pup, the runt, tri-colored with black, tan and white markings, its tiny jellybean shaped eyes outlined in solid black like it's wearing a mask, waddles over to Sky. The pup has a white marking in roughly the shape of Texas along her right shoulder, and Jesse immediately thinks of her as Lone Star. Sky watches the pup until it comes to sit at her feet. She draws her hand to her mouth and takes a slow step back. The pup moves forward, sits again, and looks up at Sky.

"She wants you to play." The woman, who has introduced herself as Miss Mary, encourages.

Sky doesn't look at Miss Mary but kneels before the pup. It reaches its wet nose to sniff her bare knee. She touches the pup's nose with a small finger.

"Baby," she whispers, and with a thumb-nail size pink tongue, the pup licks Sky's finger.

Again at the sound of Sky's voice, Jesse's chest swells, and the good he felt earlier at hearing her speak, the likes of which he'd nearly given up on, returns.

He has to find money for two pups. On the telephone, Miss Mary said it would be two weeks before the puppies would be ready. With any luck at all, he has time to raise the money. Then he hopes she doesn't expect a deposit to hold them. He has a lone twenty in his wallet and a near empty gas tank.

A giggling Katie rolls on the grass, pups chewing at her curls. Sky squats near Star and traces the map of Texas with a timid finger. Miss Mary watches the girls with the pups, and Jesse prays she has a special tenderness for what she sees.

"Daddy," Katie whispers, her arms wrapped around his waist. "Can we get Sky a puppy too?"

He looks into her pleading face and remembers how much he hated hearing, "we'll see." It always meant no, and he'd rather have heard the truth than to have clung to false hopes. He wants a better answer for Katie and Sky, but he doesn't have one.

"You girls can choose if it's okay with your daddy, but like I said, these babies will need to stay with their mama till they're older and stronger."

Sky looks up at him, but doesn't speak. The runt runs off a little ways, turns and sits, her playfulness inviting Sky to chase after her. When she doesn't, the pup gives a little bark. Sky makes a soft sound and runs toward the pup. They run in tight circles, Sky giggling. Both seem happy with their version of a girl and puppy merry-go-round.

"I believe Sky's picked already."

"I think you're right. They do make a pretty picture." Miss Mary looks at him, and her eyes shine.

"What're you asking for these fine pups?" He braces for the answer, and hopes his worry doesn't show too much on his face.

"One hundred, cash." She looks him square in the face without blinking.

"That'd be apiece, right?" He hasn't seen two hundred extra dollars at one time in over a year. Her firmness crushes his hope of buying even one, much less two.

He feels the girls' disappointment from clear across the yard where they've stopped chasing about and stand staring at him. Why did he bring them here to fall in love with these pups before asking the price? He doesn't have anything of value left to trade but his old twelve gauge shotgun, and he doesn't take Miss Mary to be one who'd favor a rusted gun over two pups.

She looks over at Sky for a moment, seeming to weigh something of considerable importance. "You know, I've been meaning to have those big oak limbs yonder trimmed from over the house." She points to a sizable limb.

"Oh yes ma'am, if you're willing to work a trade. I mean, I could do that. Anything you might need that's worth a couple of these fine pups, I stand ready to do. I'll cut those limbs down and into fireplace lengths, split them, stack it there in the woodshed, blow off your roof, clean up and haul off all the trash. Yes, ma'am, you bet." Right away, he figures he needs to cut back on the eagerness, sound less like this is his only chance at getting these pups.

"If you're the kind who keeps his word, that'll be fine."

He ignores Katie's deep sigh and reaches out to shake on the deal. Miss Mary takes his hand, hers warm and strong in his. He sizes her up as the kind of woman who'd hold a man's feet to the fire.

"Then which one of these pups are you going to want, other than the one loving on that shy daughter of yours?"

"We'll want that little one for sure. But if it's okay, I'd like to talk to the girls before picking the second pup."

KATIE LEANS THROUGH the open window and waves, calling a loud good-bye to Miss Mary, who waves back. The runt pup runs to the end of the walkway and sits as they begin pulling away, and Sky turns onto her knees and watches the pup. She begins to softly cry, and it's the first time he's felt she cries in the way of a sad little girl, which is likely a good cry.

"You better be telling the truth about that big limb. Miss Mary will get real mad if you lie to her. She won't let her pups go home with a liar."

"Cool it. Consider those limbs firewood." He winks, and the weight of his promise sits on his chest. But he means to bring back the joy he saw on Sky's face if he has to tackle that limb in his sleep. He'll ask Cole for his help. A little manly work should do him some good. Show him it can be satisfying.

Katie peers around Sky, who now sits chewing the hem of her shirt, and they both stare at him like cats stalking their prey.

TWENTY-ONE

Beau meets them in the driveway and Katie puts her hand out, offering him the new scent. She explains that he's going to have a little sister, and Beau barks and runs ahead. The girls follow, lumbering up the steps with their backpacks and jackets.

The telephone rings and Jesse hurries into the kitchen, expecting to hear Cole offering one of his many excuses as to why he's late. He's just glad the kid remembers to call.

"Hey, Jesse, it's me." Dodie's voice is high pitched, and she works for casual. Anything she has to say, he can't think of in that way.

"We're good." He responds out of habit, not sure she even asked.

"I'm here. At Mama's. Back to take care of some business."

"That right?" After the initial shock of hearing her voice, the part about being here on business worries him. What business does she have that required her to slip back into town without letting him know she was coming? He remembers her last phone message, cheerfully declaring that she continued to search for an apartment. Is she here to take the kids and needs the element of surprise?

"Sally's buying the shop. And, of course, she doesn't have cash to put down. I'm here to settle on a price and work out terms."

He doesn't say anything, but waits for the other shoe to fall.

"I was disappointed at not seeing the girls after school today. I'd wanted to surprise them."

"Yeah, they would've been surprised all right. But we had business of our own after school." He doesn't guard against his sarcasm, but enjoys turning it up a notch.

"Can you bring them to the H J Express on the interstate? I'd like to have supper with them before I go back." Her tone has grown distant, and he figures that she's picked up on his attitude.

"Why's that, after all this time?" His pent-up anger flares, and he wants absolute control over what happens between her and his kids. Her invitation doesn't include him, and if she's planning some end run, he wants to know what to expect.

"Jesse? They're my children and I want to see them. I have the right."

"Yeah, I guess you do, but they've got rights, too. Ain't right that you should expect to just waltz back in and start making demands."

"Jesse, please. Don't make this harder. I just want to see the kids. I miss them so."

Harder than what, he thinks, but her pleading softens his resolve and he searches for a satisfying way to back down a notch.

"I'll put Katie on, and if she's okay with it, I'll bring them over."

He regrets putting the heat on Katie, but Dodie readily agrees and he's stuck with his decision. He calls the girls from their room where they've changed out of their school clothes into home clothes, something he requires, although he recognizes it's likely a throwback to his childhood when outgrown sizes were passed down. He tells Katie and Sky their mom's on the telephone and that she wants to talk to them.

"Not the machine, but live?" Katie takes a step back and leans against the doorway, her arms crossed and her hands shoved under her armpits. Sky stands blinking up at Katie, and she takes hold of her sister's hand.

"Okay, but why can't she just leave a message like before?" It sounds as though Katie wants a little control, too.

"She's here, in town. Don't you think maybe you should talk to her?"

Katie takes the phone and holds it away from her as if it has suddenly grown sharp teeth. Sky continues to cling to her hand.

"Hello. Yes, ma'am. Okay … her too. Cole's out of jail. But now he's got Sarah to worry about." Katie listens, looking expectantly at him, the rearing horse decal on her tee shirt sharply rising and falling.

"Can you wait a minute?" She covers the phone and whispers, "She wants us to eat supper with her, and she doesn't mean McDonald's." Sky prances in place, not a happy dance, but more as if she has to go to the bathroom real bad.

"Do what you want. I'm betting Sky will go along with whatever." He thinks Sky nods ever so slightly, but maybe not.

She puts the telephone back to her ear. "Can Daddy come too?"

"No, no, Katie." He shakes his head.

"Forget it, he said no." She pauses a moment. "Okay, but we've got school tomorrow."

She hands him the telephone and charges down the hall, and he doesn't think her sudden burst of energy comes from the excitement of seeing her mother, but from her newest anxiety. Sky and Beau follow, and the bedroom door slams shut.

"I'll drop them off afterward, if that's okay. I'd like to pick up a few things of mine." He wonders what those would be. He's searched the house and found nothing of hers. Maybe she means to take things he thinks of as theirs, or even his.

"Cole has practice until five."

"Practice? Cole?"

There's a fill in the blank pause, but he's unwilling to share even that much of the life he and the kids are making without her. They agree on six o'clock in front of the restaurant. He hangs up the phone, and sifts through the many layers, wringing every possible meaning from the words that passed between them. Whatever else she means to do, she hasn't changed her mind about divorce. He's reconciled to divorce, but fears her intention to file for full custody and worries that he has little to no chance of stopping her.

He's ashamed that he'd once felt nothing but relief at learning she meant to come for the kids. Even as late as learning her plan to petition the court for full custody, he'd believed it best for all of them. But that was before he and Cole talked and he started to think he and the kids could make it on their own.

There was a time after Iraq, and again when he lost his job, that she was the better parent, and for that he bears his guilt. Maybe driving a forklift and working through the night like a blind armadillo doesn't stack up to the security her new career may offer. But she was the parent to abandon the kids with only a note propped on the kitchen table, and now she plans on taking them away from him on the strength of what a new job may promise.

An unexpected emptiness grips him, and he places his hand over his heart, as if he can rub the pain away. Full custody would mean he'd slip back into being an absent father, and all the gains he and his kids have made would surely be lost.

His anger builds, and he wants to go to the girls and tell them to forget supper with their mom, that he's taking them to Chucky

Cheese in Tallahassee. They've never been there before, but he imagines it's a place they'd like. Then he gets a picture of Katie and Sky's earlier confusion, and he doesn't want to make matters worse. Maybe he needs for Dodie to see him with the kids. See that he has changed for the better. Show her that he's no longer the worthless man she believed him to be.

The girls have less than an hour to get ready. He searches for clean jeans and presses Katie's blue cotton shirt while the girls are in the tub. When they're dressed and ready to go, Katie pulls on last year's school jacket, and the sleeves are too short and Sky's jacket has spots of yellow paint. Katie's jeans are high-waders, and her brown school shoes badly scuffed. He thinks shoe polish, but there's only black under the bathroom sink. He may be a better father, but not a better provider. It seems that everything comes down to money.

"Cole should have been here an hour ago. Did he say anything about after school?" He tugs at Katie's sleeves as though he could stretch them to cover her wrists.

"Cole's not my job. I've got Sky, remember?" She flops onto the couch, grabs the remote, and turns up the sound until he yells for her to shut off the TV.

"Katie, look, I don't like being jerked around either, but help me out here if you know Cole's whereabouts."

"Okay, so maybe he's off somewhere with Sarah." She shrugs, and he accepts that she told him the little she knows. She gets off the couch and walks into the kitchen like a member of the Special Forces on a priority mission. Sky doesn't follow, but continues to play itsy-bitsy spider behind the lampshade. He follows Katie, watches her fill Beau's food bowls and sit on the floor while he crunches dry food.

"Come on, Katie, buck up. I'm not taking you to face a firing squad. I bet you can order fish sticks, French fries, and even a strawberry Popsicle."

"No, they don't have popsicles in fancy restaurants."

"Cole's going to be there, and I think you did the right thing by agreeing to go. Don't you want to see your mom?"

Her lips pucker and her eyes search his face. "Not if she's taking us to live with her. I know you'll stop looking for Dakota, and Mama won't let Beau come. And you don't love him the way I do."

Beau stops crunching and licks Katie's face.

"Is that what you think? That she's going to steal you away in the night? Your mom won't do that. That's TV bull crap. You'll be right here when I bring Dakota home. And I'm crazy about Beau. Just ask him if you don't believe me." He grins, but she doesn't.

"Then can Beau come with us?" Katie gathers the dog across her lap and hugs him. Maybe Beau is the one love Katie counts on.

"Girl, you know dogs can't eat at restaurants." He tries again to be funny, but she still doesn't smile. "Okay, okay, if it'll make you feel better he can ride over and stay with me while you have supper."

Cole comes into the kitchen carrying an armload of books and wearing a sheepish look.

"Welcome home, stranger."

"James dropped Sarah off before he gave me a ride home." He draws a deep breath and piles his books on the kitchen table.

"You mean James hangs around for three hours for you and Sarah to practice being brainy?" He remembers the incident at the gas station and how easily Cole talked and laughed with Sarah before Keith showed up. He wonders if James and Cole are playing self-appointed bodyguard or Cole is simply bargaining more time with Sarah. Either way, he worries.

"Something like that. Without Sarah, we're toast. She's a brain."

"Pretty, too." Katie arches her eyebrows.

"Shut up, you miniature freak."

"You're not the boss of me." She stands with her hands on her hips, swaying, and dear God he hates the Cora he sees in her.

"Okay, you two. Go to your separate corners. Cole, I don't want you to go ballistic, but your mom's in town and she wants you kids to meet her for supper. The girls are ready, and you're fine the way you are."

Cole tosses his jacket onto the back of a kitchen chair. "She leaves, and not one time does she bother to explain. Now she pops back into our lives and requires a command performance from us? And we're supposed to be grateful? No damn way. Not me."

"What's a command performance? I don't think I'll like it either." Katie takes off her jacket, and Sky fumbles with the zipper on hers.

"Whoa down, guys. Think of it as something other than my cooking." He winces at having nothing better to say.

"That's not a damn bit funny, Dad. I've got my own problems to worry about, and it doesn't include kissing Mom's absent ass." Cole picks up a thick book from the pile and slams it down again, punctuating his meaning.

"Okay, I get it. But maybe you'll want to try thinking about it her way …." His voice trails off, and even he's not persuaded.

"Let her come here. We're all here, and this is our home." He goes to the fridge and takes out a bowl of leftover chicken and dumplings, puts it into the microwave, slams the door, and sets the timer.

Katie isn't alone; they're all feeling jerked around and they have a right. But he isn't sure Cole's hard line is best until he learns what other surprises Dodie might have in store. When Cole sits at the table and begins eating out of the bowl, Jesse gives up and herds the girls and Beau through the front door. Katie gripes that Cole should have to go too, while Beau runs to the truck and back to the porch steps as if he has a watch that reads late.

"Katie, hush for one dang minute and get yourself, Sky, and that hairy bark in the truck."

Cole is sitting on the floor, talking quietly on the phone when Jesse comes back into the kitchen. He slips a hand over the mouthpiece, and from the sadness in his eyes, Cole clearly has mixed feelings about his decision.

"You sure you don't want to change your mind?" Jesse stops in the doorway, guessing that Cole's talking to Sarah.

"I can't. It'll make me crazy. And I don't want to end up screaming at Mom." His eyes tear and he looks down, cradling the telephone to his ear.

Jesse goes back out to the truck. The girls and Beau wait silently, and they all wear long faces.

TWENTY-TWO

Dodie waits in her car while he parks, then gets out and slowly walks toward them. Katie climbs out of the truck and runs to meet her mama. Sky stands next to the open door, a wet finger lost inside her chapped cheek, and doesn't follow her sister.

"Go on, baby girl. It's your mama."

Dodie calls to Sky, and she starts to where her mother is kneeling, embracing Katie. Jesse bristles. He wants Dodie to feel jealousy at Sky's reluctance to leave him.

Cole's right to have stayed away. Dodie can't expect to show up and have the kids forget and forgive as though waking to discover she'd abandoned them overnight was normal.

Jesse stays in the truck, not trusting his emotions that have begun to swing back and forth between wanting to comfort Dodie and wanting to blame her for all the misery he feels for himself and the kids. Staring through the rear-view mirror, he studies her, as if he could know her intentions. She's as thin as she was in high school, and he remembers how pretty she was in the lavender gown she wore standing next to him on the homecoming float. Now, her shoulders sag with the same kind of weariness he's come to know.

Dodie glances toward the truck, and he believes Cole's absence is especially hurtful. She takes a hand of each of the girls and they start for the restaurant. Sky looks back his way, then turns and follows Dodie.

He shifts the truck into gear and slowly pulls away, and Beau leans even farther out the window, barking for whatever he fears. Suddenly, he hears Katie screaming his name, and he watches as she breaks away from Dodie's grip and chases after the truck. He stomps the brake, and before he can fully slide off the seat and stand, Katie grabs him around his waist, sobbing. Sky has run after Katie, and now they both look at him with tears washing down their upturned faces.

"Katie, Sky, it's all right. Your mama's going to bring you straight home after supper." He embraces both and looks back at Dodie, who stands with bowed head, her fists clenched at her sides. What did she expect? Her visit out of the blue has reduced them to emotional fruitcakes.

"No, Daddy, you're supposed to stay where I can look out and see you." Katie clings to him as though turning loose means he's swept away forever. He pulls free of her grip and squats between the two.

"Look at me. Beau and I are going to get supper and then we're coming back."

"But why can't you come inside and sit at another table? We won't even look at you."

"Leave Beau in the truck all alone? You don't want that."

Katie looks up at the dog, his tongue wallowed to one side, trying to touch her, and she nods. It's as if she looks to Beau to be the keeper of the promise.

Dodie stands apart from them with what he takes to be disbelief on her face, and in the moment, he feels sorry for her. Maybe that's why he's moved to lie.

"Cole's upset at not coming. But ... he's got practice. The last before the big district tournament." He thinks debate contests aren't likely called tournaments, but it's the best he's got at covering Cole's absence.

"But Daddy ...." Katie means to set his lie straight, but he squeezes her hand and she gets it. He hates that he's teaching her to lie, even if he thinks of it as a white lie.

"Maybe I'll still get a chance to see him before I have to leave. If not, then Thanksgiving at Mama's. Please give him my love and tell him how much I miss him."

He gently moves Katie and Sky back toward Dodie, and he watches until the three have entered the restaurant.

He drives away, savoring the good he'd felt having the girls cling to him rather than her. His first thought was to put them back into the truck and speed away, leaving Dodie alone with only her new life for comfort. But he'd hurt for her, accepting that he, too, had abandoned her and their kids.

He pulls into the yard and the house stands dark, except for the single porch light he doesn't remember leaving on. He walks into the kitchen and Cole and his books are missing. He starts down the hallway, expecting to find him sleeping or studying in his room. Not until he returns to the kitchen does he find the note on the fridge. Cole has gone to Sarah's for debate practice.

His first impulse is to worry that Cole's decision may cause him to do something foolish, but there's comfort in knowing that, if anyone can talk sense to Cole right now, it's likely Sarah. He would have called James for a ride, and the last person he needs to hang with tonight is James. Then he settles on Cole being too smart to follow James's lead.

He reheats pinto beans and rice and decides to eat in front of the TV, maybe watch a little ESPN, catch up on the news; something to say to Marlene about the NBA when he sees her next. He can stomach only half the beans and rice, and sets the plate on the floor for Beau. He stretches out on the couch, thinking to close his heavy eyelids for a minute before heading back.

He's jarred out of a deep sleep by the sound of Katie screaming his name, and he's confused, believing it's a dream, until he feels the impact of her fists pounding his chest. Her face is beet red, tears flooding, and she's shouting.

"You're a rotten liar, and you made Beau a liar."

"Katie, stop." He catches her wrists and holds her away from him. "Stop it right now."

He swings his feet onto the floor, sitting upright, and behind him, Sky screams and runs toward the bedroom.

Cole comes from his room, shouting, "What's all this damn racket about?"

Cole's sudden appearance further confuses Jesse. How had he failed to hear his return?"

"You promised you'd come back for us." Katie pulls free of his grip.

Dodie has followed the girls, her face pale and drawn.

"Mom, what are you doing here?" Cole stops and stares as though in a stupor, his eyes stretched wide and his mouth open.

"Oh, Cole, I prayed you'd be here. We need to talk." She clutches her hands to her breasts.

"I'm not here for you." He walks into the kitchen, grabs his backpack off a chair, and turns toward the front door, his body rigid with defiance.

"Cole, please wait." Dodie moves to stop him, but he sidesteps, avoiding her. "You must know I'm doing all of this for you and the girls."

She begins to cry and Cole turns to face her, his eyes blazing. "Oh, sure, Mom, and I'm supposed to go on blaming Dad? Well, I can't do that. He stayed, and you didn't."

"Cole, you know how he was. I had no other choice."

"Choice?" Cole's voice breaks. "I was with you. You could've said something. And then I'd have had no reason to steal Miss Dee's car."

"Oh, my God, I'm so sorry."

"Sorry? You're sorry? Mom, I went to jail for you. Do you ever think about that?" He turns and slams out of the house, and Jesse hears what he knows is James's truck tearing away.

Dodie collapses against the wall, her hands covering her face, and Jesse turns away from her to face Katie.

"Okay, I know I promised. And I never meant to lie." Exhaustion easily explains his having overslept, but he can't let Dodie know he works nights and leaves Cole alone with the girls.

"You always say that. But you stopped looking for Dakota."

"Good God, Katie. I've tried with that, I'm still trying, but I'm no damn cowboy."

"And you're a no-good daddy, too." Katie runs from the room, Dodie following her.

"Sweetheart, please open the door for Mama."

"No, go away. I hate you both."

Dodie comes back into the room and stands on the opposite side of the cluttered coffee table. Jesse slumps back on the couch, wave after wave of weariness assaulting him, mind and body. His life has become a succession of slamming doors.

"She was fine in the restaurant, but the moment she realized you weren't waiting, she made a terrible scene. Refused to get into the car, upsetting Sky. Both of them were inconsolable."

He stands, awkwardly, his hands in his pockets. "I do wish we could've found an easier way. But I guess some failures are so big that easy can't be had."

"Yes, but I do believe you've changed." She doesn't smile, but in the moment, her frown fades.

He follows her onto the porch and stands watching as she approaches her car. Opening the door, she turns and calls, "I still want the kids at Mama's for Thanksgiving." She gets into her car and drives away, leaving him to sort through her newest demand.

Back inside, the fractious heat has dissipated, and he allows himself to feel somewhat vindicated by Cole's fervent defense of him. And although Cole was right to confront his mom, he's bound to have regrets he'll need to sort out as well.

WHEN HE'S LET BEAU OUT for his nightly prowl, he puts together his standard fare of two peanut butter and grape jelly sandwiches, pouring the last of the day's coffee into the thermos. He goes to the back door and whistles Beau home. He has begun to worry that Cole won't make it back before time for him to leave for work. He wishes he'd accepted Marlene's offer to put Cole on her cell phone account.

He phones Marlene at the bar, and when she answers, he tells her Cole's running late and that he has no one to stay with the girls.

"It's slow here, so why don't I run these few guys out and come over. I'll stay with the girls until Cole gets home. I'm sure he'll be along soon. Don't worry. I'll be there within ten minutes after you're gone."

"Katie and I had a big fight, and there's no time to straighten things out."

"Don't worry, Jess. It'll be okay, you'll see."

Katie sleeps with Sky curled like a cat into the small of her back, and he hopes that Curtis Dobbs is a man of his word.

He turns the key in the deadbolt and shakes the handle. Standing on the top step, he looks across the front yard flooded in bright moonlight and decides that Marlene may have had a few beers with the customers, but she works sober. He puts the key where she knows to look and walks off the porch, gets into his truck, and drives out of the yard. He glances back one last time before turning onto the highway and speeding toward work.

There's no time to call home before starting his shift. The night super stood next to the time clock and frowned as he clocked in with only three minutes to spare. He takes his work orders and mounts his machine, and he'll need to wait until his first break to call home.

He counts the rings, and after ten, he finally gives up. He glances at his watch. It's one-thirty, and even if Cole hadn't made it home, Marlene would have stayed. If that boy isn't in trouble, he's going to wring his neck when he sees him next.

The super comes from the night office onto the warehouse floor and yells, "McKnight, you got an emergency call."

He breaks into a full sprint, and the super takes her time reminding him that the work crew gets two emergencies a year put through to the back, and she's making note.

"Dad, I said I'm sorry. James didn't have a spare. I ran a mile to the all-night diner and used their phone, but you'd already gone. I called Miss Susan and she stayed with the girls while Miss Dee came to pick up James and me."

"Goddamnit, Cole. You scared the shit out me. Why didn't you answer the damn phone? It rang ten times."

"I know. But by the time I woke up enough, I didn't make it. I knew you were going crazy, so I called right back."

"Are the girls okay? Were they scared? What happened to Marlene?"

"Did you know Sky walks in her sleep?"

"Hell no, what happened?"

"Nothing bad. She's got a lump on her head. Katie said she ran into the wall. Miss Susan gave her an ice pack for Sky. But she didn't do all that screaming. Cried, but not all that much."

"Jesus God. Where was Marlene during all this?"

"Some drunk put up a fight about closing. A couple of regulars had to kick his ass out. But she got here soon after Miss Susan. Everyone's gone now." He pauses, and Jesse hears a deep sigh. "Sorry for all the trouble, but I don't know what else I could've done. We broke up in plenty of time, but then everything blew up."

"Okay, but don't you dare let those girls out of your sight. You hear me?"

"If it'll make you feel better, I'll sleep on the floor next to their bed."

"No, that's not necessary. I'll see you in the morning."

He hangs up thinking that, if Cole had put his sisters before Sarah, the evening might have gone differently. Then, blaming Cole for the misery he feels would be easy, but he's had enough of finger-pointing for one night.

It's seven-thirty and his relief man hasn't shown, and the day super asks him if he wants overtime. He's so sleep deprived he could puke, but he calls home, and Cole swears he'll get the girls ready for school and stay at the bus stop until they are aboard. He downs a cup of piss-poor vending machine coffee, takes his orders, and climbs back on the forklift.

TWENTY-THREE

Jesse works until noon, then punches out, and he's surprised when he steps into a much chillier day. An overnight rain moved in hard and fast, leaving in its wake a drop in temperature. He hopes Cole sent the girls off to school wearing jackets. If not, Trudy will find something warm for Sky, but he worries about Katie.

Dead at the wheel, he swerves onto the shoulder, jerking himself awake. Reaching home, he doesn't stop for food, but goes straight to bed. He pulls the covers over his head. Sleep comes first as pressure behind his eyes, and slowly he lifts weightlessly into white silence, unshackled from his exhaustion.

He's rousted from his deep sleep by Beau's barking and a sharp bang on the front door. He pulls on his jeans, grabs a flannel shirt, and walks barefoot to the front door, his boots in his hand. Through the peephole, he sees Buddy standing on the porch, his back to the door, looking across the yard, in the direction of the busted corral. He turns at the sound of the door.

"Hey, champ. Heard you work nights, sorry to get you up."

"What brings you out in the cold?" He braces for bad news about Cole.

"Ain't exactly about family, but we do need to talk. Don't think it'll keep."

"Come on in. I need coffee, how about you?" Jesse pulls on his boots, motions Buddy to a seat at the table, and starts a fresh pot. He takes a two-day old box of donuts from the cabinet, setting the box on the table between them, only to discover that it's empty.

"Guess I've got donut rats."

"Don't matter none. I'm off donuts. Wife's got me on rabbit nibbles and dry chicken. Then I slip off to Margie's every chance I get for real chicken. Hell fire, if you believe the TV, it's a God's wonder any of us southern boys live long enough to begat offspring." Buddy laughs too big not to have given some thought to his wife's warning.

They sit for a moment without talking, Buddy's habit of figuring an easy way to start the business end of his visit. But Jesse is too worried for lengthy politeness.

"If it isn't about Cole, then what?" By now Dodie's absence is old news.

"Hear tell you recently lost a horse." Buddy pauses and Jesse wonders what makes the mare his business.

"That's about the size of it, if you leave out the part about a bunch of us chasing her for better than two hundred hours." He isn't sure how he came up with the number, but his sore ass would argue for something higher.

"It just might be that she's running too close to the highway. That'd make her a public nuisance." He looks down at the cup and then back.

"Never tracked her nowhere near a highway. Don't believe she'd run that close to humans." If Buddy wants to play sheriff, let him put a stop to that wild bunch chasing her on ATVs. Then, the forest isn't Buddy's jurisdiction.

"Might be she's running out of good grazing, fresh water, or minerals. Something's made her chance moving closer in."

"Did those complainers happen to mention anything about a foal running with her?"

"No. Is there a foal in the picture?"

"Don't know for sure. It's just that the previous owner thought there might be."

"Uh huh, that could mean she's on the move. Nursing mamas need minerals she might not be getting."

"Never thought about that."

In his mind, the tick-tock, tick-tock of his mama's old clock hanging from the wall drives him faster toward the inevitable. He has less time than he'd thought to wait for a sentimental old cowboy who makes promises at the drop of a Stetson.

Buddy scrapes back his chair from the table, rests a booted ankle over his knee, and rubs the fine black leather with his blunt fingertips.

"I'm doing all I know to do. And so far it ain't amounted to much." Jesse pulls himself up straight and clears his throat. "It ain't exactly been easy, things being what they are. But a short while back, I met a Texas cowboy. He claimed to have a buddy who's something of an expert on mustangs. He offered to bring him here first chance he got and give me a hand."

Buddy stares into the cooling coffee, twisting the cup a few turns, and finally looks at Jesse. "It ain't that I don't appreciate you're fighting a prairie fire with gasoline. But now days, citizen complaints get put in the damn computer and not on scraps of paper I carry in my pocket. If some innocent person gets hurt, then I'm up to my ass in what I knew and when I knew it. And why the hell didn't I do something."

He stands, and Jesse walks him out to the cruiser. Buddy walks around the vehicle, kicking the front tire the way he might when buying a used car, rather than delivering a warning.

"Jess, a month's all I can stall on this complaint before I got to get some of my riding boys in there after that horse." He gets into the cruiser and drives away.

Buddy had stopped short of laying it out, but his narrowed gaze drove home his point. He means to send hired guns into the forest to run the mare down and shoot her, and maybe her foal, on sight.

Jesse hugs his arms tightly across his chest and shivers in a sudden wind. What he knows is that he has little chance of saving the mare outside of Curtis Dobbs's offer. He goes back into the house, takes the business card from his wallet, and punches in the number.

"Dobbs Quarter Horse Ranch," a woman answers, and Jesse remembers the story of Dobbs's wife dying young with cancer and wonders how much of Curtis's story was made up. Still, he asks to speak to Curtis.

"May I ask if you're a business associate of Mr. Dobbs?"

"No, not exactly. It's just that I met him. And he said I was to call."

"You'll need to speak with the ranch foreman if you're inquiring about employment."

"No, ma'am. It's not about a job," he laughs, put off that she thinks he's begging for work. "I sure ain't looking to move to Texas." He's got an ear for disrespect, and he finds it hard accepting that the friendly old cowboy he met in Hardee's would want her speaking for him.

There's a long pause, and it's clear he's pissed her off. "Your name, please, and a number where you may be reached."

He tells her, and it's the first answer she doesn't respond to with another question.

"Mr. McKnight, Mr. Dobbs is due back from Nevada on Friday. I'll be happy to give him your message, and perhaps he will want to call you."

He thanks her and hangs up the phone. He studies the card and realizes that he'd missed "owner" printed after Curtis's name. It would seem that Curtis Dobbs isn't just some aging, road-weary cowboy who enjoys making up wild stories to entertain desperate strangers. At least the part about being a real cowboy and knowing about horses is true. The card states that he breeds and trains top quality quarter horses.

Jesse stares at the floor between his work boots, and his creeping doubt grows to the size of a water tower lodged under his ribs, making it harder to breathe. He can't imagine why Curtis Dobbs would take the time and expense to haul his ass back to Florida to help a near-perfect stranger run down a mustang. If he ever hears from the man, it will be because he does care about the fate of a crazed mustang mare or that his dead wife's name really was Katherine.

SATURDAY MORNING, AND JESSE has two days he can use to repair the corral. He drives toward home with a plan for stopping off at FRM and ordering corral boards with the last of his line of credit.

He swears and bangs on the steering wheel, swinging the truck around at the next divide. It's the Saturday he agreed to work in exchange for the two pups. He stops and calls Miss Mary, and sure enough, she expects him and doesn't seem one bit inclined to put the work off until some other Saturday. He reassures her that he'll be over as soon as he can pick up a few supplies and his helper.

He stops by the FRM, and instead of ordering corral boards, he charges a new chain for his saw, a gallon of chain oil, a spark plug, and a heavier rope than the frayed one he owns.

Reaching home, he goes into the kitchen where Cole's sitting at the table eating cold butter on white bread.

"We're out of breakfast food and down to the last roll of toilet paper."

"Yep, I know." Last week he'd swiped a roll from work. "What you got planned for the day?"

"Same old, same old. Why?" He stuffs the loaded bread in his mouth.

"I really could use your help." He explains that he's agreed to work out the price of two Corgi pups and that the owner expects him today.

"Two pups? What do we need with three dogs? Beau rules this house."

"Yeah, well, one's for Sky, and she actually talked to it." He hesitates to tell Cole about the second pup. But he'll know soon enough.

"The other's for Miss Marlene. You know, for all the help. You and me, with the girls."

"Yeah, Katie told me what happened to poor Sylvester. A dog hunts or he dies. Is that the Clyde Parrish Rule?" Cole's voice takes on a hard edge.

"Clyde was wrong, trying to make that little pup into something he wasn't suited to." Jesse hears a bigger truth in his concern, and the look of surprise that crosses Cole's face means he has as well. "Marlene was happy having that pup hang out at the bar with her."

"You're damn right, I want to help earn Miss Marlene a pup. One he has no say about."

Jesse slaps Cole on the shoulder. "All right, let's get rid of the midgets and get to work."

They drop the girls next door, and when he tells Dee and Susan about meeting Curtis Dobbs, Susan claps her hands, but Dee rolls her eyes in a way he takes to mean suckered.

By five o'clock, he and Cole have trimmed the three large oak limbs that extended over the roof and lowered them to the ground with the new rope and a pulley. He sawed the limbs into fireplace lengths while Cole stacked them in the woodshed to season. Cole rakes the trash and loads it in the bed of the truck while Jesse gathers the tools and rolls the rope.

Miss Mary comes out with two large cups of hot cocoa and some freshly baked oatmeal raisin cookies with take-home packages for Katie and Sky. Jesse explains that he will return with a log splitter to finish the job, and they take their leave.

Jesse looks over at Cole, and he's brushing loose sawdust from his pants. "Oak gum sticks sawdust to your clothes like glue."

Cole shrugs. "They're old. Besides, I like the smell of the wood." He sounds surprised and even pleased.

"We did a good day's work, and she seemed satisfied."

"I'll come back if you want more help."

"You bet I'll need your help. You're a damn good worker."

Cole reaches over and flips the radio dial to the station that can make Jesse cringe, but he doesn't complain. For the first time in a long time, being with Cole feels easy.

"How'd you do on that big paper? About presidents, right?"

At first Cole looks surprised, but then he smiles. "The paper was a comparison of the use of executive power by the last five presidents."

Jesse tries to remember the last five presidents, in any order.

"It was good enough that my AP teacher wants me to enter it in a state contest. But that would mean I'd go up against Sarah."

"If she's the girl you say, I bet she'd be okay with that." Maybe it's not Sarah, but Cole, who doesn't want to invite the competition.

They pick up the girls, and there's a big pot of hot chili and baked potatoes wrapped in aluminum foil to take home for supper. Susan declares chili is a meal best cooked by the gallon.

Cole passes his bowl for the third time, and Katie frowns.

"Pig, leave some for Beau. He's out of dog food." She glares at Jesse and he raises his hands, declaring guilty as charged.

"Back off. Who knows when we'll get another chance at a good meal?"

"Next week at Grandma's, that's when."

Cole looks at Katie and then at Jesse. "Tell me she's talking out her ass."

"I'm not. I'm talking Mama's coming back and us going to Grandma's for Thanksgiving. If you ever stayed around, you'd know."

"Nobody asked me."

"So," Katie shrugs. "You're not the boss. Daddy is." She sits forward in her chair, spoiling for a fight.

Cole glares across the table at Jesse. "Is she right? Did you agree? And just when did you plan on asking me what I wanted?" He snorts through his nose. "Sure as hell you weren't invited."

"It's something your mom mentioned when she was here before." He feels the weight of one step forward and two steps back with Cole.

"Great. Then silence is consent, right?"

"I was caught off-guard. And yeah, I'm guessing she took it that way."

Cole stands so abruptly, his chair slams back onto the floor. "Screw that, I'm not going a step. I'm not those two. I get a say in where I spend Thanksgiving." He stomps out of the kitchen to the sound of Sky's screams and Beau's frantic barking.

Katie gives Jesse that "what did I do" look, and he thinks about cutting her tongue out. Explosion in this house is always one spark away, and Katie's never without a dry match.

"Get the hell off of that chair and do something with your sister. You started this mess."

"But I didn't know it was a secret."

"Maybe not, but things just might run a bit smoother around here if you'd learn to keep your mouth shut."

"All right, then you deal with Sky." She calls Beau and the two run from the kitchen onto the porch. The only good in their angry exchange is Sky's decision to stop screaming and to chase after Katie and Beau.

His impulse is to risk a call to Dodie and try negotiating a different plan for Cole, but he doesn't want to piss her off. His sense is that her pending visit is about a great deal more than the traditional Thanksgiving dinner at Cora's. He stares at the messy table he's left to clear away, and wishes that just once everyone could leave the table full and happy.

TWENTY-FOUR

Jesse steps off the back porch, a steaming cup of coffee in his hand, thinking Thanksgiving is early for a morning this cold. He walks in the direction of the corral, a crystal layer of dew crunching under his boots. The first light of day reflects off the thin layer of ice atop the worn path, and he imagines he might see his reflection. Across the way, a male cardinal perches on a bare branch of the red maple he planted the day he, Dodie and Cole moved into this house, and the bird's brilliant color flashes in the sunlight like a tree ornament.

He pulls his wool-lined denim jacket closed and walks on toward the shabby outbuilding he intends to weatherproof. Stretching his already over-extended credit on the strength of the extra cash he'll have from holiday overtime he agreed to work, he's ordered sixteen-foot corral boards, posts, and sheets of galvanized tin. He intends to have the corral rebuilt and a new roof on the shed, standing ready should he hear from Curtis Dobbs. If he ever gets his hands on the mare, he intends to hold her.

Dodie wants the girls delivered by ten for the clan's gathering, so he'll drive them over before starting the repairs. Squeezing a few bucks out of living expenses, he managed to buy Katie and Sky new jackets that cover their wrists. In spite of his years of bitching about going to Cora's for holiday meals, he'll miss her bountiful table, and the pride he'd felt sitting next to the prettiest woman at the table. Then he won't miss the Simon-says criticisms passed behind cupped hands by Dodie's disapproving kin, highlighting his many failures to live up to his youthful hype.

He returns to the house and prepares a breakfast of hot oatmeal and cheese toast and has it ready when the girls come into the kitchen. They take seats at the table and he asks about Cole.

Katie shrugs, declaring it not her job to know the whereabouts of her brother. She pulls the brown crust off the edges of the toast, laying it to the side while Sky picks the raisins out of her oatmeal and crushes them between her finger and thumb like plump ticks.

Instead of challenging Katie's insolence or Sky's gross game, he stands at the sink, watching through the kitchen window as patches of ice melt in the creeping path of the sun's warmth.

Cole came home late again last night, violating the midnight curfew set as a condition of his probation. Whenever he's cautioned him on the likelihood of trouble, Cole has dismissed his warnings as hand-wringing while claiming that his probation officer is a pale ghost hiding in his tiny office with a bottle hidden in his file cabinet. He asked if that meant the man's a drunk and a derelict. Cole sneered and said, "Sure enough, Dad, but you've missed the fact that he's paid to watch losers. No one cares how he does his job. But if it makes you feel better, I show up for my sessions on time, and I feed him the bullshit he files in a report no one reads. He's done and I'm out of there, leaving the freak to booze and jerk off."

Cole staggers into the kitchen, a sleep-deprived roughness about him that Jesse knows all too well. He cups a hand over his right eye and grimaces, nursing a big league shiner, the likes of which Jesse hasn't seen since viewing his own teenage reflection.

"That's a good one, but Halloween was weeks ago." He means to low-ball the bruise until he knows more.

"Call it punctuation to a simple misunderstanding." Cole's pained expression is edged in a glimmer of boyish pride.

"What does the other guy look like?"

"Surprised?" Katie giggles, a string of yellow cheese hanging from her mouth.

"Shut up, piss ant." Cole takes two pieces of toast from the pan on the stove and sits.

"For once could you just stow it? I want to hear the original tale."

"When Mom sees that, she'll go bat-shit crazy." Katie covers her mouth.

"Damn, girl, watch your mouth." Jesse remembers having had his mouth washed with harsh soap for far less.

Cole dips bits of dry toast into his oatmeal and sucks on the crusted bread.

"It hurts that bad to chew?"

"Forget it. It's just high school shit. It'll blow over."

Katie cuts her eyes over at him, waiting for equal treatment under the rule of no swearing at the table.

"Okay, I'll buy that, but oblige me. I love a good story."

"I got into it a bit with Keith. Too much to drink and he can get crazy." Cole looks away from Jesse's steady gaze.

"You got the shiner stepping between those two?"

Cole nods.

"That dickhead Keith is mean." Katie screws up her face and jabs her spoon in the air like a weapon. Beau charges from beneath the table, barking in the direction of the back door.

"Jesus Katie, get up and go get dressed. Take Sky and that damn crazy dog with you." At this point, his mama would have used a bar of soap. When he doesn't relent, Katie spins and stomps down the hallway on bruised heels. Sky and Beau follow.

"You're right to stand up for the girl. But …." Frustrated, he shouts, "Damn it, Cole, lose the attitude."

Cole looks back at him, and this time he doesn't show a trace of disrespect, only bewilderment.

"Sarah, Dad. Why can't you say her name? Her name is Sarah, and she's my best friend."

Jesse thought Cole would have said James was his best friend. It's clear Sarah has become something more. The stakes are higher than he'd imagined.

"All right, fair enough, but if you keep stepping between Sarah and that thug, you're going to be called to do something that'll head you back to court. And I guarantee there'll be no get-out-of-jail-free pass."

"You don't get it, do you?"

"I do, but it's not your fight unless Sarah breaks it off with this guy."

"And you're hardly one to give advice on relationships." The weariness in Cole's voice means nothing is settled, but Jesse has lost confidence in issuing warnings. He remembers how he felt about Dodie at sixteen, and there would have been no backing down had his enemies arrived in Sherman tanks. That realization scares him the most for Cole.

"You're right, I've made more than my share of mistakes, but that doesn't mean I didn't learn a little along the way."

"But that doesn't change anything."

"No, I guess not."

Cole walks to the sink and dumps the oatmeal, tossing the toast in the trash.

"You should've said something earlier about that eye. I know a thing or two that could have kept the swelling down."

"Oh, yeah, I saw those old westerns too, but I don't think hotdogs work the same as T-bones."

"Maybe not. Do you still plan on staying away from your Grandma's today?"

"I don't know. I'm just not sure. But, if you don't mind, I'd like to use the phone." Cole touches his eye, and Jesse wishes that fixing his son's hurts could be easy like when he was a child.

Jesse nods, stands, and walks toward the sound of the girls' giggles, intending to hurry them along. And although he has plans, he feels a cold lump of loneliness growing in his chest at the prospect of spending the day without the kids. He imagines many such days ahead.

JESSE STOPS THE TRUCK behind a line of late model SUVs and pickups parked along the tree-lined street. He's relieved that the overflow of men gathered on the front porch doesn't, or pretends not to, notice their arrival. The ache he felt earlier returns, and he wants the kids to hurry out of the truck so he can leave.

Yet Katie lingers, and in a rare gesture, she slips her hand into Cole's, and they, along with Sky, stand on the sidewalk staring in the direction of the manicured front lawn where a five-foot tall inflated turkey squats among a pile of pumpkins.

"Damned if Grandma didn't flip the pumpkin wagon." Cole's nervous laugh squirts forth like an unexpected fart. He touches his trophy eye, takes a deep breath, and the three walk on.

"Eat some pumpkin pie for me," Jesse calls though the open window as he drives away.

He glances back, watching through the rear-view mirror as Dodie approaches the kids. She's wearing a red sweater he doesn't remember and dark slacks. He's always liked her in red, and he thinks he could learn to like her short hair. But he's sure he isn't ready to be adrift; a man alone with no place special to be.

He drives into the yard and Beau's raising hell. He hears the phone and rushes into the house.

"Hey, Jesse. Curtis here. Me and my man plan on being down your way late Sunday if that suits you."

"Lord yeah, that's mighty fine." He doesn't bother explaining that Buddy's visit has bumped up the urgency to recapture the mare.

"Going to need a suitable place to stable two spoiled geldings. Can you arrange for that?"

"You bet. And you and your man are welcome to bunk here. It ain't a Holiday Inn, but the roof don't leak."

"Appreciate it, but space to park the RV is all I'll need on that score. I'll call you for directions to your place off of I-10 when I get close." Curtis hangs up before Jesse can thank him.

Hauling a double horse trailer and driving an RV can't be cheap, but right now he can't worry about that. Maybe Clyde can advance him a few hundred more if he hasn't already gone to the well too many times.

He goes to work on the corral with renewed hope and stays with the job, except for a short break for a pb & j, until time to clean up and go for the kids.

He pulls the truck to a stop at Cora's, and right away he spots Katie and Sky occupying the porch swing, but he doesn't see Cole hanging with the older cousins.

Katie looks up and waves, dragging the toes of her shoes along the floorboards, slowing the swing. She runs into the house and returns with Dodie in tow, but still there's no Cole.

He gets out of the truck and stands on the sidewalk, bracing for whatever it is that Dodie may want from him. Cora comes onto the porch and gives him a half-hearted wave that he returns in kind.

"Hey, Jess. Thanks for sharing the kids." Dodie even smiles, but it isn't one that reaches her eyes. "Can you meet me tomorrow morning about some business?" Her words are rushed, and she tugs at the hem of her sweater.

"What kind of business?"

"I'd rather not say just now." She glances at the girls and then back at him. "Please just agree to meet me at Stuart Brown's at nine tomorrow morning. And I'd like for the girls to stay overnight. Mom will keep them while we're at Stuart's."

The name Stuart Brown hits him like a felled tree, but not nearly as hard as her request that the girls stay overnight. He's inclined to give her nothing of what she wants. Yet it can't be smart to piss her off the day before they're going before her lawyer to argue the terms of their divorce. He'll need all the goodwill that still remains between them.

"Jesse, please. I swear this isn't an ambush."

He looks at Katie, standing next to Dodie, and she shrugs, maybe meaning to spare his feelings. Sky slips a hand into her sister's, and he reads nothing in her face. Against his better judgment, he consents.

"Is Cole staying over?" Again, he searches among those gathered on the lawn, who are now stealing glances in their direction.

"No, Cole isn't here. He got a call soon after you dropped the kids. A little later, James arrived. They talked and then drove away. Cole didn't say why, only that he had to go. "

"Do you know Sarah's last name?"

"Longley. Sarah Longley."

"The high school principal Longley?"

"Yes, she's the youngest of his four daughters." Dodie sighs, but he doesn't catch her meaning, unless it's the thought of having four daughters.

Pat Spears

He drives away, and Cole's earlier problems with the principal begin to make sense. If a teenage Katie or Sky's choice of best friends included a jailbird with a brain and a ready-to-kick-ass sidekick with a doping mama, he'd worry. He understands Longley's hand-wringing, but his tactics were wrong. He thinks about calling Longley, but if Sarah and James came for Cole, maybe they're working things out. Getting Longley involved sounds like trouble for all three kids. He'll need to trust Cole.

The thought of facing Dodie across the table at Stuart Brown's looms larger and larger, and Jesse thinks about calling Marlene, talking the situation over with her. Then he gets what he hopes is a better idea.

STOPPING AT A PAY PHONE, Jesse searches among the piles of mail on the dash and retrieves the number. He makes the call and asks Miss Mary if she'll agree to release one pup and hold the other until he's finished the work. He tells her that today is his friend's birthday. He feels bad lying to her, and even worse that he doesn't actually know Marlene's birthday. He explains that, even though he hadn't picked a pup, he wants the sweetest boy in the litter.

"Young man, I want to believe you're the good man you appear to be, but it's just bad business. And I don't do bad business."

"I know it's a lot to ask, but you can trust me."

There is a long pause. "All right, but if you renege, I'm coming for that pup."

She explains that she has a house full of company, and that he's to come no earlier than seven. He hates the four hour delay, but reassures her that she has nothing to worry about, and that he'll be prompt.

He returns home, and after he dumps dirty clothes from the laundry basket, he grabs one of his old flannel shirts. Satisfied that the basket will work fine as a temporary bed for the pup, he changes back into his work clothes and resumes his repairs on the corral. He has only until Sunday to finish preparing for Curtis's arrival.

He walks Beau to the mailbox and waits while the dog chases an imaginary critter along the fence row before returning. He refills Beau's bowls, turns on ESPN for company, and explains that he's on a special mission.

Miss Mary meets him at the door, still wearing a doubtful look, and for a moment, he worries that she's changed her mind. But she hands him a tri-colored male with markings much like Star's. He cuddles the pup close and sweet talks it, and she looks only a bit relieved.

"Here, take this blanket, it's got the mother's scent, and this is his favorite toy. Don't wash them until he's settled into his new home." She hands him a plastic bag containing dog food with feeding instructions attached.

"I thank you. And don't worry. This pup's going to a mighty sweet lady. It'll have a good life. I'll bring him back by from time to time so you can see how good he's doing."

SILENCE SURROUNDS THE BAR's deserted parking lot, and he's sure the regulars spent the day perched atop deer stands deep in the woods, sipping whiskey from flat, half-pint bottles, waiting with high powered rifles for some sex-crazed buck to wander into view. As he expected, Old Blue, Clyde's special rigged van, isn't parked in its spot. Then, he's known all along that Clyde would never miss Thanksgiving in the woods with his dogs.

He leaves the truck halfway between the bar and the cabin, as if his presence is a split decision. He tucks the basket under one arm, looks toward the soft light pouring from the cabin's windows like a friendly jack-o-lantern. The cold air stings his face, and the spicy smell of charred oak rises from the stone chimney of the cabin. Shoving his free hand deep inside his jacket pocket, he hurries toward the porch. Marlene opens the front door wearing a heavy coat.

"Hope I didn't scare you."

She doesn't seem scared, just surprised. He stands watching her through the screen, and he can't remember ever needing more from a woman, and it's a need he can't even name.

"No, I was expecting a customer who wanted a little something extra to help them make it through a cold night." She invites him in, explaining that Clyde's out with his dogs, and when she asks, he tells her the girls are staying overnight with their mom.

"What do you have in the basket?"

He pulls back the shirt, and the pup stands on its hind legs with its front paws resting on the side of the basket. He looks up at Marlene and whimpers. The apprehension Jesse sensed at his unexpected arrival seems to vanish at the sight of the pup.

"Oh my God, he's beautiful."

"Found him wandering alone back of the warehouse and thought you might agree to give him a home."

"Hush, he's no stray."

She takes the pup in her arms and it licks her chin, its tiny pink tongue like a rose petal. Marlene laughs softly and rubs her face into his soft folds, her eyes shining like Christmas morning.

They sit on the floor, and he watches the beginning of a special love affair between Marlene and the pup. She puts him down, and he gets so excited he puddles. Handing him to Jesse, she gets paper towel from the kitchen and cleans the floor.

She invites him to help himself to a drink while she takes the pup outside for more serious business. When she returns, she retrieves a dog crate from storage and a tick-tock clock from a shelf over the kitchen stove. She fills a water bottle with warm water and wraps both the clock and bottle with the scented blanket. The pup sniffs the blanket, cuddles next to its warmth, and closes its eyes.

While she settles the pup, Jesse steps to the fireplace and tosses more oak wood on the fire, its orange sparks spit and crackle up the chimney. He stares into the flames, thinking how wrong it is for him to be here with Marlene, and how grateful he is that Clyde chose this night to leave her alone.

She comes from the kitchen, a bourbon in her hand, and takes a seat on the couch, inviting him to join her. The complications of doing so stop him for only a moment. They sit quietly, their shoulders touching, and he watches the flames curl and sway in a hypnotic dance, wrapping him in their warmth. He inhales deeply, wishing to let go of everything but the good in the moment, but his relief is fleeting.

"You've gotten awfully quiet. Are you okay?"

"I'm meeting Dodie at her attorney's in the morning. And I'm scared of losing my kids again."

She sits quietly before saying, "I know that fear." Her eyes grow darker, and he wonders if she speaks from a loss of her own.

"Don't moms always get their kids?"

"No, not always. But most often, unless there are reasons to challenge her fitness."

"That's what I'm afraid of."

She doesn't look at him, and he worries she's considering other possibilities he doesn't even know to fear. With all the bad decisions he's made, he wonders how a judge could possibly trust him to take care of his kids alone. "Truth is, I mess up more than I don't."

"None of us ever get parenting perfect. But remember that Judge White saw a reason to trust you. And you're doing a good job."

"Do you think my leaving the girls alone at night will work against me with a judge?"

"They aren't alone, they're with Cole. But if it eases your mind, I'll stay overnight with the kids until the terms of the divorce are settled."

"What about Clyde?" He sits upright, putting more space between them.

"It isn't his decision." A deep shadow crosses her face. "He's fine nights without me."

"I just thought …." He pauses. "What I mean is, I don't want to make trouble between you and Clyde. Or between me and Clyde."

"I understand you may be confused. And about you and Clyde," she takes a deep breath, "that stays between the two of you."

A veil of caution settles between them, and yet love presses upon him so gently he doesn't know when it came.

She puts together a leftover Thanksgiving meal for him, setting a thermos of hot coffee next to the bag, and he thanks her. The food will get him through the night, and the coffee will help keep him awake on the drive.

He steps off the porch into the yard and turns back, remembering his earlier question.

"October fifth, but why?" He notes a pleasing lilt in her voice.

"Sorry we're late, but happy birthday from me and the kids."

As he crosses the clay parking lot, the motion sensor captures him and the security light hums and flashes, spotlighting him in what he thinks of as a bright circle of guilt.

"Hey there, Little Brother. What you up to?"

Jesse swings about, his pulse racing, and he peers into the darkness beyond the circle of light. Then he doesn't need to see. Clyde's slurred voice comes at him like a sniper's bullet; true and deadly.

"Damn, don't you ever stay home? How's a man to catch up to you? Ain't about to stomp through a snake-infested swamp looking to find your sorry ass."

"Like the song goes, Little Brother: If I'd known you were coming …." Clyde's laugh sounds forced.

"Waited for you … there, with Marlene, but now I'm running late. Gotta get to the job."

"Is that right?" The cold silence of the clearing echoes what Jesse hears as Clyde's unspoken accusation.

"And you'd best get your sorry ass in out of the cold before it freezes."

"I think I just might."

Jesse lowers his head and walks into a stiff wind blowing out of the north. How long did Clyde sit in his van, and why didn't he come inside?

TWENTY-FIVE

Jesse drives home after his shift in a worried fog, his eyes stinging as if road gravel has collected under his heavy eyelids. He pulls the truck to a stop in the yard, and right away he notices tread marks. The hair on the back of his neck bristles like a wary, junkyard cur and he hurries out of the truck.

He walks onto the porch, littered with beer cans and paper trash from Hardee's. Shattered glass from the overhead light bulb grinds beneath his boots, and electrical wiring hangs from the ceiling socket. The door lock has been jimmied, but the deadbolt remains solid.

He inserts his key and unlocks the door, but something heavy is wedged against it from the inside. He bangs on the door with his fist, shouting for Cole, and when there's no answer, he rams his shoulder against the door several times with the same result. The only response is Beau barking and jumping against the door from the inside. He turns away, intending to check the back door, when he hears footsteps from inside.

The door opens, and Cole stands in the doorway, a baseball bat in his hand. "Thank God it's you."

"Are you okay? What the hell happened here?" Jesse hopes that something like a late night party is to blame, but he doesn't really expect that from Cole, who looks like he's pulled a week of graveyards. He follows his son into the kitchen. Cole drops onto the nearest chair, his head bowed, and he repeatedly runs his fingers through his hair.

"I asked you a question." Jesse circles the table as though he has taken up Beau's nervous habit.

"You're not going to like the answer."

"Shit, boy, I already don't like it." He takes a seat at the table, the suspense treading on his last nerve.

"Keith thought it would be macho to pay me a visit. He and three of his drinking buddies started in about one and hung around until nearly three."

"Why? What happened to cause you to leave your grandma's?"

"Dad, please. I can't talk about that now."

"Jesus God, Son. Where does all this end up?"

"I don't know. It's not up to me."

"Not up to you? You can stop any time you want." He says this, but the hurt look in Cole's eyes tells him he's wrong. "Okay, but why didn't you call me? Call Buddy?"

"I tried calling James, but I think they cut the land line."

Jesse gets out of the chair, puts on a pot of coffee, and stands at the counter, watching the muddy liquid drip into the pot.

"You know you really need to drink less coffee."

"Yeah, I know, but it's a damn sight better than whiskey, don't you think?"

Cole nods.

"I'm guessing from the fact you're in one piece and the house is still standing that they never made it through the door."

"They tried forcing the locks, and when that didn't work, they backed off, settled on yelling threats and calling me out."

"Did you get a look at who was with him?"

"I know what you're thinking. But getting Sheriff Buddy in on this will only make matters worse for Sarah. Keith was drunk, pumped, showing off for his new girlfriend."

"I thought Sarah was his girlfriend."

"Not any more. She broke up with him."

Jesse tries hard to remember what he would have wanted when he was Cole's age. He understands that his son's pride takes a big hit if he calls in Buddy. "Okay, for now. But what's it going to take to back this asshole off?"

Cole shakes his head. "I don't know, he's all about balls and fists."

When he can't come up with anything worth saying, Jesse tells Cole about his scheduled meeting with Dodie at Stuart Brown's office.

"Why does she need a lawyer? What's to hassle over? She dumped us kids and this house is trash." Cole pushes up out of the chair and goes onto the front porch and starts gathering beer cans.

Jesse decides to forget breakfast and use the time to clean up. He'll wear his good slacks, thinking that he's worn them for two funerals, an appearance before a judge and now to a divorce lawyer's. If his luck doesn't change soon, those pants are going to wear thin.

THE CLOCK ON THE WALL at Hardee's reads eight-forty, and Jesse brushes biscuit crumbs from his shirt, wondering why he doesn't notice food crumbs on jeans. He drives the two blocks to the lawyer's office and parks on the street behind Dodie's car. The ugly brown paint has flaked off in hunks, and the passenger door still hangs warped from the time she drove it into a parked UPS truck. At least the browns and the rust are a close match.

The woman behind the desk greets him, hands him bottled water, and directs him to an empty conference room where she informs him that Ms. McKnight and Mr. Brown will join him shortly. He takes a seat at the table, feeling alone, yet exposed, in the manner he thinks a zoo animal must.

The fake paneling and the drab carpet remind him of all the times he's stood accused while someone in authority waited to wield an ax. The rows of oversized books lining the shelves smell like moldy yellow cheese. Sweat stains circle his armpits, and he takes the handkerchief crammed in his pocket, one he'd last used at his daddy's funeral, and wipes his face. He drinks from the bottle the woman left and wipes the water ring off the table with his sleeve.

A side door opens and Dodie steps into the room, followed by Stuart Brown. She's wearing a cranberry colored suit with a pink blouse, and his breath catches, feeling her in the familiar way he'd thought he was past.

He stands and she greets him with strained politeness, suited for strangers. His anger flashes at what feels like her deliberate mockery of their past intimacy. Though he expects her to at least ask about Cole, she doesn't. Instead, she takes a quick seat across from him, crosses her legs and folds her hands in her lap. Her face is drawn, and there are dark circles under her eyes. He decides that she too hadn't had much sleep.

Stuart Brown extends his hand and it's child-like inside Jesse's large, calloused one, making him imagine he shakes hands with a pocket-sized charlatan.

Stuart Brown clears his throat. "Please, Mr. McKnight, won't you be seated?"

"And how 'bout you cut the phony formality? We ain't exactly strangers here." Jesse isn't proud, but he'd put Stuart Brown's arrogant face in the dirt a time or two in grammar school.

"No, we certainly are not." Brown sneers.

Jesse swallows hard and pushes back in the chair, hearing pay-back in Brown's tone for wrongs long harbored.

"Our business this morning will be brief. We will go over certain business matters and then deal with child custody issues regarding the welfare of the McKnight children."

The fact that Brown labels their kids as custody issues fuels the smoldering fire in Jesse's belly, and he only half-listens as Brown explains that his client recently sold her beauty enhancement business and that the proceeds from the sale of said business are not subject to any property settlement since said business was solely in her name.

While Stuart Brown attempts to cast the sale of a failed two-chair fantasy shop off as one of those corporate takeovers featured regularly on TV, Jesse contains his seething bile by picturing the comic valuing of inventory: hair spray, shampoo, hair perms, hair coloring gunk, clippers, straight razors and multiple-sized pink rollers. Brown doesn't disclose the selling price or terms of the agreement between Dodie and Sally, and Jesse hopes Sally had Dodie pinched between a rock and a hard place. His resentment pushes him to the satisfying thought of interrupting to tell Dodie about him and Sally. But he won't risk what little leverage he has with her.

"The house you currently occupy is another matter altogether." He clears his throat and glances at Dodie, who doesn't look at him but at her hands folded in her lap. "Said property is jointly-owned, and the two of you are to share equally in the proceeds from its sale." He looks at Jesse as if he should be grateful to have such a great legal mystery unraveled.

What Jesse hears means eviction for him and the kids because there's no way on God's green earth he can buy her share. He barely makes the mortgage payment, plus late fees that typically run forty-five days.

Brown hastens to add, "It's acknowledged that a quick sale in today's depressed market may prove difficult. Therefore, my client has expressed a willingness to negotiate a rental agreement." He continues, explaining something he calls fair rental assessment, and Jesse understands that she expects him to pay rent on her ownership share of the house, and that he owes three months of rent in arrears.

"It's taking it in the rear, all right." Jesse pushes back, coming to his feet, and he eyes the door.

"Surely you don't expect to continue living rent free. After all, my client has living expenses and educational expenses on a rather limited income."

"Finally, there's something we've got in common other than our soon-to-become-homeless kids."

"Please, Jesse, let's not make this any harder." Dodie reaches across the table, motioning for him to sit.

"I'm out of here unless you agree to divide the mortgage five ways. I'll pay one part for myself and half of three parts for the kids, and not one damn dime of rent." He rests on the balls of his feet, fully prepared to leave.

Brown turns to Dodie and whispers. She shakes her head to whatever he says.

Jesse leans on the table, the imprint of his sweaty palms showing on its polished surface.

"Very well, Ms. McKnight generously agrees to contribute half of three parts of the mortgage as child support and to forfeit any claims to her right to rent. Now, sir, will you please be seated so we may conclude our business here today?" Brown fidgets with the knot on his tie.

The fact that a shyster lawyer, brandishing a legal meat cleaver, has reshaped Dodie into a generous provider stuns Jesse. He considers the legal consequences of cold-cocking Brown.

Dodie reaches across the table but she doesn't actually touch him. "Please, Jesse. Let's settle this. You said yourself in Valdosta that our children need to know what to expect from us." She tears up, but in his anger, he doesn't trust her tears. She's earned whatever misery she feels. Still, he drops back into the chair.

Brown once again clears his throat and explains that Ms. McKnight acknowledges that he currently provides adequate care for the children, and due to their current enrollment in the public schools of this jurisdiction, coupled with her pursuit of a professional certificate, she agrees that the three children shall remain in his care until she has had sufficient time to complete her schooling and find suitable employment. Brown shuffles papers as though he imagines the deal final.

Jesse moves to the front of his chair and the lawyer leans back, creating greater space between them. He doesn't look at Brown but directly at Dodie.

"You want me and the kids to go on living the way we are until you decide otherwise?" He stares in disbelief, struggling to regain his balance.

"That is correct," Brown replies.

"Shut up, fool. I ain't talking to you. I want to hear it out of her mouth."

"McKnight, I speak for my client. I have prepared a child custodial agreement that requires your signature and then we're done here." He flips the papers around and pushes them across the table, holding out a pen to Jesse.

"I'll sign divorce papers right now, but not one damn thing that says I'll be in or out of my kid's lives all on her whim." He grabs the papers and slings them across the room. "I'll take my chances before a judge before I'll let her steal my kids."

Jesse hurries from the conference room and doesn't look back. He gets into the truck and speeds away, believing that he needs to beat Dodie back to Cora's. He'll get the girls before she can try some legal gimmick to stop him. He'll hide them before he'll allow her to take them.

IN A NEAR PANIC, JESSE DRIVES what seems the longest five miles he's ever traveled. When he's pulled the truck to a quick stop, he hurries along the walkway. Katie opens the door, smiling as though her parents haven't sat across the table from each other, bargaining her future.

Her smile quickly fades and she says, "Oh no, Daddy, is Cole back in detention?"

"No, baby, it isn't about Cole." The whole truth is far too complicated.

Katie continues to look doubtful but holds her question. Sky runs from the direction of the kitchen, and Jesse believes he sees a brief smile on her tiny face.

"Get your stuff, girls, we're going home."

"But Mama said we're to stay here until she gets back." Katie screws up her face so that the row of freckles across the bridge of her nose wrinkles. He doesn't think she means to argue, but that she's confused.

"Go ahead, baby, the plan's changed. I just left your mama."

Cora comes into the living room holding the phone, her fury lodged just beneath the surface of her restraint in the presence of the girls.

He doesn't want to talk to Dodie, but Katie stares at him, her bottom lip beginning to tremble. He takes the phone onto the porch, shielding his side of the conversation from both the girls and Cora. He's just left the worst combat zone of his life, and he knows he can't ever again trust Dodie.

"Oh Jess, thank God you're still there. I'm sorry Stuart made it all sound so cold. I never meant for it to go that way. I want more time with the girls before I leave."

"No way after what happened back there." His words are ground through his clenched teeth and his hands shake.

"Please, I swear you won't regret it. Put the girls in your truck and wait. I promise you can drive away after we talk if you still feel threatened."

"Know that I won't give up my kids. That day in Valdosta, I didn't know how I'd feel. Now I do. I'll fight you. And I'll fight you to win." He'll ask Dee for the lawyer help she'd offered for Cole.

"How was I to know you'd change? Even when you were home, I could never count on you."

"Then why was it that you left them with me?"

"Please, don't you see, the way I left, I couldn't take them with me."

There's a long agonizing pause, his heart pounding in his chest, and he's never before had so much at stake.

"Jess, I now know that you've had a change of heart."

For the first time in a very long time, he hears his name spoken the way she had when she still loved him. "But what does that mean for our kids?"

"It means I'm willing to rethink custody."

The promise of a better future with his kids is worth the risk. He agrees to wait. He goes back inside and tells Katie and Sky to stay inside with Cora, and that he's waiting to talk to their mom.

He takes a seat on the tailgate of his truck, struggling to control his gnawing fears. He's no match for Dodie. He can't remember the last time he won an argument with her. But what he wants, and what he's willing to do to have what he wants, is clear to him.

When he spots her car turning onto the street, he slides off the tailgate and stands watching her park the car and get out. She hurries to where he waits.

"Thank you for waiting. Would you like to go for coffee or something where we can talk away from the girls?"

"No, here is fine." He's unwilling to leave the girls alone with Cora.

"But first tell me about Cole. His black eye horrified me. I couldn't believe he'd get into a fight. Please tell me what you know. He refused to tell me anything before he left with James."

"It seems he got between Sarah and her ex-boyfriend. He was home this morning. We talked before I left."

"How serious is his involvement with Sarah?"

"If you're asking if it's sexual, I can't say."

"Oh, God, I so don't want him to make the same mistake we made."

"No, I don't either. But I think you know there's not much we can do. Our talking won't change anything they're thinking."

Tears fill her eyes, and he doesn't know if she cries for their loss or for what she fears for Cole. Both, he thinks, if she's feeling what he feels.

"Jess, I know how hard it is to be a single parent, and I understand what my absence has put you and the children through. But I think you also know that, no matter how much we want not to hurt our children, there's no going back for us."

"I do." He breathes deeply, and for the first time the truth between them leaves him feeling hopeful.

She studies his face and then smiles. It's the smile he once trusted.

"Please, Jess. Let the girls stay through lunch. They're safe here with me. Mom misses them. She'll bring them home after I've left for Valdosta."

"I think they'd like that. And I got work to do back at the house." He follows Dodie back into the house, and the girls run from the kitchen.

"Are you still mad? Are we staying with Mama?"

He turns to Dodie and she smiles.

"No, baby, and you can stay if you'd like."

"Okay, if you'll look after Beau."

"Only if I can get hugs before I go."

He stoops, and Katie smiles, rushing into his arms. Sky hangs back until he says, "Please, Sky. Your daddy needs a hug from you."

She joins Katie in the circle of his arms, and he's never before felt so good and so terrified in the same moment.

He goes back outside, gets into his truck, and pulls away. But not before returning the girls' waves as they stand perfectly framed in the big picture window. Then he knows better than to trust today's perfection. There's always tomorrow.

TWENTY-SIX

Approaching the lane, Jesse spots Keith's red Mustang pulling onto the highway and speeding away. He thinks about running the kid down and kicking his bully ass, but that would only serve to escalate the war between him and Cole.

Slowing the truck, he turns onto the lane and drives toward the house. Ahead, Beau is lying on the ground, and he doesn't offer to move out of the path of the truck. Jesse swears aloud and slams on brakes. He jumps from the idling truck and kneels on the ground next to the dog.

Beau raises his head slightly and whines. Sand matted in blood soaked fur covers his right shoulder. Jesse runs a slow hand under the injured shoulder, along his ribs and cups his hip, gently lifting. Beau's eyes are wild with pain, and he snaps at Jesse's hand.

He gently lays Beau back on the ground, removes his jacket, and spreads it over the trembling dog. From the direction of the house, he hears the sound of sand crunching beneath feet as Cole runs full speed toward him.

"Dad, what happened? Is he bad hurt?"

"Don't know. Run to the shed and bring back a piece of scrap plywood big enough for a stretcher. Get two belts and a blanket from the house, and hurry." Cole turns and runs back the way he came.

To calm his frayed nerves, he focuses on recalling Beau's age. The dog blinks up at him and closes his eyes. Jesse hopes it means he's saving his strength, readying to make a hard push at living.

Cole returns, and together they lift Beau onto the makeshift stretcher and wrap the blanket around the board, securing it with the two belts.

"We've got to hurry. Get him to Doc."

"Will he be there on a holiday weekend?"

Jesse places the board across Cole's knees, bracing it against the dashboard. He speeds onto the highway, and they drive the anxious miles at an illegal speed.

"I was right on top of whatever happened. Saw Keith batting it onto the highway. And we know Beau's too smart to run under the wheel of a moving car."

"Are you saying Keith did it on purpose?"

"I'm saying if he did, I'm kicking his ass straight into Hell. What did you see or hear?"

"I was doing trig homework when Beau started barking out front. He stopped, but when he didn't come back, I got worried. First thing I saw was you kneeling in the lane."

When they reach the parking lot, it's empty, and there are no lights in the office. Jesse swears and puts the truck into a quick turn, thinking to head for Tallahassee and the emergency animal hospital. He has less than thirty dollars in his pocket, and no check book, not that his meager balance can cover expensive treatment. He'll worry about that after he's found help for Beau.

"Dad, stop. I think that's Doc's old Chevy." Cole points toward the rear of the office.

Jesse drives to the rear entrance, parks and bangs on the back door.

Doc opens the door. "Jess, what in the world's wrong?"

"My little girl's dog is hurt. I think he's bad off."

Jesse takes the board off Cole's knees and follows Doc into the office.

"Well, it's a good thing for Beau that I've got a mighty sick old dog that needed checking on before I left for the game in Gainesville." Doc places Beau on a metal table and mutters something about a nasty tear. He runs his hand along Beau's back and hips, then walks to the phone on the wall and punches in a number. He talks in a low voice to someone and hangs up.

"Doc, has he got a chance?"

"Let me wait on that, boy. I don't know if anything's broken. Then I'm worried about a lung puncture. The X-ray tech's on her way, soon as she can find someone to watch her toddler. I'll treat the little guy for shock and clean those wounds. Rolled under a tire, I'd venture to say."

"I found him lying in the lane, down in a tire rut."

"That likely saved him. He didn't suffer a full rollover."

"Doc, my little girl …."

"Jess, you got a little money on you?"

"A precious little, but I'll get more. Do whatever it takes."

"Ain't about that. I just want you and this boy here to go spend some of what you've got. Leave this pup to me. I'll do what I can."

Jesse puts a hand on Cole's shoulder and together they walk out to the truck and drive to one of the local fast-food joints. When they've gotten drinks and taken seats, Cole says, "Is Beau going to make it?"

"You heard Doc. And I think he meant to prepare us for the worst."

"I know I'm to blame. If not for my mess with Keith, this never would have happened."

"No, you're not to blame. Keith is. But you've got to figure a way to let up on this thing."

"Yeah, I know. I'm trying."

Jesse stands. "Gonna get a refill. You want something more?"

Cole shakes his head.

Jesse sits back down and Cole glances at the clock on the wall.

"Before we go, I need to know how it went with you and Mom at the lawyer's."

"Real bad, but afterwards, your mom and I talked."

"And how'd that go?"

"Better, I think. She still wants the divorce. But I think she may have started to see some things differently."

"About us kids?"

"Could be." He wants Cole to share in his hope, but he's afraid of being wrong.

When they drive back to Doc's they note two cars that weren't there before. Jesse tries not to borrow trouble, deciding that, if there were other pets in trouble, their families would have parked in the back as well. Cole sits with his hands tightly pinched between his knees, and together they breathe the same anxious air.

The back door opens and a young woman comes out but doesn't look their way. She gets into one of the cars and drives away. Jesse guesses that whatever she came to do is done.

He recognizes the elderly woman being helped to the second car as his high school English teacher. One of Doc's helpers follows, carrying a large, black plastic bag. The two women are crying, and Jesse would have never figured hard-ass Miss Jameson as the type to cry over the loss of an animal.

Jesse and Cole cross the parking lot to the door, and Jesse remembers Katie having said the day they visited Miss Mary's Corgi pups that Beau was everything she ever needed in a dog. Doc comes to the door, and without a word, he and Cole follow him through the back hallway. Beau is lying on the same table with tubes connecting him to plastic bags hanging from a metal stand.

"He's one more tough little son-of-a-bitch." Doc, a Baptist deacon, and a man Jesse has never heard swear, grins broadly, seeming to never tire of his standing joke. Then Doc's tone turns serious, and he explains that, as he suspected, the muscle tissue across Beau's shoulder is badly torn. The good news is that, although the x-rays showed three fractured ribs, he was spared a lung puncture. Doc has stitched him up, leaving an opening for the wound to drain, and is giving him antibiotics and pain medication to get him through the roughest part.

"I need you to understand that this pup's not out of the briar patch. Then if his heart holds out, he may just get lucky, and those wounds will drain and heal. Come morning, I'll know more."

"What do I tell Katie?" His voice breaks. "She's been through a lot already."

Doc chews on his smokeless pipe and studies Beau. "If she's as tough as this little mutt, then you may want to tell her the truth."

"And exactly what would that be, Doc?"

"He's hurt bad, but he's got a fighting chance."

"Doc, I know you're in a hurry to leave town, but could you wait long enough for me to go get Katie, bring her here to see for herself?"

"I plan on staying here until I know which way he's going. So go on, bring her here."

Jesse goes to the front office and calls Marlene. She answers and there's music in the background; not the kind on the jukebox but classical, he thinks.

"Marlene, can you come help me with Katie?"

"Katie? What's happened?"

"It's Beau." He explains and she doesn't interrupt.

"Where do I come?"

"Not to Cora's, I don't think. Just come straight to Doc's. I hate to ask, but can you plan on staying the night? I don't know how Katie and Sky are going to handle this, and I need the overtime."

She doesn't hesitate, and when he hangs up the phone, he drops into an office chair, fighting back his dread.

He and Cole drive to Cora's, and when he tells Katie that Beau had an accident and that he's at Doc's getting patched up, she runs out of the house without another word. Cora hurries Sky into her jacket and hands Katie's to Cole. The four of them crowd into the truck and Katie sits on the edge of the seat, staring straight ahead. She doesn't ask a single question, and she doesn't cry. He drives to Doc's as fast as he dares.

Doc opens the door and Katie looks up at him. He puts an arm around her shoulders.

"Little darling, I know your daddy's told you that Beau's mighty sick. Seeing him might be a bit scary. He's got tubes and needles, but those don't hurt him. It's a way of giving him medicine. Medicine he needs to feel better."

"Can I see him now? I promise not to cry."

"Sure you can. And crying's all right."

Katie slips her hand into Doc's and they walk along the hallway.

Jesse has waited for Sky to decide to get out of the truck. When she does, he offers her his hand and she takes hold. They follow Doc and Katie.

Doc pulls a tall stool up to the gleaming table and Katie scrambles up. She looks at Beau, softly calling his name. Tears form in the corners of her eyes, and she brushes them away.

"Beau, please, you can't leave me too." She gently rubs him between his ears, and he opens his drug-clouded eyes and blinks.

Jesse stands next to Katie, his arm around her shoulders, and she leans her head into his chest.

The bell on the outside door rings and Jesse swallows hard, glad for an excuse to leave the room. Marlene's face is pale, and she fidgets with her car keys. Doc nods at her and steps back, making space for her at the table next to Katie, who turns and buries her face in Marlene's shoulder. She holds Katie close and whispers words that Jesse wishes he'd known to say. Sky walks over to Marlene and raises her arms, then lays a hand on Katie's back and pats with the strange wooden stiffness Jesse has come to expect from her.

After a time, Doc declares that they should stand back and give Beau time to rest. They begin to move toward the door, except for Katie, who announces that she intends to stay with her dog. She speaks with such resolve that Jesse looks to Doc for his reaction.

"That's fine, little lady. You can help keep an eye on your friend, straight through the night." He asks that Cole bring a cot and blanket from his office.

"What about you, Doc?" Jesse asks.

"Got plenty of paperwork piled on my desk to keep me busy. There's a kitchen right down the hall, and I've slept many a night in the recliner in my office." His face sags and his rounded shoulders are stooped, and Jesse decides that Doc has to be in his seventies. He came to the McKnight family farm at times of difficult deliveries, and he doesn't remember Doc ever losing one of their farm animals.

"See you in the morning, baby." Jesse bends and hugs Katie.

"Don't worry, Daddy. He'll be okay now that he knows I'm here."

COLE RIDES HOME WITH JESSE and Marlene takes Sky in her car. He's sure Sky would not stay alone with Cole, and he doesn't want to put that kind of responsibility on his son. They drive into the yard, and the house reeks of emptiness. He'd felt robbed of Katie's endless chatter on the drive home.

Marlene pulls her sedan to a stop and Jesse carries Sky into the house. He misses Beau's noisy greeting at the front door. Marlene follows him into the girls' room and offers to get Sky ready for bed.

When Jesse walks into the kitchen, Cole is filling Beau's bowls with food and fresh water. He turns to Jesse. "If that bastard Keith shows up here again, I'm calling Sheriff Buddy."

Jesse nods and leans against the sink. "If that happens, you talk to Buddy, even if you have to call him at home. Miss Marlene plans on staying overnight to help with Sky." He's ashamed that he still thinks of Sky as a tiny bomb that can go off without warning.

Cole sighs and looks relieved.

When it's time to leave for work, Jesse drives away, considering a call to Doc, but decides against disturbing him. If the worst happens during the night, Doc will call the house and Marlene will go to the office and bring Katie home. He doesn't want to think about bringing Beau home in one of those black plastic bags.

JESSE PUNCHES OUT and drives directly to Doc's, his dread eased by the thought that, had Doc called, Marlene would have let him know. He pulls the truck into a space next to a battered station wagon, gets out, and rings the emergency bell. Hands shoved deep in his pockets, he waits.

An elderly black man he remembers from Doc's visits to his parents' farm over the years opens the door and declares that the office is closed and that he will need to come back later.

"Doc ain't had no decent rest. Had some little kid sleeping up here the whole night long. You people forget the man's old." Samuel glares at Jesse as though Doc growing old is somehow his fault.

"Dang it, Samuel, let the man in." Doc's voice comes from somewhere at the end of the long hallway.

Samuel pushes the door open and steps back for Jesse to pass, but it's clear he intends to hold a grudge.

Jesse stops at the room where he left Katie and Beau. The room is empty and the folded cot stands propped against a wall. It has to mean Beau's out of the woods. He doesn't want to think about what else the cleared room could mean. He calls to Doc and continues down the hallway, glancing into more empty rooms.

"Back here, Jess, clear to the end on your right."

Katie is sitting in Doc's big chair, a bagel in one hand and a cup of hot chocolate in the other. Beau watches from a nearby crate, his head drooped to one side, wearing a hangover the size of Jesse's worst. Still, the dog stands, his nose pressed against the crate.

"See, Daddy, I told you. Beau's all better. Doc fixed him good as new. You like his big bandage?" Katie beams, and her curls are a jumbled mess of flashing color. She puts down the cup and runs to grab him around his waist, staggering him back a step.

"I don't know what this young lady said, but that little dog beats all I've ever seen. He's got to be as sore as a well-traveled road, but he's on the mend." A satisfied smile floods the deeply chiseled lines of his face.

"Does that mean he's set to leave?" Jesse's so relieved he collapses into a side chair.

"Only if you agree to bring him back early Monday morning."

"I'll do that, Doc. But you'd better scat if you're to make the kickoff." Doc brags that he hasn't missed a Thanksgiving weekend Florida vs. FSU game since its beginning in 1958.

"My wife's on her way. And believe me, if we miss a minute, she'll have my hide. Here, take this and you see that he doesn't miss a dose. Can you do that?"

When he's reassured Doc, he and Katie are allowed to wrap Beau in the purple blanket he arrived in, and Jesse carries him to the truck, placing him in the seat between them. He drives away slowly, and Katie waves and blows kisses at Doc, who stands on the stoop, waving back.

"This is the happiest day of my life." She places a hand lightly on one of Beau's front paws, and the dog raises his head.

"You did real good back there. Beau might not have made it without you." Jesse wonders how "happiest day" might stack up against the day he brings the mare back. Then it isn't a fair question for either.

"What's Sheriff Buddy going to do about Keith hurting Beau?"

"I'm not sure getting him in on this is the right thing to do."

Her eyes narrow. "No, that's wrong. We've got to take up for Beau."

"Baby, I hate what happened to Beau as much as you do. Keith deserves to have the foot of the law on his neck. But there's Cole to think about."

"What's Cole got to do with Keith hurting Beau?"

He realizes she doesn't know about Keith's attempted break-in. Nor does she understand how complicated things could get.

"Katie, if I don't handle things just right, Cole could go back to detention. He and James got into a fight with Keith."

"But that's not Beau's fault."

"No, you're right. Nothing that happened to Beau was his fault."

"Then, I don't care what happens to Cole. I'm not taking his side against Beau." She turns away and stares out the window.

"Katie, it's not true you don't care. And it's not about taking sides." He has no plan for delivering the kind of justice Katie demands. But he spares her the stale speech about life as sometimes unfair. She knows plenty about that, and he'd hated hearing the same as a kid. For the balance of the drive, an uneasy silence wedges between them like a ghost passenger.

He turns into the lane, relieved to see Marlene's car, and at the warm glow of light streaming from the kitchen window, his weariness lifts. But the good he feels mixes with the bitterness of his guilt.

The girls make a comfortable bed for Beau in their bedroom, and Katie relocates his food and water bowls, declaring that Beau doesn't need to make the long trip to the kitchen. They sit on the floor, next to Beau's bed, refusing to come into the kitchen for the pancakes Marlene has made.

No food in the bedroom is the one remaining house rule Dodie had insisted upon that Jesse has continued to enforce. But Beau's homecoming demands an exception. He carries a tray with glasses of milk and plates stacked with golden brown pancakes covered in maple syrup and butter. He doesn't bother cautioning them to take care not to dribble syrup on the carpet. But he does explain the cost to Beau should they feed him pancakes.

"Throwing up with three cracked ribs would hurt worse than a hundred bee stings."

Katie groans, and he thinks he's made his point.

He stands in the kitchen door, watching Marlene move calmly through the storm that is his life, and he knows that when she goes, she'll take the calm with her. She puts away the last of the dishes and reaches for her jacket hanging on a chair.

"Oh, Jess, I didn't hear you come in."

"Just now." He's embarrassed that she caught him secretly watching.

"How are the girls and their patient?" She smiles.

"Squared away at the moment. Poor Beau may get more nursing than is good for him. Cole's not in his room." He means to stall her departure.

"He's next door using Susan's computer. He called to say he's on his way."

"Good. He'll need to watch the girls while I catch a wink or two."

"I'd stay over, give Cole more time to work on his paper, but the home health nurse comes today. And, like I said before, Clyde's more comfortable having me there."

"I got a first-hand look at how hard being Clyde is on the road back from Georgia. Felt awful that I didn't know how to offer him help. He's my best friend, I should've known."

"As bad as you felt, I think he would feel even worse if you took away only pity. Accepting is one thing, pitying is altogether different."

"Truth is, I think I do. Pity him, I mean." He can't allow her to see that his guilt pushes his pity.

Her eyes carry tenderness. And maybe it's as much for him and what he suffers as for Clyde. She places her hand on his arm, her fingertips hot on his skin, and nothing she's said changes his desire. Only what he's willing to act upon.

When she's hugged the girls good-bye, Jesse walks her to her car and stands watching until she disappears from sight.

He goes back in the house and into the bedroom he's begun to think of as his alone. The bed linens have been changed and the bed turned down. During his months of living alone, without the caring ways only women seem to know how to give, he has come to realize that he'd taken so much for granted, and he wishes he could tell Dodie he now regrets that.

He undresses in semi-darkness, the shades drawn, and gets into bed, shivering between the cool sheets. He pulls the covers over his head, squeezes his eyes shut against the wetness building behind his eyelids, a deep weariness pulling him under, and he prays sleep saves him.

TWENTY-SEVEN

The girls pull the rusted Radio Flyer with Beau aboard for a visit with Dee and Susan while Jesse and Cole work to finish re-roofing the shed. Jesse straightens his tired back and turns toward the clattering of a vehicle approaching the lane. It's Old Blue with Clyde behind the wheel.

Clyde pulls the van to a stop near the shed and leans through the open window. "Damned if it ain't Roy and Gabby patching up the OK corral." The words are his all right, but the flatness of his tone signals that his intent might not be jest.

Balancing across two rafters, Jesse hammers in the last roofing tack and looks down at Clyde. The glare off the tin roofing makes it hard to read his expression.

"I'd hoped some loafer would come along with a cold beer. Give me the excuse I need to get down off this roof." He shades his eyes and waits for Clyde's comeback.

Clyde stares long and hard at the fence and his bearded face holds no clues.

"What'cha think?"

"I think new boards won't stop her when she takes a mind to leave." His words drift like the flight of a wounded duck, and he's more than drunk. He's pity drunk. The kind that comes and stays, fueled and refueled by whiskey.

"Jesus, man, the thing's damn near five feet. Any horse would be plumb loco to try jumping. Be something akin to suicide. And I ain't never heard tell of such a thing. Then I reckon you have?" He chuckles, wanting to push Clyde's mood to something better.

When Clyde doesn't raise his gaze, Jesse gets down off the shed roof and goes to stand next to the van. Cole offers to put away the tools and to walk Katie and Sky home from next door before dark.

At last, Clyde raises his shaggy head. "I'm still thinking open range for that one."

"If by that you mean I should just let her be, then that ain't in the cards." He hasn't mentioned Buddy's threat of sending in men with guns.

"No, fool, I'm saying we should trailer her somewhere wild and set her free, like that broken down cowboy did that drugged stallion."

"Believe me, I've thought about what the old man said about some horses never getting over the wrongs done them. And the mare's likely such a horse. Then what we're living here ain't some movie."

"Maybe not, but there's wrongs men do that go beyond forgiveness." Clyde's jaws set hard while his deep blue eyes cloud. "Might be you'll keep that in mind."

"For chrissakes, man, you're drunk out of your mind. That mare's got to be caught before something worse happens."

Clyde slowly nods. "Catching's one thing, holding's another." He presses his head back against the head rest, closes his bloodshot eyes, and maybe he slips back into the tangled thoughts he arrived with.

"How about we go where it's warm and I throw together a dab of supper? A pot of hot coffee wouldn't hurt you none."

"Me eat your sorry cooking when I've got a good woman at home with supper waiting?" With that, he starts the engine and drives out of the yard.

Jesse watches Clyde drive onto the highway, and for the first time in memory, he worries that he doesn't understand all that passed between them.

When he's scraped together a meatless supper, one his mama would have called short, he oversees baths and tucks the girls into bed over Katie's loud insistence that since Dakota is her horse, she has every right to wait up for the cowboys.

Jesse slips on his jacket and carries Beau down the back steps. Bright moonlight rolls back the darkness, casting long shadows. From deep within the forest, the distant sound of dogs on the move floats toward him on the night air.

Beau bristles. A deep growl rumbles in his throat, and Jesse admires the fight still left in the hobbling dog. He stands, listening in the direction the sound came, but the dogs have moved beyond the lift of the wind to carry their menacing threat. His chest tightens with his fear that a foal must surely slow the mare's flight, pitting her against a pack of wild dogs that she'd need to turn and fight to save her baby.

He leans on the corral, looking westward, and he wants to believe that Curtis's offer was that of an honest man with good intentions. But he knows how a man's road of good intentions can become littered with failures. If it were otherwise, the mare and her foal would be safely sheltered.

He has tossed the last of the cold coffee, whistled for Beau, and turned back toward the house when the front door slams back and Cole runs onto the porch.

"Dad, it's him. On the phone. Hurry."

Jesse rushes into the house and Cole hands over the phone. He's breathing hard and his words are puffed into the phone.

"Hey Jesse, got held up a bit, but we're nearing the I-10 exit at Highway 12 East."

He gives Curtis directions from the interstate and hangs up the phone.

"Dad, did you remember to settle with Miss Dee on stabling his horses? She was asking earlier when I picked up the girls."

"Damn, I forgot."

"What about Beau?"

"Jesus, Cole. One crisis at a time. Can you call Marlene about that? And remember Doc said early. That's before nine."

Susan answers and he apologizes for the late call, telling her about Dobbs's arrival. She agrees and insists that he isn't to worry. She's happy that he'll finally have expert help in recapturing the mare. Still, there's concern in her voice and he thinks that, like him, she worries about what expert means for the mare.

STANDING IN THE YARD, JESSE WATCHES two sets of headlights approaching, vehicles slowing, drivers appearing to take measure before turning onto the narrow lane. He waves his cap in the air and feels like a fool, as if he's landing two jumbo-jets in the yard with nothing but his weak flashlight.

Curtis backs the RV next to the shed, and when he's cranked the generator, spotlights shine all around, creating a small city. He introduces Mac, who is dark skinned with a round smooth face and he's as short as Curtis is tall. Jesse fights off Mutt and Jeff jokes, determined not to say what the two have surely tired of hearing. Mac sets about unloading two fine quarter horses while Curtis levels and extends slide-outs on the motor home. Jesse figures the machine to be a good forty feet, not exactly what he thinks of as a chuck wagon.

After an hour of exercising the horses, Curtis rides one and leads the second next door, while Jesse shows the way in his truck. Curtis dismounts and shakes Dee's outstretched hand, and at her invitation, steps into the barn. He opens a stall door and nods his approval.

He and Curtis drive back to the house, a pot of Susan's hot beef stew and homemade bread riding between them on the seat. Curtis invites him into the luxury of the RV, and together with Mac they discuss plans while consuming big bowls of stew and hunks of bread.

"Your neighbor lady knows her way around a kitchen." Curtis dips bread into the stew, then studies Jesse. "So, how old's that foal?"

"Been awhile since we've seen any sign of the mare. Don't know for sure about a foal. But grazing is still good, and there's a good source of water near where we last spotted her."

"Damn, without that foal to bait her, the job will be harder. We'll need to run her down. Get ropes on her." He gets up and pours a double shot of Jack Daniels. "Chasing a mustang through a damn forest, it ain't about to be easy. We got good roping horses, but even a good horse among trees is dangerous."

"With or without a foal, she'll be on the move come daybreak. We need to be there to say good morning." Mac stands, and the meeting is over.

Jesse steps out of the RV into the cold, moonlit night and shivers, but not from the chill alone. He wants some other way, one that doesn't mean using the mare's fears to trap her. In his gnawing regret, he plays with Clyde's notion that the two of them haul the mare and foal back to Idaho or Montana or wherever the hell she came from and set the pair free into a wilderness unmarked by the harsh boot print of any man.

TWENTY-EIGHT

Jesse wakes to the dark silence of the house. He squints at the blurred numbers on the face of the clock. Seventeen minutes before the alarm, and he dares not risk oversleeping. He slides a hand from beneath the blankets, shuts off the alarm, and flinging back the covers, runs the chilly gauntlet to bump up the thermostat.

When he's dressed, he takes up his heavy jacket and carries his boots and socks into the kitchen to pour his first coffee of the day. An automatic coffee pot is the one item he fears he'd steal before doing without.

By five-ten, the three men have driven to the barn, saddled horses, mounted, and started across the pasture, crystallized grass crunching beneath the horses' prancing hooves. The normally placid mare tosses her head, snorts, and side-steps, jostling Jesse in the saddle. Mac grins, calling it "getting acquainted" horseplay. Ahead, the sandy trail lies illuminated between the dark stands of trees. After a time, the horses settle into a steady pace, and Jesse lets go of the saddle horn and relaxes a bit.

They ride deeper into the forest, and to the east, day pushes back the veil of darkness and the trees become distinguishable, one from the other. The slumbering forest stirs with a strong pulse and today could be the day he promised Katie weeks ago.

"Jesse, we're going to need to stop a mile or so this side of that water hole. If she ain't already caught our scent, she will. Best rest these horses just in case we luck up on her. I've caught fresh sign for the last mile or so."

Jesse looks in the direction Mac points.

"Yeah, and we're in luck. There's a young foal at her side." Mac looks over at Curtis, who moves a gloved hand to the lasso rope attached to the saddle.

Mac raises a quick hand, dismounts, and takes a few steps off the trail. He squats and uses a stick to poke at a pile of manure, his expression pensive.

"Is it horse?" He remembers Dee talking about herds of deer.

"Sure as shit." Mac holds up the stick. "Fresh too. Late as last night. And from the looks of it, I'm guessing they're both in pretty fair shape." Mac scans an open area for more signs.

Jesse and Curtis ride back along the trail, while Mac heads in the opposite direction. Curtis explains that Mac hopes to locate the mare's favored resting spot and set up the catch pen before dark. But first they need to choose a good place to set up a base camp.

"That's a good spot there, under that big oak. You ease on back to your place and bring them fence panels. Along with the camping gear. Don't forget the food and water containers."

The tired mare is an easy ride back, and two hours after leaving Curtis, Jesse has brushed her down and returned her to the corral. It takes an hour to load the fence panels onto his truck and wrestle the food and water containers aboard.

Still, he's pleased with himself when he reaches the camp location less than four hours after he left. He stops near the giant oak, shuts off the engine, and sits for a moment, the stillness of the deep woods closing in around him. His stomach growls, and he wishes he'd slapped together a couple of sandwiches before starting his drive back, but he hadn't wanted to take the time. He considers plundering through the food box but decides to wait until either Curtis or Mac returns. They've got to be just as hungry.

With nothing to do but wait, he takes a seat on the tailgate, strips down to his flannel shirt in the warm sun, and a heavy wave of droop-ass washes over him. His chin drops onto his chest, and he nods off until awakened by a pair of scampering squirrels chasing along the sweeping branches overhead. Jesse decides movement along the trail had spooked the pair of tree rats, so he walks to the front of the truck and spots Mac riding toward him. He touches the brim of his hat, and although Jesse knows little to nothing about the old man, he feels friendly toward him.

"See you made it okay."

Jesse nods.

"Curtis stayed back a ways off the water hole. It's still our best shot."

"So far all the luck's stayed with her." He wants Mac to know that he'd tried before rousting him all the way here from Texas.

"Not so much that. It seems she learned to hate her enemy as well as fear him." Mac's tone is hard.

"All I ever saw of her was bad. Real bad. The mare's got every right."

"Figures, and it's too bad if she didn't get her lick in."

"Not sure, but I think she at least got one winning round."

Mac nods and Jesse figures he's here partly for Curtis, and partly for his own reasons.

"What do we do now?"

"Set that fence and wait her out. See what she takes a notion to do. If she don't come after a time, then we move it. It's her dance card."

"Where you figure to put it?" Jesse looks about without seeing a likely place.

"Back a ways from that watering hole. After a bite, I'll show you. There's a salt block in the gear you brought. To a nursing mother, that draws like bees to honey."

In addition to canned food, the box contains a two-man tent, a one-burner stove, a lantern, a smutty enamel coffee pot, four cups, a frying pan and two sleeping bags. Jesse offers to set up the tent and haul the gear beneath the tree while Mac starts some food cooking.

Mac opens a can of Spam and cuts thick slices of the congealed meat with his pocket knife. He tosses several slices into a heated frying pan and the meat sizzles and curls on its ends. When it's burnt to suit him, they squat on their heels and down several fold-overs topped off by a can of ragged peaches and washed down with lukewarm coffee. Mac gathers up the remaining pieces of meat, wraps them in bread, and stashes them with a can of peaches in his saddlebag.

"Bring that truck on, and go slow, just in case Curtis is on to something."

Mac mounts his horse and leads the way, stopping a couple hundred yards or so from the water hole. Curtis walks out from among the trees, leading his horse.

They work quickly to join the sections, and when they are done, they cut brush to hide the fence, especially across the front, the most exposed side. Curtis fits the pocket-style gate with an arm and receiver that runs off a solar battery, which will allow them to close the gate from a distance of a hundred yards with a palm-size remote.

When the sun begins to drop behind the tallest pines, Jesse worries that he'll be late picking up the girls at Cora's. He wishes he'd remembered to make plans with her to keep them overnight, but too much had happened too quickly. He and Curtis lean on the truck while Mac walks the perimeter of the catch pen, testing the strength of each connection, dragging up a few more branches for cover.

"Damned if he ain't worse than my old granny when it comes to getting things just so."

"How long, you think?"

"With the way we've stunk up the place, it'll likely be a day or so before she shows."

"Maybe we'll get lucky and it'll rain."

Curtis looks skeptical, as if he thinks that's as unlikely as teats on a mockingbird.

"The way the day's warmed up and got sticky, wind coming up out of the south, there's a better than fair chance of rain."

Mac walks up, his head cocked to one side, either surprised by a prediction of rain or that Jesse has finally hit on something useful.

"I'm going to need to head on back. Got three kids to see after."

"Kids? That right?" Mac looks surprised, and Jesse figures talk of Katie was never a piece of Curtis's persuasion.

"Yeah, I got the graveyard shift, but I'll get back to camp early."

"Bring that sack of horse feed out of the trailer when you do. I packed along just enough for tonight. I figure we're going to ask a lot from these horses. They're sure to earn their oats."

"If it rains, it'll turn cold. Chill you to the bone." He grins. "This time of the year, we don't get Miami Beach weather up this far."

"Been so long since I slept in a rain, it might be nice." Curtis mounts his horse and Mac follows, Curtis calling back. "Jess, leave your truck in camp, and walk in tomorrow. Don't know what we might be in the middle of."

Whatever is in store for the mare and her foal, he can only hope that the bad she'll know at his hands means something better for her in the end. For now, he settles on the three of them being the best shot the mare and foal have of staying alive.

TWENTY-NINE

A welcoming light frames the kitchen window, and he pictures Marlene's hands with smooth and purposeful movements bending the smallest of tasks to her will. His mama said certain women had a gift of touch that healed the body and comforted the soul, and while he always suspected she thought of Dodie as selfish, he thinks she would have recognized such a gift in Marlene.

He follows the girls and Beau through the door and into the kitchen, good smells rising from the pots she tends. She turns from the stove and smiles. Katie and Sky crowd into the space between him and Marlene, and while the expressions on their faces make everything seem perfectly all right, he knows he is only borrowing the good in the moment.

"That can't be Dad's cooking," Cole calls, coming into the kitchen.

They sit and pass bowls of mashed potatoes, brown gravy, fresh green beans and hot buttered biscuits while Marlene cuts hefty slices of pot roast. He decides against telling the kids and Marlene about having seen signs of a foal, fearing that something bad might happen, and he doesn't want to put them, especially Katie, through the pain of yet another loss.

"Feel sorry for old Curtis and Mac, roughing it out there in the cold, eating fried Spam and canned peaches."

"But not bad enough to trade places, I bet." Cole speaks with his mouth full of food.

There's less than three hours before he has to leave for work, and he regrets that he needs to spend the time sleeping. He sets the alarm clock and falls into bed, leaving Marlene and Katie to clean the kitchen. Cole promises to fold the clothes Marlene washed and dried. He closes his eyes and drifts into sleep.

He wakes to the sound of a soft rain splattering against the bedroom window and he thinks of Curtis and Mac, sleeping in the chilly rain. The house is quiet except for the muted sound of the TV. He gets out of bed and pulls on today's horse-smelling jeans, then hunts a clean shirt and socks. Dressed, he staggers down the hallway to the living room where Cole is slumped on the couch watching a rerun of *Law and Order,* an American history book resting across his chest.

"Where's everybody?"

"Miss Marlene left right after the girls got settled. Something about needing to help close out the register. She plans on coming back as soon as she's finished. Her watching the midgets is the best thing ever. I hid in my room most of the evening."

Not wanting Cole to see his disappointment, he goes into the kitchen and finds his supper is packed with roast beef sandwiches and a thermos of coffee. Beau followed him into the kitchen and now sits looking up at him.

"Okay, old man." Jesse takes his jacket from the back of a kitchen chair and the dog hobbles after him.

The rain has slacked to a light drizzle, and cooler air blows out of the north. He thinks the wind shift favors their chances. There are no stars visible, but should the cloud cover clear, it will be a much colder night. Curtis will likely get his fill of sleeping in a cold rain.

AFTER HE'S MADE HIS SHIFT, he drives directly to the camp, but there is no sign of either Curtis or Mac. The camping gear, except for the rain soaked tent and camp stove, are stored beneath a stretched tarp. He touches the stove and decides they left hours ago. He walks the mile or so to where they set up the catch pen, and approaching the outer edge of the clearing, he hears the miserable cry of something that sounds like a small animal. At first glance, he can't believe what he sees standing in the middle of the catch pen. It's the tiny foal, tethered to a rope.

Dropping into a squat, he holds his breath and listens hard. From the heavy tree cover to his right, Mac whispers for him to get off the trail. Jesse spots him on the ground, leaning against a white oak tree about twenty yards further back into the foliage. He closes the distance and squats next to Mac.

"Holy shit! You said a least a day."

"Yeah, but danged if we didn't catch a piece of Texas-size luck." Mac shakes his head in amazement.

"What about the mare?"

"She went to the mineral block. Then something spooked her. She bolted, and would you believe she beat the gate? Lord, she's a fast one. Got moves this old cowboy ain't seen except on a precious few. Reminds me of them pretty little gal dancers that get up on their toes and spin about."

"Where's she now, you think?"

"Oh, you can bet the baby's milk money she's out there, watching and waiting. Curtis figured to get behind her with his rope. Then he'd have a better chance of lassoing the wind. If she goes in that pen now, it'll be her doing on account of the fuss that hungry baby's fixing to put up."

"I know it can't be helped, but I hate what we're doing." Jesse's shame churns in his stomach with a force that surprises him.

"You're right about that. But then we didn't start this meanness. That poor critter's fate, and wild herds all across the far west, was signed, sealed and set in motion the sorry day the feds sided with greedy cattlemen. Claimed mustangs overgrazed grass rightly meant for cattle. Among my people, being rooted out by greed ain't nothing new." He says this in one long breath.

The foal whinnies and scampers the length of the rope where it's flipped onto its back, landing hard on the ground. It stays down only moments before scrambling to its feet. It stands and trembles.

"That right there starts at birth."

"What does?"

"Fear of being downed. Heard tell of a mean cowboy downed a young one and bound it so it couldn't even struggle. That horse died of pure fright, right on the ground at the feet of that sonofabitch."

"That could happen to the mare? Her foal?"

"Can't say. Horses are different, same as people."

Jesse has heard enough. He takes off his jacket and spreads it on the wet ground, sitting with his back to the struggling foal. He listens for the mare, but the only sounds are those of a red-cockaded woodpecker drumming on a dead pine. The foal calls and thrashes at the end of the rope repeatedly, with the same bad result. Jesse squeezes his eyes shut. But nothing he does can shut out the cries of the foal.

Hours of bright sunlight have begun to dry the rain soaked woods. Still, there is no sight or sound of the mare. Hunger drives the foal, and it takes up a steady cry that sets Jesse's teeth on edge. When he can't take it any longer, he offers to walk back to the camp and get food and drink, although he's sure he can't keep anything down.

The long day inches forward the way it began, with the foal tethered, never as much as a glimpse of the mare. Curtis returns late afternoon and worries aloud that the foal shouldn't go more than twelve hours without milk. The harshness of the ordeal for the mare and foal causes Jesse to think about calling off the plan, but the determination registered in Curtis's face says that it's his fight now, and that he's here to finish it.

"With night coming on, I'm counting on the cries of that hungry baby to give the mare plenty to fret about." Curtis takes a can of peaches from his saddle bag and settles against the trunk of a sweet gum. He opens the can with his pocketknife and offers Jesse a peach. When he shrugs them off, Curtis eats the entire can of peach halves and drinks the juice.

As darkness approaches, Jesse leaves the forest, and he's grateful that the girls are staying the night with Cora. He doesn't think he could look Katie in the eye and offer her hope after watching and listening to the foal's struggles. If he forgets eating, then he has time for a nap.

WHEN HE OPENS THE DOOR, the telephone is ringing and he hurries to answer.

"It would seem Mr. Dobbs has turned off his cell phone again." It's the anxious voice of the young woman he'd talked to before.

Jesse explains Curtis's whereabouts, and the woman insists that what she has to tell him is a matter of the gravest concern and he must call immediately. Jesse assures her that he will get Curtis the message within the hour, realizing that should Curtis decide to handle the situation himself, staying the night with the foal has just fallen to him.

The shift supervisor comes on the phone, and Jesse explains that a family emergency means that he won't be in tonight. The super makes it clear that she thinks he's a liar, and since she gets to decide what passes as a family emergency, he's fine with lying. He's done as much for far less.

He explains the woman's telephone call to Cole and that he's going back into the forest.

"What about the midgets? Where's Miss Marlene?"

"The girls are at your grandma's for the night."

"Why? Thought you didn't want them there."

"I don't. Marlene needed time to do something she'd committed to do. She didn't say more than that."

"What can I do?"

"Whatever Curtis is up against means I'll need to wait at the catch pen. I need you to call Clyde, tell him what's happened."

"Why do you care that he knows?"

"Just do it. I ain't got time to explain." Jesse isn't sure why he cares. Only that Clyde's always been a part of every crisis he's faced. And he feels one coming on.

He drives back into the forest and stops at the campsite. Mac crawls out of the tent, fully dressed, and Jesse explains the situation before striking off down the trail to the stakeout. Curtis comes from within the trees to meet him. When Jesse explains the telephone call, Curtis swears.

"That's it? She didn't say any more than that?"

"Said only you could handle the situation. She sounded real worried. Cried a bit."

Jesse hands over his truck key, telling him not to worry, that he called in and took the night off.

"Feel bad that this'll cost you a night's pay, but she's usually ` dead on about things that need my attention. And she ain't a crier." Curtis's face is gray with worry. "You sure about that?"

"I'm pretty sure. But then it ain't like I know her."

"Right." Curtis kicks caked mud from his boot. "I'll take your truck in, and depending on what she tells me …." He pauses, stares up at the night sky. "Guess we'll need to wait on knowing what comes next." He turns to Mac. "Why don't you wait here with Jesse?"

"Thought I would."

Jesse and Mac take up a position where they can see the opening of the catch pen. Jesse snaps his jacket closed and settles on the ground. Heavy clouds drift between the clearing and the weak light of the moon, and it's as though nature flips a switch, and in that instant he's unable to see the opening of the catch pen.

"Gonna be a long night. We best take turns watching. No need for both of us to stay awake."

"Right. I'll take the first watch."

"Here, take this." Mac hands him the remote. "Them heavy clouds are on her side. So keep a sharp eye out. Her milk's building and the foal's getting weak with hunger." He sighs, twists his hips into the ground, and settles. In no time, he's lightly snoring.

Jesse fights off sleep by tapping the tips of his fingers together, but even that doesn't hold back what his mind and body so desperately need.

His eyes blink open, and he's suddenly fully awake. The clouds have cleared, and he stares toward the opening, believing the sounds that woke him came from the catch pen.

"Holy shit," he mutters under his breath.

Mac flinches, and Jesse believes he's awake.

The mare stands next to the foal, her head turned in their direction, her ears pointed. He makes out the form of the foal at her side, and he hears the smacking sounds of the foal nursing.

Mac touches Jesse's knee. He doesn't speak, but moves his thumb on his clenched fist.

Jesse is sure if either as much as exhale, the mare will bolt. Slowly, he slips his hand into the pocket of his jacket where he put the remote, but it isn't there. He gently pats the ground at his feet, his blood pounding in his ears. Three feet to his left, he spots the red dot. He leans, reaching toward the light.

The mare snorts, and although he hears what he thinks are her hooves pounding the ground, he believes she is still in the pen. Suddenly, the cloud cover thickens, and he barely makes out the mare's gray form. He gets off his knees and crouches, the remote clutched in his hand, when beneath his right boot a twig snaps. The sound echoes across the clearing like a huge tree slamming to the ground.

"Do it, boy," Mac whispers.

But the mare has broken into a full gallop, charging toward the opening, and the foal attempts to follow. He hears all of this more than actually sees what's happening. He opens his hand, and the remote remains firmly cradled in his palm. At the sound of the horse moving toward the gate, he'd tightened his grip around the remote, his thumb over the trigger, but he didn't press down.

"Damnit." Mac stands.

Jesse stumbles into the clearing, silently screaming his anguish in the direction the mare has gone, the pounding of her hooves fading in the distance. He turns toward the sound of the foal, and it stands, washed in a sudden flash of moonlight, trembling, and he hurries away.

Ahead, he catches sight of the ghostly glow of headlights cutting through the dense fog, heading straight for the catch pen. He walks toward the approaching vehicle.

Curtis pulls the truck to a quick stop, gets out calling for Mac, who rushes from the tree cover.

"What's so God awful you're driving into here?" His voice carries the weight of more worry than reprimand.

"Lightning struck the stud barn." Curtis's words come on puffs of air, his breathing labored. "Thank God Carlos got all the horses out before the barn burned to the ground."

Mac stands apart from Curtis, but every inch of him—body and soul—reaches out. "And Big Boy?"

"Burned."

"How bad?"

"Bad enough. The vet thinks he could survive the burns. Be scarred, but …." His voice catches in his throat.

"Smoke damage."

Curtis nods and turns to Jesse. "Hate to pull out on you like this. But that old horse and me ain't nothing short of brothers."

"Lord, man. I'm awful sorry. And don't bother with a word of apology. What's here can wait. Tell me what I can do to help." He heard Mac was leaving too, and that whatever happened from here on was on his shoulders.

"Awful sorry I never got to meet your young Katie." His slight smile fades and Jesse thinks it was likely overtaken by a hard memory of his Katie's passing.

"I'm sure y'all would've liked one another."

"Mac, you bring the horses. I'll have everything back at Jesse's ready. We'll load the horses, then hit the road."

"What about the catch pen and camping gear?"

"I'll leave that with you until next time I'm through this way." He extends his big hand, and Jesse grabs it, but he spares Curtis eye contact. Curtis turns and gets into the truck and drives away.

Mac steps forward and smothers him in a hug. "Gonna take some time to clear out this human scent. Maybe one of them pretty rains y'all get will come along."

"How much longer with the foal?"

"She's nursed good. But give her no more than six to eight hours." Mac slaps him on the back and mounts his horse, looks down at Jesse.

"He said brother."

"Aside from me, that horse is the closest he's got to family. After his wife went hard the way she did, he quit living. Rode that horse off into the nowhere and stayed drunk for weeks at a time. It was the promise he saw in the horse that got him living again. Big Boy has sired a bunch of champion all-around quarter horses. He owes his life and his fortune to him."

Jesse nods. "Man don't get much more in debt than that."

"What happened back there made sense. I've yet to put a rope on a wild one without some regret." He pauses. "Just know that some don't never take to the rope." Mac lays two fingers to the brim of his Stetson and rides away, leading Curtis's horse.

A full lonesome settles over the clearing and Jesse's chest swells with a grave sense of loss. He turns back toward the catch pen where the foal lies on the ground, her small head tucked under a front leg. She could be any baby sleeping with a full stomach.

He's sorry for Curtis and the horse he called his brother. But most of all, he's sorry for the heavy hammer of fate. Then he's known all along that his destiny and that of the mare loosely hang from the same star. He'll go back to the place he and Mac sat, and wait for the mare to choose her freedom or her foal.

THIRTY

Darkness settles over the woods, and trees stand poised dark against the sky, discernible shapes blend and then disappear. Jesse's stomach aches with that bent over, clutching his middle pain of hunger. He decides to leave his post and walk back to the camp, where he can scrounge for food and drink.

His search turns up more Spam and peaches, but little else. He locates the frying pan and sets about heating a meal he can take back for the night. The meat sizzles in its own fat, and he uses his pocket knife to cut into a can of the peaches.

In the distance, a set of headlights bounces toward him, and he steps from beneath the giant oak. Clyde pulls Old Blue off the narrow trail, leans through the open window and calls, "Heard them two old cowboys hauled ass back to Texas. And I'm guessing it was something big that sent them running before finishing the job."

"Was bad all right." Jesse drags the pan off the fire and shuts off the gas.

"Damn, I'm sorry to hear that. So what do you figure to do?"

"Wait her out. Ain't like I got a lot of good choices to pick from."

"No, I reckon not. And if something good don't happen?" Clyde spits tobacco on the ground and stares straight ahead, his disapproval in what he doesn't say. "TV dude said a low of twenty tonight. Then I packed along plenty of hot coffee, roast beef sandwiches, and a pound cake. If your gut's gnawing and you ain't got your mouth set for that mess there, I'd consider sharing."

CLYDE HAS PARKED THE VAN some seventy-five yards from the catch pin in a manner that enables Jesse to view the opening using Clyde's night vision binoculars. He pulls a dog crate around, sits, and studies the foal. It stands on wobbly legs, softly whinnying, and its belly has to be empty. There is not a sound from the mare, and that doesn't surprise him. Clyde's arrival likely caused her to retreat deeper into the wood. If it wasn't for the foal spending the night alone in a cold rain, he'd wish for a downpour to wash some of the human scent away.

"Damn curious, but you'd think dead legs wouldn't feel the cold." Clyde draws a heavy blanket around his legs.

Jesse looks at him and nods. "It does … seem odd, I mean. What'd the doctors tell you about that?" In all this time since the accident, it's his first time risking a question about any of the hardship for Clyde in riding that damn chair.

"If they were standing on two feet when they said it, I didn't listen." Clyde grins.

"But, it's all right? Me asking?"

"Yeah, it's fine as long as you don't ask me about finger-fucking Daisy."

"Right. When you tire of her, I'll swap you Miss November." They laugh, and Jesse takes pleasure in having lifted even a corner of the awkwardness he's felt.

They tear into the basket of food Marlene packed, and when they have wolfed down two sandwiches each, Clyde breaks off a hunk of the pound cake and passes it over with a thermos of spiked coffee.

When they've eaten their fill, he offers a doggy-smelling blanket, and Jesse pushes around some of the junk in the van to make a space to curl up. He squeezes his eyes tight against the memory of his failure while comforted by the familiar sound of Clyde's steady breathing.

When sleep doesn't come right away, he whispers, "You asleep?"

"Not now. Why?"

"I had her, but I let her get away."

"Does that mean you want to turn that little one loose? And find us a warmer place to spend the balance of the night?"

"Can't do that. This thing's gone way past what I might have wanted."

"And how's that?"

"If we don't get her out of here, Buddy's sending in men. That's men with guns, intent on running her down and shooting her on sight. Maybe even that little one out there too."

"Shoot her? What business is it of his? He's got no cause."

"Claims she's a public nuisance."

"How's that? By free-grazing and drinking Mother Nature's water?"

"That's 'bout the size of it. Wake me if you hear something."

"You mean if I hear something other than that baby crying for its mama's tit?"

Jesse pulls the blanket under his chin and pushes his boot against a dog crate, making room to stretch his legs, his hip joint pressed against the metal frame of the van. He, too, listens, but if she's on the move, the chorus of night critters cover all sounds except for those he takes as a raccoon helping itself to the Spam he tossed.

He drifts in and out of a restless sleep, and twice he gets to his knees and peers through the fogged window of the van. The foal lies quietly, and he worries anew about the cold and what has to be the foal's shrinking belly. An hour ago, it stopped neighing, and he fears it may have grown too weak.

He glances at his watch. It's an hour to daybreak. If the mare is coming, he thinks it will be then. He shifts to his less bruised hip and lies in the dark, listening for the mare.

As the faintest edge of day cuts a deep purple scar on the distant horizon, Jesse gets to his knees. Clyde sits hunkered over in his chair, the blanket pulled beneath his red bristled chin. Jesse wipes the frosty window with a gloved hand, but it's frozen on the outside. He pushes opens the back door, the sound loud and unforgiving, and what he sees causes him to scamper to his feet.

The mare stands in the middle of the catch pen, nursing the foal, and she doesn't even look in his direction. He worries that having blundered yesterday's chance to recapture her, he may have wrongly signaled that he can be trusted.

He watches the mare, and although she stands perfectly still, he senses that she hears his every movement, even the pounding of his heart. He holds his breath and dares to watch her through the peephole for a moment longer.

Now her ears, eyes, and nose are focused in his direction. Her head swings slightly and she begins to step crab-like. The foal whinnies and moves back under her side, nudging. The mare licks and nuzzles the foal, and when she looks back toward the van, she doesn't move.

He reaches inside his jacket pocket for the remote and his hand trembles. Clyde opens his eyes and struggles to sit upright in the chair. Jesse nods toward the peephole. Clyde's bloodshot eyes stretch wide, his upper body tensing with a hunter's alertness.

Still Jesse hesitates.

Clyde holds out his hand, palm up, and Jesse gives up control of the remote. He can only watch as Clyde's thumb covers the red button and presses down.

He hears the gate slam shut, followed by the motorized sound of the chair turning in the confined space of the van.

"It's done." The words are barely more than a whisper, and Jesse believes he heard in Clyde's voice an echo of his own regret.

Jesse lifts his head, but he still doesn't look at what his pursuit of the mare has come to. The moment falls far short of the satisfaction he imagined months ago.

His breathing sounds like wind sucked through dry leaves, and he whispers, "Let's just sit here. Give her a chance to settle. Maybe she won't hate so that the gate closed on her."

"Hell, Jess, that's bullshit." Clyde doesn't say this in a mean way, but in a way that says he's made his peace with whatever comes next.

Jesse slides out the back of the van and walks around in full view. Behind him, he hears the wheezing sound of the hydraulic lift, like air escaping a dying thing, and then the familiar thump of the lift as it makes contact with the ground.

He walks toward the closed gate, expecting that the mare views all her captors the same. He's a man form moving toward her on two legs with his gray color and a sour sweat rising like death. The mare answers back with all her strength, screaming and rearing, pivoting and running the full length of the catch pen. The foal tries to follow, but the rope pulls taut. The mare returns to the foal, nudging it to stand and run. The baby struggles against the rope and falls to its knees.

The mare stands perfectly still, appearing to be paralyzed, except for wave after wave of hard tremors of the sort he believes can only be her uncontrollable fear. She backs into the far corner of the catch pen, her ears pointed and her eyes focused on the gate, brightly colored leaves swirling around her striking hooves. Her neck and shoulders swell, and she gathers herself in what seems to be some final decision.

The mare gazes straight ahead, the flesh across her withers quivering and awash in sweat. She whinnies to the foal and it stops struggling and stands still, as though in a trance. The mare's eyes glaze, and she screams the most desperate sound Jesse has ever heard. Her head raised, nose in the air, she appears to dance above the ground. She bursts forward, crossing the length of the catch pen, quickly gaining full speed.

Jesse runs toward the gate, searching in his pocket for the remote, but he's given it up to Clyde. He waves his cap in the air and shouts, trying to turn her back.

The mare crashes at full speed into the cold, metal gate, her head slams back, she staggers, legs trembling beneath her, and she falls hard to the ground. The foal struggles against its unrelenting tether, unable to reach its fallen mother's side.

Jesse climbs over the gate and runs to the mare, only faintly hearing Clyde shouting that he should stay back. He kneels next to the mare's head. Her eyes are rounded white, and foam covers her dark muzzle, the stench of her is pure fear. He places a palm to her nostrils, feels the faint warm air pushing out, and the mare shivers. He pulls her head to rest across his knees in a feeble attempt to at last touch her in an act of kindness. He watches helplessly as her spirit escapes beneath his hand.

After a long silence, he stands and walks to the post where the foal is tethered and frees it. Dragging the rope, the foal scampers to its mother and nudges her, kneading her belly with its tiny hooves. The baby begins nursing, flicking its tail while suckling its dead dam.

Jesse leaves the mare and foal, climbs back over the gate, and walks back to where Clyde sits near the van with the remote still in his hand. Dropping onto the ground next to the chair, he looks off into the dense forest and there's no sign of the evil that happened here. It's as though Mother Nature turns her face away.

"That was one hell of a run." Clyde speaks reverently, shaking his shaggy head in a way that says he believes he witnessed something special.

"Katie never had a chance." Jesse looks to Clyde.

"I'd say a rope never held any promise for the mare, don't matter who held the other end."

"You reckon she felt it?" He figures the impact had broken her neck, and he wants to believe she died instantly, although he knows better.

"Hell yeah, she had to." His large hands move tenderly along his thighs. "Then, I figure she'd suffered worse."

While Clyde readies a space in the van for transporting the foal, Jesse catches up the rope and kneels next to the mare. The foal scampers the full length of the rope, stops and looks back at him. He remembers Mac saying that the foal was too young to have learned to hate, but that she was born to fear all but her kind. Maybe he can fool the foal into accepting his approach.

He removes his jacket, rubs it over the mare's head and shoulder, and rubs his hands along her neck. He wipes his horse-scented hands over his face and chest and slowly creeps along the length of the rope, hand over hand, squatting next to the foal. It stands, front legs spread, its neck stretched, reaching, and softly snorts.

Jesse lifts the kicking foal, holding her gently against his chest, and she doesn't resist. He's so relieved he thinks he'll tear up. He carries the foal toward the van, praying she won't recoil at the dog smell. He places her within the wall of crates Clyde has constructed and removes his jacket, leaving it with the foal.

Clyde spreads a tarp over the top of the fortress and turns to Jesse. "After I've dropped this baby off at Doc's, I'll get us some help with that one."

"I'm thinking Pete. Will you get him to bring his backhoe in here? Tell him I'll work it off over time."

"You mean to bury her here?"

"Yeah, what do you think?"

"That we're supposed to get a fucking permit from the forestry boys to as much as piss in these woods."

"I don't need no permit. Do you?"

"Hell no, I'll get Pete in here. With any luck, he'll be sitting idle today."

"You know where to find him?"

"Son, I know the hidey-hole of every man in this county." He grins. "If he's on a job, it'll be sometime after dark before I can get him back in here."

"Don't matter. Just get that little one to Doc soon as you can."

Clyde drives away slowly, careful to save the foal as much roughness as possible.

Quiet seeps back, wrapping the forest in near silence, and Jesse kneels beside the mare's corpse. He's drawn to her many scars, evidence of her brutal history with man, and he traces each with his fingertip: her forehead, forelock, poll, neck, shoulder, withers, back, and loin.

He gasps at the discovery of a fresh gash across her rump. When he's pushed the wound together and smoothed course hairs over its rawness, he pushes back on the cold ground at her head. Her corpse has already begun to give off a faint sour odor.

Mac said some wild horses can never surrender to the rope, and even Clyde said much the same. Maybe the mustang was always such a horse, and her instinct for freedom had driven her to her death.

HE SQUINTS INTO THE NEAR-BLINDNESS of the mid-morning sun and watches a red-shouldered hawk catch the wind currents aloft and soar. Suddenly it drops, swooping downward, its calls taking on a frantic edge. He doesn't know what to make of the hawk's appearance, likely only a coincidence, but he feels there's more. Should his regrets escape his throat, he imagines that he'd sound much like the hawk.

Jesse leaves the mare and sets about pulling the brush away from the catch pen. When he's done, he begins the slower work of disconnecting panels and carrying the loose pieces to a site at the edge of the woods, placing them in two stacks and covering them with the brush he'd removed.

He's stripped down to his tee shirt, and he needs more water than he has in his canteen. It's a quick walk to the spring, but he doesn't want to leave the horse. He fears buzzards, even the possible approach of the wild dogs that had chased her with vengeance. He drains the last of the water and walks out of the clearing, seeking the shade of a bay magnolia within clear sight of the horse.

He sits on the ground, his back against the tree, and nods off, waking to the whine of a diesel engine from the direction of the forest road. He knows it to be heavy equipment moving at a fast pace, coming with the quiver of the ground beneath him. He gets to his feet and slowly walks toward the sound of the machine, his gait that of an old man.

"Pete's right behind me," Clyde calls. He works himself from behind the steering wheel into the chair and moves to the side door.

"What's the time?"

"Late enough you'd better haul ass out of here if you've still got need of regular work. Your boss won't likely give a damn about you sitting with a dead horse."

The roar of the diesel engine fills the clearing ahead of the big machine, and Jesse notices another vehicle following close behind.

"That's my truck," he shouts. "Who the hell's driving?" He walks over to Clyde, the chair still resting on the lift.

"Cole, and if you don't like it, then maybe you'll tell me how I was supposed to get it here."

"That's good. But I ain't leaving till it's over."

"Damn, Jess. It can't get no more over."

Clyde's right, but he fights any thought of letting go.

Cole stops the truck and hurries to where he stands next to Clyde's lift.

"Grandma's got the girls, and Miss Marlene took Beau with her."

"That's real good, son. But tell me when you learned to drive."

"Just now, in the woods. But, I'm thinking high-speed drunk driving on the interstate helped." His wide grin fades, and he looks at his feet.

"Might've been risky training, but damned if I don't think it did. You did good, boy." Clyde slaps Cole on the shoulder.

Jesse glances back toward the fence panels. "I can't go till I've loaded them fence panels and gathered up that camping gear. Gonna need to settle with Pete when he's done."

"Hell, ain't nobody going to mess with them panels. And go ahead, give me them two thin dimes you got in your pocket, and I'll see Pete gets both."

"Cole, move the truck to those stacks and swing it around and back in close. We're fixing to load them before we leave out."

"Goddamn, if you're determined, I'm taking my tired ass home. Had all the fun I can stand for one day." Clyde starts up Old Blue and pulls away.

Jesse walks back across the clearing, and he doesn't turn back at the sounds of the backhoe grinding into gear and the hydraulics lowering the big blade, ripping open the ground.

By the time he and Cole have loaded the panels onto the truck and tied them down, Pete has finished covering the grave. He climbs down off the backhoe and walks toward the truck.

He leans on the truck, takes a tin from his hip pocket, and packs the side of his mouth. "Hate that back there for you. Bet that mare would've made a fine horse for your little girl." He kicks the tire a couple of hard licks. "My girl goes right on begging for one of her own. But hell, my wife wants a weekend trip to Panama City Beach." He pauses. "The way things go, ain't neither likely to have no more than their wants."

Jesse nods, although he's learned that if a want is big enough, its pursuit can turn a man's life around.

"Guess I'll leave y'all to your work." He turns back toward the machine.

Jesse calls, "If it's all right with you, I'll need time to get together what I owe you."

Pete turns back. "What kind of a sonofabitch would I be if I couldn't do a man a favor?" He walks on.

HE AND COLE DROP THE PANELS next to the empty corral, and he slams two pb & j sandwiches together while a pot of coffee makes. When he's filled his thermos, he thanks Cole again for his help and drives away.

Although he's running late, he stops at the rusted mailbox, reaches in, and beneath his outstretched hand he fingers a fat envelope. He holds it under the dashboard light, and the return address is that of Stuart Brown, Attorney at Law. He opens the glove compartment and tosses the letter inside, then spins slick tires onto the highway, flooring the old truck, wishing he could somehow outrun his sorry day.

Pulling the truck into the parking lot, he has only minutes to spare, and the shift supervisor is standing near the breakroom. When she sees him come through the door, she motions him over.

He punches his card and closes the distance between them, his jaws set, preparing to hear the worst. But what's worse than the echo of the mare's scream and the sight of her slamming into that metal gate?

He'd heard the sound of her dropping into the ground, the blade pushing her cooled body into the scarred earth. She's to rot in soil thousands of miles from where she was meant to live out her life and produce foals to replenish the herd. But man took all that away for the price of nature's grass and cool water.

"McKnight, I hope to hell you've got a damn good reason for laying out last shift." She squints, cocking her hip, setting up a clear barrier to whatever he might have come to say.

But he didn't come with a ready excuse. He looks the big woman's resistance squarely in the face and he's moved to the truth. "Someone close died a hard death, and I waited out their passing."

"McKnight, that's so lame I'm tempted to believe you. Get your ass on that machine before I change my mind." She pushes work orders into his hand.

He nods, turns, and mounts the forklift. Sounded weak, he admits, but the truth often does.

THIRTY-ONE

An approaching thunderstorm boils like an upside down wash pot, the sky dark and twisted. Then nature's fury is no match for the turbulence that has built inside of Jesse throughout the long night. He worried himself straight into screwing up a big work order with barely enough time to fix his mistake before the disgruntled semi driver pulled away from the loading dock.

By the time he drives into the sideways rain, his worry has shifted from what he'll say to Katie about the mare to the letter he stashed in the glove compartment. His anxiety swells to fill the cab, and he jerks the steering wheel a hard left, sending the truck into a jarring skid in the median of the four-lane highway, the engine stalling.

He sits for a time, working to regain control, before daring to retrieve the envelope. He reads his name and address several times, as though he might somehow make its arrival in his mailbox the fault of the rural postman.

He opens the envelope, then scans the cover letter signed by Stuart Brown claiming to act on behalf of his client, Delores

Jean McKnight. Enclosed is a six-page document titled Marital Settlement Agreement.

He reads that Delores Jean McKnight is the Petitioner and that he, Jesse W. McKnight, Jr., is the Respondent. Irretrievably broken is the marriage between Petitioner and Respondent, Stuart Brown declares, further noting the willingness of the State of Florida to hold neither at fault. Jesse agrees it's smart of the state to get out of the business of assigning blame. Yet what happened between him and Dodie came on gradually, more like a silent rot than a clear break. The paragraph on property settlement amounts to her nothing and his nothing divided, equaling two nothings.

Stuart Brown lists the children by their full names, birth dates and current residence, and it reads cold, reducing Cole, Katie and Sky to what feels to him like marital inventory. In one long phrase, the document names Jesse W. McKnight, Jr. primary physical residential custodian, and establishes reasonable visitation rights for Delores Jean McKnight as ten weeks of summer and the week including Christmas.

He stares through the rain-splattered windshield as circles of light weave and bob toward him, and nothing feels real. He doesn't know how long he's been sitting before he notices the numbness in his feet slowly moving along his legs, through his groin into the lower half of his body, to coil like a great snake in his chest, its viperous head pushing into his throat. He presses his fingertips to his throbbing temples, and when he can't bear the pain, he jumps out of the truck, and clambers up to stand on the cab.

He stands with fists raised to the dark sky, screaming obscenities, pellets of rain stinging his hot skin like razor cuts. Caught in the back draft of speeding vehicles, he spins and falls hard onto the soaked ground. Sprawled face down on the waterlogged median strip, his hot tears mock his uncontrollable laughter, and he fears that he's lost his mind.

Tears streaming down his face, he pushes to his feet. Looking up and down the highway, he prays that he's up to being primary physical residential custodian to his children.

HE DRIVES INTO THE PARKING LOT at Doc's and walks stiffly to the back door, brushing dirt and leaves from his rain soaked shirt and pants. He rings the bell and waits.

"Hey Jess, I hoped you'd come by." Doc's faded blue eyes float in pools of weariness, and the crevices in his haggard face mark all of his years of sleepless nights.

He flashes Doc a weak smile. "Sorry to track up the place. I guess I tried soaking up all the rain."

"No matter, the foal's in the barn." Doc doesn't wait to be asked the question that plagued Jesse through much of the night.

He follows Doc through the back door and onto a well-worn path between the office and the barn.

"It's young, no more than two to three weeks, I'd guess. Undersized, as you'd expect, born to a mare on the run. But it's too early to know her heart. That's what she'll need to survive."

"Are you saying she might not make it?"

"Not saying one way or the other. Only that I can do for her what I know, but she'll need more human help than she can get here."

"Doc, I don't want …." His throat constricts, his words wadding like gristle in his mouth. "I don't want something awful happening because I'm too damn dumb and piss poor to do right by her. Couldn't get along with that."

"Son, it's true you're way short on know-how, and you'd need to follow my directions to a tee. And don't go figuring on any of those shortcuts you're so damn good at."

Jesse lowers his gaze, knowing Doc means his failure to bring Beau for his follow-up treatment. "But what about all the money I already owe you?" He shoves his hands into his empty pockets and stares at his boots.

"That's not my worry here and now. I'm more concerned that you were likely never the one sitting up nights with your sick kids." He stares clear through to the truth. "The foal's going to need a clean, tight shelter against the cold weather, measured feedings every four hours, daily weighing, and camping out day and night if it takes it to comfort her when she cries for her mama."

"Doc, I work nights. And I've got two little girls and a boy on probation."

"No doubt the way you're living is a mite hard. And I get that you're drawing on borrowed help. But if you take her, none of that can matter."

Doc's tone has grown harsh, and Jesse knows his word is his bond and that he isn't in the habit of dealing second chances, especially where the welfare of an animal hangs in the balance.

"Will need to keep her here for a time. Our biggest hurdle is to get her to take the substitute mare's milk. Don't want to tube feed her if I can avoid it. But that means she's first got to take to somebody."

They enter the barn and walk between the rows of clean and freshly hayed stalls. Jesse hears the foal whinny, and her cry sounds even weaker than when she struggled against the tether. He takes on Doc's concern that the foal may have given up on ever being answered.

He approaches the stall door, and the foal scampers to a far corner. He notices his jacket on the floor and he thinks the foal was lying on it.

"It didn't help that her dehydration forced me to use a nasal gastric tube." Doc frowns, a hand rubbing the back of his neck.

"Reckon that'd be my doing."

"That can't matter now. We've got to get this little bit to suckle. Dee's one of the best, but even she failed."

Doc takes a clipboard from a nail on the wall and glances at the chart. He looks long and hard at the foal backed into the corner. "Stay put while I go mix the formula."

Doc returns with a bottle capped with a lamb's nipple and passes the bottle to Jesse. He steps into the stall, and the foal raises her head and stretches her nose toward him. "Hey there, little one, you remember me?"

"Jess, did you change …?" Doc stops in mid-question and stares. The foal takes a cautious step toward Jesse.

"Ease off that shirt." Doc whispers.

Jesse slowly unbuttons his shirt and looks to Doc.

"Wrap it around your arm and let it hang down over your hand."

Jesse kneels, and the foal stops, raises her head, and stretches her nose toward him.

"Squirt a little formula on the nipple. Let it soak into that shirt."

Jesse holds his breath, and silently pleading, he extends the bottle.

A drop of formula hangs on the tip of the nipple and the foal stretches her neck and sniffs. Stepping closer, she reaches a pink tongue to lick the single drop from the nipple. She stops and pricks her ears forward. He exhales and she steps back, seeming to study him. Then she steps forward, takes the nipple, and begins to suckle.

"Glory be." Doc grunts a sigh of relief, and Jesse blushes with a strange surge of tenderness.

The foal downs better than three-quarters of the formula before stopping and stepping away. Jesse rocks back on his heels, bone weary, but immensely satisfied.

Doc walks with Jesse to his truck.

"Bag those stinking clothes you're wearing and bring them with you when you come back with the girls. And by the way, while you were out chasing horses, that nice lady brought Beau back in, and he's mending fine. Tough little knocker, that one."

"About that, Doc …." To save money, he believed he'd sent Beau with Marlene for treatment by Clyde's kennel man. He'd not known that instead she brought Beau to Doc.

Doc turns and walks back toward the office without another word.

STEERING THE TRUCK into morning traffic, Jesse heads home, the cramping in his stomach reminding him how little he's eaten since Marlene's sandwiches and cake.

After he scrounges a meal, he calls Cora and thanks her for her help with the girls, and explains that today he means to get them from school.

"Did you catch Katie's horse? She's awful upset, and that much worry can't be good for a little girl." There's three Sundays of preaching in her tone.

"No ma'am, too much worry at any age ain't good."

He hangs up and has started down the hall when the phone rings.

"Buddy called here looking to get up with you. The horse those meddling fools were bitching about turned out to be a neighbor's that busted loose. Said to tell you he's awful sorry if that influenced the way you went about things. I told him the next time I saw him, I intended to roll this wheelchair over his big ass."

"Truth is, what he said didn't change anything." But Jesse is glad to know he was right about the horse. It helps to think he understood the mare in that important way.

"Want to say I'm grateful to you for rousting Pete the way you did. And you were right about my job being on the line. Then that part turned out all right."

He explains Doc's decision to keep the foal and asks about Beau.

"Hell fire, that ugly half-breed and that lap pup rule the roost. Marlene talked about toting him home after the girls get out of school."

"If she's coming anyway, can you ask her if she'd mind swinging by Trudy's and bringing them with her."

"I'll do that."

Jesse wishes he could wrap the warmth of Marlene's voice around him and sleep for a week, but just now he doesn't trust himself to talk to her. He mostly wants to know if she thinks he's up for primary custodian of his kids. He knows he could be with her, but those are forbidden thoughts. He fears his mouth might betray him.

He places a call to Curtis and the woman he talked to earlier answers. He's flattered that she recognizes his name, but decides that's likely one of the things she does for Curtis. He explains the mare's death and she says she's sorry.

"Can I ask you about Big Boy?"

"I'm sure Mr. Dobbs would want to hear from you. Let me transfer you to the barn."

"Dobbs here. What do you need?"

"Curtis, it's me, Jesse. Wanted to ask you about Big Boy and get another chance at thanking you and Mac for everything."

"Big Boy's holding his own. Ain't ever gonna be that handsome brute he once was. But, thank God, his lungs are healing."

"Damn, I'm relieved. Worried on it considerably."

"He's gonna need to live on memories, since he ain't getting back the wind needed to mount mares. But, I keep explaining he can learn to live without that." Curtis laughs, and he's back to being the old cowboy Jesse met at Hardee's.

"How'd it go with the mare and her foal?"

"Baby's got a chance. But the mare didn't make it."

There's a long silence, and Curtis obliges him with the kind of wait he gave Curtis when his full throat had choked out his words about Big Boy.

"Damn sorry to hear that. But sometimes a man's just got to drop the reins. Give a smart horse her head. Take whatever comes."

Jesse nods, and it's the best he can do. He wonders if an old cowboy's best horse wisdom can apply to a woman. He's sure Dodie would resent such a notion, label it demeaning in one or more of those terms she used for him when he meant to only better understand things he didn't know how to express.

"You take the care needed to raise that little filly the gentle way, and your Katherine will have her one fine horse."

"I'll see to it. You be well and mention me to Mac."

He places the phone in its cradle, and accepts with regret that he'll likely never run across Curtis or Mac again, but he'll hold on to the good in having done so. He sets the clock, removes his clothes right down to his skin, and crawls between the covers, wishing for a dreamless sleep.

THIRTY-TWO

Before he's fully awake, Jesse believes he hears Katie calling his name and the pounding of footsteps in the hallway. He lifts onto an elbow, and Katie hurls through the air, landing on his bare chest, her bony knees digging into his ribs.

"Daddy, you did it. You brought Dakota home."

"What the hell?"

"She's next door for safekeeping, right? We've got to go now. I want to see her."

"Katie, get off me, girl." His dread feeds his gruffness, and he lifts Katie off his chest and onto the bed.

"Oh Daddy, I love you." She hugs him and plants sloppy kisses on his bearded face.

"Katie, please stop. You've got it all wrong. I tried, but I failed. I failed you. I failed Dakota. I'm so sorry." His voice is shrill, and his pain is every bit what he'd imagined. He grabs her by her shoulders and holds her firmly in his grasp, fighting back his own tears.

"No, Daddy. That's not right." Her body goes stiff and her arms hang at her sides, her face flooded with tears. He relaxes his grip and she moves to stand next to the bed.

"I never meant for any of this to happen. I only meant …."

In a chillingly calm voice, she says, "And that's what you always say."

"Please. This is different. Hear me out."

She runs from the room, never looking back, though he repeatedly calls her name. He imagines her jumping from the porch and riding away on her bike. And this time she may not stop, but ride on to God knows where.

He flings back the covers, meaning to go after her before she can reach the end of their drive, but he's stark naked. He scrambles into jeans, his boots, and with shirt in hand, runs onto the porch.

Marlene stands, shopping bags in her arms, staring after Katie.

"What on earth? Where's Katie going?"

"She thinks I quit trying."

"Did you tell her what happened?"

"She didn't give me a chance."

They watch as Katie reaches the end of the lane and turns toward Dee and Susan's.

"Wait here, I'll go after her." Marlene sets the bags on the porch.

"No. I'll go."

He drives next door to find Katie sitting on the top step of Dee and Susan's front porch, her face resting in her hands, and her body convulsing with her sobbing. He stops the truck, his relief welling up to mix with his grief, and he's grateful that she doesn't run away at his arrival.

He thinks about earlier, on the highway, when he believed that he had reached the end of his will to go on, and Katie has to feel the same. Whatever he does, he'll need to convince her that the death of the mare wasn't her fault, and that her dream need not die with the horse. Yet he has no idea what he will say.

He walks over to her, waiting for what he isn't sure. When she turns away, refusing to look at him, he swallows hard and decides to trust his gut.

"Katie, I'm sorry I yelled just now. I was scared and I'm still scared. I don't know what to say, but I do know we've got to talk about what happened."

"I already know." When she turns back to him, her stare is hard, her eyes unforgiving.

"No, I don't think you do."

"I know you're a quitter, just like Mama said. And I'll never get a chance for Dakota to like me."

"I know that's how you feel, but I'd still like to tell you how it was. Then you decide if you believe I'm a quitter."

Although the muscles in her face remain taut, she glances down at the space next to her, and he takes that as an invitation to sit. Taking her jacket from him, she wraps it around her knees and leans onto her elbows. Her gaze is focused straight ahead, and her bottom lip quivers.

"Your Uncle Clyde and me waited her out." He pauses, staring off into nothing, and knows that his shame won't permit him to tell her the full truth of his having baited the mare with the hungry cries of her tiny foal.

"What does that mean?"

"It means that Dakota went into the catch pen for her own reasons. And I can't say why, exactly."

"Did that mean she wanted to come back and be my horse?"

"No, Katie, I believe she never stopped wanting to run free in the way she was born to do."

"You can't know that's why."

"You're right, I can't." He'd boasted to Clyde that any horse crazy enough to charge a five foot fence was suicidal. And although such a notion defies all logic, he can't help but believe that was exactly what he witnessed.

"But wait, Daddy, if she's hurt, Doc can fix her like he did Beau."

"Not this time, baby. Not even Doc can fix her."

"Then there's Jesus. Grandma says He fixes things if we pray. He still owes me from when Mama went away and didn't come back."

Her tone is pleading, and he knows it's desperation that has her wishing for a miracle. The same as he'd felt, though there's nothing left for either but the hard truth.

"Katie, Dakota's dead."

Her small chest rises and falls in the rhythm of her pain, and she gulps for air. She has to want to spit in the face of every promise she's ever heard: Jesus's, her mother's, and especially his.

"Tell me what happened. I want to know." Her tone, eerily flat, delivers a profound chill to his bones, and he shudders.

"Tell me, Daddy, please."

"Okay, I'll tell you the way I remember."

"No, tell me the truth."

"Remember when she broke free of the corral?"

Katie nods, her fingertips covering her mouth, her gaze intense.

"It happened like that." Although the first time, he remembers clearly that the mare had spun about, releasing her full fury against the top rail. "She tried the gate, but this time it held. She fell back onto the ground and never got up."

"Did it hurt, what she did?"

"If you mean did she suffer, I can only tell you that she never made a sound. I touched her, there in the end." He runs his thumb over his scented fingertips, and holds his hand out to Katie. "Smell. It's the scent of her."

Katie leans and sniffs his fingers, but continues to sit apart from him.

"Why'd you do that? Touch her, I mean."

"I wanted her to know that we never meant to hurt her." He wants Katie to believe that the mare had held their intentions separate from all others.

She exhales, and he believes she looks through her pain, for she stares into the distant horizon, ablaze in hues of deep purple, intermittent flashes of rose into the palest of pinks.

"Will you take me there?"

"Yes, baby. It's in a pretty meadow with a clear spring of water. A place she chose."

Slowly, her hand comes to rest in his upturned palm, as if by doing so, she too touches the fallen mare. Katie leans into him, and burying her face into his chest, she whispers, "Why's everyone I love always leaving?"

"I don't know, baby, that's a really hard one." He leans and kisses the crown of her head, her curls tickling his face. "But what'd you say to me and you going home?"

They stand, Katie's hand in his, and walk off the porch toward the truck.

He opens the front door, and in the kitchen, Marlene is putting away the last of the groceries. She turns toward them and Katie whimpers, running into her arms. Sky and Beau draw near. When their tears have stopped, he motions to the girls, and they leave Marlene to come stand at his knees.

"You need to know that Dakota had a baby. It's at Doc's."

"Is it hurt too?" Fresh tears form in Katie's eyes.

"No, no, she's fine. It's just that she's tiny and needs Doc's help to get stronger." He rushes on before losing his courage. "I know you're glad about the foal, but I think it's best that she live with Miss Dee and Miss Susan. They know a lot about horses and you can see it every day."

"No Daddy, that's wrong. Dakota left her baby with you."

"Katie, that's only what you want to believe. Horses don't have such an instinct."

"You don't know that. You said yourself you're no cowboy."

"Katie, that baby's going to need constant care, and I have to work and you kids have to go to school. Tell me how we're supposed raise a baby?"

"We'll take care of her just like you take care of us. You didn't know how, but you're better now."

"Is that right? What you just said about taking care of you kids?"

"Yep, but you can't stop being brave."

He looks into her eyes, and he sees every reason he'll ever need to try. She must see something in him, because she smiles. It's not the perfect one that can warm him clear through to his chilled doubts, but quiet and still. Yet it's enough that he tastes its promise.

"All right, but you have to agree that if the foal gets into trouble and we don't know enough to help her, you'll give her up to someone who does."

He turns to Marlene, seeking answers to questions he hasn't yet asked, and she stands, a dish towel wrapped around her hand as if it bandages some unseen hurt. He worries that he can't know what she's thinking.

The girls cheer and jump up and down, clapping their hands while Beau circles the table and barks. The girls hug Marlene, and if she has any doubt about his decision, it doesn't yet show. He sits in the center of an emotional whirlwind, equal proportions of joy and fear.

"Okay then, who wants to go to Doc's? See the baby."

If he could afford the cell phone Cole keeps asking for, he could call him. Tell him to meet them at Doc's. He'll need Cole's help more than ever, and he knows Cole should have been in on the decision. But there's no time to do things the right way.

DOC LEADS THE WAY to the barn while Jesse explains to the girls that they will need to walk quietly and stand at a distance so they don't frighten the foal. Still, the foal scampers into a far corner, turns, and watches.

"Jesse, did you bring along them scented clothes like I told you?"

He reaches for the bag of clothes. His failure to shower should work to their advantage.

"Good, now get in there and do like before."

Jesse approaches, kneels, and the foal stands. He wraps his arm in the shirt and slowly extends the nipple to the foal.

She steps back, but right away he notices that she's calmer than before. He squirts a drop of formula on the nipple. The foal pricks her ears, steps closer, then takes the nipple and begins to suckle.

The girls stare at the foal, and at the sound of their soft giggles, the foal stops and watches them, its muzzle covered in white foam. Jesse slips his arm out of the shirt and motions for Katie. He shows her how to hold the bottle and to approach.

"Hey baby, I'm Katie. I loved your mama."

The foal steps back at the sound of her voice.

"Don't be afraid," Katie softly pleads.

The foal stretches its neck, reaching to sniff Katie's fingertip. It blinks and tosses its head, but stands its ground.

"Go slow, Katie." Jesse stands outside the stall, Marlene's hand pressed against his back.

Sky peers over Katie's shoulder at the foal and whispers something that Jesse can't make out. Katie takes Sky's hand and leads her around to kneel at her side.

"Look, baby. She's my little sister. Her name's Sky. She doesn't talk much, but she's nice, too."

Jesse's chest swells and he needs fresh air. He steps past Marlene and hurries back along the rows of stalls, into the cool evening. He leans against the wall of the barn, his arms clutching his torso, hoping that he's somehow settled his wrong with the mare.

Doc follows him outside. He reaches into his pocket and pulls out a tin of tobacco, takes a pinch between thumb and finger, and places it against his inside cheek. "I take that scene back there to mean you've made up your mind."

"Yes sir. I'm ready to learn all you can teach me."

"If she'll suckle for the vet tech, then you need not come by tonight. If the tech needs your help, I'll instruct her to call before you leave for work."

"I'll stop off in the morning."

"Good. Now let me go have one last look. My wife started raising cane an hour ago about my supper getting cold." Doc spits a dark stream of tobacco in the flower bed and starts for the barn, his gait slow and a bit unsteady.

Marlene is leaning over the half-wall and watches as the girls sit quietly on the floor. Katie holds up the empty bottle for Doc to see and the foal lies sleeping on Jesse's jacket.

"Perfect pictures," Doc whispers. "But if we ain't careful, we're going to stare all the good looks off that baby. What do you know of her sire?"

"The old man bragged the stallion was a champion roping horse. Saw the horse myself, and I don't doubt for a minute he was telling the gospel truth." Jesse blushes, guilty of prideful boasting.

"In that case, you'll want to get a copy of the sire's pedigree if there's one to be had."

When it's time to leave, the girls hold back, and when they do finally relent, they tiptoe out, throwing kisses back to the sleeping foal.

They start for home and an exhausted Sky falls asleep on Marlene's lap while Katie sits quietly, pushed up close to him. He leans and asks what she's thinking.

She squints at him. "Sire's a horse word for daddy, right?"

"Yeah, baby. And what I said back there about the foal's daddy is the whole truth. Your Uncle Clyde will tell you the same."

"I love the foal, but I wish she looked more like Dakota. Don't you?"

"Dakota loved her baby. I don't think it mattered to her."

"Like you love me?" She wears a lingering doubt, and he still isn't sure what she means to ask.

"Uh, yeah, baby. The way I love you." He glances across at Marlene, but she doesn't meet his gaze.

"You know what else?"

He looks at her and grins, wondering if her mind is ever still.

"I don't want anything more for Christmas."

"Good, it'll likely work out that way." He's jarred by the thought of Christmas coming on the heels of what he already owes Doc, Clyde, Curtis, and Marlene for all her trips to the grocery store and to Wal-Mart.

"It's already perfect with Beau, Star, and the baby."

"Oh yeah, it'll be a hoot. We'll call it the McKnight family zoo. Add a couple of white rhinos, a hump-backed camel, and some of those monkeys with bright red behinds. Put up signs at the mailbox inviting curious folk to stop and pet them for money. I'll quit the graveyard shift in favor of standing at the road and selling tickets. You two can clean the cages and pens while Miss Marlene runs the concession stand. What do you say to that?"

"That you're silly. Monkeys don't have red butts. Orangutans do." She giggles, clapping her hands and chanting "orangutan, orangutan, orangutan," like a crazed sports fan.

Sky's eyes blink open and she sits up.

"Try it, Sky, it's a fun word." Jesse joins Katie's chanting.

Sky reaches across Katie, touches his forearm with a fingertip, and giggles, joining the two of them, continuing to chant after they've stopped.

"Dang, little girl, when did you start talking so much?"

"She talks a lot now." Katie wears her Braves rally cap, and the cab of the truck fills with their laughter.

From behind them on the highway, he hears the abrupt squeal of a siren and glances back at Buddy's cruiser. Circular flashes of light send his mind reeling, and he grips the steering wheel in both hands. He brakes hard, sending the truck onto the shoulder of the road. His reflex is to reach out and pin Katie firmly against the seat. The engine stalls, and he hurries out of the truck. Katie calls his name, and Marlene pleads with her to hold still.

Buddy stands next to the cruiser.

"It's Cole, Jess. And it's bad." Buddy turns, and his normally red face is the washed out color of fear. He gets back into the cruiser and slams the door.

"Wait a goddamn minute. What's bad?"

"Ain't got time. Just get in."

Marlene stands next to the truck. Her words, caught up in the noise of oncoming traffic, scatter like crows, squawking the certainty of death.

THIRTY-THREE

Buddy steers the cruiser back onto the highway and they speed north.

"You might want to strap yourself in. I'd hate to write you a ticket." Buddy's forced grin fades and he swallows hard.

"Goddamnit, Buddy. Tell me now or I'm tearing your fucking head off."

"Steady, Jess. And first off, Cole ain't hurt. But he's got a load of trouble that'll only get worse unless we find him before Georgia law gets on him."

"What the hell are you talking about? What kind of trouble?" Jesse swallows the mucus that clots his throat and pulls the seat belt tighter, working at readying himself for whatever he's to hear.

"I was headed to your place for a talk when the dispatcher told me Longley's insisting that I issue an Amber alert on Sarah."

"Kidnapped? Are you saying Sarah's been kidnapped? And you think Cole knows something that'll help you find her?"

"I think she's with Cole." The small town of Jenson is nothing but a blur as they speed across the state line into Georgia.

"If she's with Cole, she ain't kidnapped. Jesus, man, you've got to know that."

"I do, but Longley's bound to push one of our weak-spined politician into thinking he can earn votes by putting the heat on me." He pauses. "That's why we've got to find those kids before Cole, and, I figure, James, become fugitives. Then this whole mess gets way complicated." Buddy slaps the steering wheel a hard pop.

"What do you think sent those crazy kids running into Georgia?"

"Thought you might tell me." Buddy stares ahead, and Jesse wants a better chance at knowing what he's thinking but not saying.

"It's true Cole's sweet on her, but I don't know a damn thing about him having a part in her going missing. I can't be sure where he's been for the last two nights—I haven't been home." If Buddy cares to look, he'd see a negligent father's guilt written on his face.

Buddy grunts. "Heard about Pete's trip into the forest. And I'm awful sorry about what happened there. Turned out I was wrong about your horse."

Jesse nods. "Right or wrong, I can't think it would've changed anything."

They hit Thomasville going eighty, siren squealing, lights flashing, and Jesse sits back, his boots pushed against the floorboards, death winking at him from every direction.

"One of my deputies learned from some on-lookers that Cole and Keith Harper got into it big time. And that crazy James Harvey waded in."

"Damn those kids. I've worried about James all along, but I gave Cole more credit. Thought he was smarter than that."

"He's smart all right. But we both know that a teenage boy's brain goes soft with a hard-on. Then he's lucky the fight took place off the school grounds, made it my business and not Longley's."

Jesse thinks Buddy may be splitting hairs when it comes to jurisdiction. Longley's influence will work to condemn Cole and James to the pen until Sarah's married with a house full of brat kids. The leniency he'd once afforded Longley has washed away with the undertow of Cole's newest troubles.

"Can't say exactly whether it's true or not, but a girlfriend told one of the lady deputies that Sarah's knocked up."

"Are you telling me Cole's to blame?" Jesse's throat constricts, and in the pounding of his heart, he hears echoes of his own hard road to busted dreams.

"Can't say, Jess. That's why I need to talk to those kids. Longley strikes me as the type who'd rather charge rape than face the fact his baby girl gave it up freely." Buddy's steady gaze says he has a plan, and that he expects his help.

"But why Georgia? There's help to be found in Tallahassee, right?"

"One of my deputies checked with Tallahassee first."

"Is this when you tell me where we're going?" He believes he knows, but he's going to need to hear it from Buddy.

"I'm thinking Cole may have asked his mom for help. Would she help the girl do such a thing?" Buddy's broad face is that of a cop seeking answers, as well as registering his judgment.

"Maybe, but I don't know that Cole would go to her."

"That same girlfriend hinted as much."

Jesse thinks about the thick envelope that holds his and Dodie's divorce settlement, and if Cole isn't with his mom, a visit might set her to rethinking their settlement. If he is, she already knows, and he may be in deeper trouble.

"All right, you've got whatever you need from me. But how did you get her address?" Had Sally known all along, and Buddy somehow forced her hand?

"Put the ole twitch on Stuart Brown's puny dick and he gave it up. But not without lawyering guff. It'd seem the boy's as rotten as his old man, but slicker. Then his old man owes me a drunk driving charge under the rug. Turns out Dodie lives over near the tech school, but I reckon you knew."

BUDDY PULLS THE CRUISER behind James's truck, blocking any notion either kid might have about driving away. He points to the second floor of the concrete block building that looks more like a cheap motel than an apartment building. Jesse gazes across trash scattered over brown stubble that's meant to pass as a green space and knows Dodie was right not to move their kids to this dump.

Buddy gets out and stands waiting, and when Jesse can't seem to move off the seat, motions him out of the cruiser. Jesse stands, leaning slightly against the door frame, and he's a bit dizzy.

"You all right there, Jesse?"

"Just need to get my legs under me. That's all." He moves toward the stairs, his legs feeling numb, and he wants to believe it's from sitting too long. But the truth is, he's scared in the way of a point man caught out in the open.

"We've got the element of surprise should Cole or James decide to try escaping through a back door. We want to make our entry quick, before they can think about trying something stupid."

They climb the stairs and walk along the outside walkway to apartment number 207. Buddy pauses, puffing hard, and Jesse can't picture him in pursuit of anything faster than molasses on a cold morning.

Buddy lays a blunt finger to the door bell, and Jesse makes out Cole's hushed voice on the other side of the door, followed by a breathless quiet. Buddy looks to him.

"Call your boy. Get'em to open the door. I ain't no TV cop. I hate busting up doors."

Jesse presses his face to the door. "Cole, I know you're in there. Open up. Let's not do this the hard way."

Breaths are held on each side of the door, and Jesse listens for any movement. Behind him, Buddy's big body tenses, and Jesse reaches his hand back, meaning to hold Buddy steady.

"Dad? Is that you?"

"Yeah, it's me all right. Open the damn door." Jesse shifts to the balls of his feet, preparing, if needed, to lay a shoulder into the door.

The door opens a crack, and Cole peeks out, his eyes wild with fear. Jesse rests the heel of his hand against the door and pushes. Cole steps back into the darkened room, and Jesse gets a glimpse of James standing in the room's shadows.

"Dad, before you go off, I swear I can explain everything."

"Good, you'll need to do just that. But first, answer Sheriff Buddy's questions."

Buddy steps forward, his bulk framed in the doorway, blocking much of the light from the street. "Hey, Cole. I'm sure glad to see you. We've got things to settle."

He looks toward the two doors leading off the living room. "But first, where do I find Sarah Longley?"

James shuffles his feet as if he means to make tracks, and Buddy shifts his weight toward him, his hand on his revolver. James checks his movements. He raises his hands, palms out, and Jesse has never considered that James might be packing, but he's guessing Buddy had.

"Son, you're going to need to slide your ass down and take a seat on the floor. And you stay real still. I'll want to talk to you when I'm done with your buddy."

"Shit, yeah, Sheriff. I ain't moving a fucking hair." James's profane mouth, set in his round, child-like face, seems so odd it brings a strange smile to Jesse.

Buddy removes his Stetson, shifts his gun belt, and walks deeper into the room. He squares off with Cole, and says, "Now that we're clear I ain't come here to play, how 'bout you answer my question?"

"She's in my mom's bedroom … resting." Cole's face is drawn and pale.

"Let's me and you go wake her up. Have a little talk about how and why she's here and not home with her parents." Buddy follows Cole along a short hallway, and Jesse hears a door open and close.

"Mr. McKnight, you gotta know Cole and me …." James starts to get to his feet.

"Stay down. Talk to me ass-prone."

"Sarah called me, crying. Asked me to pick up Cole and for us to meet her at Hardee's." He draws his legs up tight against his body, locking his arms around his knees, pushing his tailbone hard against the wall.

"And?" Jesse glances into the alley that serves as a kitchen and listens for Dodie's voice.

"She started in begging Cole to call his mom about us driving her here. Cole kept telling her he couldn't. That it'd mean his fucking probation. Then she sent me for drinks, and when I came back, Cole had changed his mind." James shrugs. "Then he ain't worth buzzard shit against her."

"And you are?"

"Yeah, I am. But hell, Cole's my best friend. I got worried he'd do something really stupid."

"And this," Jesse waves his hand, "ain't?"

"Yes, sir. It's fucking bad, but …." He shrugs.

Jesse nods. He tries not liking the kid, but the boy is so damn honest he hurts for him. Coming here may have been all Sarah's idea, but he fears that doesn't change much against what Cole and James face.

"Can I get up now? I gotta take a leak something awful."

"You ain't stupid enough to attempt jumping two floors to the ground, now are you?"

"Hell, no. I don't reckon my old truck could outrun the law. And I'm flat busted." He turns his jean pockets inside out and grins like a boy with no idea what lies ahead. James is all about now.

"Yeah, I see your point. Go on."

James rushes into the hall bathroom and slams the door behind him, locking it. He's likely flushing his stash of weed, but Jesse doesn't want the stupid kid to get charged with possession on top of everything else.

Buddy comes to stand in the tiny hallway. "We're going to start back, now that Sarah feels somewhat better. I'm going down to the cruiser and radio the dispatcher. Have a deputy go over to her folks to let 'em know she ain't kidnapped." He pauses, twisting his big Stetson in his hands. "The rest of what she is … well, I figure that's family business."

"That means she's done it already?" Jesse whispers, his ambivalence robbing him of a stronger voice.

"I'm afraid so. But thank goodness she went to a clinic and at least got it done by a real doctor. Not by some coat-hanger wielding quack who could have killed her."

"Jesus, Buddy. Did Cole say it was his?"

"Unless rape's suspected, and she says it ain't, then I don't figure it's the law's business to ask." He sucks on his lower lip and stares beyond Jesse at nothing in particular.

"I don't know what I should feel." Jesse drops into a chair.

"You want to talk to him before we head back?"

"Yeah, I'm thinking it ain't about to get any easier."

"Can't see how it could." He pauses. "I'll take James on out to the cruiser. Ask him a few questions. Let her folks know I'm bringing her home."

"Did Cole say where his mom is?"

"Would seem she's got evening classes until around ten."

"You aim to wait around? Hear her part in all of this?"

"Don't look like she did more than open the door to three kids in trouble. Give them floor space overnight. Sarah claims she made all the arrangements at the clinic herself. Hinted at having her mama's permission." He shakes his head.

"That being the case, why didn't she drive her?"

Buddy looks puzzled, as if he'd missed something in all of this. "What about Longley?"

"Don't appear he knew. Then, at home, it seems he knows no more than the rest of us when it comes to teenagers, especially our daughters." He glances at the floor, and when he looks back at Jesse, his rheumy eyes bare what may be his own regrets.

Cole comes from the bedroom, his shoulders slouched and his thin face drained of color, and Jesse remembers the dread he'd felt the night he'd faced his parents. Dodie was at his side, a scared, pregnant, girl-bride neither of his parents had met before that night.

"Dad, I know it's bad, but I can explain."

"That's real good. Cause I'm going to need to hear something that sheds light on this situation. And so far, I'm a man in the dark." Jesse glances about the kitchen, and the counters are clear. Not even a coffee pot. "You had supper?"

"A road-kill burger an hour or so ago." He frowns, leans, his arms wrapping his middle.

That was more than he'd had, but right now he's sure he can't swallow as much as white bread soaked in chicken broth. He sits back in the thinly padded chrome chair and looks across the table at Cole. Not wanting this to become an interrogation, he holds his tongue and nods.

"To start with, Sarah's mom called just now. Said Sarah's old man had raved on to the sheriff that I instigated the whole trip here. Like I'm to blame for what happened."

"Maybe I don't fully agree, but I do see his point." His dad had said that a real man faced up, took responsibility for his namesake. But just now, those words seem small and less certain.

"I was wrong to bring Sarah here, but the decision about the abortion was hers alone."

"But don't you love Sarah? Didn't you want the kid?" He looks at his son and knows more clearly than ever that his decision to marry Dodie and for her to have Cole was right, at least for him. If she had wanted differently, she'd never said so. Then how could he have really known? They had never talked about an abortion.

"Why ask me if I love Sarah? Or if I wanted her baby? It was never my decision."

Now it's Jesse's turn to look bewildered. "Son, you had a say in the decision, same as Sarah." He leans in, closing the distance between them, searching the slightest muscle twitch in Cole's distraught face for what he's to believe.

His son's bloodshot eyes stretch wide and he shakes his head in quick, jerky motions. "No, Dad, you've got it all wrong. It wasn't mine and Sarah's baby."

Unable to bear the transparent pain in Cole's face, Jesse abruptly stands and walks to the kitchen sink, runs cold tap water over his wrists until the hot sickness in the back of his throat subsides.

He turns back to Cole. "It was that scum bag, Keith. Did he force her?" Jesse collapses back into the chair.

Cole sits upright, his gaze locked into Jesse's. "Rape, you mean?"

He nods.

"You can't even remember high school, can you? How it is with us kids?" Through his tears, he whispers, "If you did, you'd know she was shamed into having sex."

Every ounce of tenderness Jesse has ever felt rebounds in such an acute and surprising way, his heart splinters like seasoned oak

under a sharp ax. He wants Cole to be wrong, and that a young
Dodie and Sarah had never trusted the likes of him and a boy
he's never met but has decided to hate. He remembers that a well-
meaning teacher once told him that high school was a rehearsal
for life. He hadn't known then, but he now knows she was wrong.
High school was real enough, and at that age, he'd thought it was
the whole deal, the shape of his life to come.

"Yeah, son, I do. I surely do."

"If you do, then don't you honestly think you'd be better off if
Mom had done what Sarah did?"

"Cole, in some ways, I was no different than Keith. I pressured
your mom for over a year. We were way too young, but we wanted
to marry and to have you." They'd dropped out at Christmas and
the night of their senior prom, while their classmates celebrated,
they'd huddled together in his dad's old truck, her swollen belly
between them, while they watched couples arrive at the high school
gym. He'd tried comforting her, saying proms were for kids who
wanted to play at grownup. Still, she'd cried into his shoulder, and
he'd felt to do the same.

"But you both settled."

"Maybe, but now your mom's getting her chance. And hell,
the truth is, I'd already blown any real chance I had. I didn't want
college ball bad enough to work for it off the field. You didn't
short-change me, son. I did that myself."

"I've wanted to be with Sarah for over a year, and I don't
honestly know what I would've wanted if the baby had been ours."

Old hurts surface for Jesse, and he remembers his mom's
sorrow, lamenting that she'd always believed him to be a good
boy. The worst was his daddy's silent shame, and he'd never again
looked at him with the same pride as before. The daily reminder of
that loss, more than the promise of a factory job, had driven him to
take his young wife and son and leave the farm.

Sarah comes from the bedroom, and he and Cole stand. Even with her swollen face, she is strikingly pretty; a dark brunette with smooth hair hanging heavy and straight to her narrow shoulders. Her green eyes reflect a depth much older and wiser than her age. Except for the present situation, he thinks Cole may have been getting good advice all along.

Cole stutters through a clumsy introduction, and he looks at Sarah the way Jesse had once looked at Dodie.

"Mr. McKnight, I'm so sorry I got Cole into trouble. He only meant to help." She hiccups a sob and presses her fingertips to her lips.

"It's okay. Don't worry about me." Cole reaches for her hand and Jesse is moved by his tenderness.

"Cole did right … helping you, I mean. And I'm awful sorry … about the other." His words hang empty. He hadn't known how to comfort Dodie, nor does he know what he should have said to Sarah. What he wants most is for Cole to know how proud he is of the young man he's become.

Buddy and James come back through the door, and whatever Buddy has said to James has lifted weight from his enormous shoulders.

To Sarah, he says, "Your folks have been notified that you're safe by one of my lady deputies. We need to get you home, straighten things out all around. Jesse, I'm guessing you'll agree to ride back with these boys and see to it that they don't get any wild notions about revenge."

Jesse nods, understanding that Buddy's warning includes him.

"I'll see you back home. And maybe by then, I'll have things worked out with Sarah's parents."

"What about my probation officer? Am I in trouble with him?"

"He could be a problem." Buddy frowns. "I'm going to need to pay him a visit. See what comes of our talk."

Jesse and the boys follow Buddy and Sarah to the cruiser. She gets into the back seat, and Jesse watches her behind the heavy wire screen. And while he feels pity for her, his greater relief is that Cole and James aren't huddled behind that screen, handcuffed and on their way to jail.

Buddy opens the door of the cruiser and turns back to Jesse. "And by the way, I agree old Beau was too damn smart to try tackling a speeding car. You can tell Miss Katie she's not to worry. I'll take care of that one as well."

"How'd you know about Beau?"

"Heard it from Doc, and he got it from a reliable source." Buddy winks, lowers his inside shoulder against the wind, and folds his big frame back into the warmth of the cruiser.

He should have known Katie and Doc had talked. He'll need to say to her that he was wrong, and that she and Beau deserved better from him. He stands in the parking lot, bracing against the chill, and it's not the cold that he feels but what the future is to say about the fate of his son.

THIRTY-FOUR

Jesse empties his wallet, squeezes in thirty dollars worth of gas, crossing his fingers that it's enough to get back home. He estimates that he has barely enough time to drop the boys and make the start of his shift.

The exhausted boys sleep, and he pushes the old green truck hard until the temperature gauge climbs into the red and he's forced to cut back on his speed. With less than forty minutes to spare, he pulls the truck to a quick stop in the driveway, rousting the boys.

"James, you take your ass straight home, and Cole, you stay put."

"Let me stay over. My mama ain't as much as noticed I'm missing."

"All right, but you call her. I don't care what you think, she's still your mama. And you need to let her know you're okay."

When the three enter, Marlene and Cole hold each other close, and she reaches to takes James's hand. Cole pulls away and slowly walks along the hallway to his room, James following.

Marlene watches both until they pass through the door and pull it closed behind them. She turns to Jesse, her eyes filled with tears. "Oh, Jess, when you left with Buddy, I was so afraid."

"I'm sorry. I should've called, but everything happened so fast, I barely kept up."

Every word he's left unspoken for all these months swirls in his brain, sizzling like droplets of fat in a fire, and it's his own pain as much as Cole's that moves him to take her into his arms. He kisses her, and it's an awkward kiss.

She pulls back and places a fingertip to his lips.

"God, I know it's wrong. But I swear I love you. I can't help it."

At first, she doesn't speak, and he doesn't know what her silence means. She takes him by the hand and leads him into the kitchen, and maybe she does so out of concern that they are seen or heard.

"I know you believe you do, and please know that I love you, but not this way." Her voice is strong and her rejection clear.

"Marlene, please. Earlier in the truck, with Sky and Katie, and just now with Cole, tell me you felt something. Something like I felt. You're part of all the good that's happened with my kids and me. I can't lose that."

"I know you're afraid, and that you somehow believe I can guarantee against your failure. But you're wrong. You've done so much already."

"But can't we do it together?"

"No, Jess. I'd regret too much the loss it would cause."

"You mean between Clyde and me?"

"Yes, there's you and Clyde. And I'd hurt for that as well." She pauses. "But more importantly, there's me and Clyde."

"You mean you and Clyde are … what I mean is …." He struggles to ask without asking because he doesn't want to know.

"If what you mean to ask is whether Clyde and I are lovers, the answer is no, not in the way I think you mean. I stay with Clyde because I care deeply for him. He befriended me when I wasn't sure I could ever again think of myself as worthy. He did so unconditionally, never asking to know my past or why I ran."

Jesse slumps into a chair, recounting the times, far too numerous to know, when Clyde came to his rescue, never asking for anything in return. He's wished a million times over he'd made a different decision the night of Clyde's wreck. He can never get that decision back, but now maybe he's getting a second chance to make a better choice for himself and his two best friends.

"Can we still be friends?"

"Yes, if you'll accept that I don't want anything to happen between us that we'd regret."

"But, what about just now? The kiss, I mean?"

"It doesn't count." She laughs, gently mocking.

"Still, I want you to know that I was once considered a damn good kisser. Then I guess you might say I'm a bit rusty." He forces a grin.

She hands him his battered lunch box and thermos, and playfully motions him through the door. He steps into the cold, clear night to the goodness in her laughter, and he's warmed by the promise that she'll forever be a presence in his life, no matter how many women he comes to love.

THIRTY-FIVE

After a stop at Doc's to feed the foal, Jesse arrives home and the house is silent, except for the phone message that directs him to Buddy's office within the hour. He quickly showers and changes into clean jeans and his only pressed shirt. He drives directly to the jail, and the duty officer directs him to Buddy's office.

Across the desk from Buddy, Longley and his red-faced wife sit solemn and silent, neither doing more than looking up as he enters.

Buddy stands. "Morning, Mr. McKnight. Good of you to come. Take a chair, if you will. I'll make this as quick as possible."

Jesse takes Buddy's formality to be for the Longleys. "What's this about, Sheriff?"

"That hardly seems the question you should be asking under the circumstances." Longley's hard glare causes the hair on Jesse's neck to bristle, and he squeezes his hands into fists. In a blistering instant, Longley becomes every self-important sonofabitch he's ever wanted to punch.

Buddy reads Jesse, and leans across the desk. "Mr. Longley, let's get something straight right from the get-go. Cole McKnight has not been charged with any crime. His dad is here at my request. So, you're gonna need to sit back and relax."

"But the boy's already a criminal. He clearly violated his probation when he transported my daughter across a state line. You can't make that go away, now can you?"

Buddy sits back, his big hands together with only his blunt fingertips touching.

"No, and that's a fact. Notifying the court is up to his probation officer, and he shows no interest in that direction, since it's clear Cole never intended to escape the reach of the court. And he didn't force your daughter. She stated she asked them to drive her, and he and James Harvey agreed."

"I see. Then that leaves me no choice but to talk with Judge White myself."

"Ralph, please, you're not to blame Cole. Sarah says he only meant to help." Mrs. Longley's strained voice is that of a squashed woman, and Jesse is beginning to understand why she may have sent her daughter off alone.

"It's best you keep out of this. You have a soft spot where Sarah and that … that boy are concerned." Longley twitches in anger and Jesse wonders how much his loss of control over his wife and daughter drives his will to make Cole and James the villains.

"Mrs. Longley, when did you learn that your daughter had left the state?"

She glances over at her husband, her shoulders lifting. "She called soon after arriving in Valdosta. She was determined to go through with the abortion. But she didn't want her father and me to worry."

Longley swivels about in his chair, facing his wife. His cold eyes bulge with contempt. "You knew all along. Why didn't you …?"

"Stop her? Because we both know your obsession to become school superintendent would override whatever Sarah needed." Her scorn, thick like hot tar, sticks to every word.

"Mr. Longley, I'll ask you the same question."

"Nothing until your call, telling me that you'd located Sarah."

"I see, and how about you?" He looks directly at Jesse.

"Not until you caught up to me on the highway."

"It'd seem you parents were the last to know. And that none of you had a part in this." He pauses. "Unless, Mrs. Longley, you may want to consider that your failure to talk to your husband resulted in me and my deputies undertaking an unwarranted pursuit at county expense. Then, don't get me wrong, I was pleased, with Mr. McKnight's help, to locate your daughter and bring her home safely."

"That's it? You're content to blame my wife, and therefore have it fall back on me?" He slides to the front of the chair and stands, his contempt focused on Buddy, and he isn't a man who forgives and forgets.

"No sir, I'm saying this is now a family matter. Not one for law enforcement." Buddy stands with a smile the envy of any two-faced preacher and extends his big paw.

The Longleys leave, and Buddy walks Jesse out of the office.

"You big bastard. You could've at least told me the part about the probation officer, saved my last nerve for my next crisis."

"Sorry about that. But I first needed to put a foot to his neck. It's a God's blessing the man's a drunk. Took little from me to have him see the error in his thinking and to have him shred his report to the court. Then my notion is he'll pickle his liver early. Leave justice to those who give a damn."

JESSE HAS FINISHED WIRING the shed and is pitching bedding hay in the two stalls when Marlene and the girls return, the car loaded with bags of groceries. He puts away his tools and crosses the yard.

Oliver, Marlene's corgi pup, trails the girls onto the porch, and Beau stiffens.

"Damned if this place ain't getting a bit overrun with dogs." He's surprised at his sudden flash of rancor.

"Make yourself useful. Grab some bags." Marlene continues moving toward the door, calling back over her shoulder, "I'm away too much now, and Clyde can't watch Oliver."

He goes to the car and there are more bags of groceries, dog food, even a twelve pack of beer. A shopping bag with shoe boxes, one each marked with Katie and Sky's sizes. He puts the last of the bags on the kitchen table, and watches Marlene put away more groceries than he buys in a month.

"He really isn't that much trouble. But Oliver is my responsibility." She turns back to her task.

He decides her choice of "responsibility" was deliberately demeaning.

"I decided to shop, save you the time. I know you need to take the girls to feed the foal."

"Look, you've got to stop this. I work. I've got money to feed us."

"I was in town and you and your money were here." She shrugs. "Pay me for the groceries if it'll make you feel better." She turns back to rearranging, making room for all she's bought.

"Pay you? I can't do that. This is more than I can afford. From now on, I'll do the shopping."

"If I'm here at meal times, I'm doing the cooking. You're a miserable cook. And if I'm cooking, I'll do the shopping."

"And the shoes?"

"Sky's are badly worn, and those were on sale." The set of her shoulders is enough to back off any sensible man, and it isn't that he doesn't know he's picked a stupid fight. He just can't stop.

"Haven't you heard? I fix blowouts."

She slams a box of oatmeal onto the counter and turns to face him, her eyes narrowed. No doubt he's gone too far.

"Look, don't get me wrong. I'm grateful, but ...."

"Please, stop with the pathetic whining. Surely you don't think I do what I do for your gratitude."

In silence, he watches her overstuff the vegetable cooler and attempt to close the fridge door. It pops open and she slams it again and again before it catches. "You never buy foil or trash bags or even light bulbs. Toilet paper, for godsakes."

"Because we can't eat those things, that's why. Take the bulb from my bedroom. I sure as hell don't stay up nights reading."

"And while we're on the delicate subject of your gratitude, you can shove it up your prideful ass." She goes back to rearranging the cabinet.

He grabs the back of a kitchen chair and works at steadying himself. The kitchen steams with their heat and he needs air. He rushes onto the porch, slamming the door back on its hinges, and he already wishes he hadn't.

At the sound of something bouncing off the kitchen door, he hurries off the back porch, catching the toe of his boot on a raised nail, and pitches forward onto the rough cement walkway. He spills, face down, his arms and legs sprawled in all directions, and he imagines he must look like a weather vane. He lies moaning, his chin and the heels of his hands stinging with the pain of torn flesh.

Through his misery and embarrassment, he looks up to see Katie and Sky, trailed by the two dogs, running toward him. He scrambles to his feet and stands, holding his bleeding chin in his bleeding hand.

Katie screams for Marlene, who comes to stand on the top step, exclaiming, "What on earth happened?" She turns away, attempting to smother her erupting laughter.

"Katie, call Sheriff Buddy." He points toward Marlene. "Tell him that mean woman pushed me. Tried to kill me."

"Daddy, you're full of bean farts." Still, she wrinkles her nose at the sight of blood, Sky a smaller copy of the same.

He sits on the side of the tub while Marlene cuts away ripped skin and dabs the open wounds with iodine. Katie and Sky stand in the tub, the two dogs crowded at his feet. The girls giggle each time he cries out in pain, and he thinks Beau wears a bigger grin, but he doesn't know young Oliver well enough to read his expression.

Marlene closes the bottle and smiles. "I was a nurse in a former life, and I've never met a bigger cry baby."

"And I never figured you for the type who'd bounce a man off a cement slab and then wash his wounds in iodine."

"Now you know. But I do think Santa needs to bring you a gift certificate for a haircut." She brushes his shaggy hair off his forehead.

"I thank Santa, but I still get free haircuts at Willie's."

"That's because Mr. Willie's got some old football picture of Daddy and Uncle Clyde on his wall from way back before football was on TV."

He growls at the girls and they run, giggling, and he chases. Behind him, Marlene laughs, and he warms to the goodness in the moment, making of it all that he's allowed.

THIRTY-SIX

Dee swings the horse trailer around and backs it flush with the shed door. The girls rush from the truck and stand waiting for Dee to unlatch the metal gate and lower the ramp. Jesse has ridden from Doc's inside the trailer, enclosed along with the foal in the hay barricade he made to cushion the transport.

"Hurry, Daddy. Freedom wants to see her new home."

"Hold up, girl." He grasps the lead rope and works to maneuver the foal from within the barricade. She stiffens, spreads her front legs, and balks. A pygmy goat, the foal's stall mate, tied at the front of the trailer, calls to the foal, and it answers back.

"I could bring the goat out first, but why don't you just carry the foal? What we're asking may be too much for her just now." Susan stands at the back of the trailer, twisting her shirttail and looking on.

"Please, Daddy. Freedom's scared." Katie drums her dirty fingertips against her front teeth and prances with anxiety.

Jesse stoops and gathers the foal in his arms, and she struggles against his chest, her long, dangling legs making a punching bag of his groin. Her shrill panic calls can still torment him the way they had when the hungry and frightened foal called to the mare. He carries the foal inside the shed, sets her down in the larger of the stalls and stands watching. She circles, nickering, testing the four corners of the stall. Without the mare to teach her, she fears everything new until she learns differently.

"Katie, you and Sky come in here and sit down. Stay real still, but talk softly to her the way you did at Doc's."

"Don't worry. We know what to do."

Katie's voice is strained, and while her irritation is warranted, he's coping with anxiety similar to that he suffered the day he drove Dodie and Cole from the Tallahassee hospital to his parents' farm in his dad's ancient truck that smelled of hogs.

Today, in a borrowed rig, debt up to his ass, leaning on the goodness of friends and neighbors, he brings home yet another baby. One which he has agreed to give up should his best effort be overridden by his ignorance. He takes a deep breath and goes back to the trailer for the bleating goat, then leads it into the smaller stall.

He, along with Dee, Susan, and the girls, watch the foal, her flaring nostrils pushed between the slats, and she sniffs the nanny goat. The nearness of the girls and the presence of the goat work to settle the foal. She walks to the center of the stall and stands, tossing her head, nickering softly.

"See, I told you. Freedom likes her new home." Katie approaches the foal, her hand extended, fingertips touching the foal's white blaze; a perfection of her sire's.

"Good Lord, Katie, take it easy." He edges toward the stall gate, to do exactly what, he isn't sure.

Susan places a restraining hand on his shoulder. "Trust Katie," she whispers. "She knows the foal better than any of us."

The foal shakes her head from side to side and prances in place.

Katie giggles and begins walking in circles around the foal in the way she plays with Beau and Oliver, and the foal follows her.

Jesse exhales sharply, his tension driving a burst of silliness, and he says, "Go easy greasy, we've got a long way to slide." He grins over at Dee, and waits for her predictable show of scorn.

"Damn, I can't believe how long it's been since I heard that bit of junior high." To his surprise, she punches him on his upper arm.

"Ouch, that hurt."

"Hush your mouth, McKnight. That felt too good. Can't remember the last time I gave a guy a frog." She draws her chin down and makes a scary face.

"You two kids." Susan steps between them, playing at separating two rowdy children.

He turns toward the playful commotion of the girls and foal. Sky has stopped chasing Katie, and watches him. He winks at her, and she now watches all three. Her baffled look slips into a shy smile, and she rejoins Katie and the foal.

JESSE ENTERS THE SHED and calls, "Dang it, Katie, I've told you I want this stall clean enough for a picnic. And don't forget I want a fresh sample of manure every day." He holds out the bucket and small shovel. "If she gets the runs, you really won't like this part of your job."

"But Freedom's bigger. Why do I still have to pick up dooky?"

"Do it or I'll pin a diaper on her and make you change it."

Sky picks up fresh manure with her hands and puts it into the bucket.

"Yuck, Sky. Use the shovel."

Wiping her nasty hands across the front of her jacket, she looks at him, a mischievous twinkle in her eyes, and his breath catches.

She means to tease. He picks up a pinch of dried manure and tosses it in her direction, and she runs behind the haystack, giggling.

SPRING ANNOUNCES ITS ARRIVAL with the return of the pecan tree's shaded circle, its branches feathered in tender, lime-green foliage. Jesse and Marlene sit at the freshly painted, yellow picnic table, watching Katie train Beau to lead Freedom. She claps her hands and skips along next to dog and horse, cheering their efforts.

Shading his eyes against the sun's glare, Jesse looks toward the lane where Sky's pup, Star, wearing a pink cape made from one of Katie's old tee shirts, sits like a homecoming queen in the Western Flyer Sky got from Santa. Sky pulls the wagon a little farther down the lane than the day before, and just now she stops, looks back, and waves. Soon, she'll want to pull the wagon next door to Dee and Susan's, and he hopes he'll be ready when the time comes.

Beau stops, drops the lead rope, and sits looking up at Katie. Freedom tosses her head in what seems like friendly persuasion, and Katie stands, her hands on her hips. Jesse sees Clyde's brand of sheer gutsiness rather than Cora's haughtiness. The trio makes another circle before quitting, and maybe it's about establishing her authority.

When she's brushed the filly, she turns her into Dee and Susan's pasture to frolic with the young colt born to their prize mare in February. Kneeling, Katie takes a brush from her hip pocket, and Beau rolls over onto his back, closing his jellybean-shaped eyes.

"I wish Clyde was here to share this moment. He's so proud of Katie."

"Yeah, he … is."

He stares at Marlene, and the sadness bleeding through her dark eyes harbors a truth that only pain can expose. The image of the photograph Dodie sent him in Iraq, showing a a grim-faced Clyde cradling infant Katie, fires in Jesse's consciousness, and he can no longer deny it for what it is.

"God, Jesse … I never meant …."

Behind the shed, he empties his gut, his agony driving him back and forth in a frantic pacing. His madness leaves him wheezing, and he squats, pushing back on his heels in a rhythmic motion of momentary insanity.

Marlene rushes toward him. Her lips are moving, but he hears only the hammering of his own heart, his silent screams resounding inside his head. She attempts to gather him in her arms, but he pushes her away. She slams into the shed wall, collapsing onto the ground, and although he has a moment of regret, he turns and runs.

Reaching his truck, he speeds out of the yard, sending the vehicle skidding onto the asphalt, and he screams profanities at the horror-stricken face appearing in his vision. The cab of the truck is tomb-like, the landscape a colorless blur, his consciousness fragmented, registering only his grief.

THE FRONT DOOR OF THE BAR stands open like a putrid wound, and Jesse stands in its gash, waiting for his eyes to adjust to the cavernous darkness. Behind him, warm light pours through the door, pushing back the darkness, but not the cold stiffness in his every joint. His battered mind distracts itself, registering familiar odors: beer, whisky, cigarettes, sweat, piss, stale popcorn, and busted dreams. The stench settles in his gut and stings his wet eyes.

Clyde is slumped forward onto a table, his head resting on his folded arms, and at his elbow, an empty bottle overturned, resting on its side. A drunken Clyde is a melancholy man, boiling in the purest of meanness, and closed to reason. Then Jesse hasn't come here to reason.

He steps closer, the squeal of a loose board beneath his boot, and Clyde lifts his head, pushing himself upright in the wheelchair. His eyes narrow, his irises floating in clots, and Jesse feels he treads upon bloody eyeballs.

"Aw, Little Brother, come on in, I've been expecting you. Why'd it take you so damn long?"

"You sonofabitch, I trusted you. And for that you fucked my wife. Stole my daughter."

"That's it? That's all you got?" Clyde reaches into the side pocket of the wheelchair, takes out his Smith and Wesson 38, and pushes it across the table, the whisky bottle smashing onto the floor. "Go on. Take it. I've cleaned and reloaded it every day for better than eleven years."

Jesse stares down at the gun.

"Go on, pick it up. Be a whole man." Clyde's voice cracks like a stone against a tin roof.

Seething in despair, Jesse picks up the gun and presses its ridged grip into his sweaty palm. Sliding his index finger against the cold hardness of the trigger, he raises the gun and stares into Clyde's eyes, the whole of his guilt reflected there.

Clyde rips open his shirt, buttons spinning across the table and onto the floor. "Here, right here, Little Brother." He pounds his chest with his huge fist, his red chest hairs bristling against his bluish-pale skin. Jesse raises the gun level with the patch of red hair between Clyde's hard nipples, and Clyde doesn't as much as flinch.

"Goddamn you, Clyde. I should kill you." He lowers the gun, presses the thumb piece forward, holding the cylinder open. The cartridges drop onto the table where he sweeps them into his hand. He puts the gun back onto the table between them. His knees buckle and he grabs a chair, drawing it opposite Clyde, and he sits.

"Why? Just tell me that much."

Clyde closes his eyes, his head bouncing ever so slightly on his thick neck. Then he lifts his face, and Jesse realizes that he's always known the truth of why.

"All right, then. But tell me for how long? While I was on tour? Before then, even?"

"Don't see how that matters. Once or a thousand times. Some wrongs are so bad there's no number that matters."

"You sonofabitch, it was during Iraq."

"I let her use me to punish you, siding with what I'd always wanted." His eyes glisten, and he hunches forward.

"The day you showed up drunk. Me and Cole roofing the shed …."

"Yeah, then, too."

Jesse nods.

"I've tried telling you every second since it happened. Even in my worst nightmares, where I blew my brains to kingdom come." His voice is a hoarse whisper. "I told myself that you were too messed up after Iraq. Truth is, I didn't tell you because I was too ashamed."

Jesse meets the intensity of Clyde's gaze and then looks away, staring into the motes of dust swirling in beams of fading light, his moment of clarity stretching through all time: past, present and future, and although he should hate Clyde, he can't figure a way through the balance of his life without him. Even with what happened between Clyde and Dodie, he isn't ready to let go of what they've had.

"I want to try hanging on to whatever good we got left. Give us some time. Maybe a chance at healing over the raw of it."

"Don't know I believe in forgiveness."

"Yeah, you do."

"How's that?"

"There's me and what I wanted with Marlene … if she'd felt the same."

"That was always between the two of you." His gaze drops, but not before Jesse reads relief in his eyes.

"You may be right. But one thing I do know for sure. And that's if you ever as much as think about claiming my daughter, I'll come back. And then, I'll bring my own gun."

"I swear I want no more of Katie than I do of Cole and little Sky. Just to be around. Watch them three kids grow up. Help whenever I can."

Jesse pushes back from the table, and stands. "You might want to call Marlene. Let her know we ain't killed one another."

"She'd want to know that." His grin breaks slowly across his pained face. "Then trying to love two fools can't be easy."

Jesse nods and starts for the door.

"See you in the funnies, Little Brother," Clyde calls quietly.

Jesse stops and turns back. "Not if I see your ugliness first."

It's something they've said to each other from their earliest beginnings, and maybe the moment deserved more, but it is enough for him.

He crosses the clay lot to his truck, starts the engine, and drives toward home. Behind him the sun has dropped below the stand of darkened pines, and the day's colors drain from the sky as if Mother Nature sucks them through a straw.

About the Author

Pat's short stories have appeared in numerous journals, including the *North American Review, Appalachian Heritage, Seven Hills Review,* and anthologies titled *Law and Disorder* from Main Street Rag, *Bridges and Borders* from Jane's Stories Press and *Saints and Sinners: New Fiction from the Festival 2012.* Her short story "Stranger At My Door" received honorable mention in the 2013 Lorian Hemingway Short Story competition and "Whelping" was a finalist for the Rash Award and appears in the 2014 issue of Broad River Review. In 2009 she was nominated for a United States Artists grant. She lives in Tallahassee, Florida.